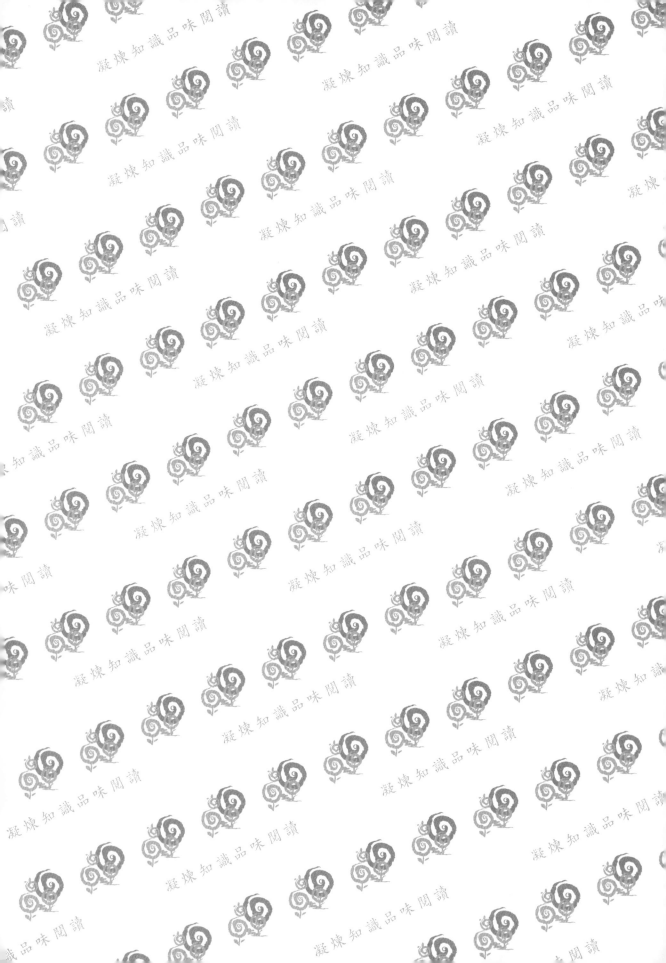

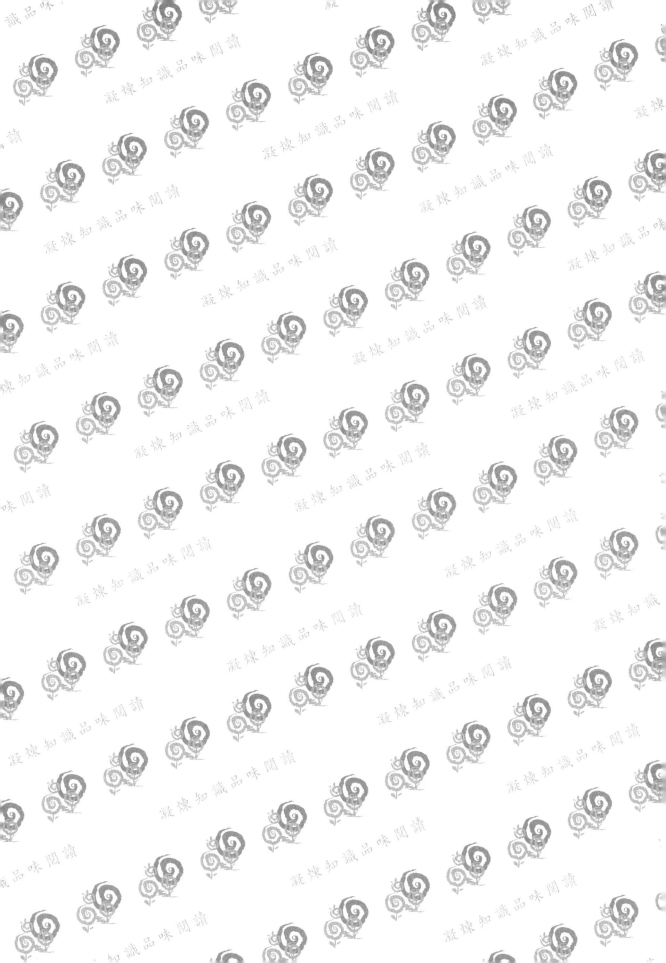

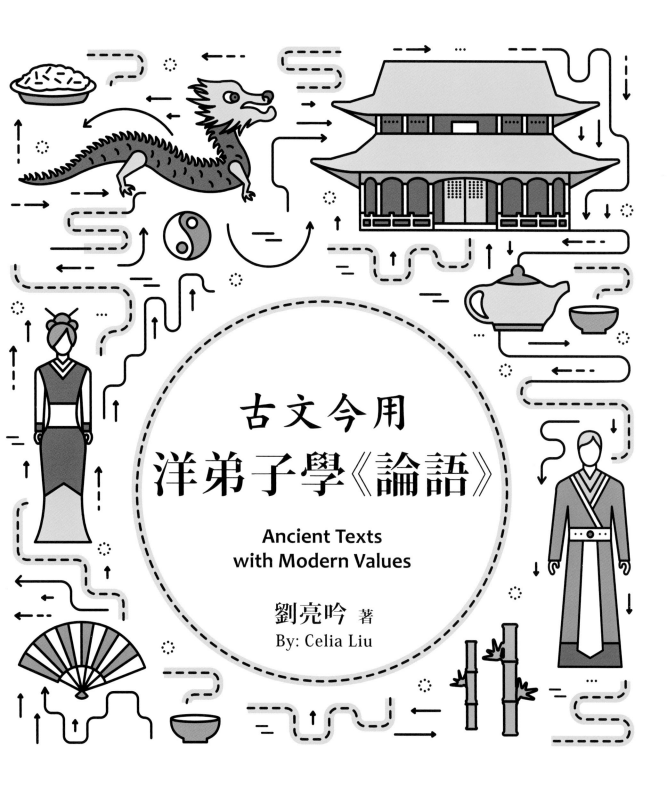

# 古文今用
# 洋弟子學《論語》

## Ancient Texts
## with Modern Values

劉亮吟 著
By: Celia Liu

五南圖書出版公司 印行

# 推薦序一
# Prefix 1

　　《古文今用─洋弟子學《論語》》一書是劉亮吟教授用中華民族兩千五百年傳統的聖經《論語》簡單的「古名言」為主題，使諸多中級華語文學習者，能更早些了解雋永精湛的文言與中國文化精髓。

　　全書共十章，內容包括論語中的孝、朋友、君子或小人、學習、禮、快樂、音樂、仁愛、道德、政治等名句。每章名句逐字翻譯，再連結成句，譯英舉例。十分合乎學生從古到今理解認知的學習過程。

　　每章編輯有白話翻譯，並加註生詞之拼音、英譯、詞類，更進一步擴充例句練習。附加短篇孔子生平故事，廣被漢語學子，認識儒家思想，了解中華文化根源。

　　本書可貴之處在於每章舉附：【短篇評論】提供古今中外核心價值比較，【ACTFL OPI 模式的模擬口試】提供口語練習的話題實例以及角色扮演等活動、以 TOCFL 和 HSK 詞彙做整理的【生詞的延伸學習】、還有以篆、隸、草、行、楷五種書法字體所呈現的漢字之美。此書還替老師們提供了【活動設計和討論話題教案】，為教師們建議各項相關的語言學習活動和實用的課程討論話題。特別是【美國總統引用中文古名言實例】更加深中華名句的使用價值。

　　全書編纂中英文，文辭深入淺出，引經據典，出處可尋，巨細靡遺，是洋學生學習中華古文名句的濫觴。也是當代華語文教材中，古文學習最充實、簡易實用，值得採用的一部教本。

　　謹此推薦。

台灣師大華語文教學系名譽教授

葉德明

12/5/2021

# 推薦序二
# Prefix 2

This book on famous quotations from the Confucian Analects, with its accompanying rich assortment of useful teaching and learning aids, has much to offer the American college or university student of Chinese language and culture.

The Analects, of course, were composed in Classical Chinese, which was the normal written language of China (and several other East Asian countries) from the fifth century BCE until the 1920s. Although challenging, acquiring an elementary knowledge of Classical Chinese is important for several reasons.

First of all, cultural literacy in Chinese requires some familiarity with Classical Chinese, which is the language in which the great bulk of China's literature, history, and philosophy was written. Secondly, knowledge of Classical Chinese is very useful for raising one's proficiency in Modern Chinese, since both formal spoken and, especially, formal written Chinese have been heavily influenced by it. Finally, some familiarity with Classical Chinese can be useful for the non-native in gaining "cultural credibility" in Chinese society. Nothing seems to impress native speakers more than a foreigner who can understand-or, even better, recite from memory-a Tang poem or some quotations from Confucius!

Because of the innovative design of the author's book, no prior background in Classical Chinese is required and it is even possible for students who have not previously studied any Chinese to learn from it. I completely agree with her that study of Confucius' Analects can help learners in "understanding Chinese ways of thinking and values and applying Chinese wisdom to social interactions today." It is a pleasure for me to recommend her book to students and instructors alike.

Cornelius C. Kubler 顧百里
Stanfield Professor of Asian Studies
Dept. of Asian Languages, Literatures & Cultures
Williams College, Massachusetts, U.S.A.

# 推薦序三
# Prefix 3

　　這是一本深入淺出而又實用的漢語學習補充教材。《古文今用—洋弟子學《論語》》內含十章，重點收錄了儒家思想中關於：孝、悌（兄弟朋友）、品德行為、學習態度、禮樂和政治等主題的論語名言，體現了中華文化傳承的重要價值觀，條理分明地引領學習華語的非母語者進入古漢語的經典文學領域。

　　一直以來，我們都期望對於跨文化的學習者介紹中華文化精髓的寶典，但由於傳統語言學習的過程中，這些非母語的學習者限於華語水平，若不是到高級階段很少有機會能接觸到古文的學習。這本書摘錄簡短的論語名言，並加以逐字翻譯白話解釋原文，讓學生可以很容易地學習到古代漢語的語言模式，這可以為華語非母語者打開學習古代漢語的通道，對他們的華語學習有很大的幫助。

　　本書的另一特點是美國領袖在公開的演說中的名言引用實例，讓洋弟子能跟自己熟悉的領導人進行學習連結。對於華語非母語的外國學生來說，將所學的論語經典名句運用到實際的演說或寫作當中是非常好的引導學習目標，也是一個吸引人的語言運用策略。

　　更難能可貴的是，本書做了文化與語言學習及測驗評量的連結，除了對書中摘錄的每一個名言分別有：逐字翻譯、白話解釋原文、延伸對話與生詞、孔子故事、論語名言的現代價值評論等，還依據 ACTFL OPI 的口語測驗模式為老師們安排了：「模擬口語考試討論話題」。這部分可以使得論語名句的學習充分和現代社會議題做結合，讓學生有機會做實用的口語討論練習。

　　教學方面在附錄中提供了活動設計、討論話題以及延伸生詞學習，面面俱到，真是非常值得推薦的跨語言跨文化的雙語教材！！！

國立臺灣師範大學華語文教學系暨研究所教授

曾金金（Tseng, Chin-Chin）

# 關於本書和作者
# Introduction of this book and the author

【簡介】

　　這是一本適用於英語國家的漢語課程或通識教育文化課程的教科書，也是提供全球所有漢語非母語的學習者（CSL-Chinese as Second Language Learners）「自學」關於中華儒家文化的引導手冊。本書作者在新澤西州立學院（The College of New Jersey）創設的「中國哲學」課程成功通過該校課程委員會核准，列為教導世界觀及國際視野（Global-Worldview and Ways of Knowing）的「通識教育」（Liberal Learning Curriculum）課程。這本書就是作者以多年的教學心得所發展出的課程教材。從研讀簡單的孔子名言出發，提供美國大學生認識中華傳統核心文化的機會。本書所列舉的名句，涉及孔子的人本主義（Humanism）、家庭倫理（Family values）、學習知識（Learning）、忠恕社交處事原則（Benevolence and Social Rules），以及禮樂治國的仁政思想（Governing with rites and rituals）等。

　　本書前序先以美國總統曾經引用中國古語名言的成功演說為範例，引導全球廣大正在學習漢語的 CSL（漢語非母語學習者）成年學生接觸《論語》名言。從簡單易學的《論語》短句著手，探討傳統東方社會的核心文化價值與現今西方社會觀念的相互比對，達到跨文化學習的最優效果。

　　本書擷取《論語》篇章中關於：1 孝順（家庭）、2 朋友（社交）、3 君子或小人、4 學習、5 禮、6 快樂、7 音樂、8 仁愛、9 道德、10 政治等十大類的重要名句。在每一個篇章分別介紹代表性的孔子名言，逐字分析並提供延伸學習的常見詞彙，並在每一章提供短篇孔子生平故事，接著以參考 ACTFL OPI（美國外語教師協會）口語考試的模式發展討論話題、以 TOCFL（華語學測考試）和 HSK（漢語水平考試）的詞彙庫連貫該課名言的生詞，擴充學習常用詞彙的引導，讓學習古名言和現代用語連結，同時並進。

　　中國古典經書，尤其是記載儒家思想的《論語》，有著富含中華核心文化的重要價值。雖然近年來學習漢語的外國學生增加，但是在美國大學的漢語課程設計上，中國古典文學屬於高級漢語程度，對於非華裔背景的 CSL 學生來說，通常需要經過多年的漢語課程才能達到高級漢語水平。本書的設計是擷取易懂的《論語》名言，提供漢語水平在初、中級，並對於中華傳統文化有興趣的成年學生，透過逐字介紹、英文翻譯、白話註解以及延伸意義的討論，使學生能夠直接接觸到富有中華文化核心價值的《論語》名言原文。

很多外國演說者尤其在對有華裔聽眾演講的場合，特別喜歡引用孔子的名言，希望能和聽眾拉近文化距離。他們通常在網上所搜尋到的英文翻譯版並沒有中英對照。透過這種方法引用「Confucius said」的英文翻譯，容易失去原文的真實語意，也容易訛以傳訛，網絡上沒有附註漢語原文出處，並且錯誤不實之「孔子說 - Fake Confucius quotes」更是在網路上充斥無所不在。

演說者以英文引用 Confucius Said 時，華裔聽眾通常無法確知演講者所引的名言為何，失去跨文化溝通的意義。筆者認為演說者在引用中文名言時，若能先以漢語拼音唸出漢語原文，再接上英文演說，可以吸引華裔聽眾的信服和讚賞，更能增加演說的跨文化效力。筆者認為在美國曾經學習過中文的大學生即使還沒有到高級階段，也應該可以有足夠能力儘早接觸《論語》中的名言短句，也能透過學習這些富俱意義的短句，擴展語言及文化的學習。

全世界廣大的 CSL 學習者，應該有機會接觸富含中華文化核心價值的古文。歸納導致漢語教師對於教導學生們學習古文卻步不行的原因，除了認為學習古代漢語（古文）太難以外，其實真正的原因在於 1) 適用的教材太少 2) 配合外語學習教學法的研究缺乏。

本書針對以上幾項困難的瓶頸予以突破，挑選富有文化核心意義價值的簡短《論語》名句，加以分類並詳細的介紹分析，並且精心設計每一句名言的「延伸學習」，以及提供適用的課程教案。為了顯示在這些名言價值的不同時空背景、以及東西文化背景之對比，本書邀請多位專家以及美國學生對每一句《論語》名言撰寫短篇英文評論，反映這些傳統核心文化已經在今日的世界呈現並融合了跨文化的現代價值。

本書的設計特點如下：

# 一、【以原文學習真實語意】

對所摘錄的《論語》名言中的漢字都逐字解釋，讓學生能直接理解每一個漢字的意義，而不是只讀英文翻譯，沒有看到中文原文。學生能領會到古文雖然「精簡」，但其實並不難懂。這些名句中每一個字都仍然是現在常用的詞彙，不僅易學也很實用。對成年學習者來說，只要學過拼音，都能接觸古文，逐字了解其意涵。對於曾經學習過一兩個學期的漢語課程的 CSL 學生，更能夠利用這些簡短的古文，延伸學到更多的詞彙。

## 二、【延伸學習詞彙、句型和短篇孔子生平故事】

　　除了對孔子名言中的每一個漢字都能詳細理解之外，還利用這些漢字做「延伸學習」，提供相關造句詞彙，延伸例句，還有孔子生平短篇故事。本書設計從孔子的論語名言中的字詞出發，逐字延伸擴展，讓學習者利用學習到更多同義字以及相關的常用詞彙。對每一個詞彙，本書都加註參考【漢語水平考試－HSK】和【華語文能力測驗TOCFL】的等級數，讓學習者能夠從「學習古文」出發，進而增加對現代漢語的運用能力。

## 三、【跨文化價值教案】

　　從研讀《論語》名句出發，將中華文化精髓介紹給在全世界學習漢語的學生（洋弟子）。作者在這些名句的討論活動教學教案（teaching plan）中，以美國大學協會－Association of American Colleges & Universities (AAC&M) 所制定的美國大學通識教育為準則，配合美國外語教師協會（American Council on the Teaching of Foreign Languages－ACTFL）所訂定的語言學習評量準則為標的，提供給讀者各項相關的語言學習以及文化課程討論活動，並針對這些論語名言的主題，提供教師們實施課程教案的實用建議。

## 四、【古今中外核心價值之比較】

　　本書特別邀請不同領域的人士和美國大學生，對這些《論語》名言做「縱向」古今時空歷史，以及「橫向」東西文化異同做對比，並提供簡短評論（commentary）。這些評論由來自不同國家的政府官員（政治界）、醫生（醫學界）、金融顧問（商業界）、教授（學術界）、以及美國大學生（年輕的新生代）等之筆，讓讀者可以透過這些英文短評論（commentary），了解到孔子的儒家思想經過了兩千五百多年的流傳，仍能在現今國際化的社會中維持重要的文化意義，甚至已經衍生出在不同文化中皆所注重的普世價值。

　　作者也已經和一些美國大學生一起錄製了數個講述演示孔子名言的短視頻，提供給讀者參考學習 。鼓勵學生可以經常以孔子名言作為座右銘或是在演說中應用。本書出版時也可以將每一個名句都做出簡短的視頻，這些教學視頻可以伴隨遍佈世界各地的讀者學習達到更好的習得效果。

It is well-recognized that many of the deeply rooted Chinese social and behavioral principles can be sourced from the teaching of Confucianism. Chinese people adhere to many traditions in their families that were passed down, generation to generation, from their ancestors.

To learn about the teaching of Confucius, one should start reading The Analects—the book that recorded the teaching of Confucius and provides the original discussion between him and his disciples.

To help learners in Chinese language and culture courses learn about The Analects, which was written more than 2,000 years ago, the author selected essential topics from The Analects and designed a set of teaching materials for American college students to learn about the greatest Chinese philosopher's teachings and sayings.

This book provides the original texts of The Analects with Pinyin—the pronunciation, explanation of each word with its essential meaning, and translation of the entire quote. The original text is analyzed into individual words or phrases, and they are annotated with the pronunciation and meaning of each phrase. Readers can attain the meanings from the basic words and phrases and thereby understand the entire quotes.

In this book, each quote comes with modern, everyday examples. The author explains these quotes with illustrations of how Chinese people approach different life lessons and scenarios. Furthermore, the appropriate modern applications of each quote in Chinese society are presented with commentary by American students and esteemed contributors from different professional fields. The most compelling examples are American presidents quoting the philosopher's words in their speeches to the Chinese people. Readers can utilize a similar strategy of quoting the words of Confucius in delivering their speeches to a cross-cultural audience.

While teaching in the higher education environment, Liu found that most American students who start to learn the Chinese language in college have an immense interests in understanding Chinese culture, especially how Chinese ways of thinking function in business or political settings. However, these interests are often not served in the curriculum of a Chinese language course.

In a language course, most curriculum focus on the drills of basic vocabulary, sentence structure, and grammar occupy the lesson plans. Instructors of these language courses often have difficulty finding appropriate supplemental materials to discuss these important cultural points. Many adult learners who are learning the Chinese language consider the ancient text too difficult to learn and do not have the means to access it.

In the curriculum for Chinese as second language learners, most programs do not expose students to these ancient text materials — Gu Wen（古文）— until students reach advanced language competency. However, many college students who are taking Chinese language courses as electives won't have time to take as many Chinese courses as needed to reach the advanced level in their college years while accumulating the necessary courses in their major discipline. This is a commonly missed opportunity for college students who have learned Chinese as a second language — not being exposed to the essential materials of Chinese philosophy and culture. Furthermore, appropriate Chinese textbooks for intermediate-level students to learn the Chinese culture and philosophy in Chinese texts are very limited. Therefore, Liu has devoted years of her teaching to this area and decided to create appropriate learning materials to answer this need.

The design of this book starts with examples of how American presidents quoted the Chinese philosopher's words in their speeches.（美國領袖的名言引用實例）These speeches demonstrate a cross-cultural communications strategy for the current global platform.

Seeing the benefit of this cross-cultural approach using the Chinese quotes in the U.S. presidents' speeches, readers are encouraged to utilize these Chinese philosophical proverbs and apply them to a presentation or social conversations.

A suggested teaching guide ( 推薦教學指引 ), including learning activities and assignments（課程活動設計與課後作業）, and cultural discussion topics（文化討論話題）is provided as instruction resources.

Famous quotes from the Analects are organized into ten categories in this book.

Chapter 1    Quotes related to filial piety【孝順】
Chapter 2    Quotes related to friendship【朋友】
Chapter 3    Quotes related to being a good scholar (Jun-Zi) or a pitiful man (Xiao- Ren)
             【君子 或 小人】
Chapter 4    Quotes related to learning【學習】
Chapter 5    Quotes related to propriety【禮】
Chapter 6    Quotes related to the happiness in life【快樂】
Chapter 7    Quotes related to music【音樂】
Chapter 8    Quotes related to benevolence【仁愛】
Chapter 9    Quotes related to virtues【道德】
Chapter 10   Quotes related to politics【政治】

In each chapter, three quotes are fulling explained and provided the following sections and practices:
1. Learn the original text and its meaning（逐字翻譯）
2. Explanation with the modern text（白話解釋原文）
3. Extended learning with sentence practices（延伸對話與生詞）

4. Stories about Confucius' life and his teaching（孔子故事）

5. Commentary about this ancient text with modern values（現代價值評論）

6. Suggested topics for oral proficiency interview (OPI)（模擬口語考試話題）

7. Extended vocabulary learning on HSK & TOCFL（延伸生詞學習）附錄

## Who is this book for?

The target audience is the wide range of adult learners who are interested in understanding Chinese ways of thinking and values and applying Chinese ancient wisdom to the social interactions today. The book will be suitable to learners whose Chinese language competency levels ranges from intermediate to advanced levels. This book can serve as a textbook for philosophy courses, a supplemental textbook in language courses, or as a book for self-study learners.

### 1. Textbook for language course

This book is suited for all learners whose Chinese language competency ranges from intermediate to advanced levels. It can serve as supplemental material for Chinese culture and philosophy in Chinese language courses at any level.

### 2. Self-study learners

This book is suited for all CSL (Chinese as Second Language) learners whose Chinese language competency ranges from intermediate to advanced levels. It can serve as a self-study material because all quotes are explained fully in English with many ways of practices.

### 3. Textbook for cultural course

This book can serve as a textbook for cultural topic courses, related to the Chinese philosophy or Chinese ancient literature. The author has been teaching a liberal learning cultural course (general education course 大學通識教育課程 ), Chinese Philosophy and Calligraphy, at the College of New Jersey with these materials. These quotes are explained and discussed in English, then students would write these quotes with Chinese calligraphy exercises. Calligraphy writing samples of some Confucius quotes writing are provided in the book.

This book elucidates the importance of Confucian teaching and its current applications. Instructors using this book for cultural courses, can shift the focus from the language teaching to the cultural discussion topics.

It provides valid discussion topics related to social rules and the ways of thinking in Chinese society. Instructors can guide the students to explore the modern values of these ancient texts in today's cross-cultural society.

The genuine Confucius' quotes with citation to the correct chapters and verses in the Analects, provide students an invaluable opportunity to learn about Chinese classic literature. It is an important reminder for students to find genuine literature books to avoid fake Confucius' quotes on the internet.

The English translation for the Analects quotes was adapted from James Legge's (1815~1897) translation. We are deeply grateful for James Legge's master work.

## Short Biography of the author – Dr. Celia Liu

Dr. Celia Liu received her Doctor of Education degree from the Graduate School of Education of The University of Pennsylvania. She has been teaching Chinese language and culture courses in the World Language Department at The College of New Jersey (TCNJ) since 2010. She also has an M.A.T. (Master of Arts in Teaching) from Rutgers University, an MBA (Master in Business Administration) in Public Accounting and M.S. (Master of Science) in Taxation from Fordham University's Graduate School of Business.

With this cross-disciplinary background, Dr. Liu's teaching experiences covers Chinese Languages and Philosophy courses, International Transitional Seminar and

Accounting courses at The College of New Jersey and the Rutgers Business School. She holds certification of eligibility for K-12 World Language Education and Early Childhood Education in the State of New Jersey. She has a full certification as a tester for the ACTFL (American Council on the Teaching of Foreign Languages) Oral Proficiency Interview examination.

She has conducted numerous Internet Teaching Training workshops, seminars and webinars sponsored by the Taiwan Overseas Community Affair Council (OCAC), the National Council of Associations of Chinese Schools (NCACLS) and at ACTFL for Chinese language teachers regionally and nationwide. She also served as an instructor for technology-teaching courses at STARTALK program.

She composes language-teaching contents for curriculum, training workshops, and was the principal writer for the online Mandarin course material for K-12 students sponsored by Freeman Foundation at Rutgers University in 2010-2013. Being heavily involved with community services, Dr. Liu served many positions in local organization, immersion schools, and community Chinese schools boards and was frequently invited to local organizations, schools, and college students' events as a guest speaker on cross-cultural topics. Since 2020, she was elected as a board member of NECTFL (Northeast Conference on the Teaching of Foreign Languages). NECTFL is one of the five largest regional associations of its kind in the United States, working alongside the American Council on the Teaching of Foreign Languages (ACTFL), representing educators from Maine to Virginia but exercising leadership nation-wide. In 2022, Dr. Liu is awarded a Fulbright Hayes Group Project grant and she will serve as the project director leading a US-Taiwan cross-disciplinary research project.

# 推薦教學指引
# Teaching Guides

## 課程活動與課後作業Class Activities and Assignments

第一章　孝順
## Quotes related to filial piety

(一) **Oral discussion**

Instructors can engage students to hold an oral discussion on the topics provided below about "filial piety".

1. Please talk about the family activities you and your parents enjoy doing together.【Narration/Description】
2. Please discuss your opinion about whether an adult-child should live with their parents after they are married or not.【Discussion on abstract opinion】

口語練習

1. 請談談你和你父母親最喜歡一起做的事情。【描述／敘述】
2. 請討論孩子結婚以後，應不應該和父母住在一起？【討論／表達意見】

(二) **Essay writing**

Instructors can assign short essay writing with the topics below.

1. Please write about an unforgettable memory which happened in your family.
2. Do you remember how your parents took care of you when you were sick? Please describe what you remember about your parents' care.

寫作練習

1. 請描寫一件你和父母曾經經歷過、最難忘的或最感動的一件事。
2. 你記得小時候生病時父母照顧你的情形嗎？請回想並描寫在你小時候，父母如何照顧你？

## (三) **Applying the quotes in a skit/a presentation/a speech**

1. A group of students can create a drama (a play/skit) to illustrate a story related to "filial piety" – being kind to their parents. They can use a Confucius' quote related to "filial piety" in the written script for a play (skit).

2. In a video assignment, students can make speech telling a childhood story, or talking about their relationship with their parents. They can also share some suggestions about how to treat their parents with respect and practice filial piety. They should apply a Confucius' quote in their speech.

### 引用名言的任務型活動

1. 讓學生做一齣關於「孝順父母」的短劇演出,在短劇的對話中使用關於「孝順」的論語名言。

2. 讓學生錄製一段演說視頻,講一段童年的回憶,或分享他們和父母的故事,可以在演說中提出如何尊敬父母的建議,並使用關於「孝順」的論語名言。

## 第二章　朋友
## Quotes related to friendship

### (一) **Oral discussion**

Instructors can engage students to hold an oral discussion on the topics provided below about "friendship".

1. Please describe the things that you enjoy doing with your good friends. 【Narration/Description】

2. Please discuss your opinion with examples about how we should treat our good friends and what we should not do to our friends. 【Discussion on abstract opinion】

### 口語練習

1. 請說明你和你的好朋友最喜歡一起做的事情。【描述／敘述】

2. 請討論並以實例說明:我們應該怎麼對待我們的好朋友,和我們不應該怎樣

對待我們的好朋友。【討論／表達意見】

## (二) Essay writing

Instructors can assign short essay writing with the topics below.

1. Please write a letter to a friend whom you have not seen for a long time. Tell him/her about some recent updates about your life.
2. Please write a journal entry and describe a shared experience that you had with your friend.

### 寫作練習

1. 請寫一封信給一位很久沒有見面的老朋友，告訴他／她關於你的現況。
2. 請寫一篇日記，描述你和你的朋友一起做過的一件很有意思的事情。

## (三) Applying the quotes in a skit/a presentation/a speech

1. A group of students can create a drama (a play/skit) to illustrate a story related to "friendship" to demonstrate what are good friends. They can use a Confucius' quote related to "friendship" in the written script for a play (skit).
2. In a video assignment, students can make a speech wishing a friend "Happy Birthday" talking about their experiences related to friendship. They should apply a Confucius' quote in their speech.

### 引用名言的任務型活動

1. 讓學生做一齣關於「朋友／友誼」的短劇演出，在短劇的對話中使用關於「朋友」的論語名言。
2. 讓學生錄製一段視頻，在視頻中祝朋友「生日快樂」，談談和朋友曾經共同有的回憶，並使用關於「朋友」的論語名言。

# 第三章　君子或小人
## Quotes related to a gentleman or a pitiful man

## (一) Oral discussion

Instructors can engage students to hold an oral discussion on the topics provided below about "being a gentleman or a pitiful man."

1. Please describe a person with good behaviors and characteristics who you consider a gentleman ( 君子 ).【Narration/Description】
2. Please describe a person with bad behaviors and characteristics who you would consider a pitiful man ( 小人 ).【Narration/Description】

口語練習

1. 請說說你曾經遇過的一位好品行的「君子」是怎樣的一個人。【描述／敘述】
2. 請說說你曾經遇過的一位品行不好的「小人」是怎樣的一個人。【描述／敘述】

## (二) Essay writing

Instructors can assign short essay writing with the topics below:

1. Please write an essay to discuss what a gentleman or an educated person can contribute to the society.
2. Please write an essay to discuss what a person with bad behaviors can do harm to the society.
3. Please write a journal entry describing something that you did which could be considered as a gentleman with good behaviors.

寫作練習

1. 請寫一篇短文討論一位「君子」（品行好的人）可以為社會貢獻什麼？
2. 請寫一篇短文討論一位「小人」（品行不好的人）可以為社會造成什麼傷害或損失。
3. 請寫一篇日記，描述自己曾經做過的，像是一位「君子」的好行為。

(三) **Applying the quotes in a skit/a presentation/a speech**

1. A group of students can create a drama (a play/skit) to illustrate a story, or their experiences related to "being a gentleman or a pitiful man" describing what are good or bad characteristics or behaviors. They can use a Confucius' quote related to "being a gentleman or a pitiful man" in the written script for a play (skit).

2. In a video assignment, students can make a speech explaining what a gentleman could contribute and what a pitiful man could do to harm the society. They should apply a Confucius' quote in their speech.

## 引用名言的任務型活動

1. 讓學生做一齣關於「君子或小人」的短劇演出,在短劇的對話中分別扮演「君子」或「小人」,演示什麼是良好的行為,什麼是不好的行為,在劇中也可以引用一個關於「君子或小人」的論語名言。

2. 讓學生錄製一段演說視頻,在演說中解釋「君子或小人」的論語名言。解釋「君子」或「小人」對於國家和社會造成的影響。

# 第四章　學習
# Quotes related to learning

(一) **Oral discussion**

Instructors can engage students to hold a discussion on the topics provided below about "learning."

1. Please talk about a learning experience in which you felt happy or frustrated. 【Narration/Description】

2. Please describe how did you decide on your learning and career goal. 【Narration/Description】

## 口語練習

1. 請談談你在學習的時候,曾經感覺快樂或挫折的一個經驗。【描述／敘述】

2. 請談談你是如何決定自己的學習和職業目標。【描述／敘述】

## ㈡ Essay writing

Instructors can assign short essay writing with the topics below.

1. Please write about the most effective way of learning in your learning process.
2. Please describe the person who had the most influence in your learning process.

## 寫作練習

1. 請回想並寫下在你學習的過程中，對你的學習最有效的方法是什麼？
2. 請描述在你的學習過程中，對你影響最大的一個人。

## ㈢ Applying the quotes in a skit/a presentation/a speech

1. A group of students can create a drama (a play/skit) to illustrate a story related to "learning".  They can use a Confucius' quote related to "learning" in the written script for a play (skit).
   ⑴ My favorite learning experiences
   ⑵ My most memorable learning experience
   ⑶ An inspiring course in my college
2. In a video assignment, students can make speech talking about their learning experiences and their studying habits. They can also share some suggestions about learning and apply a Confucius' quote in their speech.

## 引用名言的任務型活動

1. 讓學生做一齣關於學習經驗的短劇演出，在短劇的對話中使用關於「學習」的論語名言。
   ⑴ 我最喜歡的學習經驗
   ⑵ 我最難忘的學習經驗
   ⑶ 大學課程給我的啟發
2. 讓學生錄製一段演說視頻，在演說中分享他的學習經驗、學習方式，也可以分享他們對學習的建議，並在演說中使用關於「學習」的論語名言。

# 第五章　禮
## Quotes related to propriety

## (一) Oral discussion

Instructors can engage students to hold a discussion on the topics provided below about "rites and etiquettes".

1. Please describe what, in your opinion, are the important etiquettes or proper manners in our daily social interactions.【Narration/Description】
2. Please discuss whether you notice that people from different cultural backgrounds conduct etiquettes differently.【Discussion on abstract opinion/ making comparison】

口語練習

1. 請說明你認為什麼是日常生活中重要的社交禮儀。【描述／敘述】
2. 請討論你注意到文化背景不同的人，有什麼不一樣的禮儀習慣？【討論／比較／表達意見】

## (二) Essay writing

Instructors can assign short essay writing with the topics below.

1. Please describe a practice of a foreign rite or an etiquette which is different from your own culture.
2. Please describe an important rite or etiquette of your culture, which related to a wedding or related to a funeral.

寫作練習

1. 請描述一個你曾經聽過，或是經歷過的不同文化的禮儀。
2. 請描述一個在你的文化中很有意義的重要禮儀。（可以是在婚禮中、或是葬禮中的禮儀。）

## (三) Applying the quotes in a skit/a presentation/a speech

1. A group of students can create a drama (a play/skit) to illustrate a story

related to "rites or etiquettes" to demonstrate what are good manners. They can use a Confucius' quote related to "rites or etiquettes" in the written script for a play (skit).

2. In a video assignment, students can make a speech, pretending they were the school principal, the mayor or the president talking on the topic of good etiquettes. They should apply a Confucius' quote in their speech.

## 引用名言的任務型活動

1. 讓學生做一齣關於「禮節」的短劇演出，表演什麼是好禮節，並在短劇的對話中使用關於「禮」的論語名言。

2. 讓學生錄製一段演說視頻，設想自己是一位校長，市長或是主席對學生演說，在演說中使用關於「禮」的論語名言。

---

# 第六章　快樂
# Quotes related to happiness in life

## (一) Oral discussion

Instructors can engage students to hold an oral discussion on the topics provided below about "the happiness in life".

1. Please narrate the happiest experience (or a happiest day) that you had in the past. 【Narration/Description】

2. Please describe your opinion about what a happy life would be like. 【Discussion on abstract opinion】

## 口語練習

1. 請說明你曾經經歷過最快樂的一件事。【描述／敘述】

2. 請談談你認為一個人應該追求什麼樣的快樂人生？【討論／表達意見】

## (二) Essay writing

Instructors can assign short essay writing with the topics below.

1. Please write about an unforgettable memory which made you feel very happy.

2. Please write an essay to describe your future wishes or what in your opinion a happy life would be like.

## 寫作練習

1. 請寫一段短文描述一件你曾經經歷過、最難忘的一件最快樂的事。
2. 請寫一段短文描述你對未來的願望或是描述你心目中的快樂人生。

## (三) Applying the quotes in a skit/a presentation/a speech

1. A group of students can create a drama (a play/skit) to illustrate a story related to "happiness in life". They can use a Confucius' quote related to "happiness in life" in the written script for a play (skit).
2. In a video assignment, students can tell a story about a happy (or an unhappy) experience or to discuss what they consider happiness in life is. They should apply a Confucius' quote in their speech.

## 引用名言的任務型活動

1. 讓學生做一齣關於「快樂的人生」的短劇演出，在短劇的對話中使用關於「快樂」的論語名言。
2. 讓學生錄製一段演說視頻，在演說中講述一個自己感覺最快樂（或不高興）的一個經驗，或是發表關於人生中真正的快樂是什麼。在演說中使用關於「快樂」的論語名言。

# 第七章　音樂
# Quotes related to music

## (一) Oral discussion

Instructors can engage students to hold an oral discussion on the topics provided below about "music".

1. What type of music do you enjoy the most? Please describe the music that you like, and discuss what are the effects it brings to you when you listen to the music.【Narration/Description】

2. Do you think learning music could change a person's temperament, please explain why do you think so?【Discussion on abstract opinion】

口語練習

1. 請談談你喜歡哪一種的音樂，並說說當你聽這些音樂的時候，它會為你帶來什麼樣的感受。【描述／敘述】

2. 你認為學習音樂會改變一個人的個性嗎？請說明你的看法。【表達意見／抽象觀念】

(二) **Essay writing**

Instructors can assign short essay writing with the topics below.

1. Please write an essay to describe how the music could cultivate ( 陶冶 ) people.

2. Some people strongly support music lesson as an important subject for all school-aged children. Do you agree with this opinion or not? Please write an essay to express your opinion on this topic.

寫作練習

1. 請寫一段短文描述並說明你認為「音樂如何能夠陶冶人心」。

2. 許多人認為音樂對學齡兒童是一項重要的課程。你同意這個看法嗎？請寫一段短文說明你的看法。

(三) **Applying the quotes in a skit/a presentation/a speech**

1. A group of students can create a drama (a play/skit) to illustrate a story about music, or their learning experiences related to "music". They can use a Confucius' quote related to "music" in the written script for a play (skit).

2. In a video assignment, students can make a speech talking about their experiences related to learning or playing music. They should apply a Confucius' quote in their speech.

引用名言的任務型活動

1. 讓學生做一齣短劇演出，主題是關於「音樂」的故事，或是學習音樂的經驗。在短劇的對話中使用關於「音樂」的論語名言。

2. 讓學生錄製一段演說視頻，在演說中敘述他們學習或表演音樂的經驗，並且使用關於「音樂」的論語名言。

# 第八章　仁愛
# Quotes related to benevolence

## (一) Oral discussion

Instructors can engage students to hold an oral discussion on the topics provided below about "being benevolence".

1. Please describe how people usually demonstrate their kindness to the family?【Narration/Description】
2. Please describe how people usually demonstrate their kindness to the friends?【Narration/Description】
3. Please describe how people usually demonstrate their kindness to the animals?【Narration/Description】

### 口語練習

1. 請說明人們通常會如何表示對家人的愛心。【描述／敘述】
2. 請說明人們通常會如何表示對朋友的愛心。【描述／敘述】
3. 請說說人們通常會如何表示對動物的愛心。【描述／敘述】

## (二) Essay writing

Instructors can assign short essay writing with the topics below.

1. Please write an essay to describe an experience that you had received a kindness or a favor from a stranger.
2. Please write a letter to your teacher, or an old friend to express your gratitude on the kindness or favor they had provided to you.

### 寫作練習

1. 請寫一段短文描述一位陌生人曾經給過你的幫助或恩惠。
2. 請寫一封信給你的老師或是你的老朋友，向他們曾經給予你的恩惠道謝。

## (三) Applying the quotes in a skit/a presentation/a speech

1. A group of students can create a drama (a play/skit) to illustrate a story, or their experiences related to "being benevolent and kind". They can use a Confucius' quote related to "benevolence" in the written script for a play (skit).

2. In a video assignment, students can make a speech describing how to exercise humanity kindness and care to people and to animals. They should apply a Confucius' quote in their speech.

引用名言的任務型活動

1. 讓學生做一齣描述他們曾經經歷過的仁愛的故事，或是介紹如何表現「仁愛」的短劇演出，在短劇的對話中使用關於「仁愛」的論語名言。

2. 讓學生錄製一段演說視頻，在演說中提到關於「對人友好、對動物友善」的故事，並且在演說中使用關於「仁愛」的論語名言。

## 第九章　道德
# Quotes related to virtues

## (一) Oral discussion

Instructors can engage students to hold an oral discussion on the topics provided below about "virtues".

1. Please describe and explain in your opinion what are three types of virtues and ethical actions.【Narration / Description】

2. Please describe what are "big virtues" and what are "small virtues." Please discuss according to your own opinion on this topic.【Discussion on abstract opinion】

口語練習

1. 請舉三例說明你認為什麼是有道德的行為。【描述／敘述】

2. 請討論什麼是「大德」？什麼是「小德」？請談談你對各種「道德」的看法。
【討論抽象觀念和表達意見】

The Analects, Chapter Zi-Zhan, verse 11 子夏曰：「大德不踰閑，小德出入可也。」

## (二) Essay writing

Instructors can assign short essay writing with the topics below.

1. Please write a short essay to narrate a story about ethical behaviors or to describe a person with good virtues.

寫作練習

1. 請寫一段短文描述有關道德的行為，或描述一位具有良好道德的人物故事。

## (三) Applying the quotes in a skit/a presentation/a speech:

1. A group of students can create a drama (a play/skit) to illustrate a story related to "virtues and ethical behaviors".  They can use a Confucius' quote related to "virtues and ethical behaviors" in the written script for a play (skit).
2. In a video assignment, students can tell a story about virtues and ethical behaviors or to discuss what behaviors they consider are virtues and ethical. They should apply a Confucius' quote in their speech.

引用名言的任務型活動

1. 讓學生做一齣關於「道德」表現的短劇演出，並且在短劇的對話中使用關於「道德」的論語名言。
2. 讓學生錄製一段演說視頻，在演說中使用關於「道德」的論語名言。

# 第十章　政治
# Quotes related to politics

## (一) Oral discussion

Instructors can engage students to hold an oral discussion on the topics provided below about "leadership and government".

1. Please describe your leadership experience in participating with a student

organization. 【Narration/Description】

2. Please discuss a possible policy change if you were the school principal, the mayor or the president of your country. 【Discussion on abstract opinion】

3. Please make comparison on the leadership or political position of an ancient king and the modern government leader.

## 口語練習

1. 請說明你參加學校社團時曾經擔任社團職務的經驗。【描述／敘述】

2. 請討論如果你是學校校長，或市長，或國家領導人，你會有什麼政策的改變？ 【假設情境】

3. 請比較古代的國王和現代的政府領導人在領導或政治地位有什麼不同？

## ㈡ Essay writing

Instructors can assign short essay writing with the topics below.

1. Please write an essay to describe a policy or a rule of your school.

2. Please write an essay to describe a policy or a regulation of your country's law.

3. Please write a letter to your school principal, your major, or your country's president to express your opinion on a situation or provide suggestions on a policy.

## 寫作練習

1. 請寫一段短文描述你的學校的一個政策或規定。

2. 請寫一段短文描述你的國家的一個政策或法律規定。

3. 請寫一封信給你的學校校長，或市長，或國家領導人，說明你對某一件事的意見，並提供你對政策的建議。

## ㈢ Applying the quotes in a skit/a presentation/a speech

1. A group of students can create a drama (a play/skit) to illustrate a story related to "governing or leadership" to demonstrate about good leaders. They can use a Confucius' quote related to "governing or leadership" in the written script for a play (skit).

2. In a video assignment, students can make a speech pretending they were the school principal, the mayor, or the president. They should apply a Confucius' quote in their speech.

引用名言的任務型活動

1. 讓學生做一齣關於「政治」議題的短劇演出，在短劇的對話中使用關於「政治」的論語名言。
2. 讓學生錄製一段演說視頻，假設以校長，或市長，或是總統的身分來發表演說。在演說中使用關於「政治」的論語名言。

# 文化討論話題Topics for Culture Discussion

## 第一章　孝順
## Quotes related to filial piety

1. 請分享你見過的孩子「孝順」父母的例子。

   Please share examples of children treating their parents respectfully in which illustrate the virtue of filial piety.

   【中級、高級 – 描述／敘述 Intermediate to Advanced Level – can narrate and describe】

2. 請比較說明在中國人和美國人的家庭裡，照顧老年人的方式有什麼相同或不同？

   Can you describe any difference or similarity in how people take care of their elders in Chinese families and in American families?

   【高級 – 說明比較 Advanced Level – can make comparison】

3. 請說明，如果你在事業上成功了，賺了很多錢以後，你會計畫如何照顧你的父母？

   Would you share your own plan on how you would take care of your elders if you became successful and rich?

   【優秀級 – 假設情境申述 Superior Level – can hypothesize】

4. 你認爲什麼是「孝順」？在你的文化背景裡，該怎麼做才算是對你的父母做到了「孝」？

In your opinion or according to your cultural background, what action is considered "filial piety"- a virtue of respect for one's parents and ancestors?

【優秀級 – 表達個人意見和申述抽象觀念 Superior Level – can support opinion and discuss abstract concept】

5. 在中華文化中，做出讓祖先光榮的事情是「孝順」的一部分。你同意這種觀念嗎？爲什麼？

In Chinese culture, it is considered filial piety if one can make an achievement to honor his/her family. Do you agree with this traditional concept? Why?

【優秀級 – 表達個人意見和申述抽象觀念 Superior Level – can support opinion and discuss abstract concept】

# 第二章　朋友
# Quotes related to friendship

1. 請說明，你的好朋友曾經爲你做的，讓你很高興的事情。

Please describe the things that your good friends did for you in the past which made you happy?

【中級、高級 – 描述／敘述 Intermediate to Advanced Level – can narrate and describe】

2. 請說明，你會願意爲你的好朋友做什麼事？

Please describe the things that you would be willing to do for your good friend.

【中級、高級 – 描述／敘述 Intermediate to Advanced Level – can narrate and describe】

3. 請依照你的看法，提出五個「怎樣才算是好朋友」的例子。

Please list 5 examples, in your opinion, which are considered demonstrating good friendship.

【中級、高級 – 描述／敘述 Intermediate to Advanced Level – can narrate and describe】

4. 你認爲和朋友要怎樣維持好的友誼？請舉例說明。

How do you maintain good friendship? Please provide some examples.

【中級、高級 – 描述 / 敘述 Intermediate to Advanced Level – can narrate and describe】

5. 你認為交跨文化（有不同的文化背景）的朋友有什麼好處？可能有什麼困難？為什麼？請舉例說明。

Please describe the benefits or difficulty of having cross-cultural friends? You can use examples to explain your opinion.

【優秀級 – 表達個人意見和申述抽象觀念 Superior Level – can support opinion and discuss abstract concept】

## 第三章　君子或小人
## Quotes related to a gentleman or a pitiful man

1. 請介紹一位著名的學者，或是一位世界的領導人，說說他們有什麼樣的性格？

Please introduce a well-known educated man/a scholar or a world leader; and describe the virtue or the characteristics of this person.

【中級、高級 – 描述 / 敘述 Intermediate to Advanced Level – can narrate and describe】

2. 你認為受過教育的人，能夠為我們的社會做什麼？

What do you think an educated person can contribute to our society?

【中級、高級 – 描述 / 敘述 Intermediate to Advanced Level – can narrate and describe】

3. 請說明一位令你敬佩的人，他有什麼特別的性格或是作為。

Please describe a person who you admire and respect. What are the characteristics or conducts which makes this person respectful?

【中級、高級 – 描述 / 敘述 Intermediate to Advanced Level – can narrate and describe】

4. 你曾經遇過品行不好的人嗎？他們做了什麼不好的行為，請描述一下。

Have you ever met someone who carried bad conduct or behaviors? Please describe those bad behaviors.

【中級、高級 – 描述／敘述 Intermediate to Advanced Level – can narrate and describe】

5. 你認為一個品行不好的人能夠因為受到教育的引導而變成一個品行良好的人嗎？請談談如果你是一位老師，你會怎麼做來陶冶並且改善一個人的品行？

Do you think education can cultivate and transform a person with bad conducts into a person with good conducts? If you were a teacher, what would you do to improve your students' moral conducts?

【優秀級 – 表達個人意見和申述抽象觀念，並做假設 Superior Level – can support opinion and discuss abstract concept and making hypothesis】

# 第四章 學習
# Quotes related to learning

1. 你認為什麼是好的學習方法？請舉三個例子。

Please describe three good learning styles.

【中級、高級 – 描述／敘述 Intermediate to Advanced Level – can narrate and describe】

2. 請談談你的一個學習經驗和學習過程。（你學了什麼？你是怎麼學習的？）

Please describe what learning process you have experienced.

【中級、高級 – 描述／敘述 Intermediate to Advanced Level – can narrate and describe】

3. 請談談你學中文的學習方法。

Please describe your studying style or methods for learning the Chinese language.

【中級、高級 – 描述／敘述 Intermediate to Advanced Level – can narrate and describe】

4. 請比較你的學習方法和你朋友的不一樣的學習方法。

Please compare your learning style with another different learning style of your friend.

【高級－說明比較 Advanced Level – can compare】

5. 有人說，女孩子比較擅長文科，男孩子比較擅長理科。你同意這樣的說法嗎？為什麼？

Some people say that the female students are better in liberal arts, while the male students are better in Math or Sciences. Do you agree with this statement? Why?

【高級－說明比較 Advanced Level – can compare】

【優秀級－表達個人意見和申述抽象觀念 Superior Level – can support opinion and discuss abstract concept】

6. 由於科技的進步，很多人覺得他們可以依靠網上資源來「自學」任何一項學科或技能。你贊同這個說法嗎？你認為依靠網路上的資源「自學」和傳統式由老師引導的學習，各有什麼優點或缺點？

Some people say that they can learn anything with the resources online. Do you agree with this statement? Please discuss the pros and cons for "self-learning" with resources online or learning with a teacher in a traditional classroom?

【高級－說明比較 Advanced Level – can compare】

【優秀級－表達個人意見和申述抽象觀念 Superior Level – can support opinion and discuss abstract concept】

# 第五章　禮
# Quotes related to propriety

1. 請說明三件合乎「禮」的好行為。

Please describe three things which you consider good behaviors (social etiquettes) and righteous conducts.

【中級、高級－描述／敘述 Intermediate to Advanced Level – can narrate and describe】

2. 請舉例說明什麼是一個家庭裡合乎「禮」的行為？請舉例說明一個在學校

裡合乎「禮」的行為？請舉例說明一個在工作的地方合乎「禮」的行為？請說明並比較這些在不同場合背景應該注意的合乎「禮」的行為。

Please provide an example of a righteous conduct which is suitable at home, a righteous conduct which is often seen at school and a righteous conduct which is often seen at the workplaces? Please explain these appropriate conducts (social etiquettes) and righteous behaviors in different settings and surroundings.

【中級、高級 – 描述／敘述 Intermediate to Advanced Level – can narrate and describe】

【高級 – 說明比較 Advanced Level – can compare】

3. 你有沒有經歷過一個很難做到合乎「禮」的情形？請分享你的經驗。（譬如，選擇合適的禮物送給不同文化的人。）

Have you ever experienced any difficulty in carrying out the righteous conducts? Please share about this experience. (For example, giving an appropriate gift to someone from different culture.)

【中級、高級 – 描述／敘述 Intermediate to Advanced Level – can narrate and describe】

4. 你有沒有曾經在一個不同文化的國家，因為不了解他們的習俗而做錯了一個行為的情形？請分享你的經驗，並對不了解這個文化的人提供一些建議。

Have you ever made a social misconduct in a country which has different culture because you did not understand their social customs? Please share your experiences and provide some advice for people not familiar with the culture.

【中級、高級 – 描述／敘述 Intermediate to Advanced Level – can narrate and describe】

5. 請談談你所知道的「社交禮儀」在西方社會和華人社會裡有什麼不同的表現方式。你認為為什麼在不同的地方會有這種不同的社交禮儀？

Do you have any examples which the social etiquettes in the Western society and in the Chinese society are different? Please explain why do you think they are different?

【高級 – 說明比較 Advanced Level – can compare】

【優秀級 – 表達個人意見和申述抽象觀念 Superior Level – can support opinion and discuss abstract concept】

## 第六章　快樂
## Quotes related to happiness in life

1. 請說明三件讓你覺得很快樂的事情。

    Please describe three things which make you happy.

    【中級、高級 – 描述／敘述 Intermediate to Advanced Level – can narrate and describe】

2. 小時候，什麼事情讓你很快樂？長大以後，什麼事情讓你很快樂？這些有什麼不同呢？

    What made you happy when you were a young child? What makes you happy after you become an adult? Please compare the differences in what you consider happiness is as a younger child and as an adult.

    【中級、高級 – 描述／敘述 Intermediate to Advanced Level – can narrate and describe】

    【高級 – 說明比較 Advanced Level – can compare】

3. 讓你感覺快樂的事情，有沒有和「學習」或「工作」有關的？為什麼這些事情會讓你快樂？請說明。

    Are the things which make you happy related to learning or working? Please discuss why these things would make you happy.

    【中級、高級 – 描述／敘述 Intermediate to Advanced Level – can narrate and describe】

    【優秀級 – 表達個人意見和申述抽象觀念 Superior Level – can support opinion and discuss abstract concept】

4. 什麼樣的快樂是「短期」的快樂？什麼樣的快樂是「長期」的（可以持續很久的）？請用你的經驗做例子說明，這兩種快樂有怎樣的差別？

    What kind of happiness do you consider "short-term"? What kind of happiness do you consider "long-term"? Please give examples of the two, and explain how you think these two types of happiness are different with your own experiences about them.

    【高級 – 說明比較 Advanced Level – can compare】

    【優秀級 – 表達個人意見和申述抽象觀念 Superior Level – can support opinion and discuss abstract concept】

# 第七章　音樂
## Quotes related to music

1. 請說明，你知道的音樂有哪幾種？他們的特色是什麼？他們有什麼不一樣？

   Please list the types of music you know of and talk about their characteristics and differences.

   【中級、高級 － 描述／敘述 Intermediate to Advanced Level － can narrate and describe】

   【高級 － 說明比較 Advanced Level － can compare】

2. 你認爲「音樂」對我們的生活有什麼好處？In your opinion, what benefits does music provide for our lives?

   【優秀級 － 表達個人意見和申述抽象觀念 Superior Level － can support opinion and discuss abstract concept】

3. 請談談你和你的好朋友（或室友）喜歡的音樂有什麼相同或不同的地方。

   Can you describe any difference or similarity in the types of music that you prefer compared with the types of music that your best friend or your roommate likes?

   【中級、高級 － 描述／敘述 Intermediate to Advanced Level － can narrate and describe】

   【高級 － 說明比較 Advanced Level － can compare】

4. 請討論西方流行音樂和東方流行音樂有什麼相同或不同的地方。

   Please discuss the difference or similarity in the Western pop-music and the Eastern pop-music.

   【中級、高級 － 說明比較 Advanced Level － can compare】

5. 有些人認爲學習音樂（或一個樂器）可以改變一個人的性格，你同意這個看法嗎？請對這個話題表達你的意見。

   Some people state that learning music (or a musical instrument) can cultivate people and change their characteristics. Do you agree with this statement? Please provide your opinion on this topic.

# 第八章　仁愛
## Quotes related to benevolence

1. 請（舉例）說明三個你認為是善良和仁愛的行為。

   Please list three examples of behaviors being kind and benevolent.

   【中級、高級 – 描述／敘述 Intermediate to Advanced Level – can narrate and describe】

2. 你認為每個人對「愛」會有不一樣的表達方式嗎？譬如，你是怎麼表達你對父母的愛？你的朋友是怎麼表達他們對父母的愛？你們的表達方法有不一樣嗎？可以舉例說明嗎？

   Do you think everyone expresses their love to people in a very different way? For example, how do you express your love to your parents? How do your friends express their love to their parents? Can you share an example about this topic?

   【中級、高級 – 說明比較 Advanced Level – can compare】

3. 你聽過「無差異化的愛（兼愛）」和「有差異化的愛」嗎？愛有大和小的分別嗎？請舉例討論你認為什麼是小愛，什麼是大愛？請舉例說明什麼是「兼愛」和「差異化的愛」。你認為「兼愛」和「差異化的愛」會有衝突嗎？你會比較贊同哪一種？

   What is the universal love (impartial love) and the differential love? Do you think love can be differentiated as "big love" (love to general population) or "small love" (love to one's own family or close friends)?

   Please give examples to illustrate "universal love" and "differential love." Do you think the universal love could conflict with the differential love? Please share your opinion on this topic.

   【中級、高級 – 描述／敘述 Intermediate to Advanced Level – can narrate and describe】

   【中級、高級 – 說明比較 Advanced Level – can compare】

4. 你覺得你的父母是如何表示他們對你的愛？請舉例說明。

   How do your parents express their love to you? Please explain by examples.

   【中級、高級 – 描述／敘述 Intermediate to Advanced Level – can narrate and describe】

5. 如果你將來成為父母了，你愛你的小孩的方式會不會和你父母愛你的方式不一樣？請討論你會用什麼方式來對你的孩子表達你對他們的愛。

   Please also describe how will you express your love for your child if you become a parent. Would you do it differently from the way your parents express their love for you?

   【優秀級 – 假設情境申述 Superior Level – can hypothesize】

## 第九章　道德
## Quotes related to virtues

1. 請舉例說明三個你認為是有道德的行為。

   Please list three examples of good ethical behaviors.

   【中級、高級 – 描述／敘述 Intermediate to Advanced Level – can narrate and describe】

2. 你覺得道德有大和小的分別嗎？請（舉例）說明你認為什麼是小道德，什麼是大道德？

   Do you think the virtues can be differentiated as "great virtues" or "small virtues"? Please make examples of what could be a great virtue and what could be considered a small virtue?

   【中級、高級 – 說明比較 Advanced Level – can compare】

   【中級、高級 – 描述／敘述 Intermediate to Advanced Level – can narrate and describe】

   子夏曰：「大德不踰閑，小德出入可也。」

   子夏說：「大的道德節操上不能逾越界限，在小節上有些出入是可以的。」

【原文出處 Reference】

【論語第十九·子張篇·第 11 節】 *The Analects，Chapter 19 Zi-Zhang，verse 11*

Zi Xia said, "When a person does not transgress the boundary line in the great virtues, he may pass and repass it in the small virtues."

3. 你覺得一個人的「道德」是怎麼養成的？道德是天生的？還是長大慢慢學習養成的？

Do you think people are born with good virtues innately or we grow to have virtues through learning?

【優秀級 – 表達個人意見和申述抽象觀念 Superior Level – can support opinion and discuss abstract concept】

4. 在現代的社會裡，你覺得道德是不是可能會和利益有衝突？請說明一個「利益和道德衝突」的例子。

In today's modern society, do you think sometimes obtaining virtues could be conflicted with material profits? Please think about an example in which virtues and profits are conflicted.

【中級、高級 – 描述／敘述 Intermediate to Advanced Level – can narrate and describe】

【優秀級 – 表達個人意見和申述抽象觀念 Superior Level – can support opinion and discuss abstract concept】

5. 你覺得東方和西方的道德標準有不同嗎？請以例子說明，什麼是在東方和西方國家都同樣被特別注重的道德。

In today's modern, are there different standards for virtues in the Western countries or in the Eastern countries? Please provide some examples that illustrate the virtues which are valued in both the West and the East.

## 第十章　政治
## Quotes related to government and good leaders

1. 你覺得一位好的國家元首（領導人）應該有什麼特質？

What characteristics do you think a good leader of a country should have?

【中級、高級 – 描述／敘述 Intermediate to Advanced Level – can narrate and describe〕

2. 你認為在你的國家的（美國的）歷史上誰是一位好總統（國家領導人）？為什麼？

Who do you think is a good president (leader) in the history of the United States of America (or in your country)? Please explain why.

〔中級、高級 – 描述／敘述 Intermediate to Advanced Level – can narrate and describe〕

3. 如果你是一位國家元首，你會有什麼新的政策來改善人民的生活？

If you were the president, what new policy would you implement to improve the citizen's life in your country?

〔優秀級 – 假設情境申述 Superior Level – can hypothesize〕

4. 如果你是一位國家元首，你會有什麼新的政策來改善國際間的和平？

If you were the president of your country, what new policy would you implement to improve world peace?

〔優秀級 – 假設情境申述 Superior Level – can hypothesize〕

5. 請說明最近發生的一件（國內或國外的）政治事件，並且提出你對於這件事的看法。

Please describe a political event that happened recently in your country or internationally. Share your opinion on this matter.

〔優秀級 – 表達個人意見和申述抽象觀念 Superior Level – can support opinion and discuss abstract concept〕

# 目錄
# CONTENTS

## 關於【孝順】的三個論語名言：
**Three top quotes about "Filial Piety":**

父母在，不遠遊，遊必有方。

While his parents are alive, the son may not go abroad to a distance. If he does go abroad, he must have a fixed place to which he goes."

【論語第四 · 里仁篇 · 第 19 節】*The Analects, Chapter 4 Li-Ren, Verse 19*


父母唯其疾之憂。

Parents are anxious lest their children should be sick.

【論語第二 · 為政篇 · 第 6 節】*The Analects, Chapter 2 Wei-Zheng, Verse 6*


父母之年，不可不知，一則以喜，一則以懼。

The years of parents may by no means not be kept in the memory, as an occasion at once for joy and for fear.

【論語第四 · 里仁篇 · 第 21 節】*The Analects, Chapter 4 Li-Ren, Verse 21*

名言一 **父母在，不遠遊，遊必有方。**
**Quote 1**

While his parents are alive, the son may not go abroad to a distance. If he does go abroad, he must have a fixed place to which he goes."

## (一)逐字翻譯
## Learn the original text and its meaning

父母在，不遠遊，遊必有方。
fù mǔ zài, bù yuǎn yóu, yóu bì yǒu fāng.

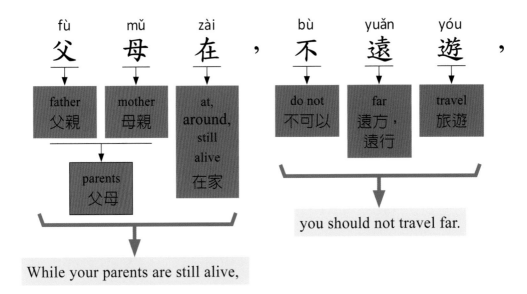

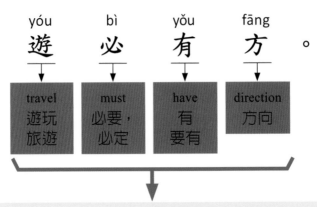

If you need to travel, you should always tell your parents where you are.

## ㈡白話解釋原文
## Explanation with the modern text

父母在，不遠遊，遊必有方 。

While his parents are alive, the son may not go abroad to a distance. If he does go abroad, he must have a fixed place to which he goes.

### 1.白話解釋
父母還在（＝還健在＝活著）的時候，孩子不應該到遠方旅遊，因爲父母會擔心孩子的安全，也會想念孩子。孩子旅遊的時候，一定要告訴父母你的去向。

While your parents are still living, children should not travel far. This is because the parents will worry about their children's safety, and they will miss their children. When the children need to travel, they should tell their parents where they are traveling to.

### 2.生詞

| | 生詞<br>Vocabulary | 拼音<br>Pin Yin | 英文<br>English | 詞類<br>Part of Speech |
|---|---|---|---|---|
| 1 | 健在＝活著 | jiàn zài =huó zhe | at, alive, around | adjective |
| 2 | 應該 | yīng gāi | should | verb |
| 3 | 遠方 | yuǎn fāng | far places | noun |
| 4 | 旅遊 | lǚ yóu | to travel | verb |
| 5 | 擔心 | dān xīn | to worry | verb |
| 6 | 安全 | ān quán | safety | noun |
| 7 | 想念 | xiǎng niàn | whereabout | verb |
| 8 | 去向 | qù xiàng | direction | noun |

## ㊂延伸對話與生詞
### Extended learning with sentence practices

1.會話

A：你的父母在不在家？

Are your parents at home?

B：在。他們在家，請等一下。

Yes. They are at home. Please wait for a minute.

A：下個月我會去中國旅遊。

I am going to travel to China next month.

B：你旅遊的時候，要記得給你的父母發短信，向他們報平安。

Whenever you are traveling, you should send a text message to your parents to let them know that you are safe.

2.生詞

| | 生詞<br>**Vocabulary** | 拼音<br>**Pin Yin** | 英文<br>**English** | 詞類<br>**Part of Speech** |
|---|---|---|---|---|
| 1 | 在家 | zài jiā | at home | Vs |
| 2 | 請 | qǐng | please | verb |
| 3 | 等一下 | děng yí xià | wait a minute | noun |
| 4 | 下個月 | xià gè yuè | next month | noun |
| 5 | 中國 | zhōng guó | China | noun |
| 6 | 發短信 | fā duǎn xìn | to send a text message | verb |
| 7 | 報平安 | bào píng ān | to report one's safety | verb |

## ㈣ 孔子故事
### Stories about Confucius' life and his teaching

## 孔子的出生和他的父母
Confucius' early childhood and his parents.

孔子在西元前551年（B.C.E.）周朝春秋時代的魯國（現在的中國山東省曲阜）出生。孔子的爸爸名字是孔紇（叔梁紇），他有九個女兒和一個殘障的兒子。雖然孔紇（叔梁紇）已經快七十歲了，可是他還想要有一個健康的兒子。於是，他又娶了一位年輕的女子，就是孔子的媽媽，顏徵在。他們到小山丘上去祈禱[1]，希望能生一個兒子。後來孔子出生了，他們就叫他「孔丘」，字「仲尼」。孔子三歲的時候，他的爸爸就去世了。孔子的媽媽自己一個人把孔子養大。

Confucius was born in 551 B.C.E. in the State of Lu (in present-day Qufu, Shandong Province, China), during the Spring and Autumn period of the Zhou dynasty. Confucius' father, Kong-He (or Shu-Liang-He), an official from the Lu State, had nine daughters and a crippled son from his first marriage. In his older age (near 70's), he asked Confucius' mother, Yan Zheng-Zai, to marry him*. They prayed for a son on a hill. When they had Confucius next year, they name him, "Qiu", meaning "Hill." His capping name (literary name) is Zhong-Ni. Confucius' father passed away when Confucius was three years old, so his mother raised him on her · own.

### 【原文出處 Reference】

[1] In KongZi Shijia, it was recorded that Confucius' parents had a "wild union"(野合) then gave birth to Confucius. Some translated this as extra-marital union or had a child out of wedlock.
【史記・孔子世家・第1節】*Shiji, Kongzi Shijia, Verse 1*
【孔子家語・第39章・本姓解・第1節】*Kongzi Jiayu, Chapter 39 Ben-Xing-Jie, Verse 1*

## ㈤論語名言的現代價值評論
## Commentary about this ancient text with modern values

Ancient Text：父母在，不遠遊，遊必有方。

While his parents are alive, the son may not go abroad to a distance. If he does go abroad, he must have a fixed place to which he goes.

【論語第四・里仁篇・第 19 節】 *The Analects, Chapter 4 Li-Ren, Verse 19*

**Modern Values Commentary by: Alexander Viola**

Traveling and ultimately living away from your parents is a granted part of a typically envisioned successful American life. Young adults are expected to take off from their nests: off to college, to career, and beyond, fashioning brilliant, independent lives and eventually roosts of their own. So ingrained is this ideal, it would be almost unreasonable to have a child not roam as they come of age. However, Confucius importantly—and perhaps knowingly—doesn't preclude the very possibility of travel, but merely adds a condition. Let your parents know where you are. If not roving away from your parents is impossible, following that one rule certainly is possible—it is no more than an easy call or brief text message, nowadays. So easy and so brief as to often make it a forgettable thing for a busy person. Even at the frequent entreaties of parents, doing so misses our minds on occasion. What might help us to remember is to really understand why they ask this communication of us, something the conciseness of this quote invites us to ponder. I think having empathy towards our parents leads us to the answer, as simple and as human as it is: they worry about us. They just want to know that we are safe, happy, and healthy where we are—wherever we are. Once we truly comprehend that, as we see the humanity of our own parents and understand the mercy that such a simple message might mean, I imagine it will become quite difficult not to send it.

Alexander Viola 韋明達
Computer Science Major,
The College of New Jersey, USA

## ㈥ 模擬口語考試討論話題
### Suggested topics for oral proficiency interview (OPI)

**父母在，不遠遊，遊必有方。**

While his parents are alive, the son may not go abroad to a distance. If he does go abroad, he must have a fixed place to which he goes.

【模擬口試考題】

1. 你外出時，會不會先告訴你的父母？為什麼？請說明你覺得為什麼應該告訴父母你的去向，或是不必告訴父母。

   Do you always let your parents know when you go out? Do you think we should let our parents know where we are going; why or why not?

   【中級、高級 – 描述／敘述 Intermediate to Advanced Level – can narrate and describe】

2. 下個月你想要和朋友去旅遊，你們要去比較遠的地方過夜。你會怎麼跟你的父母說這件事，讓他們放心讓你和朋友出去玩？

   （我來扮演你的父母，你來跟我說你想和朋友去旅遊的事情。）

   Next mouth, you want to travel with your friends to a far place overnight. How would you tell your parents so that they will not be worried about your travel? (I will play the role of your parents. Please talk to me about your weekend plans.)

   【中級、高級 – 角色扮演 Intermediate to Advanced Level – role play】

## 名言二　孟武伯問孝。子曰：「父母唯其疾之憂。」

**Quote 2**　Meng Wu asked what filial piety was. The Master said, "Parents are anxious lest their children should be sick."

### (一) 逐字翻譯
**Learn the original text and its meaning**

孟武伯問孝。子曰：「父母唯其疾之憂。」

mèng wǔ bó wèn xiào. zǐ yuē : "fù mǔ wéi qí jí zhī yōu."

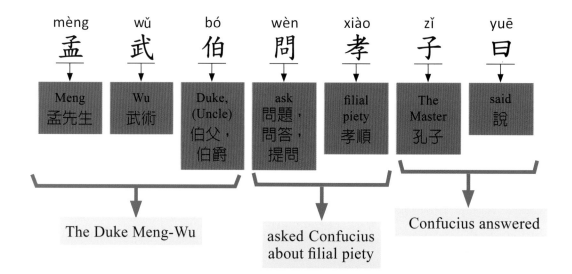

Meng Wu Bo asked why one should perform filial piety. Confucius answered: "Parents worry and care so much when the child is sick." (Knowing this kind of unconditional love, a child should always be grateful for his parents and exercise the filial piety virtue.)

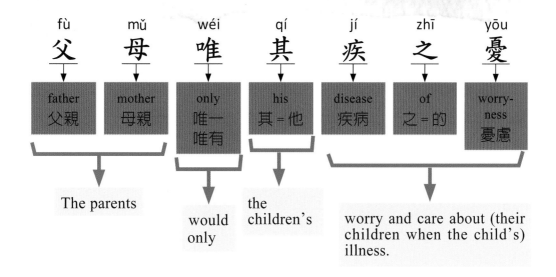

| fù | mǔ | wéi | qí | jí | zhī | yōu |
|---|---|---|---|---|---|---|
| 父 | 母 | 唯 | 其 | 疾 | 之 | 憂 |
| father<br>父親 | mother<br>母親 | only<br>唯一<br>唯有 | his<br>其＝他 | disease<br>疾病 | of<br>之＝的 | worry-<br>ness<br>憂慮 |

The parents

would only

the children's

worry and care about (their children when the child's) illness.

## ㈡ 白話解釋原文
### Explanation with the modern text

孟武伯問孝。子曰：「父母唯其疾之憂。」

Meng Wu Bo asked why one should perform filial piety. Confucius answered: "Parents worry and care so much when the child is sick." (Knowing this kind of unconditional love, a child should always be grateful for his parents and exercise the filial piety virtue.)

### 1.白話解釋

孟武伯問孔子：「我們為什麼要孝順父母呢？」孔子說：「想想當你生病的時候，父母是如何地擔心我們，照顧我們。」

如果你可以了解父母是這麼辛苦地照顧我們，我們長大後就應該孝順父母。

Meng-Wu Duke asked Confucius: "Why do we need to exercise filial piety and treat our parents well?" Confucius said: "Think about it when you are sick, how much our parents worry about us and take care of us?"

### 2.生詞

| | 生詞<br>Vocabulary | 拼音<br>Pin Yin | 英文<br>English | 詞類<br>Part of Speech |
|---|---|---|---|---|
| 1 | 孝順 | xiào shùn | filial piety | noun |

| | 生詞<br>Vocabulary | 拼音<br>Pin Yin | 英文<br>English | 詞類<br>Part of Speech |
|---|---|---|---|---|
| 2 | 當⋯的時候 | dāng … de shí hòu | as, when | preposition phrase |
| 3 | 生病 | shēng bìng | to be sick | adjective |
| 4 | 如何地 | rú hé dì | how | adverb |
| 5 | 擔心 | dān xīn | to worry | verb |
| 6 | 照顧 | zhào gù | to take care of | verb |
| 7 | 辛苦地 | xīn kǔ dì | strenuously, working through tough time | adverb |
| 8 | 長大 | zhǎng dà | to grow up | verb |

## (三) 延伸對話與生詞
### Extended learning with sentence practices

### 1. 會話

A：我生病的時候最希望能夠喝到媽媽做的雞湯。

When I am sick, I wish I could drink my mom's chicken soup.

B：是啊！小時候，我們生病的時候，媽媽細心地照顧我們。

Indeed, when we were little, our mother always took care of us when we were ill.

現在我們長大了，爸爸媽媽老了，我們一定要照顧他們。

We are grownups now. Our parents are getting old; we must take care of them.

### 2. 生詞

| | 生詞<br>Vocabulary | 拼音<br>Pin Yin | 英文<br>English | 詞類<br>Part of Speech |
|---|---|---|---|---|
| 1 | 希望 | xī wàng | to wish | verb |
| 2 | 喝到 | hē dào | to drink | verb |

| | 生詞<br>**Vocabulary** | 拼音<br>**Pin Yin** | 英文<br>**English** | 詞類<br>**Part of Speech** |
|---|---|---|---|---|
| 3 | 雞湯 | jī tāng | chicken soup | noun |
| 4 | 細心地 | xì xīn dì | carefully | adverb |
| 5 | 照顧 | zhào gù | take care of | verb |
| 6 | 長大 | zhǎng dà | to grow up | verb |
| 7 | 老 | lǎo | old | adjective |
| 8 | 誰 | shuí | who | pronoun |

## ㈣ 孔子故事
## Stories about Confucius' life and his teaching

### 孔子長相
Confucius' appearance.

在司馬遷寫的《史記・孔子世家》中描述地孔子：孔子出生的時候，他的頭頂很高，像一座小山丘，四週高，中間低，像一個倒蓋的屋頂。所以他的名字叫「丘」。長大的孔子身高很高大，有人叫他「長人」。

In the Records of Grand Historian, Shi-Ji, Kongzi-Shijia 史記孔子世家，written by Sima Qian (145 B.C.E – 86 B.C.E.) described Confucius' appearance. "He was born with a flat top on his head, that was why he was named "Hill.""

Confucius was very tall as a grown-up, reaching 9 nine feet, 6 inches in ancient measurements. (approximately 185 cm). Sima Qian called Confucius: "the tall man" in the Records of Grand Historian.

【原文出處 Reference】

司馬遷的《史記・世家・孔子世家》「生而首上圩頂，故因名曰丘云。字仲尼，姓孔氏。」孔子長九尺有六寸，人皆謂之「長人」而異之。
【史記・孔子世家・第 1 & 5 節】 *Shiji, Kongzi Shijia, Verse 1 & 5*
【孔子家語・第 9 章・本姓解・第 1 節】 *Kongzi Jiayu, Chapter 9 Ben-Xing-Jie, Verse 1*

## ㈤論語名言的現代價值評論
## Commentary about this ancient text with modern values

Ancient Text：父母唯其疾之憂。

Meng Wu asked what filial piety was. The Master said, "Parents are anxious lest their children should be sick."

【論語第二・為政篇・第 6 節】 *The Analects, Chapter 2 Wei-Zheng, Verse 6*

**Modern Values Commentary by: Dr. Gloria A Bachmann**

"Parents worry and care so much when the child is sick," truly taps into the expansiveness of maternal and paternal unconditional love. No parent can dismiss the strong bond of love that bridges their care to the medically ill child. However, Confucius's saying goes beyond the sick room. These wise words also gently remind the parents that the tender feelings that emerge when a child is sick should be embraced under all other circumstances as well. That is, the young child who misbehaves, the teen child who occasionally disobeys, the young adult child who becomes a poor communicator---all scenario, although disturbing to the parents, should never-the-less, illicit the same love that emerges when the child is sick. As Confucius so wisely reminds us, that same parental love that is given to the sick child should permeate the discipline when the well-child deviates.

Gloria A Bachmann, MD
Interim Chair, Department of Obstetrics,
Gynecology & Reproductive Sciences
Associate Dean for Women's Health
Director, Women's Health Institute
Rutgers Robert Wood Johnson Medical School

## ㈥ 模擬口語考試練習
## Suggested topics for oral proficiency interview (OPI)

孟武伯問孝。子曰：「父母唯其疾之憂。」

Meng Wu Bo asked why one should perform filial piety. Confucius answered: "Parents worry and care so much when the child is sick."

【模擬口試練習】

1. 你認為我們為什麼要孝順父母？請提出三個理由。

   Why do you think we should exercise filial piety and treat our parents with respect and care? Please list three reasons for filial piety.

   【優秀級 – 表達個人意見和申述抽象觀念 Superior Level – can support opinion and discuss abstract concept】

2. 你記得小時候你的父母是怎樣照顧你的嗎？請分享最令你難忘的一個兒時回憶，說明你的父母是如何地照顧你的。

   Do you remember how your parents took care of you? Please share your most unforgettable childhood memory about how your parents took care of you when you were young.

---

名言三 / Quote 3

**父母之年，不可不知，一則以喜，一則以懼。**

**The Master said, "The years of parents may by no means not be kept in the memory, as an occasion at once for joy and for fear."**

---

## ㈠ 逐字翻譯
## Learn the original text and its meaning

父母之年，不可不知，一則以喜，一則以懼。

fù mǔ zhī nián, bù kě bù zhī, yī zé yǐ xǐ, yī zé yǐ jù.

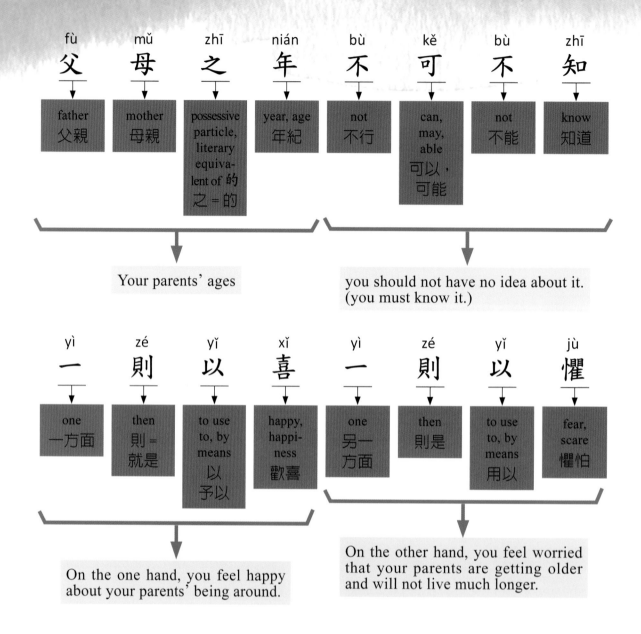

| fù 父 | mǔ 母 | zhī 之 | nián 年 | bù 不 | kě 可 | bù 不 | zhī 知 |
|---|---|---|---|---|---|---|---|
| father 父親 | mother 母親 | possessive particle, literary equivalent of 的 之 = 的 | year, age 年紀 | not 不行 | can, may, able 可以，可能 | not 不能 | know 知道 |

Your parents' ages

you should not have no idea about it. (you must know it.)

| yì 一 | zé 則 | yǐ 以 | xǐ 喜 | yì 一 | zé 則 | yǐ 以 | jù 懼 |
|---|---|---|---|---|---|---|---|
| one 一方面 | then 則 = 就是 | to use to, by means 以 予以 | happy, happiness 歡喜 | one 另一方面 | then 則是 | to use to, by means 用以 | fear, scare 懼怕 |

On the one hand, you feel happy about your parents' being around.

On the other hand, you feel worried that your parents are getting older and will not live much longer.

## ㈡ 白話解釋原文
### Explanation with the modern text

父母之年，不可不知，一則以喜，一則以懼。

The Master said, "The years of parents may by no means not be kept in the memory, as an occasion at once for joy and for fear."

## 1.白話解釋

父母的年紀，我們不可以不知道。一方面，覺得很高興，因為他們還健在，另一方面也害怕他們越來越老了。

We need to be aware of our parents' ages. On the one hand, we are very happy because they are still healthy and alive; on the other hand, we are worried that they are getting older.

## 2.生詞

| | 生詞<br>Vocabulary | 拼音<br>Pin Yin | 英文<br>English | 詞類<br>Part of Speech |
|---|---|---|---|---|
| 1 | 年紀 | nián jì | age | noun |
| 2 | 一方面…另一方面… | yī fāng miàn … lìng yī fāng miàn … | on one hand, and on the other hand | phrase |
| 3 | 健在 | jiàn zài | healthy | adjective |
| 4 | 害怕 | hài pà | to fear | verb |
| 5 | 越來越老 | yuè lái yuè lǎo | older and older | adjective phrase |

## ㈢ 延伸對話與生詞
### Extended learning with sentence practices

### 1.對話

A：你知道你父母的年紀嗎？

　　Do you know your parents' ages?

B：我當然記得。有的時候，我們會忘記自己的父母漸漸變老了。

　　Of course I remember. Sometimes, we forget our parents are getting older.

A：對啊！我們要好好把握和父母相處的時間。他們還在的時候，要讓他們高興。

　　That's right. We should make every opportunity to spend time with them. We should make them happy while they are around.

## 2.生詞

| | 生詞<br>**Vocabulary** | 拼音<br>**Pin Yin** | 英文<br>**English** | 詞類<br>**Part of Speech** |
|---|---|---|---|---|
| 1 | 忘記 | wàng jì | to forget | verb |
| 2 | 漸漸 | jiàn jiàn | gradually | adverb |
| 3 | 變老 | biàn lǎo | getting older | adjective |
| 4 | 把握 | bǎ wò | to hold | verb |
| 5 | 相處 | xiāng chǔ | to get along | verb |
| 6 | 時間 | shí jiān | time | noun |
| 7 | 還在 | hái zài | still around | adjective |

## ㈣ 孔子故事

### Stories about Confucius' life and his teaching

孔子的家人 ── 太太、兒子、女兒

Confucius' family, his wife, son, and daughter.

孔子在 19 歲的時候，娶了妻子，亓官氏。第二年亓官氏就生了一個兒子，魯昭公派人送了鯉魚來祝賀孔子有了兒子，孔子就把他的兒子取名爲「孔鯉」。

孔子也有一個女兒，他把女兒嫁給了公冶長 *

Confucius married Qi Guan-Shi when he was 19 years old. They had a son the next year. The Duke of Lu sent carp fish as a gift for their newborn. Confucius decided to name their son - Carp. Confucius also had a daughter. He married his daughter to a scholar Gong-Ye-Chang.

【原文出處 Reference】

子謂公冶長，「可妻也。雖在縲絏之中，非其罪也」。以其子妻之。
【論語第五・公冶長・第 1 節】*The Analects, Chapter 5 Gong-Ye-Chang, Verse 1*
【孔子家語・第 39 章・本姓解・第 1 節】*Kongzi Jiayu, Chapter 39 Ben-Xing-Jie, Verse 1*

孔子葬母

Confucius provided an honorable burial for his mother.

孔子三歲時，他的父親就死了。孔子的母親沒有告訴孔子，他的父親的墳墓在哪裡。後來，孔子 17 歲的時候，他的母親也去世了。爲了讓母親安葬，孔子到處打聽，後來有一位諏（zōu）人輓（wǎn）父的老母親告訴了孔子他父親葬在哪裡，最後終於找到了父親的墳墓，才能讓孔子的母親和父親葬在一起。

Confucius' father passed away when he was three years old. His mother did not tell Confucius where his father was buried before she died. Confucius' mother passed away when he was 17 years old. In honoring his mother, Confucius asked around and searched for his father's burial site. Finally, with an old neighbor's help, he was able to find his father's tomb and bury his parents together.

【原文出處 Reference】

孔子母死，乃殯五父之衢，蓋其愼也。耶人輓父之母誨孔子父墓，然後往合葬于防焉。

【史記・孔子世家・第 2 節】*Shiji, Kongzi Shijia, Verse 2*

## ㈤ 論語名言的現代價值評論

### Commentary about this ancient text with modern values

Ancient Text：父母之年，不可不知，一則以喜，一則以懼。

The Master said, "The years of parents may by no means not be kept in the memory, as an occasion at once for joy and for fear."

【論語第四・里仁篇・第 21 節】*The Analects, Chapter 4 Li-Ren, Verse 21*

**Modern Values Commentary by: Tomas Athan,** 沈永明

Leaves that are green turn to brown. I wonder, do they ever stop to remember the spring or think to autumn?

As a child, I remember being overcome with emotion when the impermanence of life flashed before my mind's eye. I was safe and happy and with my mom and dad back then, and yet I knew that it would pass. I intuited this forthcoming reality and felt a deep sense of grief.

It turns out the young and sensitive intuition was well reasoned. If one takes a couple of average assumptions about their parents' life expectancies and the anticipated number of visits they might have per year in adulthood, it is not uncommon that by the time that person turns 18 years old they will have spent upwards of 90% of all the shared days they will ever have with their parents.

When we look into the eyes of the people who brought us life, there is only one time we can ever truly see them — in the present moment. Everything else is either memory or fantasy. In this way, Confucius says we cannot not be aware of our parents' age.

And yet, so often our eyes see our parents through distorted lenses that are rosy (喜) or foggy (懼). By reflecting on and accepting the impermanence of life, we come closer to celebrating this shared time right now. Remember often that we all have to die. Death can be sad — that's okay — feel what you feel. It can also be peaceful and liberating. If you're lucky enough to have a parent or two in your life, be sure to cherish them.

Tomas Athan, 沈永明

Manager at Environmental Enterprise,

Trenton, New Jersey, USA

## ㈥ 模擬口語考試討論話題
### Suggested topics for oral proficiency interview (OPI)

父母之年，不可不知，一則以喜，一則以懼。

The Master said, "The years of parents may by no means not be kept in the memory, as an occasion at once for joy and for fear."

【模擬口試練習】

1. 請說明，上一次你父母的生日，你是怎樣爲父母慶祝的？

   Please describe how you celebrated your parents' last birthday.

   【中級、高級 – 描述／敍述 Intermediate to Advanced Level – can narrate and describe】

2. 你認爲老人應該和家人住在一起，還是應該去住養老院？請談談你的看法。

   Do you think senior citizens should live with their families or in nursing homes? Please share your opinion on this.

   【優秀級 – 表達個人意見和申述抽象觀念 Superior Level – can support opinion and discuss abstract concept】

【孝順】入則孝出則弟【論語第一 · 學而篇 · 第 6 節】*The Analects, Chapter 1 Xue-Er; Verse 6*

When at home, one should be filial, and abroad, respectful to his elders.

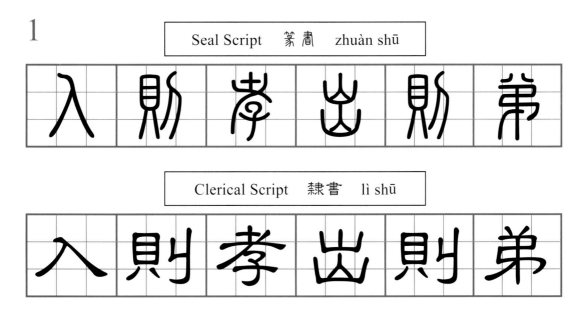

| Cursive Script 草書 cǎo shū |
|---|

| Running Script 行書 xíng shū |
|---|

| Standard Script 楷書 kǎi shū |
|---|

## 關於【朋友】的三個論語名言：
## Three top quotes about "Friendship":

四海之內，皆兄弟也。

To the superior and benevolent man (educated person), all within the four seas will be his brothers.

【論語第十二‧顏淵篇‧第 5 節】 *The Analects, Chapter 12 Yan-Yuan, Verse 5*


與朋友交，言而有信。

In our interaction with friends, one's words should be sincere.

【論語第一‧學而篇‧第 7 節】 *The Analects, Chapter 1 Xue-Er, Verse 7*


老者安之，朋友信之，少者懷之。

My wishes are, to provide the aged comfort; to show the friends sincerity; to treat the young tenderly.

【論語第五‧公冶長篇‧第 26 節】 *The Analects, Chapter 5 Gong-Ye-Chang, Verse 26*

# 名言一 四海之內，皆兄弟也。
**Quote 1** To the superior and benevolent man (educated person), all within the four seas will be his brothers.

## (一) 逐字翻譯
## Learn the original text and its meaning

四海之內，皆兄弟也。
sì hǎi zhī nèi, jiē xiōng dì yě.

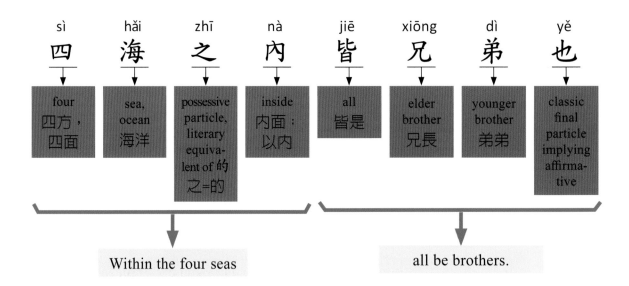

| sì | hǎi | zhī | nà | jiē | xiōng | dì | yě |
|---|---|---|---|---|---|---|---|
| 四 | 海 | 之 | 內 | 皆 | 兄 | 弟 | 也 |
| four 四方，四面 | sea, ocean 海洋 | possessive particle, literary equivalent of 的 之=的 | inside 內面；以內 | all 皆是 | elder brother 兄長 | younger brother 弟弟 | classic final particle implying affirmative |

Within the four seas        all be brothers.

## (二) 白話解釋原文
## Explanation with the modern text

四海之內，皆兄弟也。
The superior man is respectful to others and observant of propriety – then all within the four seas will be his brothers.

全段原文：
司馬牛憂曰：「人皆有兄弟，我獨亡。」子夏曰：「商聞之矣：『死生有命，富貴在天。』君子敬而無失，與人恭而有禮。四海之內，皆兄弟也。君子何患乎無兄弟也？」

Si Ma Niu, full of anxiety, said, "Other men all have their brothers, I only have not." Zi Xia said to him, "There is the following saying which I have heard - 'Death and life have their determined appointment; riches and honors depend upon Heaven.' Let the superior man never fail reverentially to order his own conduct and let him be respectful to others and observant of propriety - then all within the four seas will be his brothers. What has the superior man to do with being distressed because he has no brothers?"

## 1. 白話解釋

司馬牛難過憂心地說：「大家都有兄弟，只有我沒有（亡＝無＝沒有）兄弟。」

子夏說：「我曾經聽說過這句話：『生和死都是命中註定的，財富和尊貴地位也是由天決定的』。君子認真地做事，不犯錯，對人恭敬而且有禮貌。世界四海以內的人就都是我們的兄弟。我們何必憂患沒有兄弟呢？」

司馬牛說：別人都有兄弟，而我卻沒有兄弟。子夏安慰他說：全世界的人，都可以做你的兄弟啊。

## 2. 生詞

| | 生詞<br>Vocabulary | 拼音<br>Pin Yin | 英文<br>English | 詞類<br>Part of Speech |
|---|---|---|---|---|
| 1 | 安慰 | ān wèi | to comfort | verb |
| 2 | 全世界 | quán shì jiè | the whole world | noun |
| 3 | 難過 | nán guò | to be sad | verb |
| 4 | 憂心 | yōu xīn | to worry | verb |
| 5 | 命中註定 | mìng zhōng zhù dìng | destiny, fate | noun |
| 6 | 財富 | cái fù | wealth | noun |
| 7 | 尊貴 | zūn guì | dignity | noun |
| 8 | 犯錯 | fàn cuò | to make a mistake | verb |

| | 生詞<br>Vocabulary | 拼音<br>Pin Yin | 英文<br>English | 詞類<br>Part of Speech |
|---|---|---|---|---|
| 9 | 恭敬 | gōng jìng | respectfully | adverb |
| 10 | 憂患 | yōu huàn | to be worried | adjective |

## ㈢ 延伸對話與生詞
### Extended learning with sentence practices

1.會話

A：我去歐洲留學的時候，我交到了很多來自不同國家的好朋友。

When I studied abroad in Europe, I made a lot of friends who came from many different countries.

B：是啊，這些好朋友讓我能夠感受到「四海之內，皆兄弟也」。

That's great! These good friends really made me feel that "all within the four seas are my brothers."

2.生詞

| | 生詞<br>Vocabulary | 拼音<br>Pin Yin | 英文<br>English | 詞類<br>Part of Speech |
|---|---|---|---|---|
| 1 | 歐洲 | ōu zhōu | Europe | noun |
| 2 | 留學 | liú xué | to study abroad | verb |
| 3 | 交朋友 | jiāo péng yǒu | to make friends | verb |
| 4 | 不同 | bù tóng | different | adjective |
| 5 | 國家 | guó jiā | country | noun |
| 6 | 能夠 | néng gòu | to be able to | verb |
| 7 | 感受 | gǎn shòu | to feel, to receive | verb |

## ㈣ 孔子故事
### Stories about Confucius' life and his teaching

三種好朋友，三種壞朋友

Confucius said: "There are three types of good friends and three types of bad friends."

　　孔子說：對我們有益處的朋友有三種，有害處的朋友也有三種。和正直的朋友、誠實的朋友、有見識的朋友交往是有益的。和走歪路的朋友、愛逢迎（拍馬屁）和花言巧語的朋友交往，是有害處的。

　　Confucius said, "There are three friendships which are helpful to us, and three which are injurious. Friendship with the upright; friendship with the sincere; and friendship with the man of much observation - these are advantageous (helpful). Friendship with the man of specious airs; friendship with the insinuatingly soft; and friendship with the glib-tongued - these are injurious (harmful)."

【原文出處 Reference】

孔子曰：「益者三友，損者三友。友直，友諒，友多聞，益矣。友便辟 pián pì，友善柔，友便佞（pián nìng），損矣。」
【論語第十六‧季氏篇‧第 4 節】*The Analects, Chapter 16 Ji-Shi, Verse 4*

## ㈤ 論語名言的現代價值評論
### Commentary about this ancient text with modern values

Ancient Text：四海之內，皆兄弟也。

　　　　"To the superior and benevolent man (educated person), all within the four seas will be his brothers." Zi Xia.

【論語第十二‧顏淵篇‧第 5 節】*The Analects, Chapter 12 Yan-Yuan, Verse 5*

**Modern Values Commentary by: Alexander D'Andrea (Lex) 杜宏敬**

　　Zi Xia's words remind me of a truth I unearthed during my freshman year of college. Having been born an only child, I often thought in my younger years that

I lacked a connection that many of my friends had. However, I came to realize I could find people to call my family anywhere I went.

People often get lost in their thoughts, obsessing over regrets, wondering when their untimely demise may fall upon them. One might think they only have their biological family, whereas a wise man has a biological and chosen family. By chosen family, I am referring to loved ones and friends a person meets along their life's journey.

Zi Xia offers key wisdom: Rather than worry about the date of your journey's end and what you lack, enjoy the adventure with the friends you have and look for what you can learn along the way. You can gain a new perspective by looking at life from different angles. Perhaps you think a person who has a full glass is better than someone with an empty one. I think the person with an empty glass has the opportunity to fill it with new memories. One who lacks what another has is no worse or better just different.

When searching for your chosen family, you may look for other people who also have an empty glass. Remember that you can find people with empty glasses in every country on Earth. Do not be nearsighted in your search for those who can genuinely support, challenge, and love you. As Zi Xia says, your brothers can be found "within the four seas," not just one. For me, I found people I could relate to in my life all around the world. While studying abroad in Taiwan, I immersed myself in the culture and gained a greater appreciation friendship from overseas as brotherhood.

Alexander D'Andrea (Lex) 杜宏敬

Political Science Major

The College of New Jersey

## ㈥ 模擬口語考試練習
### Suggested topics for oral proficiency interview (OPI)

## 四海之內，皆兄弟也。

To the superior and benevolent man (educated person), all within the four seas will be his brothers.

【模擬口試練習】

1. 請介紹一位你的好朋友。請說明這位好朋友的興趣愛好，或談談你們喜歡一起做的事情。

   Please introduce one of your friends. You can talk about their hobbies or describe what you like to do with this friend.

   【中級、高級 – 描述 / 敘述 Intermediate to Advanced Level – can narrate and describe】

2. 你覺得你與朋友的感情和兄弟姊妹有什麼不同？有什麼是一樣的？

   Please discuss the differences or the similarities in the relationships between your siblings and your friends.

   【中級、高級 – 比較 Intermediate to Advanced Level – to be able to compare】

3. 你有很多不同文化背景的朋友嗎？請介紹一下這位和你有「不同文化背景」的朋友。也請說說你們的文化有什麼不同。

   Do you have many friends from different cultural backgrounds? Please introduce your friends who have a different cultural background from yours. Please describe the differences in cultural practices between you and this foreign friend.

   【中級、高級 – 描述 / 敘述 Intermediate to Advanced Level – can narrate and describe】

4. 你認為交朋友應該找興趣愛好跟你一樣的，還是不一樣的？請以你的經驗說明比較？

   Do you think it is a good idea to find friends with the same interests and hobbies or those with different hobbies? Please describe and compare with your personal experiences.

   【中級、高級 – 比較 Intermediate to Advanced Level – to be able to compare】

## 名言二　與朋友交，言而有信。

**Quote 2** In our interaction with friends, one's words should be sincere.

### (一) 逐字翻譯
**Learn the original text and its meaning**

與朋友交，言而有信。

yǔ péng yǒu jiāo, yán ér yǒu xìn.

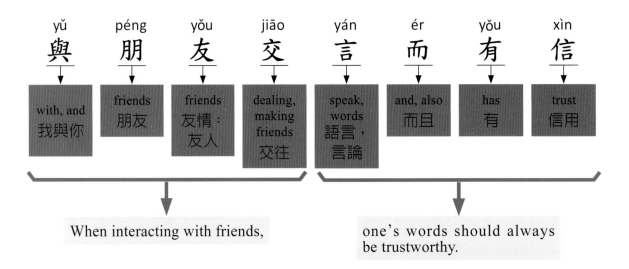

| yǔ | péng | yǒu | jiāo | yán | ér | yǒu | xìn |
|---|---|---|---|---|---|---|---|
| 與 | 朋 | 友 | 交 | 言 | 而 | 有 | 信 |
| with, and 我與你 | friends 朋友 | friends 友情；友人 | dealing, making friends 交往 | speak, words 語言，言論 | and, also 而且 | has 有 | trust 信用 |

When interacting with friends,　　one's words should always be trustworthy.

### (二) 白話解釋原文
**Explanation with the modern text**

與朋友交，言而有信。

In our interaction with friends, one's words should be sincere.

1.白話解釋

和朋友交往，說話一定要講信用。

When associating with your friends, you should always keep your words and your promise.

## 2.生詞

|   | 生詞<br>**Vocabulary** | 拼音<br>**Pin Yin** | 英文<br>**English** | 詞類<br>**Part of Speech** |
|---|---|---|---|---|
| 1 | 交往 | jiāo wǎng | to associate | verb |
| 2 | 說話 | shuō huà | to talk | verb |
| 3 | 講 | jiǎng | to talk, to keep (a promise) | verb |
| 4 | 信用 | xìn yòng | promise | noun |

## ㈢ 延伸對話與生詞
### Extended learning with sentence practices

### 1.會話

A：你覺得對待朋友，應該最重視什麼？

What do you think is most important in terms of interactions with friends?

B：我認為朋友之間，一定要守信用。

I think keeping one's words or promises is most important among friends.

### 2.生詞

|   | 生詞<br>**Vocabulary** | 拼音<br>**Pin Yin** | 英文<br>**English** | 詞類<br>**Part of Speech** |
|---|---|---|---|---|
| 1 | 對待 | duì dài | to treat | verb |
| 2 | 重視 | zhòng shì | to value | verb |
| 3 | 之間 | zhī jiān | within, among | preposition |
| 4 | 守 | shǒu | to keep | verb |
| 5 | 信用 | xìn yòng | a promise | noun |

## ㈣ 孔子故事
### Stories about Confucius' life and his teaching

孔子是多才多藝的聖人嗎？

Was Confucius a sage with multi-talents?

　　太宰問子貢：「你的老師是聖人嗎？為什麼如此多才多藝？」子貢說：「老天本來就要他成為聖人，又要他多才多藝。」孔子聽到後說：「太宰瞭解我嗎？我小時候生活艱難，所以會做一些粗活。貴族會有這麼多技藝嗎？不會有的。」

　　A high officer asked Zi Gong: "May we not say that your Master is a sage? How many various abilities does he have?" Zi Gong said, "Certainly, Heaven has endowed him unlimitedly. He is about a sage. And, moreover, his ability is various." The Master heard of the conversation and said, "Does the high officer know me? When I was young, my condition was low, and therefore I acquired my ability in many things, but they were mean matters. Must the superior man have such a variety of ability? He does not need variety of ability."

【原文出處 Reference】

> 大宰問於子貢曰：「夫子聖者與？何其多能也？」子貢曰：「固天縱之將聖，又多能也。」子聞之，曰：「大宰知我乎！吾少也賤，故多能鄙事。君子多乎哉？不多也。」
> 【論語第九·子罕篇·第 6 節】 *The Analects, Chapter 9 Zi-Han, verse 6*

## ㈤ 論語名言的現代價值評論
### Commentary about this ancient text with modern values

Ancient Text：子曰：「弟子入則孝，出則弟，謹而信，汎愛眾，而親仁。行有餘力，則以學文。」

The Master said, "A youth, when at home, should be filial, and, abroad, respectful to his elders. He should be earnest and truthful. He should overflow in love to all, and cultivate the friendship of the good. When he has time and opportunity, after the performance of these things, he should employ them in polite studies."

【論語第一 · 學而篇 · 第 6 節】 *The Analects, Chapter 1 Xue-Er, verse 6*

## Modern Values Commentary by: Dr. Marybeth Gasman

Modern society often has a disregard for respect, especially for elders. In recent years, there have been verbal attacks and mocking of older individuals because their views on social issues aren't changing as rapidly as youth want them too. Although society needs change, there is much to learn from the perspectives of elders – both friends and parents. They have engaged the world long before the youth and have benefited from lessons learned – lessons that can be shared. Yes, there will disagreements and growth is needed across all generations – but sometimes patience is needed to explain the reasons for growth and to listen to tentative resistance. When teaching others, respect is imperative.

Marybeth Gasman, PhD

Samuel DeWitt Proctor Endowed Chair in Education &

Distinguished Professor

Department of Educational Psychology

Graduate School of Education,

Rutgers University - New Brunswick

Executive Director

Samuel DeWitt Proctor Institute for Leadership,

Equity, & Justice

& Rutgers Center for Minority Serving Institutions

## ㈥ 模擬口語考試練習
## Suggested topics for oral proficiency interview (OPI)

與朋友交，言而有信。

In our interaction with friends, one's words should be sincere.

【模擬口試練習】

1. 請說明為什麼朋友之間可以互相信任是很重要的？請以你自己所經歷過的事情來討論為什麼朋友之間相互信任很重要。

Please discuss why it is important for friends to be able to trust each other mutually. You can share an experience of yours related to this topic.

【優秀級 – 表達個人意見和申述抽象觀念 Superior Level – can support opinion and discuss abstract concept】

2. 請說明你和朋友之間曾經一起約定過什麼嗎？

Please talk about any promises you have made with your friends?

【中級、高級 – 描述／敘述 Intermediate to Advanced Level – can narrate and describe】

3. 論語裡，孔子說：「與朋友交，言而有信」。如果你的朋友請你幫忙，你答應了，後來你發現朋友請你做的事情是你不願意做的，你怎麼辦？

In the Analects, Confucius said: "Keeping your promises with your friends is essential." Imagine and discuss what you would do if you promised to help your friends and later realized that you could not keep that promise?

【優秀級 – 假設情境申述 Superior Level – can hypothesize】

名言三 **老者安之，朋友信之，少者懷之。**
Quote 3

My wishes are, to provide the aged comfort; to show the friends sincerity; to treat the young tenderly.

## (一)逐字翻譯
## Learn the original text and its meaning

老者安之，朋友信之，少者懷之。
lǎo zhě ān zhī, péng yǒu xìn zhī, shào zhě huái zhī.

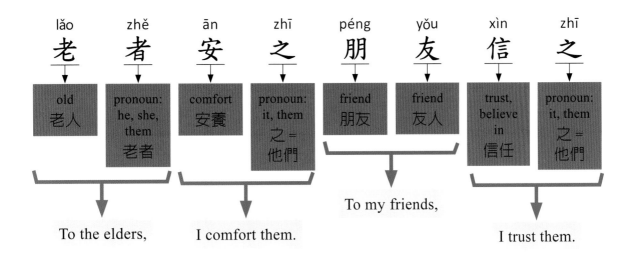

| | | | | | | | |
|---|---|---|---|---|---|---|---|
| lǎo | zhě | ān | zhī | péng | yǒu | xìn | zhī |
| 老 | 者 | 安 | 之 | 朋 | 友 | 信 | 之 |
| old 老人 | pronoun: he, she, them 老者 | comfort 安養 | pronoun: it, them 之=他們 | friend 朋友 | friend 友人 | trust, believe in 信任 | pronoun: it, them 之=他們 |

To the elders, I comfort them. To my friends, I trust them.

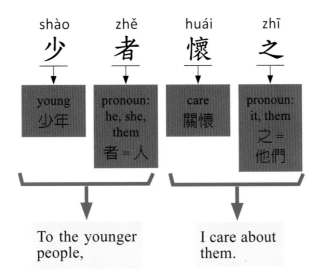

| | | | |
|---|---|---|---|
| shào | zhě | huái | zhī |
| 少 | 者 | 懷 | 之 |
| young 少年 | pronoun: he, she, them 者=人 | care 關懷 | pronoun: it, them 之=他們 |

To the younger people, I care about them.

## (二)白話解釋原文
## Explanation with the modern text

老者安之，朋友信之，少者懷之。

They are, in regard to the aged, to give them rest; in regard to friends, to show them sincerity; in regard to the young, to treat them tenderly.

全段原文：

顏淵、季路侍。子曰：「盍各言爾志？」子路曰：「願車馬、衣輕裘，與朋友共。敝之而無憾。」顏淵曰：「願無伐善，無施勞。」子路曰：「願聞子之志。」子曰：「老者安之，朋友信之，少者懷之。」

Yan Yuan and Ji Lu being by his side, the Master said to them, "Come, let each of you tell his wishes." Zi Lu said, "I should like, having chariots and horses, and light fur clothes, to share them with my friends, and though they should spoil them, I would not be displeased." Yan Yuan said, "I should like not to boast of my excellence, nor to make a display of my meritorious deeds." Zi Lu then said, "I should like, sir, to hear your wishes." The Master said, "They are, in regard to the aged, to give them rest; in regard to friends, to show them sincerity; in regard to the young, to treat them tenderly."

以上為全段原文（Above is the original paragraph of this quote）

### 1.白話解釋

顏淵和子路在孔子身邊。孔子說：「你們來說說看自己的志向吧？」子路說：「我願意把自己的車馬、皮衣都拿來和朋友們分享。就是用壞了，也不會遺憾。」

顏淵說：「我不會自誇，不宣揚自己的功勞。」

子路向孔子說：「我們希望能聽聽老師的志向。」

孔子說：「（我的志向是）安養老年人，信任朋友，關懷年輕人。」

## 2. 生詞

| | 生詞<br>Vocabulary | 拼音<br>Pin Yin | 英文<br>English | 詞類<br>Part of Speech |
|---|---|---|---|---|
| 1 | 志向 | zhì xiàng | will, goal | noun |
| 2 | 願意 | yuàn yì | willing to | verb |
| 3 | 分享 | fēn xiǎng | to share | verb |
| 4 | 用壞 | yòng huài | broken after use | verb |
| 5 | 遺憾 | yí hàn | to regret | verb |
| 6 | 自誇 | zì kuā | to self exagerate | verb |
| 7 | 宣揚 | ān wèi | to publicize. | verb |
| 8 | 功勞 | quán shì jiè | achievement | noun |
| 9 | 安養 | ān yǎng | to take care of elders | verb |
| 10 | 信任 | xìn rèn | to trust | verb |
| 11 | 關懷 | guān huái | to care | verb |

## (三) 延伸對話與生詞
### Extended learning with sentence practices

### 1. 會話

A：我想聽聽看你的人生志向和對未來的願望。

I would like to hear about your career goals and wishes for the future.

B：我的志向是想要有一份安定的工作，讓我的家人快樂。

I would like to have a secure job and make my family happy.

### 2. 生詞

| | 生詞<br>Vocabulary | 拼音<br>Pin Yin | 英文<br>English | 詞類<br>Part of Speech |
|---|---|---|---|---|
| 1 | 志向 | zhì xiàng | will, goal | noun |
| 2 | 未來 | wèi lái | future | noun |
| 3 | 願望 | yuàn wàng | wish | noun |
| 4 | 安定 | ān dìng | secured | adjective |

## ㈣孔子故事
## Stories about Confucius' life and his teaching

孔子貧苦的成長（吾少也賤，故多能鄙事。）

Confucius grew up in poverty.

孔子的父親去世後，孔子的母親一個人把孔子養大。雖然他小時候的日子過得很苦，可是孔子很孝順也不怕吃苦。因為他做過很多不同的小工作，所以他學到了很多不同的技能，也成了多才多藝的人。這個故事也鼓勵所有的年輕人，從工作經驗中學習和磨練。

After Confucius' father passed away, his mother raised Confucius up as a single mother. Despite this hardship in his childhood, Confucius was a very good son of his mother, and he was not afraid of taking on challenges in life. He was very bright and talented. He took on various menial jobs and through these experiences he acquired ability in many fields.

Confucius took on many menial jobs at a young age to help lessen his family's financial burden. This story shows that Confucius encouraged all youngsters to work hard and learn from all working experiences.

【原文出處 Reference】

子曰：「吾少也賤，故多能鄙事。」
【論語第九 · 子罕篇 · 第 6 節】*The Analects, Chapter 9 Zi-Han, verse 6*

不怕艱難困苦，才會出人頭地（歲寒，然後知松柏之後凋也。）

After the tough challenges, the qualified will prevail.

孔子說：「天冷時，才知道松柏最後凋謝。」

經過艱難的挑戰，有能力的才會通過難關。

The Master said, "When the season of the year becomes cold, then we know how the pine and the cypress are the last to lose their leaves."

Only after the tough challenges, the qualified will prevail.

> 子曰：「歲寒，然後知松柏之後凋也。」
> 【論語第九‧子罕篇‧第 28 節】 *The Analects, Chapter 9 Zi-Han, Verse 28*

## ㈤論語名言的現代價值評論
### Commentary about this ancient text with modern values

Ancient Text：老者安之，朋友信之，少者懷之。

> My wishes are, to provide the aged comfort; to show the friends sincerity; to treat the young tenderly."

【論語第五‧公冶長篇‧第 26 節】 *The Analects, Chapter 5 Gong-Ye-Chang, Verse 26*

**Modern Values Commentary by: Juliana Rice**

Confucius expresses his intentions the people in his life by segmenting them into three categories: the aged, his friends, and the young. When thinking about providing the aged comfort, my mind immediately jumps to the big picture, ever present questions that tend to be eclipsed by the smaller picture filled with easily answered questions- most likely due to modern day which has groomed us to value immediate gratification almost above anything else. Am I happy? Did I make the impact that I wanted to? Did I help those around me to grow? Did I allow those around me to help me grow? Comforting the elderly goes beyond physicality, extending into assurance. Confucius seems to allude that if we are able to provide some semblance of assurance, we should. And I can't say I disagree.

Shifting into the sincerity in which we treat our friends, our friends are those around us who we allow to go beyond the walls we knowingly or unknowingly build and make a home in our minds and hearts. They are our chosen family. Friendship is one of the most intimate bonds that you can have with a human being because it is an unconditional kind of love that does not inherently exist like it does with our sisters, our fathers, our in-laws and so forth. Because of that, sincerity is the irreplicable, intangible distinction that evolves an acquaintanceship into a friendship.

Just as we comfort the elderly and treat our friends with sincerity, we must finally, treat the young tenderly. Being young means being naive, starting with a blank canvas and intricately crafting yourself into the person you want to be. But that does not mean that we are free of the ramifications of the actions and words of others. We assure the elderly their life was a life lived and so we must help the young so that they live their lives in a fashion that is worth living. That means being tender in the words that you say, actions you take, and the love you give.

Perhaps... Confucius was onto something.

Juliana Rice 付瑩花

National Account Associate at MJH Life Sciences

## ㈥ 模擬口語考試練習
### Suggested topics for oral proficiency interview (OPI)

老者安之，朋友信之，少者懷之。

My wishes are, to provide the aged comfort; to show the friends sincerity; to treat the young tenderly."

【模擬口試練習】

1. 假設你有能力可以做到任何你想做的事情，你的人生目標會是什麼？

   If you are able to achieve anything you want to do, what would you set as your life goals?

   【優秀級 – 假設情境申述 Superior Level – able to hypothesize】

2. 照顧弱勢是不少國家的政策，請舉例說明您所知道的這類社會福利政策，並討論為什麼政府應該照顧窮人或失業者？如果一個社會或者政府不照顧這些人，會有什麼問題？反之，這一類的社會福利政策也有可能造成什麼社會問題？請發表您對這些議題的看法。

Many countries have comprehensive policies for social equality and welfare. Please describe the policies you know of which are designed for this purpose, and discuss the reasons why a government needs to help the poor or the unemployed? What problem could it create if a government does not take care of the poor, and on the contrary, what problems could these welfare policies also create? Please discuss your opinion on this topic.

【優秀級 – 表達個人意見和申述抽象觀念 Superior Level – able to support opinion and discuss abstract concept】

【朋友】四海皆兄弟【論語第十二·顏淵篇·第5節】 *The Analects, Chapter 12 Yan-Yuan, Verse 5*

When at home, one should be filial, and abroad, respectful to his elders.

2

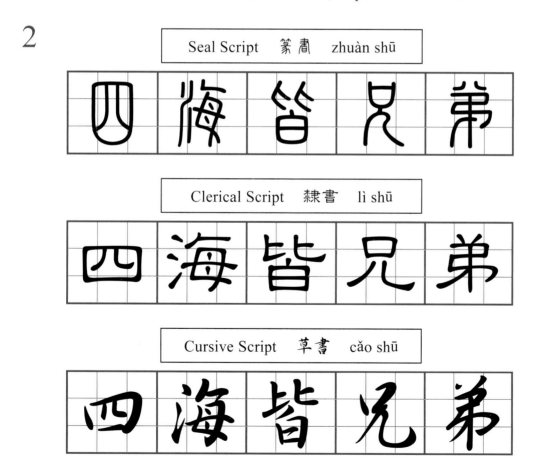

Seal Script　篆書　zhuàn shū

Clerical Script　隸書　lì shū

Cursive Script　草書　cǎo shū

四海皆兄弟

四海皆兄弟

關於【君子或小人】的三個論語名言：

Three top quotes about "A gentleman or a pitiful man":

君子不器。

The accomplished scholar is not a utensil.

【論語第二·為政篇·第 12 節】*The Analects, Chapter 2 Wei-Zheng, Verse 12*


君子求諸己，小人求諸人。

What the superior man seeks, is in himself. What the mean man seeks, is in others.

【論語第十五·衛靈公篇·第 21 節】*The Analects, Chapter 15 Wei-Ling-Gong, Verse 21*


君子謀道不謀食。

The object of the superior man is truth. Food is not his object.

【論語第十五·衛靈公篇·第 32 節】*The Analects, Chapter 15 Wei-Ling-Gong, Verse 32*

## (一)逐字翻譯
## Learn the original text and its meaning

子曰：君子不器。

zǐ yuē: jūn zǐ bú qì.

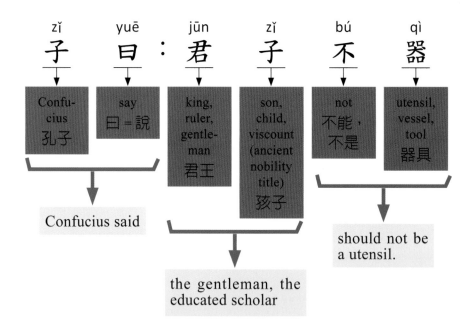

## (二)白話解釋原文
## Explanation with the modern text

子曰：君子不器。

The Master said, "The accomplished scholar should not be like a utensil or a vessel."

### 1. 白話解釋

孔子說：「一位君子不應該像是一個器具或是一個容器。」

The Master said, "The accomplished scholar should not be like a utensil or a vessel."

什麼是「君子」？（jūn zǐ）

君子是有學問，並且品行好的人。

What is a gentleman (an educated man)?

A gentleman has knowledge and good conduct.

什麼是「小人」？（xiǎo rén）

小人是品行和行為都還需要改進的人。

What is a pitiful man (a mean man)?

A pitiful man needs to improve on his behaviors and conduct.

2. 生詞

| | 生詞<br>Vocabulary | 拼音<br>Pin Yin | 英文<br>English | 詞類<br>Part of Speech |
|---|---|---|---|---|
| 1 | 器具 | qì jù | tool | noun |
| 2 | 容器 | róng qì | vessel | noun |
| 3 | 學問 | xué wèn | knowledge | noun |
| 4 | 品行 | pǐn xìng | conduct | noun |
| 5 | 需要 | xū yào | to need | verb |
| 6 | 改進 | gǎi jìn | to improve | verb |

## ㈢ 延伸對話與生詞
### Extended learning with sentence practices

1. 會話

A：為什麼孔子說：「君子不器」？

　　Why did Confucius say: "A gentleman cannot be like a utensil"?

B：因為一個器具或是容器，通常都只有一個固定的用途。

　　It is because a vessel or a utensil usually has only a fixed purpose.

孔子鼓勵他的學生，要學習各種不同的知識和技能，不能只有一種技能。

Confucius encouraged his students to learn various different knowledge or skills and to not be limited to just one-single skill. (Confucius promoted cross-disciplinary training.)

## 2. 生詞

| | 生詞<br>Vocabulary | 拼音<br>Pin Yin | 英文<br>English | 詞類<br>Part of Speech |
|---|---|---|---|---|
| 1 | 器具 | qì jù | tool | noun |
| 2 | 容器 | róng qì | vessel | noun |
| 3 | 通常 | tōng cháng | usually | adverb |
| 4 | 固定 | gù dìng | fixed | adjective |
| 5 | 用途 | yòng tú | purpose | noun |
| 6 | 鼓勵 | gǔ lì | to encourage | verb |
| 7 | 學習 | xué xí | to learn | verb |
| 8 | 各種 | gè zhǒng | various | adjective |
| 9 | 知識 | zhī shì | knowledge | noun |
| 10 | 技能 | jì néng | skill | noun |

## ㈣ 孔子故事

### Stories about Confucius' life and his teaching

孔子打過什麼工?

What kind of part-time jobs Confucius had during his growing-up?

孔子少年時期家裡很貧苦。長大的過程中曾經打過很多工。孟子在書中記載說:孔子曾當過幫人管帳的會計工作,也做過幫人餵養放牧牛羊的工作。而孔子當時做這些微小的工作都是為了解決生活上的窮困。

Confucius lived in poverty when he was young. Throughout his childhood, he took on many small jobs. Mencius recorded in his book that Confucius took small jobs such as handling bookkeeping, as well as taking care of the livestock. All these small jobs were to earn a living to solve his financial difficulty.

孔子嘗為委吏矣，曰：「會計當而已矣。」嘗為乘田矣，曰：「牛羊茁壯，長而已矣。」
【史記・孔子世家・第 2 節】*Shiji, Kongzi Shijia, Verse 2*
【孟子・萬章下・第 14 節】*Mencius, Chapter Wan-Zhang II, Verse 14*

## ㈤ 論語名言的現代價值評論
### Commentary about this ancient text with modern values

Ancient Text：君子不器。

An educated gentleman or a scholar should not be a utensil.

【論語第二・為政篇 – 第 12 節】*The Analects, Chapter 2 Wei-Zheng, Verse 12*

**Modern Values Commentary by: Mark Cheng**

An entrepreneur, as defined by the classic French term, means to start and undertake. Nowadays this means to own and manage. On a broader scale an entrepreneur is someone who conceptualizes, forms, owns, manages and markets their original ideas while taking on risks to do so. Far from the notion that a businessperson simply clocks hours at the office day in day out, an entrepreneurially minded businessperson actively thinks outside the box while implementing constant improvements to offer better goods and services. Overall, one needs to be nimble, fungible, and dynamic in order to sustain high levels of entrepreneurship.

As the global pandemic disrupted all areas of life in 2020, I regularly refer to Confucian ideologies regarding balance; obstacles; achievement. I must admit I've been extremely fortunate this year, despite intense socioeconomic challenges affecting the world, in that I've exceeded even my own expectations in terms of professional and academic footprints. Through pure curiosity plus a willingness to learn about sweeping industry changes, I've been handed various avenues to offer transformative insight within my Firm and two universities in New York; Ohio. From seeing positive reception in people around me, the satisfaction gained far outweighs and outlasts any material earned.

Mark Cheng (Management Consultant)

## ㈥ 模擬口語考試討論話題
## Suggested topics for oral proficiency interview (OPI)

子曰：「君子不器。」

The Master said, "The accomplished scholar is not a utensil."

【模擬口試練習】

1. 你對未來有什麼打算？你覺得你未來可能會從事什麼方面的工作？請談談這個工作對社會的貢獻。

   Please talk about your plans for the future. What area of profession do you think you may be working in the future? Please discuss what contribution this job would provide for society.

   【優秀級 – 表達個人意見和申述抽象觀念 Superior Level – can support opinion and discuss abstract concept】

2. 請介紹你的興趣愛好是什麼？並且說明爲什麼你喜歡這些興趣愛好。

   Please share what your hobbies and interests are and explain why you enjoy these hobbies and interests.

   【中級、高級 – 描述／敘述 Intermediate to Advanced Level – can narrate and describe】

3. 你的主修專業是不是你的興趣所在？請討論一個人的工作是不是應該配合他的興趣愛好。

Is your major study in the area of your interests or hobby? Please discuss whether one should choose his/her career in the area of one's interests or hobby?

【優秀級 – 表達個人意見和申述抽象觀念 Superior Level – can support opinion and discuss abstract concept】

## 名言二 Quote 2　君子求諸己，小人求諸人。

**What the superior man seeks, is in himself. What the mean man seeks, is in others.**

## ㈠逐字翻譯
## Learn the original text and its meaning

君子求諸己，小人求諸人。

Jūn zǐ qiú zhū jǐ, xiǎo rén qiú zhū rén.

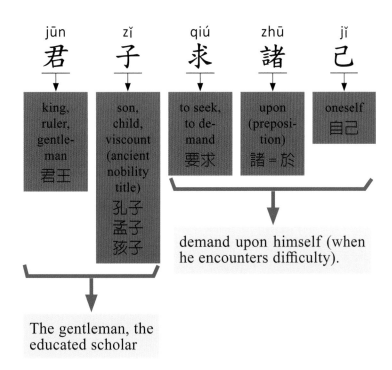

|  |  |  |  |  |
| jūn | zǐ | qiú | zhū | jǐ |
| 君 | 子 | 求 | 諸 | 己 |
| king, ruler, gentleman 君王 | son, child, viscount (ancient nobility title) 孔子 孟子 孩子 | to seek, to demand 要求 | upon (preposition) 諸＝於 | oneself 自己 |

demand upon himself (when he encounters difficulty).

The gentleman, the educated scholar

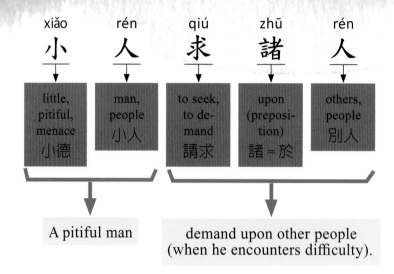

| xiǎo | rén | qiú | zhū | rén |
|------|-----|-----|-----|-----|
| 小 | 人 | 求 | 諸 | 人 |
| little, pitiful, menace 小德 | man, people 小人 | to seek, to demand 請求 | upon (preposition) 諸＝於 | others, people 別人 |

A pitiful man

demand upon other people (when he encounters difficulty).

## ㈡白話解釋原文
### Explanation with the modern text

君子求諸己，小人求諸人。

What the superior man seeks, is in himself. What the mean man seeks, is in others.

### 1.白話解釋

一位有品行的君子，遇到問題會先在自己身上找原因，反省如何改進。

而那些小人，只好把問題推到別人身上。

When a superior man runs into difficulty, he would examine his wrongdoing first, self-review, and seek improvement; while the pitiful man would blame his problem on others.

### 2.生詞

| | 生詞 Vocabulary | 拼音 Pin Yin | 英文 English | 詞類 Part of Speech |
|---|---|---|---|---|
| 1 | 品行 | pǐn xìng | conduct | noun |
| 2 | 遇到 | yù dào | to meet | verb |
| 3 | 問題 | wèn tí | question | noun |
| 4 | 找 | zhǎo | to look for | verb |
| 5 | 原因 | yuán yīn | reason | noun |

| | 生詞<br>**Vocabulary** | 拼音<br>**Pin Yin** | 英文<br>**English** | 詞類<br>**Part of Speech** |
|---|---|---|---|---|
| 6 | 反省 | fǎn shěng | to introspection | verb |
| 7 | 如何 | rú hé | how to | adverb |
| 8 | 改進 | gǎi jìn | to improve | verb |
| 9 | 推到 | tuī dào | to promote, to push | verb |

## ㈢ 延伸對話與生詞

**Extended learning with sentence practices**

1. 會話

A：你為什麼考試考得這麼差呢？

Why you do terribly on the test?

B：那個考題太難了！

The test was too hard!

A：你考試考不好的時候，你應該反省自己為什麼沒有好好用功，不應該怪老師啊！

When you did poorly in the test, you should introspect and ask yourself why you did not work harder. You should not blame it on your teacher.

2. 生詞

| | 生詞<br>**Vocabulary** | 拼音<br>**Pin Yin** | 英文<br>**English** | 詞類<br>**Part of Speech** |
|---|---|---|---|---|
| 1 | 考試 | kǎo shì | a test, an exam | noun |
| 2 | 差 | chà | inferior with | adverb |
| 3 | 考題 | kǎo tí | test questions | noun |
| 4 | 反省 | fǎn shěng | to introspection | verb |
| 5 | 用功 | yòng gōng | working hard | verb |
| 6 | 不應該 | Bù yīng gāi | Should not | Auxiliary verb |
| 7 | 怪 | guài | To blame on Someone | Verb |

## ㈣ 孔子故事
## Stories about Confucius' life and his teaching

### 孔子年少時的自學歷程
Confucius' self-learning process during his youth.

　　孔子少年時期雖然家裡很窮，但是孔子非常好學，除了孔子小時候，他的媽媽幫助他自學以外，長大後，孔子也常常謙虛求師。他 27 歲時向郯國國君郯子學習。他也曾經跟老子學禮，跟師襄子學鼓琴，向萇弘學音樂。

　　Although Confucius had a difficult financial situation during his youth, he was very committed to learning. Not only did his mother help him self-learning, but he also humbly pursued learning opportunities at age of 27 with the King of Zheng State, Tan-Zi, and with some famous teachers, he learned about the propriety with Lao-Zi, about musical instruments with Shi-Xiang-Zi, and about music with Chang-Hong.

【原文出處 Reference】

> 吾聞聖人之後，雖不當世，必有達者。今孔丘年少好禮，其達者歟？吾即沒，若必師之。」
> 【史記·孔子世家·第 4 & 6 節】*Shiji, Kongzi Shijia, Verse 4 & 6*
> 孔子師郯子、萇弘、師襄、老聃。
> 引自：韓愈的【師說】*Shishuo by Han-Yu, Tang dynasty*

## ㈤ 論語名言的現代價值評論
## Commentary about this ancient text with modern values

Ancient Text：君子求諸己，小人求諸人。

What the superior man seeks, is in himself. What the mean man seeks, is in others.

【論語第十五·衛靈公篇·第 21 節】*The Analects, Chapter 15 Wei-Ling-Gong, Verse 21*

**Modern Values Commentary by: Carly Mauro**

"Confucius reminds us of the power that an individual can have through self-motivation and self-reflection. The superior man is independent and does not rely on other for personal growth and success. In the world we live in today riddled with social media, it's easy to look for acceptance from others. We want to share our successes with our friends and families online and feel uplifted from the "likes" and "followers". You should not depend on others to build you up into the person you want to be. It's important to focus on what you want to be, not what others want you to be.

The superior man also understands his own actions and consequences before looking to others. Often when there's conflict in a school or work group project, it's easy to place the blame on others. I like to think that Confucius is telling us to self-reflect. He wants us to ask, "Did I do my best?" and "How could I improve?" instead of asking the same question of others.

We must work for everything we have because success is not guaranteed. We should be confident and work as hard as we could, but never become arrogant as your opponent can always be better than us. This quote reminds us of when we are troubled with the challenges, we should not put the blame on others. We should look into our own actions or limitation and find the area to improve. Only when we could examine and evaluate our own skills and shortcomings, we can then seek ways to improve ourselves.

While we are all trying to achieve, sometimes, we might not be able to identify what are the areas that we could improve on. Instead, we might seek the problem at the environment, or the people around us. This could cause us unable to improve or to breakthrough. There are always reasons externally and those in fact are not what we could control. What we need to breakthrough is our own limitation.

For example, the responsibility to unlearn racism to ensure that society can become a safe place for all. Thus, in today's world, we still see the importance of Confucius teaching in self-assessment and self-improvement.

Carly Mauro, 麥吉文

Class of 2019

The College of New Jersey, Mathematics major

## ㈥ 模擬口語考試討論話題
### Suggested topics for oral proficiency interview (OPI)

## 君子求諸己，小人求諸人。
What the superior man seeks, is in himself. What the mean man seeks, is in others.

【模擬口試練習】

1. 你曾經失敗過嗎？請分享你失敗的經驗。你本來的目標是什麼？爲什麼沒達到目標？失敗以後你做了什麼？可以說說你故事嗎？

   Have you ever had a goal which you did not successfully reach? Can you share a story when you had an unsuccessful experience?

   Please share your story.

   【高級 – 描述 / 敘述 Advanced Level – can narrate and describe】

2. 你曾經幫助過一位朋友解決困難嗎？請分享這個經驗。

   Have you ever helped a friend who was having a difficult time? Please share your story.

   【高級 – 描述 / 敘述 Advanced Level – can narrate and describe】

## 名言三　君子謀道不謀食。
Quote 3　The object of the superior man is truth. Food is not his object.

## (一) 逐字翻譯
## Learn the original text and its meaning

君子謀道不謀食。

jūn zǐ móu dào bù móu shí.

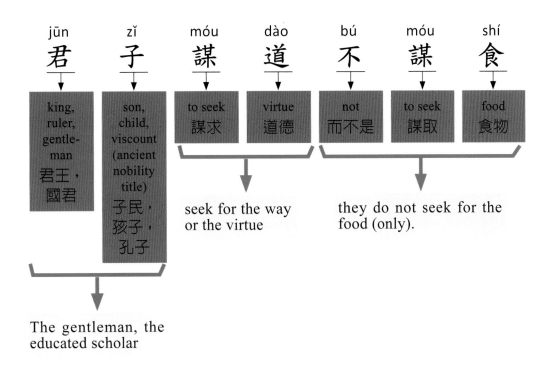

## (二) 白話解釋原文
## Explanation with the modern text

君子謀道不謀食。

The object of the superior man is truth. Food is not his object.

## 1.白話解釋

一位君子會追求道德和真理，而不是只追求食物、錢財和地位。

A gentleman will pursue virtues and truth. He would not only pursue food, wealth, nor the status or a position.

## 2.生詞

| | 生詞<br>Vocabulary | 拼音<br>Pin Yin | 英文<br>English | 詞類<br>Part of Speech |
|---|---|---|---|---|
| 1 | 追求 | zhuī qiú | to pursue | verb |
| 2 | 道德 | dào dé | merit, vertue | noun |
| 3 | 真理 | zhēn lǐ | truth | noun |
| 4 | 食物 | shí wù | food | noun |
| 5 | 錢財 | qián cái | wealth | noun |
| 6 | 地位 | dì wèi | status | noun |

## (三) 延伸對話與生詞
## Extended learning with sentence practices

### 1.會話

A：你的主修專業是哲學，畢業後會不會找不到工作呢？

Will it be hard for you to find a job since you major in philosophy?

B：我學哲學，因為我真的喜歡思考。我並不擔心找不找得到工作。

I major in philosophy because I like to study philosophy. It is not my concern whether or not I will be able to find a job.

### 2.生詞

| | 生詞<br>Vocabulary | 拼音<br>Pin Yin | 英文<br>English | 詞類<br>Part of Speech |
|---|---|---|---|---|
| 1 | 主修 | zhǔ xiū | to major | verb |
| 2 | 專業 | zhuān yè | major | noun |
| 3 | 畢業 | bì yè | to graduate | verb |

| | 生詞<br>Vocabulary | 拼音<br>Pin Yin | 英文<br>English | 詞類<br>Part of Speech |
|---|---|---|---|---|
| 4 | 哲學 | zhé xué | philosophy | noun |
| 5 | 找工作 | zhǎo gōng zuò | to look for a job | verb |
| 6 | 思考 | sī kǎo | to think | verb |
| 7 | 擔心 | dān xīn | to worry | verb |
| 8 | V+ 不 +V 得到<br>（找不找得到） | V+bù +V dé<br>dào | can obtain（得到）<br>or can not | Sentence<br>pattern |

## ㈣ 孔子故事
## Stories about Confucius' life and his teaching

孔子認為平民的志向可以強過大軍的主帥

A common man's will can be stronger than the commander of a large troupe.

　　孔子說：「大軍的主帥可以被奪走，普通的平民的志向卻不可以被奪走。」孔子認為一個人只要有堅定的志向，這個強大的意志力是別人不能奪走的。孔子將一個人的意志力和三軍的統帥做比較。比喻一個人不能沒有堅定的意志，就如同三軍不能沒有統帥。

The Master said, "The commander of the forces of a large state may be carried off, but the will of even a common man cannot be taken from him."

Confucius taught us that as long as one sets his/her willpower on a goal, no one else can take away his strong determination. Confucius compared the importance of a person's willpower to the chief commander/the general of the three soldiers. Removing the chief commander is as fatal as losing one's determination/the willpower.

　　三軍：現代的「三軍」是「陸軍、空軍、海軍」。古代的三軍意思是很大的軍隊。匹夫：普通人民，平民。

Three soldiers: in the modern time, this term (三軍) refers to Army, Airforce, and Navy. In ancient China, this term means a troupe from a large state with many soldiers.

【原文出處 Reference】

> 子曰：「三軍可奪帥也，匹夫不可奪志也。」
> 【論語第九 · 子罕篇 · 第 26 節】 *The Analects, Chapter 9 Zi-Han, Verse 26*

## ㈤ 論語名言的現代價值評論
## Commentary about this ancient text with modern values

Ancient Text：君子謀道不謀食。

The Master said, "The object of the superior man's pursuit is the truth. Food is not his goal."

【論語第十五 · 衛靈公篇 · 第 32 節】 *The Analects, Chapter 15 Wei-Ling-Gong, Verse 32*

**Modern Values Commentary by: Mark Cheng**

Throughout the era of pre/post industrialized nations, there are many examples of individuals who invested extraordinary levels of time and energy to launch and sustain their industrial legacies. In fact, such figures exist in many major regions of the world, not just 1st world economies. These leaders were true tycoons in the traditional sense, meaning they literally launched and ran businesses from the ground up. They did this not to simply survive for that "simple survival" can be attained by much simpler means; they did this because of a certain gap in socioeconomic discovery and desire in hopes to carry on a family legacy. In other words, these people truly needed to exist in the manner in which they did. Just look up the major tycoons through history books and each time the theme can correlate to this Confucius principle.

Mark Cheng (Management Consultant)

## ㈥ 模擬口語考試討論話題
### Suggested topics for oral proficiency interview (OPI)

## 君子謀道不謀食。
The object of the superior man is truth. Food is not his object.

【模擬口試練習】

1. 請談談你的人生目標或是你對未來的計畫是什麼？

   Can you share the objectives or the goals of your life, and your plans for the future?

   【高級 – 描述／敘述 Advanced Level – can narrate and describe】

   【優秀級 – 假設情境申述 Superior Level – can hypothesize】

2. 歷史上有很多「偉人」，他們對人類社會有一定的貢獻。你認為什麼樣的人可以稱為「偉人」？請舉例說明。

   There are many "great men" in history who have made certain contributions to human society. What kind of person do you think can be called a "great man"? Please give an exmple.

   【高級 – 描述／敘述 Advanced Level – can narrate and describe】

   【優秀級 – 表達個人意見和申述抽象觀念 Superior Level – can support opinion and discuss abstract concept】

【君子】君子不器【論語第二 · 為政篇 · 第 12 節】 *The Analects, Chapter 2 Wei-Zheng, Verse 12*

The accomplished scholar is not a utensil.

3

| Seal Script 篆書 zhuàn shū |
| --- |
| 君　子　不　器 |

Clerical Script　隸書　lì shū

Cursive Script　草書　cǎo shū

Running Script　行書　xíng shū

Standard Script　楷書　kǎi shū

## 關於【學習】的三個論語名言：
## Three top quotes about "Learning":

知之爲知之，不知爲不知，是知也。

When you know a thing, to hold that you know it; and when you do not know a thing, to allow that you do not know it - this is how to obtain knowledge.

【論語第二‧爲政篇‧第 17 節】 *The Analects, Chapter 2 Wei-Zheng, Verse 17*


溫故而知新，可以爲師矣。

If a man keeps cherishing his old knowledge, so as continually to be acquiring new, he may be a teacher of others.

【論語第二‧爲政篇‧第 11 節】 *The Analects, Chapter 2 Wei-Zheng, Verse 11*


三人行，必有我師焉。

When I walk along with two others, they may serve me as my teachers.

【論語第七‧述而篇‧第 22 節】 *The Analects, Chapter 7 Xu-Er, Verse 22*

名言一　知之為知之，不知為不知，是知也。
**Quote 1**

**When you know a thing, to hold that you know it; and when you do not know a thing, to allow that you do not know it - this is knowledge.**

## (一)逐字翻譯
### Learn the original text and its meaning

知之為知之，不知為不知，是知也。

zhī zhī wéi zhī zhī, bù zhī wéi bù zhī, shì zhī yě.

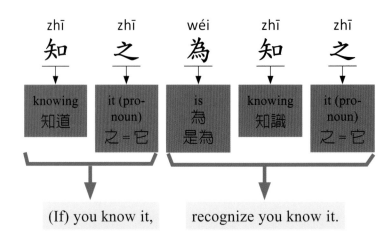

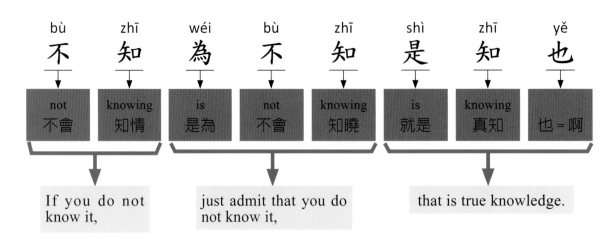

## ㈡ 白話解釋原文
### Explanation with the modern text

知之為知之，不知為不知，是知也。

When you know a thing, to hold that you know it; and when you do not know a thing, to allow that you do not know it - this is how to obtain knowledge.

### 1. 白話解釋
知道就說知道，不知道就說不知道，這樣才是學習知識的好方法。

When you know a thing, just say that you know it; and when you do not know a thing, just say that you do not know it - this is how to obtain knowledge.

### 2. 生詞

| | 生詞<br>Vocabulary | 拼音<br>Pin Yin | 英文<br>English | 詞類<br>Part of Speech |
|---|---|---|---|---|
| 1 | 知道 | zhī dào | to know | verb |
| 2 | 學習 | xué xí | to learn | verb |
| 3 | 知識 | zhī shì | knowledge | noun |
| 4 | 方法 | fāng fǎ | method | noun |

## ㈢ 延伸對話與生詞
### Extended learning with sentence practices

### 1. 會話
A：今天老師教的你都聽懂了嗎？

Did you understand what the teacher taught today?

B：我不太懂，可是上課的時候，我又不敢說我不懂。

I did not quite get it. However, I was too shy to say that I didn't understand it during class.

A：不懂的時候，就要說妳不懂，老師才會解釋清楚啊。

When you don't understand, you should just say it. The teacher will explain it.

B：你說的對，下次我不懂的時候，我會舉手發問。

You are right. Next time, I would raise my hand and ask questions when I do not understand it.

## 2.生詞

| | 生詞<br>Vocabulary | 拼音<br>Pin Yin | 英文<br>English | 詞類<br>Part of Speech |
|---|---|---|---|---|
| 1 | 老師 | lǎo shī | teacher | noun |
| 2 | 教 | jiāo | to teach | verb |
| 3 | 聽懂 | tīng dǒng | to understand after listening | verb |
| 4 | 上課 | shàng kè | at a class | vsep |
| 5 | 的時候 | de shí hòu | when, while, during | time phrase |
| 6 | 不敢 | bù gǎn | too timid to, not dare to | verb |
| 7 | 解釋 | jiě shì | to explain | verb |
| 8 | 清楚 | qīng chǔ | clear | adjective |
| 9 | 下次 | xià cì | next time | time phrase |
| 10 | 舉手 | jǔ shǒu | to raise hand | verb |
| 11 | 發問 | fā wèn | to ask | verb |

## (四)孔子故事
## Stories about Confucius' life and his teaching

孔子辦學，弟子三千

Confucius held private school and had over 3,000 disciples.

孔子 23 歲開始教學生，約 30 歲開始辦學校，推廣私學。

孔子一邊學習，一邊教學。（溫故而知新，可以為師也。）

孔子教學生學習詩、書、禮、樂。相傳孔子有超過三千位弟子，其中精通六藝的有七十二位。

Confucius started to teach the age of 23 and set up a private school at the age of 30. Confucius taught his students about Poems, Calligraphy - writing, Rites, and Music. He had more than 3000 disciples: there were 72 of them who mastered these subjects of the Six Arts

【原文出處 Reference】

孔子以詩書禮樂教，弟子蓋三千焉，身通六藝者七十有二人。
【史記・孔子世家・第 62 節】*Shiji, Kongzi Shijia, Verse 62*
孔子之施教也，先之以《詩》《書》，導之以孝悌，說之以仁義，觀之以禮樂，然後成之以文德。蓋入室升堂者七十有餘人。
【孔子家語・第 12 章・弟子行・第 1 節】*Kongzi Jiayu, Chapter 12 Di-Zi-Xing, Verse 1*

## ㈤ 論語名言的現代價值評論
**Commentary about this ancient text with modern values**

Ancient Text：學而不思則罔，思而不學則殆。

The Master said, "Learning without thought is labor lost; thought without learning is perilous."

【論語第二・為政篇・第 15 節】*The Analects, Chapter 2 Wei-Zheng, Verse 15*

**Modern Values Commentary by: Yu-Chen Huang 黃語晨**

Both learning and thought are prerequisites to be a good citizen in the modern world. It is no longer enough to just be aware of what's going on; memorizing facts and statistics about racial inequality or climate change does nothing to change the current situation. Instead, we must continually probe the information we are exposed to: *How does this align with my values? What are the implications for me and others?* Most importantly, if something doesn't seem just, we must ask ourselves: *What can I do to make a difference?* Instead of blindly following whatever sentiments they are taught, a good citizen utilizes their education to ground their beliefs and actively question the institutions around them.

On the other hand, constructing a worldview with no regard to fact can be much more harmful to society, as it often leads to blatantly misguided or prejudiced thinking. When one is guided solely by their observations, their way of thinking is easily limited by their circumstances. A person living in a bubble of privilege might never understand poverty or intolerance if not for educating themselves through others' lenses. Someone who has not been personally affected by COVID-19 might refuse to take measures to protect themselves and their communities. While learning by itself is powerless, thought by itself is dangerous. Only through a combination of the two can we utilize both learning and thought as a force for good.

Yu-Chen Huang 黃語晨，哥倫比亞大學
Computer Engineering major, Columbia University

## ㈥ 模擬口語考試討論話題
## Suggested topics for oral proficiency interview (OPI)

知之為知之，不知為不知，是知也。

When you know a thing, to hold that you know it; and when you do not know a thing, to allow that you do not know it - this is knowledge.

【模擬口試練習】

1. 在學習的時候，如果碰到不懂的地方，你會怎樣辦？請以你的經驗來說明。

   When studying, what you do if you came across something you do not understand? Please explain with an experience of yours.

   【中級、高級 – 描述／敘述 Intermediate to Advanced Level – can narrate and describe】

2. 你認爲考試對學習有什麼意義或作用？在作業裡有的錯誤，或是考試考得不好，對學生的學習會有什麼幫助？請分享你的個人經驗和你的看法。

In your opinion, what is the meaning or purpose of assessment in learning? How can having some mistakes in students' homework assignments or doing poorly in a test, be beneficial to students? Please share your own experiences and your opinion.

【中級、高級 – 描述／敘述 Intermediate to Advanced Level – can narrate and describe】

【優秀級 – 表達個人意見和申述抽象觀念 Superior Level – can support opinion and discuss abstract concept】

名言二 **溫故而知新，可以爲師矣。**
Quote 2 **If a man keeps cherishing his old knowledge, so as continually to be acquiring new, he may be a teacher of others.**

## ㈠逐字翻譯
**Learn the original text and its meaning**

溫故而知新，可以為師矣。
wēn gù ér zhī xīn, kě yǐ wéi shī yǐ.

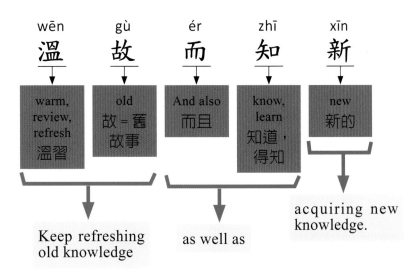

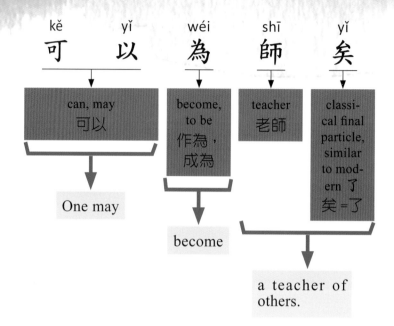

## (二) 白話解釋原文
## Explanation with the modern text

溫故而知新，可以為師矣。

If a man keeps cherishing his old knowledge, as continually to be acquiring new, he may be a teacher of others.

### 1. 白話解釋
時常溫習已經學過的知識，而且學習新的知識，就可以成為一位老師，幫助別人學習。

If a man often reviews his prior knowledge, as well as learning new thing, he may be a teacher to help others learn.

### 2. 生詞

| | 生詞<br>Vocabulary | 拼音<br>Pin Yin | 英文<br>English | 詞類<br>Part of Speech |
|---|---|---|---|---|
| 1 | 溫習 | wēn xí | to review | verb |
| 2 | 已經 | yǐ jīng | already | adverb |
| 3 | 新 | xīn | new | adjective |
| 4 | 知識 | zhī shì | knowledge | noun |

## ㈢ 延伸對話與生詞
## Extended learning with sentence practices

1. 會話

A：我每天不但要學習新課程，而且也要溫習以前學過的舊課程。

I not only learn new lessons every day, but I also review lessons that I learned before.

B：難怪你是班上成績最好的學生。我不會的地方可以請教你嗎？

No wonder you are the best student in the class. Can I ask you when I have questions?

A：當然可以。我很樂意幫忙。

Of course! I would be happy to help.

2. 生詞

| | 生詞<br>**Vocabulary** | 拼音<br>**Pin Yin** | 英文<br>**English** | 詞類<br>**Part of Speech** |
|---|---|---|---|---|
| 1 | 不但… 而且 | bú dàn … ér qiě | not only, but also | sentence pattern |
| 2 | 舊 | jiù | old | adjective |
| 3 | 難怪 | nán guài | no wonder | adverb |
| 4 | 班上 | bān shàng | in the class | noun |
| 5 | 成績 | chéng jì | grades, score | noun |
| 6 | 地方 | dì fāng | place, area | noun |
| 7 | 請教 | qǐng jiāo | to consult | verb |
| 8 | 當然 | dāng rán | of course | adverb |
| 9 | 樂意 | lè yì | to be happy to | verb |
| 10 | 幫忙 | bāng máng | to help | verb |

## ㈣ 孔子故事
## Stories about Confucius' life and his teaching

孔子有教無類，因材施教

Confucius promoted educational equality and developed individual student's talents.

孔子說：「教育的機會應該提供給所有的人，不能有因為背景或是地位的區別。」這就是孔子所主張的：「有教無類」。

孔子在教導學生的時候，也會「因材施教」。以不同的教學方法，依照每一位學生的天賦和潛力來啟發學生。

The Master said, "In teaching there should be no distinction between classes." Confucius asserted that we should offer education opportunities to all regardless of their social status. All should have the right to receive education without disparity.

Confucius also applied different teaching methods according to each students' aptitude and potential. The Master said, "In teaching there should be no distinction between classes."

【原文出處 Reference】

子曰：「有教無類。」
【論語第十五 · 衛靈公篇 · 第 39 節】 *The Analects, Chapter 15 Wei-Ling-Gong, Verse 39*
「因材施教」的例子
【論語第十一 · 先進篇 · 第 22 節】 *The Analects, Chapter 11 Xian-Jin, Verse 22*

## ㈤ 論語名言的現代價值評論
## Commentary about this ancient text with modern values

Ancient Text：子曰：「見賢思齊焉，見不賢而內自省也。」

If you see a worthy man, try to emulate him; if you see an unworthy man, examine yourself.

【論語第四 · 里仁篇 · 第 17 節】 *The Analects, Chapter 4 Li-Ren, Verse 17*

**Modern Values Commentary by: Dr. Panetha Theodosia Nychis Ott**

It is good practice to imitate the actions of those whom we respect and admire. Today, such individuals are known as role models. Our goal is to aspire to become people who embrace the good qualities we find in our role models. We often recognize those qualities because we wish to develop them in ourselves.

Conversely, we are often quick to notice and to criticize characteristics we do not admire. We often forget, however, that when we criticize others, we do so because their faults are ones which we know all too well – because we ourselves are guilty of them! When we find fault with others, it is important to first examine ourselves to see if the fault is really a personal shortcoming. All too often, criticisms are self-referential.

Dr. Panetha Theodosia Nychis Ott
Director of Admission, International Recruitment
Office of College Admission
Brown University 美國布朗大學招生部主任

## ㈥ 模擬口語考試討論話題
### Suggested topics for oral proficiency interview (OPI)

溫故而知新，可以為師矣。

If a man keeps cherishing his old knowledge, as continually to be acquiring new, he may be a teacher of others.

【模擬口試練習】

1. 你曾經幫助別人學習嗎？你認為在「教」的過程中，你同時也有「學」到什麼嗎？請分享你的經驗。

   Have you ever helped others with their learning? Do you think that this teaching experience can also help you learn at the same time? Please share your experience with this.

   【中級、高級 – 描述／敘述 Intermediate to Advanced Level – can narrate and describe】

2. 在你的學習經驗裡，有哪些是幫助你成功的因素？請舉三個例子說明。

During your learning experiences, what were the key factors to your success?
Please share three reasons for your successful learning experience.

【中級、高級 – 描述／敘述 Intermediate to Advanced Level – can narrate and
describe】

## 名言三　三人行，必有我師焉。
**Quote 3**　The Master said, "When I walk along with two others, they may
serve me as my teachers."

## ㈠逐字翻譯
## Learn the original text and its meaning

三人行，必有我師焉。
sān rén xíng, bì yǒu wǒ shī yān.

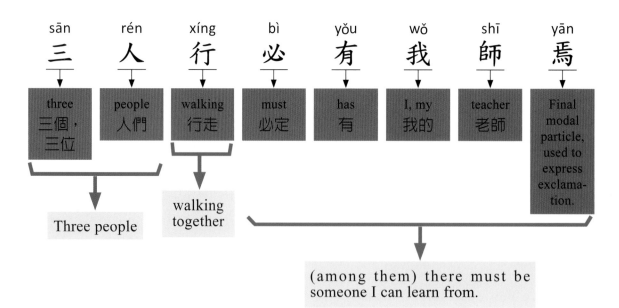

## ㈡ 白話解釋原文
## Explanation with the modern text

三人行，必有我師焉。（擇其善者而從之，其不善者而改之。）

When I walk along with two others, they may serve me as my teachers.

### 1. 白話解釋

孔子說：三個人走在一起，必定有一位可以當我的老師。我可以選擇好的行為來跟從，不好的行為就當作警惕，改善自己。

Confucius said: "When I walk along with two others, any one of them may serve me as my teachers." I can choose good conduct to follow and to learn from; as for the bad behaviors would serve as reminders for me to improve myself."

### 2. 生詞

| | 生詞<br>Vocabulary | 拼音<br>Pin Yin | 英文<br>English | 詞類<br>Part of Speech |
|---|---|---|---|---|
| 1 | 必定 | bì dìng | must have | adverb |
| 2 | 選擇 | xuǎn zé | to choose | verb |
| 3 | 行為 | háng wéi | action, behavior | noun |
| 4 | 跟從 | gēn cóng | to follow | verb |
| 5 | 當作 | dāng zuò | to take (it) as | verb |
| 6 | 警惕 | jǐng tì | vigilance | noun |
| 7 | 改善 | gǎi shàn | to improve | verb |

## ㈢ 延伸對話與生詞
## Extended learning with sentence practices

### 1. 會話

A：孔子說的「三人行，必有我師」，你同意這個說法嗎？

Confucius said: "When I walk along with two others, they may serve me as my teachers." Do you agree with this saying?

B：我非常同意。在我們身旁的人，一定有我們可以學習的優點。從他們的身上看到的優點，可以做我們好榜樣。但是，當我們看到他們身上的缺點，就告訴自己不要犯一樣的錯誤。

I agree. There must be merits that we could learn from the people around us. The good characteristics on these people could be our good model. However, when we see inferior points on them, we should be vigilant and tell ourselves not to make the same mistakes.

2.生詞

| | 生詞<br>**Vocabulary** | 拼音<br>**Pin Yin** | 英文<br>**English** | 詞類<br>**Part of Speech** |
|---|---|---|---|---|
| 1 | 同意 | tóng yì | to agree | verb |
| 2 | 身旁 | shēn páng | nearby | noun |
| 3 | 優點 | yōu diǎn | merit | noun |
| 4 | 榜樣 | bǎng yàng | model | noun |
| 5 | 缺點 | quē diǎn | shortcoming | noun |
| 6 | 犯 | fàn | to commit | verb |
| 7 | 錯誤 | cuò wù | an error, a mistake | noun |

## ㈣ 孔子故事
### Stories about Confucius' life and his teaching

孔子因材施教。孔子在同樣的問題上，對不同的學生給出不同的回答
Confucius gave different answers to different students on the same question.

　　孔子在教導學生的時候，會以不同的教法來教個性不同的學生。

　　有一次，子路問孔子：「當我聽到對的事情，是不是應該馬上就去做這件事呢？」孔子回答：「你有爸爸和哥哥，怎麼能不先問問他們的意見而馬上就去做呢？」

　　冉求也問孔子：「當我聽到對的事情，是不是應該馬上就去做這件事呢？」孔子回答：「是！你應該馬上就去做它。」

　　公西華問孔子：「同樣的問題，為什麼您給子路和冉求不一樣的回答

呢？」孔子回答説：「冉求個性退縮，我得鼓勵他前進。因爲子路比別人勇敢，我得提醒他，聽聽父兄的意見。」

Confucius used different ways to teach different students.

Zi-Lu asked Confucius: "Whether I should immediately carry into practice what I heard?" Confucius answered Zi-Lu: "You have a father and brother, how could you put something you heard to practice without consulting your father and brother first?"

Ran-Qiu asked Confucius: "Whether I should immediately carry into practice what I heard?" Confucius answered: "yes, go right ahead and do it."

Another student, Gong-Xi-Hua asked: "Why did you advise these two students differently?" Confucius said: "Qiu is very timid, that's why I encourage him to move forward. Zi-Lu is braver than others, so I try to stop him."

【原文出處 Reference】

子路問：「聞斯行諸？」子曰：「有父兄在，如之何其聞斯行之？」冉有問：「聞斯行諸？」子曰：「聞斯行之。」公西華曰：「由也問聞斯行諸，子曰『有父兄在』；求也問聞斯行諸，子曰『聞斯行之』。赤也惑，敢問。」子曰：「求也退，故進之；由也兼人，故退之。」
【論語第十一 · 先進篇 · 第 22 節】*The Analects, Chapter 11 Xian-Jin, Verse 22*

## ㈤論語名言的現代價值評論
**Commentary about this ancient text with modern values**

Ancient Text：三人行，必有我師焉。

The Master said, "When I walk along with two others, they may serve me as my teachers."

【論語第七 · 述而篇 · 第 22 節】*The Analects, Chapter 7 Xu-Er, Verse 22*

**Modern Values Commentary by: Laura Desai**

I really like the quote by Confucius "The Master said, "When I walk along with two others, they may serve me as my teachers. I will select their good qualities and follow them, their bad qualities and avoid them."" as I feel it is very applicable to my life. I have had the opportunity to work in a variety of career opportunities and I appreciate the opportunity to mentor and be mentored and observe others. I have learned so much since I began my career by observing others, not only my supervisors, but also my colleagues. I find, that in my own career, I have taken the best qualities and applied them to my own manner of interacting with others as a colleague or leader. I have also worked with various individuals who I would not aspire to mirror personally or professionally. However, through my interactions with those individuals I too have learned what I do not want to be and that is also a valuable lesson. This is what this quote speaks about very directly. I believe it is as applicable today as it was in the time of Confucius. Every experience, every person we encounter, every interaction we have in life is a learning experience if we only see it as such. There are times when the lesson is harder to accept but each experience makes our own life richer and fuller of knowledge, wisdom and experience. If we look for a lesson in all interactions and we focus on the good, we will become wise like Confucius as we interact. We will also interact in a more harmonious and balanced manner with others and the world.

Laura Desai
Former Head of School 校長
Ying-Hua International School
English-Chinese Immersion School of Princeton, NJ

## ㈥ 模擬口語考試討論話題
## Suggested topics for oral proficiency interview (OPI)

三人行，必有我師焉。（擇其善者而從之，其不善者而改之。）

When I walk along with two others, they may serve me as my teachers.

【模擬口試練習】

1. 我們可以在不同的地方學習到不同的事物，也可以向不同的人學習。請說說你曾經在什麼特別的地方學習？曾經從什麼特別的人身上學習？

   Learning can take place in different locations, and from different people. Can you talk about your most special learning experiences? From whom did you learn from and where?

   【中級、高級 – 描述／敘述 Intermediate to Advanced Level – can narrate and describe】

2. 你記不記得你最喜歡的一位老師嗎？為什麼你記得這位老師？請描述一下這位老師對你學習的影響。

   Please describe your favorite teacher. What do you remember liking about this teacher? Please also share the influence this teacher has had on you.

   【中級、高級 – 描述／敘述 Intermediate to Advanced Level – can narrate and describe】

【學習】溫故知新【論語第二 · 為政篇 · 第 11 節】*The Analects, Chapter 2 Wei-Zheng, Verse 11*

Keep cherishing the old knowledge, and continually to acquire new knowledge.

4

| Seal Script 篆書 zhuàn shū |
|---|

溫 故 知 新

Clerical Script　隸書　lì shū

Cursive Script　草書　cǎo shū

Running Script　行書　xíng shū

Standard Script　楷書　kǎi shū

第五章 【禮】 lǐ

# Chapter 5　Quotes related to propriety

## 關於【禮】的三個論語名言：
## Three top quotes about "Propriety":

不知禮，無以爲立。

Without an acquaintance with the rules of Propriety, it is impossible for the character to be established.

【論語第二十・堯曰篇・第 3 節】 *The Analects, Chapter 20 Yao-Yue, Verse 3*

君使臣以禮，臣事君以忠。

A prince should employ his minister according to the rules of propriety; ministers should serve their prince with faithfulness.

【論語第三・八佾篇・第 19 節】 *The Analects, Chapter 3 Ba-Yi, Verse 19*

上好禮，則民莫敢不敬。

If a superior man love propriety, the people will not dare not to be reverent.

【論語第十三・子路篇・第 4 節】 *The Analects, Chapter 13 Zi-Lu, Verse 4*

## (一)逐字翻譯
**Learn the original text and its meaning**

不知禮，無以為立。
bù zhī lǐ, wú yǐ wéi lì.

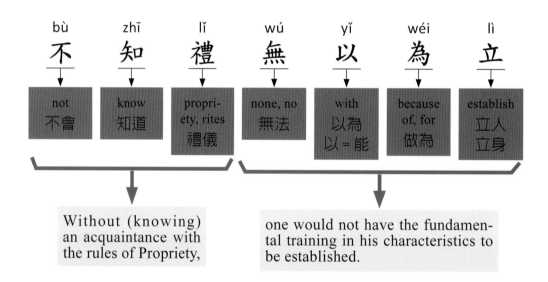

| bù | zhī | lǐ | wú | yǐ | wéi | lì |
|----|-----|-----|-----|-----|------|-----|
| 不 | 知 | 禮 | 無 | 以 | 為 | 立 |
| not 不會 | know 知道 | propriety, rites 禮儀 | none, no 無法 | with 以為 以＝能 | because of, for 做為 | establish 立人 立身 |

Without (knowing) an acquaintance with the rules of Propriety,

one would not have the fundamental training in his characteristics to be established.

## (二)白話解釋原文
**Explanation with the modern text**

不知禮，無以為立 , 不知言，無以知人也。

The Master said, "Without an acquaintance with the rules of Propriety, it is impossible for the character to be established. Without knowing the force of words, it is impossible to know men."

### 1.白話解釋
一個人如果不懂禮儀，就不能和別人好好相處。如果不懂得別人說話的含義，就無法眞正地了解對方。

If one cannot practice propriety, one cannot be established and know about the social rules; if a person cannot understand the real meaning in someone's words, one would not be able to know the characteristic of the speaker.

## 2.生詞

| | 生詞<br>**Vocabulary** | 拼音<br>**Pin Yin** | 英文<br>**English** | 詞類<br>**Part of Speech** |
|---|---|---|---|---|
| 1 | 懂 | dǒng | to understand | verb |
| 2 | 禮儀 | lǐ yí | etiquette | noun |
| 3 | 別人 | bié rén | other people | noun |
| 4 | 相處 | xiāng chǔ | to get along | verb |
| 5 | 含義 | hán yì | the meaning | noun |
| 6 | 無法 | wú fǎ | unable to | adj; adverb |
| 7 | 真正地 | zhēn zhèng dì | truly | adverb |
| 8 | 了解 | liǎo jiě | understand | verb |
| 9 | 對方 | duì fāng | the others (counterpart) | noun |

## (三)延伸對話與生詞
### Extended learning with sentence practices

1.會話

A：從小我的父母教我禮儀，學習爲人處事的道理。

Since I was young, my parents taugh us to practice good manners and how to get along with others.

B：是啊！ 如果你沒有學到良好的禮儀，將來在社會上與人交往會有困難，也會無法與他人好好相處。

If you do not learn good manners, you will encounter difficulty socially, and will not be able to get along with others in the society.

## 2. 生詞

| | 生詞<br>Vocabulary | 拼音<br>Pin Yin | 英文<br>English | 詞類<br>Part of Speech |
|---|---|---|---|---|
| 1 | 從小 | cóng xiǎo | since young age | adverb |
| 2 | 禮儀 | lǐ yí | etiquette | noun |
| 3 | 為人 | wéi rén | to behave | verb |
| 4 | 處事 | chǔ shì | to behave socially | verb |
| 5 | 道理 | dào lǐ | the rules | noun |
| 6 | 良好的 | liáng hǎo de | good, proper | adjective |
| 7 | 交往 | jiāo wǎng | to socialize | verb |
| 8 | 無法 | wú fǎ | unable to | adj; adverb |
| 9 | 相處 | xiāng chǔ | to get along | verb |
| 10 | 社會 | shè huì | society | noun |

## (四) 孔子故事

### Stories about Confucius' life and his teaching

#### 為父母守孝三年

Three years' mourning for our parents.

　　孔子遵從周禮，認為父母死後，孩子應該為父母「守孝」三年。孔子的學生宰我對孔子說：「守孝三年太長了。三年不練習禮和樂，會把這些技能都忘了。守孝一年就夠了吧。」孔子回答說：「父母死後三年不到，你就吃香飯，穿好看的衣服，你會心安嗎？」宰我說：「我會心安。」孔子對宰我說：「你如果能心安，你就去做吧。」

　　孔子說：「出生後的嬰兒要三年才會離開父母的懷抱，因為父母給我們的愛，所以父母死後三年內，君子守孝，吃魚肉不會覺得好吃，聽音樂不會覺得快樂，住豪宅也會感覺不心安。難道宰我沒有得到父母三年的照顧嗎？」

Zai Wo asked about the three years' mourning for parents, saying that one year was long enough. "If the superior man abstains for three years from the observances of propriety, those observances will be quite lost. If for three years he abstains from music, music will be ruined. Within a year the old grain is exhausted, and the new grain has sprung up, and, in procuring fire by friction, we go through all the changes of wood for that purpose. After a year, the mourning may stop." The Master said, "If you were, after a year, to eat good food, and wear fancy clothes, would you feel at ease?" "I should," replied Wo. The Master said, "If you can feel at ease, do it. But a superior man, during the whole period of mourning, does not enjoy pleasant food which he may eat, nor derive pleasure from music which he may hear. He also does not feel at ease, if he is comfortably lodged. Therefore, he does not do what you mentioned. But now you feel at ease, and you may do it then." Zai Wo then went out, and the Master said, "This shows Yu's need of virtue. It is not till a child is three years old that it is allowed to leave the arms of his parents. And the three years' mourning is universally observed throughout the empire. Did Yu enjoy the three years' love of his parents?"

【原文出處 Reference】

> 宰我問：「三年之喪，期已久矣，君子三年不為禮，禮必壞；三年不為樂，樂必崩。舊穀既沒，新穀既升，鑽燧改火，期可已矣。」子曰：「食夫稻，衣夫錦，于汝安乎？」曰：「安。」汝安則為之。夫君子之居喪，食旨不甘，聞樂不樂，居處不安，故不為也，今汝安則為之。」宰我出，子曰：「予之不仁也，子生三年，然後免于父母之懷。夫三年之喪，天下之通喪也。予也有三年之愛于其父母乎？」
>
> 【論語第十七 · 陽貨篇 · 第 21 節】*The Analects, Chapter 17 Yang-Huo, Verse 21*

## ㈤ 論語名言的現代價值評論
### Commentary about this ancient text with modern values

Ancient Text：不知禮，無以為立。

Without an acquaintance with the rules of Propriety, it is impossible for the character to be established.

【論語第二十 · 堯曰篇 · 第 3 節】*The Analects, Chapter 20 Yao-Yue, Verse 3*

**Modern Values Commentary by: Dr. Alvin Joaquín Figueroa**

Propriety does not depart from a blank slate. Experience and learning generate it. How we behave with others originate in the values we are taught at an early stage of our lives. The values of respect and good manners were instilled in me by my maternal grandmother. She raised me since I was four years old and taught me not only poetry and how to write properly and with elegance in an epoch without computers (her penmanship was absolutely beautiful), but how to honor family and friends. As an only child and as orphan, I learned how to place friends at the top of my social world. Learning to respect and celebrate my friends' pluralities and idiosyncrasies from a young age cemented relationships that I still have. My Facebook world, for instance, is a constant celebration of the friends I've had since elementary school. To this date we honor our friendships without regards to ideology. Ideology is something that gravely divides many people in my home country.

When I entered the workforce, I brought these values with me to Academia. They have helped me to see my co-workers as friends, and not only as colleagues. That for me, constitutes a rule of propriety that has made a great difference in my life. Placing the value of friendship first keeps us away from the political···or at least it eases the process.

Propriety for me is not necessarily politeness or table manners, but a standard of good social behavior towards the Other.

Dr. Alvin Joaquín Figueroa
Professor Emeritus
Department of World Languages and Cultures
The College of New Jersey

Ancient Text：子曰：不知禮，無以為立。

> Confucius said: "Without an acquaintance with the rules of Propriety, it is impossible for the character to be established."

【論語第二十‧堯曰篇‧第 3 節】 *The Analects, Chapter 20 Yao-Yue, Verse 3*

**Modern Values Commentary by: Jamie Rufe**

Anecdotally speaking, I would say most of my manners and etiquette were nurtured by my parents from a very young age. Whether it was saying "please" and "thank you," giving firm handshakes or looking people in the eye when introducing myself, my parents were persistent in making sure that these behaviors became good habits. One other area that my parents were very particular about was table manners – as I've gotten older and eaten with many different people, it's become very clear to me why parents were so strict about our table manners – your etiquette at the dinner table is not only a reflection of your upbringing, values and character, but it is also a very powerful first impression for other people. In American society, you are often judged by your social manners and etiquette.

In terms of social skill and manners, I would say the most important skill I've developed and mastered over the past 10-20 years is getting along with others and be empathetic of other people. When you can learn to respect and understand others without trying to control them or impose yourself on them, I think that is a true sign of character.

After living in China and Taiwan for over the past 10 years, I would say one of the biggest differences I've noticed in terms of social communication and etiquette is the "subtlety" of your message. Americans tend to be very direct and to the point – if they have an issue with you, they will tell you. If they don't like your deal or proposal, they'll say no. However, in ethnic Chinese societies, my impression is that despite saying somewhat nebulous messages that could be interpreted as positive or neutral, the true intent is negative. For example, if I really don't want to say yes, but out of respect for said person or situation, I would maneuver myself out of this situation by going sideways.

Jamie Rufe
Masters student,
National Taiwan Normal University,
Taipei, Taiwan

## ㈥ 模擬口語考試討論話題
### Suggested topics for oral proficiency interview (OPI)

不知禮，無以為立 , 不知言，無以知人也。
The Master said, "Without an acquaintance with the rules of Propriety, it is impossible for the character to be established. Without knowing the force of words, it is impossible to know men."

【模擬口試練習】
1. 什麼是有禮貌的行為？你覺得有禮貌的行為，對一個人能不能成功，重不重要？為什麼？請以一個經驗或是故事來說明你的看法。

   Please share your opinion about etiquettes and manners. Are etiquettes and manners important to a person's growth and success? Why? Can you tell a story related to this topic?

   【中級、高級 – 描述／敘述 Intermediate to Advanced Level – can narrate and describe】

   【優秀級 – 表達個人意見和申述抽象觀念 Superior Level – can support opinion and discuss abstract concept】

2. 人們的有禮貌行為對一個國家、社會的文明有重要的意義，假如你是一個國家的總統或是領導人，你會實行什麼政策，讓你的國人對禮儀更加重視？

   Polite behaviors and etiquettes of people are of great value to the civility of a country. If you were the president, or the leader of your country, what policy would you implement to encourage your citizens to place more emphasis on manners?

【優秀級 – 假設情境申述 Superior Level – can hypothesize】

## 名言二 Quote 2　君使臣以禮，臣事君以忠。
A prince should employ his minister according to according to the rules of propriety; ministers should serve their prince with faithfulness."

㈠ 逐字翻譯

**Learn the original text and its meaning**

君使臣以禮，臣事君以忠。

jūn shǐ chén yǐ lǐ, chén shì jūn yǐ zhōng.

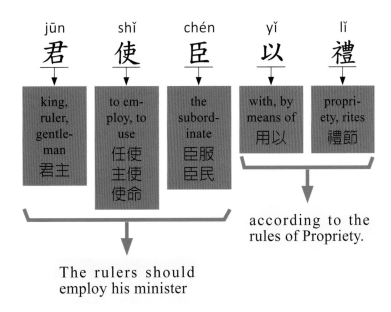

第五章 【禮】

85

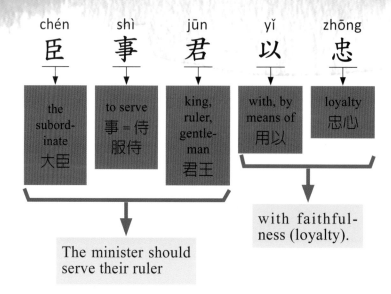

|  | chén | shì | jūn | yǐ | zhōng |
|--|------|-----|-----|-----|-------|
|  | 臣 | 事 | 君 | 以 | 忠 |

the subordinate 大臣

to serve 事＝侍 服侍

king, ruler, gentleman 君王

with, by means of 用以

loyalty 忠心

The minister should serve their ruler

with faithfulness (loyalty).

## (二) 白話解釋原文
**Explanation with the modern text**

君使臣以禮，臣事君以忠。

A prince should employ his minister according to the rules of propriety; ministers should serve their prince with faithfulness."

### 1. 白話解釋

國君對待臣子要有禮貌，臣子要忠心服侍國君。

The king should treat his minister with respect and according to the rules of propriety; ministers should serve their king with loyalty and faithfulness."

### 2. 生詞

|  | 生詞<br>Vocabulary | 拼音<br>Pin Yin | 英文<br>English | 詞類<br>Part of Speech |
|--|------|------|------|------|
| 1 | 國君 | guó jūn | emperor, king | noun |
| 2 | 對待 | duì dài | to treat | verb |
| 3 | 臣子 | chén zǐ | minister | noun |
| 4 | 有禮貌 | yǒu lǐ mào | polite | adjective |

| | 生詞<br>Vocabulary | 拼音<br>Pin Yin | 英文<br>English | 詞類<br>Part of Speech |
|---|---|---|---|---|
| 5 | 服侍 | fú shì | to attend | verb |
| 6 | 忠心 | zhōng xīn | loyal | adjective |

## ㈢ 延伸對話與生詞
### Extended learning with sentence practices

1. 會話

A：我們公司的老闆對待我們員工很有禮貌，也很尊重員工。

The boss of our company treats us politely and with respect.

B：是啊！就是因為這樣，我們員工才會對他很忠心，也很認真為公司工作。

Indeed! That is why we are very loyal to him and we work hard for the company.

2. 生詞

| | 生詞<br>Vocabulary | 拼音<br>Pin Yin | 英文<br>English | 詞類<br>Part of Speech |
|---|---|---|---|---|
| 1 | 老闆 | lǎo bǎn | boss, supervisor | noun |
| 2 | 對待 | duì dài | to treat | verb |
| 3 | 員工 | yuán gōng | employee | noun |
| 4 | 尊重 | zūn zhòng | to respect | verb |
| 5 | 忠心 | zhōng xīn | loyal | adjective |
| 6 | 認真 | rèn zhēn | diligent | adjective |
| 7 | 公司 | gōng sī | the company | noun |

## ㈣孔子故事
### Stories about Confucius' life and his teaching

孔子怎麼教自己的兒子？

How did Confucius teach his own son?

陳亢問孔子的兒子，伯魚：「你的爸爸孔子有教你特別的知識嗎？」伯魚回答：「沒有。」有一次他一個人站在那，我快步走過庭園。他問我說：『你學詩了嗎？』我說：『沒有。』孔子說：『不學詩，就不能掌握說話的技巧。』我回去學詩。又一次他又一個人站在那，我快步走過庭園。他問我：『學禮了嗎？』我說：『沒有。』孔子說：『不學禮，就不能立足於社會。』我回去學禮，就聽過這兩次。」陳亢回去高興地說：「問一件事，得到三個收穫：知道了詩的作用，知道了禮的作用，又知道了君子並不偏愛自己的兒子。」

Chen Kang asked Bo Yu, saying, "Have you heard any lessons from your father different from what we have all heard?" Bo Yu replied, "No. He was standing alone once, when I passed below the hall with hasty steps, and said to me, 'Have you learned the Odes?' On my replying 'Not yet,' he added, 'If you do not learn the Odes, you will not be fit to converse with.' I retired and studied the Odes. Another day, he was in the same way standing alone, when I passed by below the hall with hasty steps, and said to me, 'Have you learned the rules of Propriety?' On my replying 'Not yet,' he added, 'If you do not learn the rules of Propriety, your character cannot be established.' I then retired, and learned the rules of Propriety. I have heard only these two things from him." Chen Kang retired, and, quite delighted, said, "I asked one thing, and I have got three things. I have heard about the Odes. I have heard about the rules of Propriety. I have also heard that the superior man maintains a distant reserve towards his son."

【原文出處 Reference】

陳亢問于伯魚曰：「子亦有異聞乎？」對曰：「未也。嘗獨立，鯉趨而過庭。曰：『學詩乎？』對曰：『未也。』『不學詩，無以言。』鯉退而學詩。他日，又獨立，鯉趨而過庭。曰：『學禮乎？』對曰：『未也。』『不學禮，無以立。』鯉退而學禮，聞斯二者。」

## 父親死後，還能遵從父親的規矩嗎？

Follow his father's rules for at least three years after his father passed?

　　孔子說：「父親活著的時候，看孩子的志向有沒有，父親死後，就要看孩子的行動，如果父親死後三年內不改父親的規矩習慣，這樣的孩子可以算是孝順了。」

　　The Master said, "While a man's father is alive, look at the bent of his will; when his father is dead, look at his conduct. If for three years, the son does not alter from the way of his father, he may be called filial."

【原文出處 Reference】

## ㈤ 論語名言的現代價值評論
## Commentary about this ancient text with modern values

Ancient Text：君事臣以禮，臣事君以忠。

　　　　　　　"A prince should employ his minister according to the rules of proplety; ministers should serve their prince with faithfulness."

【論語第三‧八佾篇‧第 19 節】 *The Analects, Chapter 3 Ba-Yi, Verse 19*

**Modern Values Commentary by: Yu-Chen Huang 黃語晨**

　　Leaders come in myriad forms — from politicians to principals, captains to CEO's — but they all have one thing in common: they are nothing without their teams. Confucius recognized that a necessary component of an effective leadership is fostering a reciprocal relationship between leader and follower. When a prince rules with morality and respect, he acts in the best interest of his people; his ministers are expected to return the favor by serving him with loyalty and trust. Though there are few princes nowadays, this principle is still relevant for all types of leaders today.

A good leader shouldn't just be good at leading; they should also lead for good. When they are guided by virtue, their goals are ethical and beneficial to others, which serves as motivation for their team to work diligently. From my experience, volunteers rarely require extra incentives because they believe in the goals of the organization, whether it's a soup kitchen, animal shelter, or something else. I'm normally quite shy, but even I'm willing to knock on strangers' doors for a political campaign if I believe it serves good causes. In addition, team members feel more personally obligated to do their part when leaders treat them with respect and dignity. I, for one, am happy to go the extra mile for a teacher or supervisor that I admire simply because I want to make them proud. It's clear that having common values and mutual respect creates a harmonious dynamic between leader and follower, consequently increasing productivity. However, perfect harmony isn't always possible, so what happens when it is broken?

If a team isn't finding success, a good leader looks to themself before blaming others, finding a balance between enforcing rules and adjusting expectations. For example, it's not reasonable to punish Amazon warehouse workers for not fulfilling their quotas when they don't even have time to go to the bathroom. On the other hand, when a leader defies justice, it is the follower's responsibility to question them and use their own moral compass to determine what is right. This is something that, as citizens, we can all do. When our community or country's leaders stop acting in everyone's best interest, it is our duty to protest for what we believe in to help create a better world for all.

Yu-Chen Huang 黃語晨，
哥倫比亞大學
Computer Engineering major,
Columbia University

## ㈥ 模擬口語考試討論話題
## Suggested topics for oral proficiency interview (OPI)

### 君使臣以禮，臣事君以忠。

A prince should employ his minister according to the rules of propriety; ministers should serve their prince with faithfulness.

【模擬口試練習】

1. 你認為一位上司應該怎麼做，他的員工才會更努力工作？應該對員工有禮貌，還是對員工加強管理？請說說你的看法。

   What do you think a supervisor should do to make their menbers work harder? Do you think the supervisor should treat their employees politely and with respect or do you think they should enforce stricter rules to manage their staff so that they will work harder and be more productive? Please talk about your opinion on this issue.

   【高級－說明比較 Advanced Level – can compare】

   【優秀級－表達個人意見和申述抽象觀念 Superior Level – can support opinion and discuss abstract concept】

2. 如果有兩個主管，一個主管常常請員工吃飯，而需要加班的時候，不付加班費給員工；另一個主管平常很少跟員工聊天，工作的時候也比較嚴肅，員工需要加班的時候，他也會加班，也會付加班費給員工。你會選擇哪位主管？為什麼？

   Which of the following two supervisors would you choose? The one who likes to take employees to meals, but will not pay the workers extra on overtime; or the other one who seldom treats employees to meals but will pay overtime compensation. Which one would you choose to work with? Why?

   【高級－說明比較 Advanced Level – can compare】

   【優秀級－表達個人意見和申述抽象觀念 Superior Level – can support opinion and discuss abstract concept】

## 名言三 上好禮，則民莫敢不敬。

**Quote 3** If a superior man loves propriety, the people will not dare not to be irreverent.

### (一) 逐字翻譯
### Learn the original text and its meaning

上好禮，則民莫敢不敬。

shàng hào lǐ, zé mín mò gǎn bù jìng.

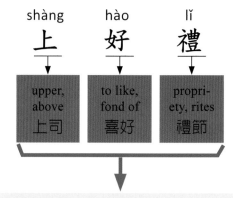

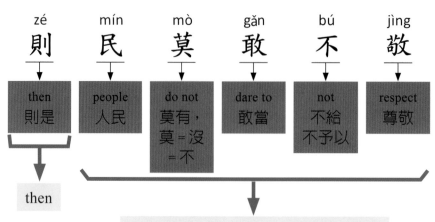

## (二)白話解釋原文
## Explanation with the modern text

## 上好禮，則民莫敢不敬。
If a superior man love propriety, the people will not dare not to be reverent.

### 1. 白話解釋
身為領導者的上司（長官）如果喜好崇尚禮節的話，那麼他的跟隨者（人民）一定會尊敬他。

If a supervisor or a leader applies and practices propriety, his employees or followers will surely respect him.

### 2. 生詞

| | 生詞<br>Vocabulary | 拼音<br>Pin Yin | 英文<br>English | 詞類<br>Part of Speech |
|---|---|---|---|---|
| 1 | 身為 | shēn wéi | to be, as | verb |
| 2 | 領導者 | lǐng dǎo zhě | leader | noun |
| 3 | 上司 | shàng sī | supervisor | noun |
| 4 | 長官 | zhǎng guān | supervisor, sir | noun |
| 5 | 崇尚 | chóng shàng | to advocate | verb |
| 6 | 禮節 | lǐ jié | manner | noun |
| 7 | 跟隨者 | gēn suí zhě | follower | noun |
| 8 | 尊敬 | zūn jìng | to respect | verb |

## (三)延伸對話與生詞
## Extended learning with sentence practices

### 1. 會話
A：我很喜歡我們的老闆。他很注重禮節和崇尚禮儀。也對大家都很有禮貌。

I like our boss. He cares about proper etiquettes and propriety. He treats everyone with respect.

B：沒錯，我覺得就是因為他對大家都很有禮貌，所以，大家也都很尊敬他。

That is right. I think it is because he acts politely toward everyone , that is why everyone respects him.

## 2.生詞

| | 生詞<br>Vocabulary | 拼音<br>Pin Yin | 英文<br>English | 詞類<br>Part of Speech |
|---|---|---|---|---|
| 1 | 老闆 | lǎo bǎn | supervisor, boss | noun |
| 2 | 注重 | zhù zhòng | to value, to emphasize | Verb |
| 3 | 崇尚 | chóng shàng | to advocate | verb |
| 4 | 禮節 | lǐ jié | manner | noun |
| 5 | 禮儀 | lǐ yí | etiquette | noun |
| 6 | 禮貌 | lǐ mào | courtesy | noun |
| 7 | 尊敬 | zūn jìng | to respect | verb |

## ㈣ 孔子故事
### Stories about Confucius' life and his teaching

孔子收學費嗎？什麼是「束脩」？

Did Confucius accept tuition?

想要成為孔子的學生，需不需要準備學費？

孔子曾經說過：「有學生自己帶來乾肉條來送我，要我做他的老師，我從來沒有不願意教導他。（我一定會教導這位學生。）」

束脩（乾肉條）是一個表示，這個故事告訴我們，孔子認為學生帶來「束脩」是對老師表示尊敬，和想學習的決心。這是一個「禮儀」的代表。

Did Confucius accept tuition from his disciples?

Confucius once said: "If anyone brings me a bundle of dry meat and asks me to teach him, I have never refused to teach such a student."

Su-Xiu (a piece of dried-meat) is a gift tha symbolizes appreciation to the teacher. This story tells us that if someone showed up with a small token of appreciation and respect for Confucius as a teacher, he would always agree to provide instructions to him. Confucius took the dry meat from the disciple as a token of respect and a sign of determination for becoming a disciple to learn from him.

【原文出處 Reference】

子曰：「自行束脩以上，吾未嘗無誨焉。」
The Master said, "From the man bringing his bundle of dried flesh for my teaching upwards, I have never refused instruction to anyone."
【論語第七 · 述而篇 · 第 7 節】 *The Analects, Chapter 7 Shu-Er, Verse 7*

## 孔子「至聖先師」，誨人不倦

Confucius, The Greatest Teacher, Confucius, The Greatest Teacher, who taught without weariness.

明世宗（西元 1530）追諡孔子爲「至聖先師孔子」，所以後人都尊稱孔子爲「至聖先師」。

Emperor Ming Shi-Zong in Ming dynasty (1530 A.D.) gave Confucius a posthumous title: "The Greatest Teacher, Confucius". Since then, people call Confucius "The Greatest Teacher".

孔子說：「人家說我是有仁道的聖人，我不敢說自己有那麼好。我只是一直很努力，喜好教學而不覺得厭倦。只是這樣而已。」公西華說：「這就是我們這些學生所學不到的。」

The Master said, "The sage and the man of perfect virtue how dare I rank myself with them? I strive to become such without satiety and teach others without weariness - this much can be said of me." Gong Xi Hua said, "This is just what we, the disciples, cannot imitate you in."

【原文出處 Reference】

子曰：「若聖與仁，則吾豈敢？抑爲之不厭，誨人不倦，則可謂云爾已矣。」
公西華曰：「正唯弟子不能學也。」
【論語第七 · 述而篇 · 第 34 節】 *The Analects, Chapter 7 Shu-Er, Verse 34*

## ㈤ 論語名言的現代價值評論
## Commentary about this ancient text with modern values

Ancient Text：禮之用，和為貴。

In practicing the rules of propriety, a natural ease is to be prized.

【論語第一‧學而篇‧第 12 節】 *The Analects, Chapter 1 Xue-Er, Verse 12*

**Modern Values Commentary by: Jessica Nicol**

Propriety, conforming to conventionally accepted standards of behavior and morality, is a compelling concept for the modern person. As globalization and technological advances continue to connect disparate ways of life, the rapidly changing world continues to erode the existing consensus on what is considered proper and improper.

Conflicting notions of "right" and "wrong" perpetually battle in public spheres. Young people striving to proliferate ideals of freedom and equality often offend the sensibilities of older generations through their endeavors. One's own sense of propriety, which might come with ease comparable to that of common sense, may be foreign and uncomfortable to another's.

The reason for this is thus: culture, that which defines our sense of morality and ultimately defines propriety, no longer stands as the primordial, homogenized monolith as it had for those who preceded us.

However, this does not mean that propriety cannot be engaged by the modern person. If the goal of propriety is to cultivate an environment of comfort in which one can feel effortlessly understood, then, when confronted with conflicting ideas of behavioral and moral norms, propriety can still be invoked through the praxes of kindness and compassion.

All whom we pass in life are equally human as ourselves, and in being such, they all wish for understanding and respect. In our endeavors, listening and understanding should be carried out on the principle that we are all joined together in our desire for a good life. This intentional creation of comfort and good faith is the modern incarnation of propriety. And ultimately, this sense of propriety should come with the same effortlessness and ease as acknowledging our own humanity.

By, Jessica Nicol

International Study Major, Class of 2021

The College of New Jersey, USA

## ㈥ 模擬口語考試討論話題
### Suggested topics for oral proficiency interview (OPI)

## 上好禮，則民莫敢不敬。
If a superior man love propriety, the people will not dare to be unreverent.

【模擬口試練習】

1. 歷史上出現過很多不同的領導人，請說說一位你欣賞的領導人，他有什麼樣的人格和能力？

   There have been many great leaders throughout history. Please name one of the leaders you admire and explain their characteristics and skills you find in them.

   【中級、高級 – 描述／敘述 Intermediate to Advanced Level – can narrate and describe】

2. 你曾經做過一個團體的領導嗎？請談談你的 " 領導 " 經驗，並且分享如何做好一位領導。

   Do you have experience being a leader for any organization or group? Please talk about the experience and share your suggestions on how to be a good leader.

   【中級、高級 – 描述／敘述 Intermediate to Advanced Level – can narrate and describe】

   【優秀級 – 表達個人意見和申述抽象觀念 Superior Level – can support opinion and discuss abstract concept】

【禮】禮之用和為貴【論語第一・學而篇・第 12 節】*The Analects, Chapter 1 Xue-Er; Verse 12*

In practicing the rules of propriety, a natural case is to be prized.

5

Seal Script　篆書　zhuàn shū

Clerical Script　隸書　lì shū

Cursive Script　草書　cǎo shū

Running Script　行書　xíng shū

Standard Script　楷書　kǎi shū

關於【快樂】的三個論語名言：

Three top quotes about "Happiness":

學而時習之，不亦説（悦 yuè）乎？

Is it not pleasant to learn with a constant perseverance and application?

有朋自遠方來，不亦樂（lè - happiness）乎？

Is it not delightful to have friends coming from distant quarters?

【論語第一 · 學而篇 · 第 01 節】 The Analects, Chapter 1 Xue-Er, Verse 01

知（智）者樂水，仁者樂山。

The wise find pleasure in water; the virtuous find pleasure in hills.

【論語第六 · 雍也篇 · 第 23 節】 The Analects, Chapter 6 Yong-Ye, Verse 23

知之者不如好之者，好之者不如樂（lè）之者。

They who know the truth are not equal to those who love it, and they who love it are not equal to those who delight in it.

【論語第六 · 雍也篇 · 第 20 節】 The Analects, Chapter 6 Yong-Ye, Verse 20

名言一 學而時習之，不亦悅（yuè）（說）乎。
有朋自遠方來，不亦樂（lè –
happiness）乎。

Quote 1 Is it not pleasant to learn with a constant perseverance and application? Is it not delightful to have friends coming from distant quarters?

## ㈠逐字翻譯

## Learn the original text and its meaning

學而時習之，不亦說（悅 yuè）乎？

Xué ér shí xí zhī, bú yì yuè hū?

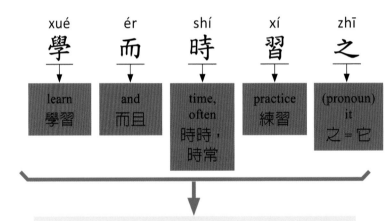

Learning with frequent practices the knowledge,

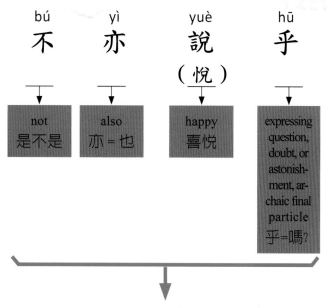

Isn't that a pleasant thing to do?

有朋自遠方來，不亦樂（lè - happiness）乎？
yǒu péng zì yuǎn fāng lái, bú yì lè hū?

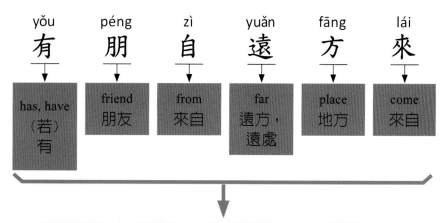

(If) you have friends coming to visit you from a far place,

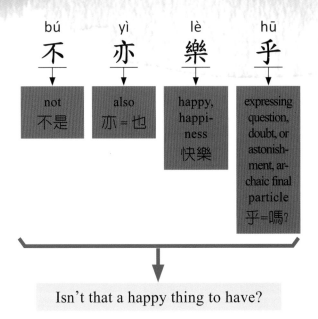

| bú | yì | lè | hū |
|---|---|---|---|
| 不 | 亦 | 樂 | 乎 |
| not 不是 | also 亦＝也 | happy, happiness 快樂 | expressing question, doubt, or astonishment, archaic final particle 乎＝嗎？ |

Isn't that a happy thing to have?

## ㈡ 白話解釋原文
**Explanation with the modern text**

### (A) 學而時習之，不亦說（悅 yuè）乎？
Is it not pleasant to learn with a constant perseverance and application?

1.白話解釋 -A

孔子說：「學習新知識，而且時時溫習、練習和複習這些知識，是一件多麼愉快的事情啊！」

Confucius said: "Learning new knowledge and studying often, practicing and reviewing the knowledge is a great pleasure in learning."

2.生詞 -A

| | 生詞 Vocabulary | 拼音 Pin Yin | 英文 English | 詞類 Part of Speech |
|---|---|---|---|---|
| 1 | 知識 | zhī shì | knowledge | noun |
| 2 | 時時 | shí shí | often | adverb |
| 3 | 溫習 | wēn xí | to review and study | verb |

| | 生詞<br>Vocabulary | 拼音<br>Pin Yin | 英文<br>English | 詞類<br>Part of Speech |
|---|---|---|---|---|
| 4 | 練習 | liàn xí | to practice | verb |
| 5 | 複習 | fù xí | to review | verb |
| 6 | 愉快 | yú kuài | pleasant, happy | adjective |

## (B) 有朋自遠方來，不亦樂（lè - happiness）乎？

Is it not delightful to have friends coming from distant quarters?

### 1. 白話解釋 -B

有朋友從遠方來拜訪，不也是一件很快樂的事情嗎？

Is it not delightful to have friends coming from distant quarters?

### 2. 生詞 -B

| | 生詞<br>Vocabulary | 拼音<br>Pin Yin | 英文<br>English | 詞類<br>Part of Speech |
|---|---|---|---|---|
| 1 | 遠方 | yuǎn fāng | far place | noun |
| 2 | 拜訪 | bài fǎng | to visit | verb |
| 3 | 快樂 | kuài lè | happy | adjective |
| 4 | 一件 | yī jiàn | A (measure word) | Measure word |
| 5 | 事情 | shì qíng | A thing, a matter | noun |

## (三) 延伸對話與生詞

### Extended learning with sentence practices

### 1. 會話 -A

(A) 學而時習之，不亦說（悅 yuè）乎？

A：我覺得今天學到的新課程很有意思。

I think the new lesson we learned today is very interesting.

B：是啊！我們明天一起去圖書館溫習、練習和複習今天學到的課程，好嗎？

That's right! Let's go to the library together tomorrow. We can study, practice and review the lesson together, all right?

A：好啊！我們還可以預習明天的課程。好好學習，加油向上！

Good! We could also review the lesson for tomorrow's class. Let's work hard and move forward together!

## 2.生詞 -A

| | 生詞<br>Vocabulary | 拼音<br>Pin Yin | 英文<br>English | 詞類<br>Part of Speech |
|---|---|---|---|---|
| 1 | 課程 | kè chéng | lesson | noun |
| 2 | 圖書館 | tú shū guǎn | library | noun |
| 3 | 溫習 | wēn xí | to review and study | verb |
| 4 | 練習 | liàn xí | to practice | verb |
| 5 | 複習 | fù xí | to review | verb |
| 6 | 加油 | jiā yóu | to work hard | verb |
| 7 | 預習 | yù xí | to preview | verb |
| 8 | 學習 | xué xí | to learn, to study | verb |
| 9 | 向上 | xiàng shàng | to improve, to move upwards | verb |

## 1.會話 -B

(B) 有朋自遠方來，不亦樂（lè - happiness）乎？

A：我的好朋友下個月要從美國來台灣玩。我真是太興奮了！

My friends are coming to visit me in Taiwan from America next month. I am so excited!

B：太好了！孔子說：「有朋自遠方來，不亦樂乎！」
我來幫你招待遠方來的朋友。

That is great! Confucius said that it is most delightful to have a friend visiting from far away. I will help you take your friends around.

A：謝謝你，我在美國留學的時候，這些美國朋友幫了我很多忙，這次我邀請他們來台灣，就是希望有機會好好地招待他們。

Thank you! When I was studying abroad in America, these friends helped me a lot. I invited them to visit Taiwan in hopes of having the opportunity to show them a good time in Taiwan.

## 2. 生詞 -B

|  | 生詞<br>Vocabulary | 拼音<br>Pin Yin | 英文<br>English | 詞類<br>Part of Speech |
|---|---|---|---|---|
| 1 | 興奮 | xìng fèn | excited | adjective |
| 2 | 招待 | zhāo dài | to treat | verb |
| 3 | 遠方 | yuǎn fāng | places from far away | noun |
| 4 | 留學 | liú xué | to study abroad | verb |
| 5 | 邀請 | yāo qǐng | to invite | verb |
| 6 | 希望 | xī wàng | to hope | verb |
| 7 | 機會 | jī huì | a chance, an opportunity | noun |

## ㈣ 孔子故事
### Stories about Confucius' life and his teaching

孔子覺得空想沒有好處

It is not beneficial to be thinking without learning.

孔子說：「我曾經整天不吃、整夜不睡，只用來思考。結果沒有得到什麼好處，還不如學習。」

The Master said, "I have been the whole day without eating, and the whole night without sleeping; occupied with thinking. It was of no use. The better plan is to learn."

【原文出處 Reference】

子曰：「吾嘗終日不食，終夜不寢，以思。無益，不如學也。」
【論語第十五·衛靈公篇·第 31 節】 *The Analects, Chapter 15 Wei-Ling-Gong, Verse 31*

孔子描述自己的性格（樂以忘憂，不知老之將至云爾。）

Confucius commented on his own personality.

　　葉公問子路：你的老師孔子是怎樣的人？子路不回答葉公。後來，孔子知道了就對子路說：「你怎麼不說：我的老師這個人啊，努力學習的時候就忘記吃飯，高興的時候就忘了憂愁，也不知道他自己的年紀越來越老了。」

　　The Duke of Yeh asked Zi-Lu (one of Confucius' students) about Confucius. Zi-Lu did not answer the Duke. (When Confucius heard about this), the Master said to Zi-Lu: "Why didn't you tell the Duke that he is simply a man, who in his eager pursuit of knowledge forgets his meals, who in the joy of its attainment forgets his sorrows, and who does not perceive that old age is approaching."

【原文出處 Reference】

> 葉公問孔子於子路，子路不對。子曰：「女奚不曰，其為人也，發憤忘食，樂以忘憂，不知老之將至云爾。」
> 【論語第七‧述而篇‧第 19 節】 *The Analects, Chapter 7 Shu-Er, verse19*

## ㈤論語名言的現代價值評論
## Commentary about this ancient text with modern values

Ancient Text：子曰：「學而時習之，不亦說乎？有朋自遠方來，不亦樂乎？人不知而不慍，不亦君子乎？」

The Master said, "Is it not pleasant to learn with a constant perseverance and application? Is it not delightful to have friends coming from distant quarters? Is he not a man of complete virtue, who feels no discomposure though men may take no note of him?"

【論語第一‧學而篇‧第 1 節】 *The Analects, Chapter 1 Xue-Er, Verse 1*

**Modern Values Commentary by: Dr. Panetha Theodosia Nychis Ott**

In this passage, Confucius describes a person completely at peace with himself or herself. Inner peace is achieved through the joy one takes in life-long learning, which is an end in itself rather than a means to an end. Similarly, the delight one takes in the gift of friendship is a pleasure in itself, rather than a possible means to an end. A person who has developed good habits and discipline in learning and who takes satisfaction in it for its own sake, just as he takes satisfaction in friendship for its own sake, will take no notice of what others may think. Absent are the emotions that plague the person whose actions are driven by a desire to be noticed by others. Note that the emphasis is on values that are not material.

The connection between virtue and the habit of discipline is explicit in this passage. Implicit is the connection between virtue and knowledge or wisdom. The person who has developed the good habit of learning and cherishes it as he/she cherishes friendship, achieves virtue and through virtue, inner peace.

By: Dr. Panetha Theodosia Nychis Ott

Director of Admission, International Recruitment

Office of College Admission

Brown University 布朗大學招生部主任

Ancient Text：學而時習之，不亦說乎？

Is it not pleasant to learn with a constant perseverance and application?

有朋自遠方來，不亦樂乎？

Is it not delightful to have friends coming from distant quarters?

【論語第一・學而篇・第 1 節】*The Analects, Chapter 1 Xue-Er, Verse 1*

**Modern Values Commentary by: Brian Ford 富柏恩**

Being able to speak Chinese as an American usually surprises people. I feel like everyone knows it's a difficult language to learn and it required plenty of perseverance and practice for me to learn how to read, write and speak. Even after graduating with a second major in Chinese Studies, I feel fortunate to have a job that enables me to apply my Mandarin abilities and continue to develop them. The usefulness and applicability of Chinese language has made my learning experience especially rewarding.

To Confucius' point, indeed it has been pleasant to learn with perseverance and application! In other words, I have seen my hard work pay off and enjoyed the fruits of my labor. I think modern wisdom and phrases like these still reflect the meanings behind many of Confucius' quotes today. – Anyone who has studied a language should understand that much deeper understanding is needed to truly learn. After all, what is language for? It's not just the naming of things; it's the lifeblood of a culture, a people. This insight provided by J.R.R. Tolkien has been completely true in my experience.

Learning Chinese brought me a wonderful connection with Chinese culture and people. Thankfully, I've been fortunate enough to study in Beijing and Taiwan through great programs at top universities, and the people were undoubtedly the most crucial aspect of both experiences. I left each program with newly established lifelong friendships, with people from around the world. This really broadened my idea of what "far" is. An hour or two drive to visit a good friend, or better yet, a friend coming to visit you, is really a beautiful thing that's not hard to do.

Visiting a friend in Texas, or Utah, or Oregon, while I live in New Jersey, is also accessible and will always make for a joyous trip. Going back to Taiwan or Beijing, or friends coming to visit me from either of those places, would truly be a delight. My point is that in each of these instances, visiting with friends who can't see you every day because of the distance between your homes will always worthwhile and delightful, regardless of the distance.

However, I think the distance adds a fonder appreciation the further you or your friends travel to make it happen. Furthermore, when there are cultural differences and foreign aspects of the visit, I think friends tend to go the extra mile to make their guests comfortable. When I visited friends' homes in Taiwan or Beijing, they were some of the most hospitable welcomes I've ever experienced. Enjoying locally grown tea leaves, or a homecooked traditional meal, or even casual conversation with a friend in their hometown, comes with heartwarming affection, mutual care, respect and excitement.

By: Brian Ford 富柏恩
International Finance Analyst,
KYBORA, International Advisory Firm

## ㈥ 模擬口語考試討論話題
### Suggested topics for oral proficiency interview (OPI)

## 學而時習之，不亦說（悅 yuè）乎？
Is it not pleasant to learn with a constant perseverance and application?

【模擬口試練習】

1. 你覺得怎樣的「學習」是一種快樂的學習方式？

   What kind of learning style do you think is the style that makes you happiest? Please describe how to achieve an enjoyable learning approach.

   【中級、高級 – 描述／敘述 Intermediate to Advanced Level – can narrate and describe】

2. 你曾經有很快樂的學習經驗嗎？請說說看這個快樂的學習經驗有什麼特別的地方。

   Have you had pariticularly happy learning experiences? Please talk about your experience. and what you think made it especially joyful in this scenario?

   【中級、高級 – 描述／敘述 Intermediate to Advanced Level – can narrate and describe】

3. 快樂的學習讓人喜歡學習，可是學習的過程中常常有考試、記憶等等讓人有壓力的事情。你認爲是不是應該取消考試，才可以有快樂的學習嗎？爲什麼？

   An enjoyable learning process can make a person enjoy learning. However, there are often thing such as memorization or tests in the traditional learning process which creates a lot of stress. Do you think we should eliminate tests in order to promote enjoyable learning? Why?

【優秀級 – 表達個人意見和申述抽象觀念 Superior Level – can support opinion and discuss abstract concept】

## 有朋自遠方來，不亦樂（lè - happiness）乎？

Is it not delightful to have friends coming from distant quarters?

【模擬口試練習】

1. 你的朋友從很遠的地方來拜訪你，你怎麼招待他？

   When your friends came to visit you from afar, how did you take them around town? Please describe this experience.

   【中級、高級 – 描述／敘述 Intermediate to Advanced Level – can narrate and describe】

2. 請為你的朋友介紹你的家人。

   Please introduce your family to your friends.

   【中級、高級 – 描述／敘述 Intermediate to Advanced Level – can narrate and describe】

3. 你的朋友從很遠的地方來拜訪你，你會帶他去看哪一個名勝古蹟？請介紹一下這個地方。

   To what local place of interest would you take friends who are visiting from afar. Please describe and introduce this sightseeing spot.

   【中級、高級 – 描述／敘述 Intermediate to Advanced Level – can narrate and describe】

# 名言二 知（智）者樂水，仁者樂山。
**Quote 2** "The wise find pleasure in water; the virtuous find pleasure in hills."

## ㈠逐字翻譯
**Learn the original text and its meaning**

子曰：「知（智）者樂水，仁者樂山。」

zǐ yuē: Zhì zhě yào shuǐ, rén zhě yào shān.

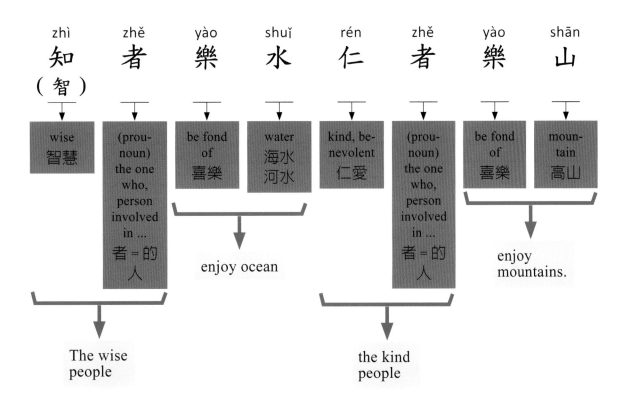

## ㈡白話解釋原文
**Explanation with the modern text**

子曰：「知（智）者樂水，仁者樂山；知（智）者動，仁者靜；智者樂，仁者壽。」

Master said, "The wise find pleasure in water; the virtuous find pleasure in hills. The wise are active; the virtuous are tranquil. The wise are joyful; the virtuous are long-lived."

【論語第六・雍也篇・第 23 節】 *The Analects, Chapter 6 Yong-Ye, Verse 23*

## 1.白話解釋

孔子說：「有智慧的人喜歡水，有仁心的人喜歡山。因為有智慧的人喜好動態的事物，有仁心的人喜好靜態的事物；有智慧的人總是快樂的，有仁心的人活得很長壽。」

Confucius said: "Wise people enjoy the ocean (or the water), and kind-hearted people enjoy the mountains. Because the wise enjoy dynamic activities, and people with kindness enjoy the calm activities; the wise people are always happy and the kind-hearted people usually live a long life.

## 2.生詞

| | 生詞<br>**Vocabulary** | 拼音<br>**Pin Yin** | 英文<br>**English** | 詞類<br>**Part of Speech** |
|---|---|---|---|---|
| 1 | 智慧 | zhì huì | wisdom | noun |
| 2 | 仁心 | rén xīn | kindness | noun |
| 3 | 喜好 | xǐ hǎo | to like | verb |
| 4 | 動態 | dòng tài | active | adjective |
| 5 | 事物 | shì wù | matters | noun |
| 6 | 靜態 | jìng tài | still, static | adjective |
| 7 | 長壽 | cháng shòu | longevity | noun |

## (三) 延伸對話與生詞
**Extended learning with sentence practices**

## 1.會話

A：你喜歡去看海，還是喜歡去爬山？

Do you like to go to the beach or do you like to go hiking?

B：我喜歡看海，因為海浪總是變化無窮。

I like watching the sea, because the waves are always charging and unpredictable.

A：我喜歡爬山，因為在山上可以看到很多植物和動物。

I like mountain climbing, because there are many plants and animals in the mountains.

## 2.生詞

| | 生詞<br>Vocabulary | 拼音<br>Pin Yin | 英文<br>English | 詞類<br>Part of Speech |
|---|---|---|---|---|
| 1 | 看海 | kàn hǎi | to watch the sea | verb |
| 2 | 爬山 | pá shān | to climb a mountain | verb |
| 3 | 海浪 | hǎi làng | wave | noun |
| 4 | 變化無窮 | biàn huà wú qióng | changeable | adjective |
| 5 | 植物 | zhí wù | plant | noun |
| 6 | 動物 | dòng wù | animal | noun |

## ㈣ 孔子故事

### Stories about Confucius' life and his teaching

三種有益的愛好樂趣，也三種有害的愛好樂趣

Three advantageous enjoyment and three harmful enjoyment.

　　孔子告訴學生，要選擇對自己有益的興趣愛好，不要喜歡做那些對自己有害的事情。

　　孔子認為有三種愛好樂趣是有益的，有三種愛好樂趣是有害的。孔子說：「對身心有益的愛好有三種，對身心有害的愛好也有三種。愛好有節制行為，讓行為適合禮和樂；愛好說別人的優點；愛好多結交有良好品德的朋友，這些都是有益的。喜歡驕傲自大，喜歡沒有限度的遊樂，喜歡沒有限度的吃喝，這些都是有害的興趣愛好。」

　　Confucius said, "There are three things men find enjoyment in which are advantageous, and three things they find enjoyment in which are injurious. To find enjoyment in the discriminating study of ceremonies and music; to find enjoyment in speaking of the goodness of others; to find enjoyment in having many worthy friends - these are advantageous. To find enjoyment in extravagant pleasures; to find enjoyment in idleness and sauntering; to find enjoyment in the pleasures of feasting - these are injurious."

【原文出處 Reference】

孔子曰：「益者三樂，損者三樂。樂節禮樂，樂道人之善，樂多賢友，益矣。樂驕樂，樂佚遊，樂宴樂，損矣。」

【論語第十六‧季氏篇‧第 5 節】 *The Analects, Chapter 16 Ji-Shi, Verse 5*

## ㈤ 論語名言的現代價值評論
## Commentary about this ancient text with modern values

Ancient Text：子曰：「學而時習之，不亦說乎？有朋自遠方來，不亦樂乎？人不知而不慍，不亦君子乎？」

The master said, "Is it not pleasant to learn with a constant perseverance and application? Is it not delightful to have friends coming from distant quarters? Is he not a man of complete virtue, who feels no discomposure though men take no note of him?"

【論語第一‧學而篇‧第 01 節】 *The Analects, Chapter 1 Xue-Er, Verse 01*

**Modern Values Commentary by: Jane Wagner 萬美珍**

According to Confucius here, someone is considered virtuous when they feel fulfilled from hard work and attaining knowledge. They will gain respect from others even if they don't gain fame from their efforts. One way to interpret the first section of the quote, in my opinion, is to not give up. It's easy to give up, but you'll feel happier with yourself after having worked past hard times and being able to use what you have learned. I've been studying Mandarin for some years now but still have a way to go before I can get close to achieving fluency. I don't know if I'll ever be fluent but giving up learning certainly won't help in any way. With hard work and consistency, I can better myself and come closer to my goal.

These friends coming from a distant place I think can be understood as fellow scholars or like-minded individuals. Deep and meaningful relationships are crucial to one's well-being, so it's only natural that being acknowledged by others for your accomplishments can deepen the joy already experienced from acquiring knowledge.

However, one who is upset by the fact that others don't recognize their efforts might question "the point" of putting in all the hard work pursuing greatness. In that case, their goal of bettering themself and learning was not in fact for the sole purpose of bettering themselves through gaining knowledge, but instead a false version of greatness, that being approval.

For example, when you go to school to receive an education, are you learning to learn, or are you learning to be applauded by others? Of course, it's okay to hope that someone might recognize your efforts- since as people, positive and meaningful relationships help build up our confidence and make us happy. But if no one ever recognized your hard work in studying, would you just quit school altogether?

In this quote, the term 'junzi' refers to a Confucian ideal of the "exemplary person." As said in *The Analects*, they are a righteous human being with virtues that enable them to follow the Dao- the Way, path; the way people ought to behave in society. Learning is a form of self-cultivation. Confucius laments that scholars who study for themselves are Junzi, unlike scholars who study for others. So by being devoted to learning, the Confucian Junzi is a morally significant person.

Jane Wagner 萬美珍

International Study Major

The College of New Jersey

## ㈥模擬口語考試討論話題
## Suggested topics for oral proficiency interview (OPI)

知（智）者樂水，仁者樂山。（智者動，仁者靜。）

Master said, "The wise find pleasure in water; the virtuous find pleasure in hills. The wise are active; the virtuous are tranquil. The wise are joyful; the virtuous are long-lived."

【模擬口試練習】

1. 你去海邊的時候，喜歡做些什麼活動？你在海邊會有什麼心情感受？

   What activities do you enjoy doing when you are at the beach? Please describe your feelings when you are at the beach.

   【中級、高級 – 描述／敘述 Intermediate to Advanced Level – can narrate and describe】

2. 你去山上的時候，喜歡做些什麼活動？你爬山的時候，或是在山上的時候，會有什麼心情感受？

   What activities do you enjoy doing when you go to the mountains? Please describe your feelings when you are in the mountains.

   【中級、高級 – 描述／敘述 Intermediate to Advanced Level – can narrate and describe】

3. 你喜歡「海」，還是喜歡「山」？請說明為什麼你喜歡「海」，或是為什麼喜歡「山」。

   Do you enjoy the ocean or the mountains? Please talk about the reasons why you like the ocean or the mountains.

   【高級 – 說明比較 Advanced Level – can compare】

   【優秀級 – 表達個人意見和申述抽象觀念 Superior Level – can support opinion and discuss abstract concept】

名言三 知之者不如好之者，好之者不如樂（lè）之者。

Quote 3 "They who know the truth are not equal to those who love it, and they who love it are not equal to those who delight in it."

## (一)逐字翻譯
**Learn the original text and its meaning**

知之者不如好之者，好之者不如樂（lè）之者。
zhī zhī zhě bù rú hào zhī zhě, hǎo zhī zhě bù rú lè zhī zhě.

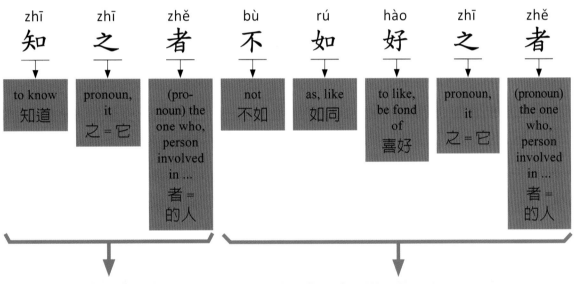

| zhī 知 | zhī 之 | zhě 者 | bù 不 | rú 如 | hào 好 | zhī 之 | zhě 者 |
|---|---|---|---|---|---|---|---|
| to know 知道 | pronoun, it 之＝它 | (pronoun) the one who, person involved in ... 者＝的人 | not 不如 | as, like 如同 | to like, be fond of 喜好 | pronoun, it 之＝它 | (pronoun) the one who, person involved in ... 者＝的人 |

Those who merely know the knowledge,

are not as good as the ones who like the knowledge.

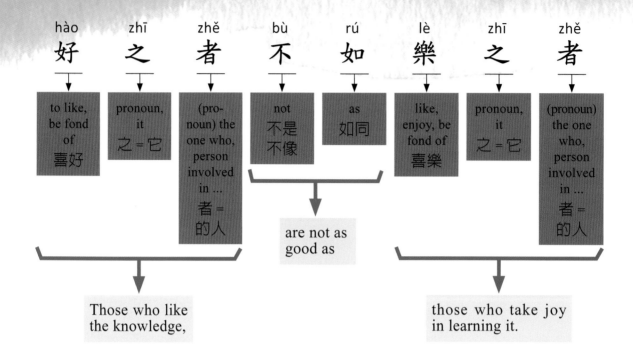

## ㈡白話解釋原文
**Explanation with the modern text**

知之者不如好之者，好之者不如樂（lè）之者。

Confucius said: "Those who know the knowledge are not equal to those who love it, and they who love the knowledge are not equal to those who delight in it.

【論語第六・雍也篇・第 20 節】*The Analects, Chapter 6 Yong-Ye, Verse 20*

### 1.白話解釋

孔子說：有知識的人不如喜好知識的人，喜好知識的人不如以學習為樂的人。孔子用這句話來鼓勵學生，要以學習為一件快樂的事情，在取得知識的過程享受學習的樂趣。

Confucius said: "Those who know the knowledge are not equal to those who love it, and they who love the knowledge are not equal to those who delight in it.

## 2.生詞

| | 生詞<br>**Vocabulary** | 拼音<br>**Pin Yin** | 英文<br>**English** | 詞類<br>**Part of Speech** |
|---|---|---|---|---|
| 1 | 知識 | zhī shì | knowledge | noun |
| 2 | 喜好 | xǐ hào | to like | verb |
| 3 | 不如 | bù rú | not as, inferior to | adjective |
| 4 | 以…為樂 | yǐ … wéi lè | to be happy for something | verb |
| 5 | 鼓勵 | gǔ lì | to encourage | verb |
| 6 | 取得 | qǔ dé | to gain, to obtain | verb |
| 7 | 學習 | xué xí | to learn | verb |
| 8 | 過程 | guò chéng | process | noun |
| 9 | 享受 | xiǎng shòu | to enjoy | verb |
| 10 | 樂趣 | lè qù | joy, fun | noun |

## ㈢ 延伸對話與生詞
### Extended learning with sentence practices

1.會話

A：上了一個學期的中文課，你的中文水平越來越好了。

After a semester of Chinese lessons, your Chinese is getting better and better.

B：我不僅越來越喜歡學習中文，更以學習中文為一件快樂的事情。

Not only do I enjoy the Chinese course more and more, but I also think learning the Chinese language is a pleasure.

2.生詞

| | 生詞<br>**Vocabulary** | 拼音<br>**Pin Yin** | 英文<br>**English** | 詞類<br>**Part of Speech** |
|---|---|---|---|---|
| 1 | 學期 | xué qī | semester | noun |

| | 生詞<br>Vocabulary | 拼音<br>Pin Yin | 英文<br>English | 詞類<br>Part of Speech |
|---|---|---|---|---|
| 2 | 水平 | shuǐ píng | proficiency level | noun |
| 3 | 越來越 | yuè lái yuè | more and more | adverb |
| 4 | 不僅 | bù jǐn | not only | adverb |
| 5 | 更 | gēng | even, more | adverb |
| 6 | 以⋯為（一件快樂的事情） | yǐ ... wéi ... | To make something as a happy matter | sentence pattern |
| 7 | 事情 | shì qíng | matters | noun |

## ㈣孔子故事
## Stories about Confucius' life and his teaching

一邊學習，一邊思考（學而不思則罔，思而不學則殆。）

Thinking and learning should go hand-in-hand.

　　孔子說：「學習時如果不思考道理，會越學越困惑；如果只是憑空思考，而不認真學習知識，卻是很危險的，因為他可能會做錯事。」

　　Confucius said: "If one engages with learning without applying his reasoning or analysis, he could be confused and puzzled. If one ponders but does not commit himself to gaining more knowledge, it is dangerous because he might choose to do the wrong action."

【原文出處 Reference】

學而不思則罔，思而不學則殆

The Master said, "Learning without thought is labor lost; thought without learning is perilous."

　　【論語第二・為政篇・第 15 節】 *The Analects, Chapter 2 Wei-Zheng, Verse 15*

## ㈤ 論語名言的現代價值評論
## Commentary about this ancient text with modern values

Ancient Text：知之者不如好之者，好之者不如樂之者。

"They who know the truth are not equal to those who love it, and they who love it are not equal to those who delight in it."

【論語第六‧雍也篇‧第 20 節】 *The Analects, Chapter 6 Yong-Ye, Verse 20*

**Modern Values Commentary by: Chloë Epstein**

I first interpreted Confucius's quote as learning something new, grappling with both the uncomfortable and fascinating sides to the fact, and then accepting its existence. After that I began to associate this idea with morbid curiosity, something I've always had since I was a child, and many of my friends and family have as well. My earliest memory of morbid curiosity is when I was around 10 years old I was given a book called *Oh, Yikes!: History's Grossest Wackiest Moments*, which appeared as a fun kids book on history, but transformed into a source of knowledge for the gross and disturbing. King Henry VIII's 6 wives, Vlad the Impaler, and numerous torture devices and deadly plagues were all topics I had first learned about through this book. As horrific as *Oh Yikes!* was, I absolutely loved it, especially compared to the history I learned in school, which consisted of memorizing dates and the Revolutionary War. Through high school and college, I have found myself going through deep wormholes of webpage after webpage on more historical oddities and disturbances. Serial killers is a topic in particular I read up on because of their status as real life monsters and the mystery of why they exist. I later found out my mother had the same interest in them when she was young as well. Just a few weeks ago, my best friend at college sent me a video series of a person narrating outrageous Wikipedia pages he had found on topics like mass hysteria, dead bodies, and historical surgeries. However, despite the horror, the videos are presented in fun animations through a comedic tone. There are some truths that are difficult to come to terms with, but comedy and creativity is the way we deal with them instead of wallowing in misery. Knowing history is a necessary part of understanding the present, but when we dive into the uncomfortable, we have to explore our own feelings on the issue in order to fully accept its existence and importance.

Chloë Epstein
Fine Arts Major, Bryn Mawr College,
Pennsylvania, USA

# ㈥ 模擬口語考試討論話題
## Suggested topics for oral proficiency interview (OPI)

知之者不如好之者，好之者不如樂（lè）之者。

They who know the truth are not equal to those who love it, and they who love it are not equal to those who delight in it.

【模擬口試練習】

1. 你曾經覺得學習一個學科或是技能是很有意思、很快樂的嗎？請說說看你最喜歡的學科是什麼？也說說你的學習經驗。

   Have you ever found learning a subject or a skill interesting and enjoyable? What is your favorite subject?
   Please share your joyful learning experience.

   【中級、高級－描述／敘述 Intermediate to Advanced Level－can narrate and describe】

2. 你的主修專業是什麼？你是怎麼決定選這個專業的？請說說為什麼選這個專業的原因。

   What is your major in college? How did you make this choice? Please talk about the reasons why you choose the specific area as your major?

   【中級、高級－描述／敘述 Intermediate to Advanced Level－can narrate and describe】

【快樂】知者樂，仁者壽【論語第六‧雍也篇‧第23節】*The Analects, Chapter 6 Yong-Ye, Verse 23*

The wise are active; the virtuous are tranquil.

6

Seal Script 篆書 zhuàn shū

Clerical Script 隸書 lì shū

Cursive Script 草書 cǎo shū

Running Script 行書 xíng shū

Standard Script 楷書 kǎi shū

# 第七章 【音樂】 yin yuè

## Chapter 7  Quotes related to music

關於【音樂】的三個論語名言：
**Three top quotes about "Music":**

興於詩，立於禮，成於樂（yuè - music）。

It is by the Odes that the mind is aroused. It is by the Rules of Propriety that the character is established. It is from Music that the finish is received.

【論語第八‧泰伯篇‧第 8 節】*The Analects, Chapter 8 Tai-Bo, Verse 8*

歌樂者，仁之和也。

Singing and music are the harmony of humanity

【禮記‧儒行‧第 18 節】*The Book of Rites , Chapter Rúxíng , Verse 18*

子與人歌而善，必使反之，而後和之。

When the Master was in company with a person who was singing, if he sang well, he would make him repeat the song, while he accompanied it with his own voice.

【論語第七‧述而篇‧第 32 節】*The Analects, Chapter 7 Xu-Er, Verse 32*

The Master said, "It is by the Odes that the mind is aroused. It is by the Rules of Propriety that the character is established. It is from Music that the finish is received."

## (一) 逐字翻譯

**Learn the original text and its meaning**

興於詩，立於禮，成於樂。

xing yú shī, lì yú lǐ, chéng yú yuè

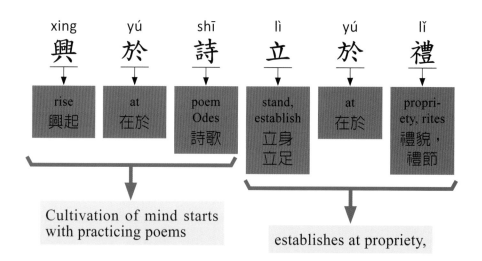

Cultivation of mind starts with practicing poems

establishes at propriety,

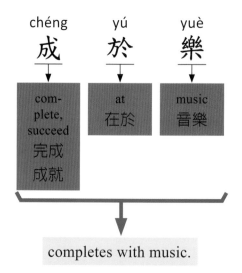

completes with music.

## ㈡白話解釋原文
### Explanation with the modern text

子曰：「興於詩，立於禮，成於樂。」

The Master said, "It is by the Odes that the mind is aroused. It is by the Rules of Propriety that the character is established. It is from Music that the finish is received."

### 1.白話解釋

孔子說，學習「詩書」讓你開始立志，學習「禮節」讓你能在社會上立足（有位子／地位），學習「音樂」使你的知識和性格都能完善。

Confucius said: "Learning the Literatures, it would help you start the determination of cultivation. Learning the rites and propriety can help you be established (with your own identity.). Learning the music can help you be accomplished with harmonious characteristics.

The process of cultivation and building characteristics (in a person) starts with learning poems (including such as nursery rhyme), then established with practicing rites and rituals, finally learning and making music would allow my personality to be accomplished.

### 2.生詞

| | 生詞<br>Vocabulary | 拼音<br>Pin Yin | 英文<br>English | 詞類<br>Part of Speech |
|---|---|---|---|---|
| 1 | 詩 | shī | a poem | noun |
| 2 | 書 | shū | a book | noun |
| 3 | 禮節 | lǐ jié | etiquette | noun |
| 4 | 社會 | shè huì | society | noun |
| 5 | 立足 | lì zú | to gain a foothold | verb |
| 6 | 地位 | dì wèi | status | noun |
| 7 | 性格 | xìng gé | characteristic | noun |
| 8 | 完善 | wán shàn | to make perfect | verb |
| 9 | 位子 | wèi zī | a position | noun |

## ㈢延伸對話與生詞
### Extended learning with sentence practices

1.會話

A：孔子說：「興於詩，立於禮，成於樂。」你可以幫我解釋這個名言的意思嗎？

Confucius said: "Learning poetry will increase our knowledge, practicing manners and rites will rectify our actions, learning music will make our characteristics become complete." Can you help me understand the meaning of this quote?

B：這句名言的意思是，「詩書」可以幫我們增加知識，學習「禮節」是良好行為的表現，學習「音樂」可以讓性格完美。也就是說，一個人如果學習「詩書」，可以讓自己的知識增長（knowledge），學習好的「禮節」可以注意自己的行為（behaviors），學習「音樂」可以完善個人的性格（characteristics）。

The meaning of this quote is: Learning poems (including nursery rhymes) can help to build characteristics. Practicing rites and rituals can help to establish social behaviors. Learning and making music can help to complete one's characteristics. That also means, one should learn poems to increase knowledge (in literature), learn good etiquettes to establish good conducts, and learn music to grow good characters.

2.生詞

| | 生詞<br>Vocabulary | 拼音<br>Pin Yin | 英文<br>English | 詞類<br>Part of Speech |
|---|---|---|---|---|
| 1 | 學習 | xué xí | to learn | verb |
| 2 | 詩書 | shī shū | poetry | noun |
| 3 | 增長 | zēng zhǎng | to improve | verb |
| 4 | 行為 | xíng wéi | conduct, behavior | noun |
| 5 | 完善 | wán shàn | to make perfect | verb |
| 6 | 性格 | xìng gé | personality, characteristic | noun |

| | 生詞<br>**Vocabulary** | 拼音<br>**Pin Yin** | 英文<br>**English** | 詞類<br>**Part of Speech** |
|---|---|---|---|---|
| 7 | 增加 | zēng jiā | to increase | verb |
| 8 | 良好 | liáng hǎo | good, fine | adjective |
| 9 | 表現 | biǎo xiàn | to demonstrate | verb |
| 10 | 完美 | wán měi | perfect | adjective |

## ㈣ 孔子故事
## Stories about Confucius' life and his teaching

孔子尊重失明的樂師

Confucius respectfully assisted the blind musician.

　　音樂大師冕來見孔子，因為冕是失明（眼瞎）的盲人，孔子就非常小心，一步一步告訴冕，「台階到了」、「座位到了」、「和面前有什麼人」。音樂大師冕離開後，子張問孔子：「您這樣是幫助盲人的方法嗎？」孔子說：「對！這就是幫忙盲人的方法。」

　　這個故事說明了孔子如何表現對失明的樂師的尊重。

　　The musician, Mian, visited Confucius. Because Mian could not see, Confucius assisted him very carefully. He told Mian about the steps, the seat, and who was in front of Mian. After Mian left, Zi-Zhang (Confucius' disciple) asked Confucius: "Was that the proper way of treating the blind person?" Confucius said: "Yes! That is the proper way to assist the blind person."

　　This story illustrated how Confucius demonstrated the respect toward the blind musician.

【原文出處 Reference】

師冕見，及階，子曰：「階也。」及席，子曰：「席也。」皆坐，子告之曰：「某在斯，某在斯。」師冕出。子張問曰：「與師言之道與？」子曰：「然。固相師之道也。」
【論語第十五・衛靈公篇・第 42 節】 *The Analects, Chapter 15 Wei-Ling-gong, Verse 42*

## ㈤論語名言的現代價值評論
## Commentary about this ancient text with modern values

Ancient Text：興於詩，立於禮，成於樂（yuè - music）。

The Master said, "It is by the Odes that the mind is aroused. It is by the Rules of Propriety that the character is established. It is from Music that the finish is received."

【論語第八 · 泰伯篇 · 第 8 節】*The Analects, Chapter 8 Tai-Bo, Verse 8*

**Modern Values Commentary by: Ellis Cain, 柯南**

In many cultures, literature and poetry are often viewed as the road to cultivating oneself, especially with regards to cultural cultivation. This cultural cultivation mainly rises from the different perspectives that one encounters when reading literature and poetry. By putting oneself in the author, narrator, or character's shoes, you can learn and develop empathy, a key skill for interacting with others. Literature and poetry are also deeply ingrained in their background culture, which allows the reader to enjoy the surface level meaning as well as learning the deeper cultural nuances, bringing about a better appreciation for the work's culture as well as your own culture. On the side of social interactions, personal cultivation comes from a better understanding of cultural norms and rules; understanding the nuances and aspects of these allows one to become more personable, compassionate, and thoughtful in any interaction. People often say that learning music also helps with the integration of the creative, big picture side of the brain and the logical, small detail side of the brain. While these mainly deal with the cultivation of personal qualities, certain musical environments also allow us serve better in a society; in an orchestra or band, you also have to learn how to work together as a team and adjust to the others around you. This may not directly transfer to social interactions, but they can help to develop teamwork and understand the part one plays in a larger goal. Reflecting on my own experiences, I can see these different aspects of cultural cultivation throughout my time learning

Chinese, studying classical Chinese and modern literature, learning the formal and informal language patterns, and exploring Chinese history and culture. These have provided countless opportunities and experiences that have deeply shaped my character to this day, whether it be the time I spent abroad in China or the Chinese, Taiwanese, or Hong Kong friends I have met in at university, all leading me to learn how to rise up, establish oneself, and connect to the world.

Ellis Cain, 柯南

Indiana University,

Cognitive Science major（專業認知科學）

## ㈥ 模擬口語考試討論話題
## Suggested topics oral proficiency interview (OPI)

興於詩，立於禮，成於樂（yuè - music）。

The Master said, "It is by the Odes that the mind is aroused. It is by the Rules of Propriety that the character is established. It is from Music that the finish is received."

【模擬口試練習】

1. 你覺得學習「詩或文學」對我們有什麼好處？ 請解釋你的看法，並舉例說明。

   Please discuss why learning literature and poetry would be helpful to a person? Please explain why or share an example from your experiences.

   【中級、高級 – 描述 / 敘述 Intermediate to Advanced Level – can narrate and describe】

   【優秀級 – 表達個人意見和申述抽象觀念 Superior Level – can support opinion and discuss abstract concept】

2. 你覺得學習「禮節」對我們有什麼好處？請討論學習「禮」對個人在社會交流互動能力有什麼幫助。並舉例說明。

Please describe the benefits of learning propriety and following good social rules for our personal growth in social interactions with others.

Please explain why or share an example from your experiences.

【高級 – 描述／敘述 Advanced Level – can narrate and describe】

【優秀級 – 表達個人意見和申述抽象觀念 Superior Level – can support opinion and discuss abstract concept】

3. 你覺得學習「音樂」對我們有什麼好處？請以個人成長、職場與社會交流互動等方面來討論。並舉例說明。

Please discuss why learning music would be helpful to us? Please describe how music could help the society to maintain harmony and to promote civilization.

Please explain why or please share an example from your experiences.

【高級 – 描述／敘述 Advanced Level – can narrate and describe】

【優秀級 – 表達個人意見和申述抽象觀念 Superior Level – can support opinion and discuss abstract concept】

---

名言二　Quote 2　歌樂者，仁之和也。
Singing and music are the harmony of humanity.

## (一) 逐字翻譯
**Learn the original text and its meaning**

歌樂者，仁之和也。

gē yuè zhě, rén zhī hé yě.

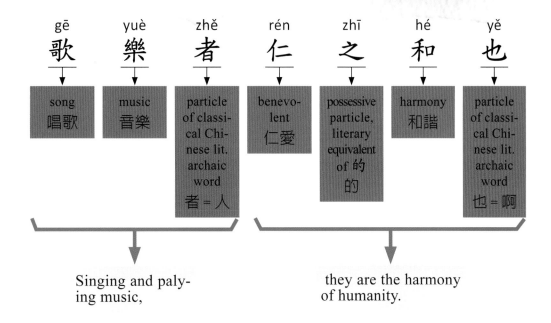

| gē 歌 | yuè 樂 | zhě 者 | rén 仁 | zhī 之 | hé 和 | yě 也 |
|---|---|---|---|---|---|---|
| song 唱歌 | music 音樂 | particle of classical Chinese lit. archaic word 者＝人 | benevolent 仁愛 | possessive particle, literary equivalent of 的 的 | harmony 和諧 | particle of classical Chinese lit. archaic word 也＝啊 |

Singing and palying music,　　　they are the harmony of humanity.

## ㈡ 白話解釋原文
### Explanation with the modern text

歌樂者，仁之和也。

Singing and playing music are the harmony of humanity and benevolence.

### 1. 白話解釋
演唱歌曲和演奏音樂都是「仁愛」的融合表現。

Singing and playing music are the harmony of humanity and benevolence.

### 2. 生詞

| | 生詞 Vocabulary | 拼音 Pin Yin | 英文 English | 詞類 Part of Speech |
|---|---|---|---|---|
| 1 | 演唱 | yǎn chàng | singing (a song) | verb |
| 2 | 歌曲 | gē qǔ | song | noun |
| 3 | 演奏 | yǎn zòu | playing (a musical instrument) | verb |
| 4 | 音樂 | yīn yuè | music | noun |
| 5 | 仁愛 | rén ài | benevolence | noun |

| | 生詞<br>Vocabulary | 拼音<br>Pin Yin | 英文<br>English | 詞類<br>Part of Speech |
|---|---|---|---|---|
| 6 | 融合 | róng hé | to blend, to fuse | verb |
| 7 | 表現 | biǎo xiàn | to display | verb |

## (三) 延伸對話與生詞
## Extended learning with sentence practices

1. 會話

A：聽到音樂的時候，我覺得心情很祥和、輕鬆。

When I hear music, my emotion is very peaceful and relaxed.

B：我也喜歡唱歌。因為唱歌的時候，我們的心充滿著和諧。

I like to sing too. When singing, our hearts are filled with harmony.

2. 生詞

| | 生詞<br>Vocabulary | 拼音<br>Pin Yin | 英文<br>English | 詞類<br>Part of Speech |
|---|---|---|---|---|
| 1 | 心情 | xīn qíng | emotion | noun |
| 2 | 祥和 | xiáng hé | auspicious, peaceful | adjective |
| 3 | 輕鬆 | qīng sōng | relaxed | adjective |
| 4 | 唱歌 | chàng gē | to sing | verb |
| 5 | 充滿 | chōng mǎn | to fill with | verb |
| 6 | 和諧 | hé xié | harmony | adjective |

## (四) 孔子故事
## Stories about Confucius' life and his teaching

孔子學琴於師襄子

Confucius' music lessons with Shi-Xiang-Zi.

　　孔子跟師襄子學彈鼓琴。孔子練了十天還不學另一首新的曲子。師襄子說：「可以學更難的曲子了。」孔子說：「我雖然已經學會彈奏這首曲子，但是還沒有學到技巧。」

　　過了幾天，師襄子對孔子說：「你已經學到了技巧了，可以學更難的曲子了。」孔子又說：「雖然我已經學會了技巧，但是我還沒領會到這首曲子所要表達的精神。」

　　過了幾天，師襄子又對孔子說：「你已經可以表達曲子的精神了。可以開始學更難的曲子了。」孔子說：「可是我還沒領會出來這首曲子是誰作的。」

　　又過了幾天，孔子對師襄子說：「我終於可以感受到這首曲子是誰寫的了。這個作曲者的情緒低沈，身材高高的，有長遠明亮的眼光，像一位統治四方的君王，如果不是周文王，還有誰能作出這首曲子呢？」師襄子聽後，起身向孔子拜了又拜說：「我的老師教我這首曲子的時候就是這樣告訴我的，這首曲子叫做《文王操》啊！」

　　這個「孔子學琴」的故事告訴我們，孔子對於學習音樂的態度和用心。

Confucius learned to play the musical instrument with Shi-Xiangzi. After playing the new piece for ten days, Confucius still wouldn't want to move forward. Shi-Xiangzi said to Confucius:" You have learned the piece, let's learn a harder piece." Confucius replied:" Although I have learned how to play the piece, I have not mastered the technique." After a few days, Shi Xiangzi came and said to Confucius:" Now you have mastered the techniques, you should move forward to learn a harder piece."

Confucius replied: "Although I have learned the technique, I need more time to learn the spirit of this piece." After a few more days, Shi Xiangzi said: "Now that you have captured the spirit of this piece, shall we move forward to learn a harder piece?" Confucius said: "I have not yet figured out who composed this music."

After pondering over the piece for a few more days, Confucius said to Shi Xiangzi: "The composer seemed to be in a dark mood, tall, with high vision. He must be a king of the four states. Who else could it be other than the King Wen of Zhou?" Shi Xiangzi was very impressed and bowed to Confucius. He said: "That was exactly what my teacher said when he taught me this music."

This story illustrated to us how Confucius took every learning to heart and his dedication to deep understanding.

孔子學鼓琴師襄子，十日不進。師襄子曰：「可以益矣。」孔子曰：「丘已習其曲矣，未得其數也。」有間，曰：「已習其數，可以益矣。」孔子曰：「丘未得其志也。」有間，曰：「已習其志，可以益矣。」孔子曰：「丘未得其為人也。」有間，有所穆然深思焉，有所怡然高望而遠志焉。曰：「丘得其為人，黯然而黑，幾然而長，眼如望羊，如王四國，非文王其誰能為此也！」師襄子去席再拜，曰：「師蓋雲《文王操》也。」

【孔子家語‧第 35 章‧辯樂解‧第 1 節】 *Kongzi Jiayu, Chapter 35 Bian-Yue-Jie, Verse 1*

【史記‧孔子世家‧第 34 節】 *Shiji, Kongzi Shijia, Verse 34*

## (五) 論語名言的現代價值評論
### Commentary about this ancient text with modern values

Ancient Text：歌樂者，仁之和也。

Singing and music are the harmony of humanity.

【禮記‧儒行‧第 18 節】 *The Book of Rites, Chapter Rú-Xíng, Verse 18*

**Modern Values Commentary by: Jessie Lin Roberts**

Music is a universal language of mankind. It is something that is common to all cultures and peoples of the world. It seems that everyone can appreciate or connect with it in some way. By organizing musical notes and playing them in harmony to a rhythm, we can create order out of chaos. Music takes the divergent, disjointed, and incompatible parts of life and brings them into harmony with each other. For me, singing and playing music is a way of communicating with others. It allows me to spread the joy that I feel to anyone out there that cares to listen. When an audience is engaged by a rhythm, some chords, and a melody, it can produce a powerful experience for all involved. This, indeed, is the way in which a voice and an instrument can bring all of humanity together in harmony.

By, Jessie Lin Roberts，林曉芸

Arts and Communication - Interactive Multimedia Major

Student at The College of New Jersey, USA

## ㈥ 模擬口語考試討論話題
## Suggested topics for oral proficiency interview (OPI)

### 歌樂者，仁之和也。
Singing and music are the harmony of humanity.

【模擬口試練習】

1. 你認為音樂可以幫助我們和別人相處得更加和諧嗎？請以自己的經驗說明為什麼？

   Do you think music can help us get along with others in a more harmonious way? Please explain your viewpoint on this topic with your own experiences.

   【高級 – 描述／敘述 Advanced Level – can narrate and describe】

   【優秀級 – 表達個人意見和申述抽象觀念 Superior Level – can support opinion and discuss abstract concept】

2. 你曾經學過彈奏樂器，或是唱歌嗎？可不可以說說學習那個樂器的經驗。

   Have you ever learned how to play a musical instrument or how to sing a song? Please describe your experience about learning an instrument or playing music.

   【高級 – 描述／敘述 Advanced Level – can narrate and describe】

3. 對你來說，在學習樂器（或是音樂）的時候，有沒有感受到音樂對人們的好處？請討論音樂對人們的好處有哪些？

   Do you think learning music could offer any benefits to people? Please talk about your opinion on the benefits of learning music.

   【優秀級 – 表達個人意見和申述抽象觀念 Superior Level – can support opinion and discuss abstract concept】

名言三 子與人歌而善，必使反之，而後和之。
Quote 3

**When the Master was in company with a person who was singing, if he sang well, he would make him repeat the song, while he accompanied it with his own voice.**

## (一) 逐字翻譯

**Learn the original text and its meaning**

子與人歌而善，必使反之，而後和之。

zǐ yǔ rén gē ér shàn, bì shǐ fǎn zhī, ér hòu hé zhī.

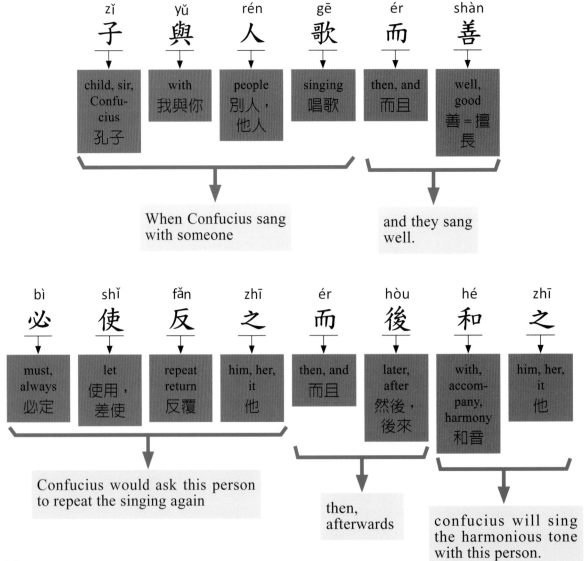

| zǐ 子 | yǔ 與 | rén 人 | gē 歌 | ér 而 | shàn 善 |
|---|---|---|---|---|---|
| child, sir, Confucius 孔子 | with 我與你 | people 別人，他人 | singing 唱歌 | then, and 而且 | well, good 善＝擅長 |

When Confucius sang with someone

and they sang well.

| bì 必 | shǐ 使 | fǎn 反 | zhī 之 | ér 而 | hòu 後 | hé 和 | zhī 之 |
|---|---|---|---|---|---|---|---|
| must, always 必定 | let 使用，差使 | repeat return 反覆 | him, her, it 他 | then, and 而且 | later, after 然後，後來 | with, accompany, harmony 和音 | him, her, it 他 |

Confucius would ask this person to repeat the singing again

then, afterwards

confucius will sing the harmonious tone with this person.

## ㈡ 白話解釋原文
### Explanation with the modern text

子與人歌而善，必使反之，而後和之。

When the Master was in company with a person who was singing, if he sang well, he would make him repeat the song, while he accompanied it with his own voice.

### 1. 白話解釋

孔子和人一起唱歌，如果對方唱得好（善），一定會請對方再唱一次，然後自己在旁邊為對方和音。

When the Master was in company with a person who was singing, well, Confucius would ask him to repeat the song, and then he would accompany it with his own voice.

### 2. 生詞

| | 生詞<br>Vocabulary | 拼音<br>Pin Yin | 英文<br>English | 詞類<br>Part of Speech |
|---|---|---|---|---|
| 1 | 唱歌 | chàng gē | to sing | verb |
| 2 | 對方 | duì fāng | the other party | pronoun |
| 3 | 善 = 擅長 | shàn | being good at | adjective, adverb |
| 4 | 反 = 返 | fǎn = fǎn | to return | verb |
| 5 | 然後 | rán hòu | then | adverb |
| 6 | 旁邊 | páng biān | at the side | adverb |
| 7 | 和音 | hé yīn | to sing in harmony | verb |

## ㈢ 延伸對話與生詞
### Extended learning with sentence practices

### 1. 會話

A：我們一起去唱卡拉 OK 吧！

Let's go to a karaoke singing place for singing together.

B：好啊！我聽說你很擅長唱歌？

Sure! I heard that you are good at singing.

A：哪裡！哪裡！我喜歡和朋友一起唱歌，也喜歡為朋友做和音喔！

No, not at all! I enjoy singing with friends, and I like to sing harmony for friends.

B：那太好了！這個週末我們就去唱歌吧！

That is great! Let's go singing together this weekend.

## 2.生詞

| | 生詞<br>Vocabulary | 拼音<br>Pin Yin | 英文<br>English | 詞類<br>Part of Speech |
|---|---|---|---|---|
| 1 | 卡拉 OK | kǎ lā | Karaoke | noun |
| 2 | 擅長 | shàn cháng | to be good at | verb |
| 3 | 和音 | hé yīn | to sing in harmony | verb |
| 4 | 哪裡 | nǎ lǐ | soft tone of denying a compliment | adverb |
| 5 | 週末 | zhōu mò | weekend | noun |

## (四) 孔子故事
### Stories about Confucius' life and his teaching

孔子很尊敬音樂，如果孔子哪天哭過了，他那一天就不唱歌了

Confucius would not sing if he had cried on that day.

孔子很尊敬音樂，他對音樂有特別的感情。孔子如果在那天哭過，心情不好，他就不在那天唱歌了。這個故事告訴我們，孔子非常注重音樂所表達的感情，因此他不希望把悲傷的情緒混入音樂中。

Confucius appreciated music fondly. He had special respect to music, and he always enjoyed singing. However, it was said that Confucius would not sing on the day if he had cried during that day.

This story tells us how much he respected the expression of music and he would not mix his sadness into the music.

【原文出處 Reference】

> 子於是日哭，則不歌。
> 【論語第七‧述而篇‧第 10 節】*The Analects, Chapter 7 Shu-Er, Verse 10*

孔子聽到好聽的韶樂，就忘了肉的好味道（孔子三月不知肉味。）
After Confucius heard the amazing Shao music, the delicious meat flavor became tasteless to him.

　　孔子在齊國聽到了韶樂這種音樂，覺得太好聽了。後來有三個月的時間，連孔子最喜歡吃的肉，他都不能感覺到肉的香味。孔子說：「我沒有想到，這個音樂會這麼的好聽。」這個故事告訴我們孔子對音樂的喜好。

　　Confucius lost the taste with his favorite food – meat for three months after hearing the music of Shao.

　　When the Master was in Qi, he heard Shao and, thought it was fascinating. The music resonated with him for a long time. He liked the music so much that for three months he could not taste the flavor of his favorite food – meat. He said, "I did not think that music could have been made as excellent as this."

　　This story told us how much Confucius appreciated music.

【原文出處 Reference】

> 孔子三月不知肉味
> 【論語第七‧述而篇‧第 14 節】*The Analects, Chapter 7 Shu-Er, Verse 14*

## ㈤ 論語名言的現代價值評論
### Commentary about this ancient text with modern values

Ancient Text：六藝 The Six Arts。

　　在孔子之前的周朝，學生已經開始學習六藝。孔子也繼續以六藝來教導學生。孔子的學生有 72 位精通六藝。

　　Before Confucius, during the Zhou dynasty (1122–256 BCE),

students were already required to learn and practice the Six Arts. Confucius continued to promote the Six Arts curriculum in his teaching.

【The Six Arts】The six courses of ancient Chinese education are: the Rites, the Music, the Archery, the Chariotry, the Calligraphy and the Math.

【六藝】禮、樂、射、御、書、數：

1. 禮（lǐ - The Rites）Human and Social Behavior: it includes etiquette/social/law/management/communication sciences.

2. 樂（yuè - Music）Musicology: it includes music performance/popular culture/ceremonies/rituals/spirituality.

3. 射（shè - Archery）Archery: it stands for martial skills/sports/gentleman's competition.

4. 御（yù）Chariot riding: it stands for martial arts/physical culture.

5. 書（shū）Literacy and liberal Arts: it includes reading/writing/literature/history/philosophy.

6. 數（shù）Quantitative Methodology and Cosmology: it stands for physics/arithmetic/mathematics.

【原文出處 Reference】

孔子論述六藝
【史記・書・第 28 章・封禪書・第 13 節】*Shiji, Shu, Chapter 28 Feng-Can-Shu, Verse 13*

**Modern Values Commentary by: Dr. Panetha Theodosia Nychis Ott**

Confucius believed that the educated person should have familiarity with different areas of knowledge and skills in order to be a fully developed human being and a good leader. He divided these into six categories. Interestingly, at approximately the same time in the West, ancient philosophers were identifying different areas with which an educated man should gain familiarity. Plato, for example, advocated for both mental and physical agility as important for the development of a human being. It is striking how similar these six areas are to the *West's seven liberal arts* and to the areas prescribed by many modern curricula. In the modern school system, students are expected to gain familiarity with and develop a respect for different areas that correspond to the categories Confucius identified. These include *behavior and communication, music and the arts, physical education, wellness, philology and language, and mathematics and science*. In order to be well educated, students around the world are offered an education that closely resembles the areas defined by Confucius. They thereby are a part of a venerated ancient tradition which brings together humanity throughout the ages.

Dr. Panetha Theodosia Nychis Ott
Director of Admission, International Recruitment
Office of College Admission
Brown University 美國布朗大學招生部主任

## ㈥ 模擬口語考試討論話題
## Suggested topics for oral proficiency interview (OPI)

子與人歌而善，必使反之，而後和之。

When the Master was in company with a person who was singing, if he sang well, he would make him repeat the song, while he accompanied it with his own voice.

【模擬口試練習】

1. 你喜歡你自己國家的音樂還是外國音樂？不同國家的音樂能反映不同的文化嗎？請舉例說明不同國家的音樂給你什麼不同的感受。

   Do you prefer music from your own country or foreign music? Does music reflect the culture of the country it represents? Please talk about the differences between the music from different countries.

   【中級、高級 – 描述／敘述 Intermediate to Advanced Level – can narrate and describe】

   【中級、高級 – 說明比較 Advanced Level – can compare】

2. 你喜歡自己一個人唱歌或聽音樂，還是喜歡和朋友一起唱歌或是聽音樂？
請說說看你喜歡聽音樂的方式，為什麼？

Do you prefer singing or listening to music alone or with friends? Please describe and explain why.

【中級、高級 – 描述 / 敘述 Intermediate to Advanced Level – can narrate and describe】

【中級、高級 – 說明比較 Advanced Level – can compare】

【音樂】立於禮，成於樂【論語第八·泰伯篇·第 8 節】*The Analects, Chapter 8 Tai-Bo, Verse 8*

It is by the Rules of Propriety that the character is established. It is from Music that the finish is received.

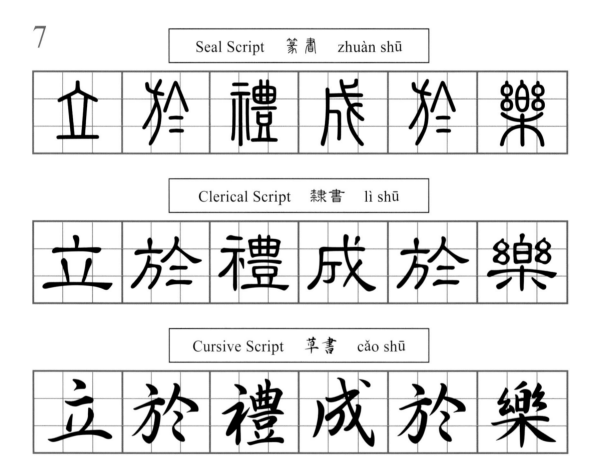

立 於 禮 成 於 樂

立 於 禮 成 於 樂

## 關於【仁愛】的三個論語名言：
## Three top quotes about "Benevolence":

己所不欲，勿施於人。

Not to do to others as you would not wish done to yourself.

【論語第十二 · 顏淵篇 · 第 2 節】 *The Analects, Chapter 12 Yan-Yuan, Verse 2*

巧言令色，鮮以仁。

Fine words and an insinuating appearance are seldom associated with true virtue.

【論語第一 · 學而篇 · 第 3 節】 *The Analects, Chapter 1 Xue-Er, Verse 3*

克己復禮爲仁。

To subdue one's self and return to propriety, is perfect virtue.

【論語第十二 · 顏淵篇 · 第 1 節】 *The Analects, Chapter 12 Yan-Yuan, Verse 1*

## 名言一　己所不欲，勿施於人。

**Quote 1**　**Not to do to others as you would not wish done to yourself.**

### ㈠逐字翻譯
**Learn the original text and its meaning**

己所不欲，勿施於人。
jǐ suǒ bù yù, wù shī yú rén.

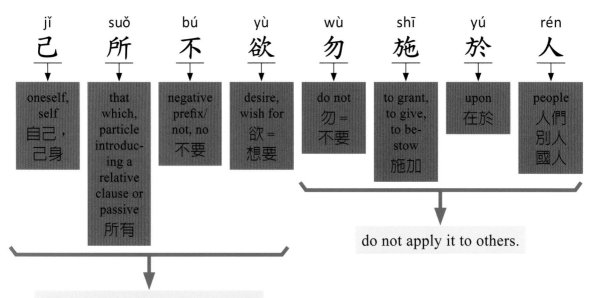

| jǐ | suǒ | bú | yù | wù | shī | yú | rén |
|----|-----|-----|-----|-----|-----|-----|-----|
| 己 | 所 | 不 | 欲 | 勿 | 施 | 於 | 人 |
| oneself, self 自己，己身 | that which, particle introducing a relative clause or passive 所有 | negative prefix/ not, no 不要 | desire, wish for 欲＝想要 | do not 勿＝不要 | to grant, to give, to bestow 施加 | upon 在於 | people 人們 別人 國人 |

What you do not like for yourself,

do not apply it to others.

### ㈡白話解釋原文
**Explanation with the modern text**

己所不欲，勿施於人。
Do not do to others as you would not wish done to yourself.

1.白話解釋
自己不想要的（不好的）感受，不要把它施加在別人身上。對待他人要將心比心，了解別人的感受，並且尊重對方。

Do not do to others what you would not wish done to yourself. Treat others with your compassion and love. Try to understand others' feelings and respect others.

## 2.生詞

| | 生詞<br>**Vocabulary** | 拼音<br>**Pin Yin** | 英文<br>**English** | 詞類<br>**Part of Speech** |
|---|---|---|---|---|
| 1 | 感受 | gǎn shòu | feeling | noun |
| 2 | 施加 | shī jiā | to apply | verb |
| 3 | 身上 | shēn shàng | body | noun |
| 4 | 對待 | duì dài | to treat | verb |
| 5 | 他人 | tā rén | other people | noun |
| 6 | 將心比心 | jiāng xīn bǐ xīn | empathy, heart to heart to feel for others | verb phrase |
| 7 | 了解 | liǎo jiě | to understand | verb |
| 8 | 尊重 | zūn zhòng | to respect | verb |
| 9 | 對方 | duì fāng | the others, counterpart | noun |

## ㈢延伸對話與生詞
### Extended learning with sentence practices

### 1.會話

A：請不要在我的背後跟別人說關於我的事情。想想看，如果換作妳是我的話，妳也一定不會喜歡別人在妳的背後談論妳。

Please do not talk about me behind my back. Imagine it. If you were me, I am sure you would not like people to talk behind your back.

B：妳說的沒錯，對不起。孔子告訴我們，「己所不欲，勿施於人」，就是自己感覺不喜歡被對待的方式，就不應該以那種不好的方式來對待別人。

You are right, I am sorry. Confucius said, "do not do to others what you would not wish done to yourself."

## 2. 生詞

| | 生詞 Vocabulary | 拼音 Pin Yin | 英文 English | 詞類 Part of Speech |
|---|---|---|---|---|
| 1 | 背後 | bèi hòu | behind | noun |
| 2 | 關於 | guān yú | about, in regard to | preposition |
| 3 | 換作 | huàn zuò | to exchange | verb |
| 4 | 談論 | tán lùn | to discuss | verb |
| 5 | 沒錯 | méi cuò | not wrong, correct | adjective |
| 6 | 感覺 | gǎn jiào | to feel | verb |
| 7 | 對待 | duì dài | to treat | verb |
| 8 | 方式 | fāng shì | manner, style | noun |
| 9 | 應該 | yīng gāi | should | auxiliary verb |

## ㈣ 孔子故事
### Stories about Confucius' life and his teaching

己所不欲，勿施於人（恕）

The golden rule – Do not do to others what you do not want done to yourself.

「恕」就是可以終身遵守的行為。

The one rule to apply for all social interactions is: Empathy.

　　子貢問孔子說：「有沒有一句話是一生遵行的準則？」孔子回答說：「就是『恕』！用同理心替別人想。如果你不想要有的，就不要把它加在別人身上。」

　　Zi Gong asked: "Is there one word which may serve as a rule of practice for all one's life?" The Master said, "Is not RECIPROCITY such a word? What you do not want done to yourself, do not do to others."

【原文出處 Reference】

子貢問曰：「有一言而可以終身行之者乎？」子曰：「其恕乎！己所不欲，勿施於人。」
【論語第十五‧衛靈公篇‧第 24 節】*The Analects, Chapter 15 Wei-Ling-Gong, Verse 24*

## ㈤ 論語名言的現代價值評論
## Commentary about this ancient text with modern values

Ancient Text：子曰：「己所不欲，勿施於人。」

The master said: "Do not do to others what you would not have them do to you"

【論語第十二 · 顏淵篇 · 第 2 節】 *The Analects, Chapter12 Yan-Yuan, Verse 2*

**Modern Values Commentary by: Dr. Hugo Yu-Hsiu Lee 李育修**

In reflecting on these ancient texts from the perspective of my work life and my daily life. I, thereby, came up with the following Bible verse from the Book of Matthew in regard to the Sermon on the Mount by Jesus that has a correspondent ancient text derive from the teaching of Confucius.

Both Jesus (written by Matthew, an author inspired by the Holy Spirit to write the New Testament Book of Matthew) and Confucius refer to their respective concluding statement that sums up as the essence of life and the essence of Law, respectively. On the one hand, Jesus said: "In everything, then, do to others as you would have them do to you. For this is the essence of the Law and the prophets" (Matthew 7:12). On the other hand, Confucius said: "Do not do to others what you would not have them do to you."

Both the Lord our God, Jesus, and human teacher, Confucius, took their retrospective glance at what they have been teaching and concluded in their respective text to draw significant modern-day implications of how we would treat people around us including family, colleagues and neighbors, among others.

Dr. Hugo Yu-Hsiu Lee, 李育修，Assoc. Prof. of Sociolinguistics, National Institute of Development Administration (Thailand) and Chinese Teacher / Consultant Roster, United Nations, Economic and Social Commission for Asia and the Pacific (UN Headquarters, Bangkok)

References / 出處：

所以，無論何事，你們願意人怎樣待你們，你們也要怎樣待人，因爲這就是律法和先知的道理。──馬太福音 7:12

In everything, then, do to others as you would have them do to you. For this is the essence of the Law and the prophets. -- Matthew 7:12

## ㈥ 模擬口語考試討論話題
### Suggested topics for oral proficiency interview (OPI)

## 己所不欲，勿施於人。
Do not do to others as you would not wish done to yourself.

【模擬口試練習】

1.「同情心」可以讓我們設身處地想想別人的感受。請以一個故事說明表現「同情心」的例子。

Empathy helps us to put ourselves in other people's positions and to understand others' feelings. Please share an example or a story demonstrating "empathy".

【中級、高級 – 描述 / 敘述 Intermediate to Advanced Level – can narrate and describe】

2. 請描述一個你曾經看見有人被霸凌的例子。你認爲那件霸凌事件可以被避免嗎？你認爲我們應該如何防止這類的事件。

Please describe an incident or an experience you witnessed when someone was being bullied. How did it happen?

【中級、高級 – 描述 / 敘述 Intermediate to Advanced Level – can narrate and describe】

Do you think it could be avoided? Please explain how to prevent this type of incident.

【優秀級 – 表達個人意見和申述抽象觀念 Superior Level – can support opinion and discuss abstract concept】

# 名言二　巧言令色，鮮以仁。
## Quote 2　"Fine words and an insinuating appearance are seldom associated with true virtue."

## (一)逐字翻譯
### Learn the original text and its meaning

巧言令色，鮮以仁。

qiǎo yán líng sè, xiān yǐ rén.

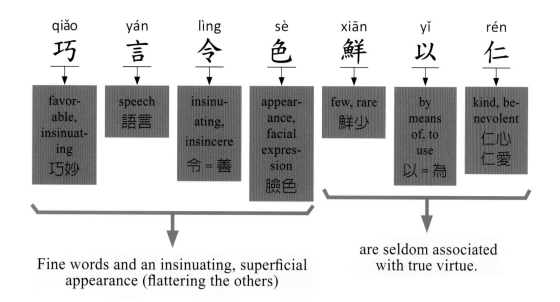

Fine words and an insinuating, superficial appearance (flattering the others)

are seldom associated with true virtue.

## (二)白話解釋原文
### Explanation with the modern text

巧言令色，鮮以仁。

Fine words and an insinuating appearance are seldom associated with true virtue.

### 1.白話解釋

說好聽的話，但卻不眞心也不老實，表現虛僞的外表，都不是眞誠的行爲，也不是仁愛的表現。

"Flattering but not sincere words and an insinuating appearance are insincere behaviors which are seldom associated with true virtue."

## 2.生詞

| | 生詞<br>Vocabulary | 拼音<br>Pin Yin | 英文<br>English | 詞類<br>Part of Speech |
|---|---|---|---|---|
| 1 | 好聽 | hǎo tīng | favorable | adjective |
| 2 | 真心 | zhēn xīn | sincere | adjective |
| 3 | 老實 | lǎo shí | honest | adjective |
| 4 | 表現 | biǎo xiàn | to display, to demonstrate | verb |
| 5 | 虛偽 | xū wěi | fake | adjective |
| 6 | 外表 | wài biǎo | appearance | noun |
| 7 | 真誠 | zhēn chéng | sincere | adjective |
| 8 | 行為 | xíng wéi | conduct, action | noun |
| 9 | 仁愛 | rén ài | benevolent, kind | adjective |
| 10 | 表現 | biǎo xiàn | behaviors, actions | noun |

## (三) 延伸對話與生詞
## Extended learning with sentence practices

### 1.會話

A：他這個人喜歡說好聽的話。

He always sweet talks to others.

B：所以我覺得他不老實,而且我總是有一個直覺告訴我說:他這個人不可靠。

That is why I don't consider him as an honest person. My instinct is telling me that he is not trustworthy.

## 2.生詞

| | 生詞<br>Vocabulary | 拼音<br>Pin Yin | 英文<br>English | 詞類<br>Part of Speech |
|---|---|---|---|---|
| 1 | 好聽 | hǎo tīng | sound good | adjective |
| 2 | 老實 | lǎo shí | honest and decent | adjective |
| 3 | 總是 | zǒng shì | always | adverb |
| 4 | 直覺 | zhí jué | instinct | noun |
| 5 | 不可靠 | bù kě kào | not reliable | adjective |

## ㈣孔子故事
**Stories about Confucius' life and his teaching**

孔子描述自己的人生里程碑

Confucius' self-described milestones in life.

　　孔子說：「我十五歲就立志於學習，三十歲就能獨立思考，四十歲對事情不困惑，五十歲就可以知道『天』（自然）的規律。六十歲時對於我所聽到的事情都可以接受，七十歲時，我可以按照自己的想法去做，也不會做錯事。」

　　The Master said, "At fifteen, I had my mind bent on learning. At thirty, I stood firm. At forty, I had no doubts. At fifty, I knew the decrees of Heaven. At sixty, my ear was an obedient organ for the reception of truth. At seventy, I could follow what my heart desired, without transgressing what was right."

【原文出處 Reference】

子曰：「吾十有五而志于學，三十而立，四十而不惑，五十而知天命，六十而耳順，七十而從心所欲，不踰矩。」
【論語第二‧為政篇‧第 4 節】*The Analects, Chapter 2 Wei-Zheng, Verse 4*

## ㈤論語名言的現代價值評論
## Commentary about this ancient text with modern values

Ancient Text：子曰：「巧言令色，鮮矣仁！」

"Fine words and an insinuating appearance are seldom associated with true virtue."

【論語第一 · 學而篇 · 第 3 節】*The Analects, Chapter 1 Xue-Er, Verse 3*

**Modern Values Commentary by: Dr. Marybeth Gasman**

The 'selfie' culture of the 21st Century, which is focused on presenting fake images of who we are in order to impress others, has resulted in the shallowing of societies. All too often, we are focused on ourselves, on impressing others, on presenting a version of ourselves that is far from truth. Instead of being concerned with the welfare of others, we are consumed with self and what others think about us. In reality, and in service to humanity, we should present ourselves in the rawest, truest forms – forms that show our heart, our dignity, and our vulnerability. I often wonder what will need to happen throughout our nations and societies to move us away from 'selfie' culture and toward one that embraces each other. What do you think will force this change?

Marybeth Gasman

Samuel DeWitt Proctor Endowed Chair in Education

& Distinguished Professor

Department of Educational Psychology

Graduate School of Education

Rutgers University - New Brunswick


Executive Director

Samuel DeWitt Proctor Institute for Leadership, Equity, & Justice

& Rutgers Center for Minority Serving Institutions

## ㈥ 模擬口語考試討論話題
### Suggested topics for oral proficiency interview (OPI)

巧言令色，鮮以仁。

Fine words and an insinuating appearance are seldom associated with true virtue.

【模擬口試練習】

1. 你曾經不小心說錯話，然後覺得很後悔嗎？請分享你說錯話的經驗。

   Have you ever made an impulsive and careless comment which you later regretted? Please share your experience.

   【中級、高級 – 描述／敘述 Intermediate to Advanced Level – can narrate and describe】

2. 你曾經受騙過嗎？那是怎麼樣的一個情況？ 可以說說那個經驗嗎？也請說一下你受騙後的感覺。

   Have you ever been cheated or been tricked by someone? Please describe the incident and your feelings afterwards.

   【中級、高級 – 描述／敘述 Intermediate to Advanced Level – can narrate and describe】

## 名言三　克己復禮為仁。
### Quote 3　To subdue one's self and return to propriety, is perfect virtue.

## ㈠ 逐字翻譯
### Learn the original text and its meaning

克己復禮為仁。

kè jǐ fù lǐ wéi rén.

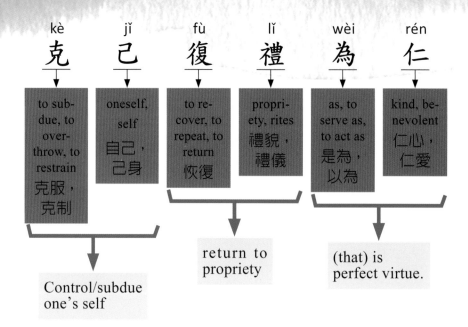

## (二) 白話解釋原文
## Explanation with the modern text

克己復禮為仁。

To subdue one's self and return to propriety, is perfect virtue.

1. 白話解釋

克制自己，以禮對待他人，對人尊敬、有禮貌，這樣就可以做到「仁愛」。

To subdue and control one's self and treat others with propriety and respect, that is perfect virtue and benevolence.

2. 生詞

|   | 生詞<br>**Vocabulary** | 拼音<br>**Pin Yin** | 英文<br>**English** | 詞類<br>**Part of Speech** |
|---|---|---|---|---|
| 1 | 克制 | kè zhì | to control | verb |
| 2 | 自己 | zì jǐ | oneself | noun |
| 3 | 以 = 用 | yǐ | with | preposition |
| 4 | 禮 | lǐ | propriety, rite | noun |

| | 生詞<br>**Vocabulary** | 拼音<br>**Pin Yin** | 英文<br>**English** | 詞類<br>**Part of Speech** |
|---|---|---|---|---|
| 5 | 對待 | duì dài | to treat | verb |
| 6 | 他人 = 別人 | tā rén = bié rén | others | noun |
| 7 | 對 | duì | to, toward | preposition |
| 8 | 尊敬 | zūn jìng | to respect | verb |
| 9 | 有禮貌 | yǒu lǐ mào | polite | adjective |
| 10 | 仁愛 | rén ài | benevolent | adjective |

## ㈢ 延伸對話與生詞
### Extended learning with sentence practices

1.會話

A：控制自己的行為，對別人要有禮貌，這樣就是「仁愛」。

Self-control in one's temper and actions, treat others with courtesy, that is true virtue and benevolence.

B：孔子說：「非禮勿視，非禮勿聽，非禮勿言，非禮勿動。」意思就是，不合乎禮節的事不要看、不要聽、不要說、不要做。每一個人都能做好克制自己，社會就會很和諧。

The Master replied, "Look not at what is contrary to propriety; listen not to what is contrary to propriety; speak not what is contrary to propriety; make no movement which is contrary to propriety." That means if we could refrain ourselves from the conducts which are contrary to propriety, and everyone can achieve this in controlling their conducts, the society will be harmonious.

2.生詞

| | 生詞<br>**Vocabulary** | 拼音<br>**Pin Yin** | 英文<br>**English** | 詞類<br>**Part of Speech** |
|---|---|---|---|---|
| 1 | 控制 | kòng zhì | to control | verb |

| | 生詞<br>**Vocabulary** | 拼音<br>**Pin Yin** | 英文<br>**English** | 詞類<br>**Part of Speech** |
|---|---|---|---|---|
| 2 | 行為 | xíng wéi | behavior, conduct | noun |
| 3 | 非 = 不是 | fēi | not | adverb |
| 4 | 勿 | wù | don't | auxiliary verb |
| 5 | 視 | shì | to see | verb |
| 6 | 聽 | tīng | to listen | verb |
| 7 | 言 | yán | to speak | verb |
| 8 | 動 | dòng | to move, act | verb |
| 9 | 合乎 | hé hū | to conform,<br>in line with | verb |
| 10 | 禮節 | lǐ jié | rites, etiquettes | noun |
| 11 | 社會 | shè huì | society | noun |
| 12 | 和諧 | hé xié | harmony | adjective |

## ㈣ 孔子故事
### Stories about Confucius' life and his teaching

孔子描述自己「好古」（hào gǔ）

How did Confucius describe himself.

　　孔子説：「我不是天生就有學問的，我只是個喜歡傳統道德、勤奮敏捷地追求知識的人。」

　　The Master said, "I am not one who was born in the possession of knowledge; I am one who is fond of antiquity (traditional virtues), and earnest in seeking to learn about it."

【原文出處 Reference】

子曰：「我非生而知之者，好古，敏以求之者也。」
【論語第七・述而篇・第 20 節】 *The Analects, Chapter 7 Shu-Er, Verse 20*

孔子認為人要以行為來推行「仁道」（人能弘道，非道能弘人。）

Confucius was an activist to exercise the principles and the ethics.

孔子說：「一個人能用行動真正地實現『道』，將『道』弘揚光大。而不能認為自己懂得『道』了，就能讓自己偉大了。」

要用仁愛來愛人，用行動來表現仁道。

The Master said, "A man can put into action to achieve ethics according to the principles which he follows; those principles cannot by itself make the man famous or be known."

It takes benevolent actions to demonstrate and exercise humanity in life.

【原文出處 Reference】

子曰：「人能弘道，非道弘人。」
【論語第十五 · 衛靈公篇 · 第 29 節】 *The Analects, Chapter 15 Wei-Ling-Gong, Verse 29*

## ㈤ 論語名言的現代價值評論
## Commentary about this ancient text with modern values

Ancient Text：克己復禮為仁。

To subdue one's self and return to propriety, is perfect virtue.

【論語第十二 · 顏淵篇 · 第 1 節】 *The Analects, Chapter 12 Yan-Yuan, Verse 1*

**Modern Values Commentary by: Christopher Licetti，林榮燦**

My understanding of the Confucius quote is that no matter how long someone has been neglecting or ignoring tradition and etiquette it is still the best practice to be able to realize when to return to following tradition. It's never too late to realize one's mistakes and be able to fix their actions. I think that a big problem in modern society that would be fixed by more people following Confucius' teaching is that when people are questioned for not following the best practices, a natural reaction for some is to become hostile and resistant rather than admitting they are in the wrong and changing their ways. One relevant example I can think of is how some people refuse to wear masks in stores and restaurants amid the coronavirus pandemic, and when some people are asked to wear them, they become angry and refuse. This is an example of people not following both parts of Confucius' teaching; that is they are not following propriety by not wearing a mask to protect others in the first place, but they also refuse to return to propriety when asked. Society would be a much friendlier place if people were more willing to act in ways to help others, and also if people were more willing to admit when they are wrong and change rather than refuse and become stubborn.

Christopher Licetti，林榮燦
The College of New Jersey

## ㈥ 模擬口語考試討論話題
## Suggested topics for oral proficiency interview (OPI)

克己復禮為仁。
To subdue one's self and return to propriety, is perfect virtue.

全段原文：
顏淵問仁。子曰：「克己復禮為仁。一日克己復禮，天下歸仁焉。為仁由己，而由人乎哉？」顏淵曰：「請問其目。」子曰：「非禮勿視，非禮勿聽，非禮勿言，非禮勿動。」顏淵曰：「回雖不敏，請事斯語矣。」

Yan Yuan asked about perfect virtue. The Master said, "To subdue one's self and return to propriety, is perfect virtue. If a man can for one day subdue himself and return to propriety, all under heaven will ascribe perfect virtue to him. Is the practice of perfect virtue from a man himself, or is it from others?" Yan Yuan said, "I beg to ask the steps of that process." The Master replied, "Look not at what is contrary to propriety; listen not to what is contrary to propriety; speak not what is contrary to propriety; make no movement which is contrary to propriety." Yan Yuan then said, "Though I am deficient in intelligence and vigor, I will make it my business to practice this lesson."

【模擬口試練習】

1. 你同意一個人如果有良好的禮貌，就會受到別人的尊敬和歡迎嗎？請舉三個良好行為的例子。

   Do you agree that a person with good manners is usually respected and welcome by others? Please share three examples which you consider to be virtuous and conducted with respect.

   【中級、高級 – 描述／敘述 Intermediate to Advanced Level – can narrate and describe】

2. 你曾經受到別人不禮貌的對待嗎？請說明為什麼會發生這樣的事？怎麼做可以避免這種情況嗎？

   Have you ever encountered someone's offensive behaviors or impoliteness to you? How did it happen and how could we avoid it?

   【中級、高級 – 描述／敘述 Intermediate to Advanced Level – can narrate and describe】

   【優秀級 – 表達個人意見和申述抽象觀念 Superior Level – can support opinion and discuss abstract concept】

3. 有些人去別的國家旅遊或者跟不同文化背景的人相處時，常常會發生文化衝突，甚至造成誤會。請舉三個文化差異的例子，並說明應該如何避免誤會。

   Some people often experience cultural shocks or misunderstanding when visiting another country or interacting with a person from a different culture. Please share one of your experiences and discuss how to avoid cultural misunderstanding.

   【中級、高級 – 描述／敘述 Intermediate to Advanced Level – can narrate and describe】

   【優秀級 – 表達個人意見和申述抽象觀念 Superior Level – can support opinion and discuss abstract concept】

4. 在全世界國際化交流越來越密切的今日，了解文化差異是一個非常重要的課題，如果你是一位大學校長，你會爲你的學校做什麼策略的改變，以鼓勵學生對世界不同國家的文化差異做更好的學習與進步？

Cultural awareness, exchanges and understanding are subjects with increasing importance in globalization today. What policies or programs would you implement to your school to help your students in this area if you were a president of a university?

【優秀級 – 假設情境申述 Superior Level – can hypothesize】

【仁】仁者人也【禮記·中庸·第 20 節】*Li-Ji, Zhong-Yong, Verse 20*
Benevolence is the characteristic element of humanity.

8

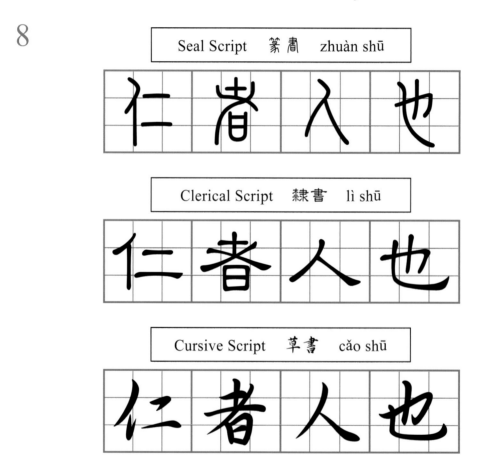

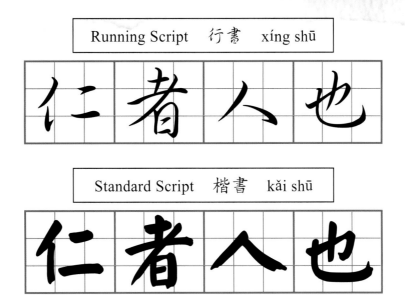

【仁】仁者愛人【孟子·離婁下篇·第 56 節】*Meng-Zi, Chapter Li-Lou II, Verse 56*

The benevolent man loves others.

9

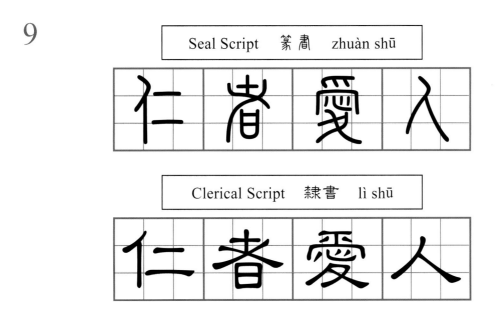

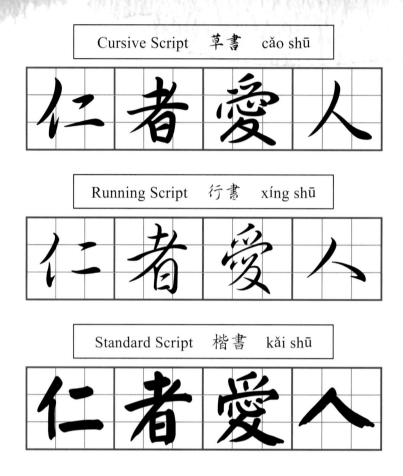

| | | | |
|---|---|---|---|
Cursive Script 草書 cǎo shū

仁 者 愛 人

Running Script 行書 xíng shū

仁 者 愛 人

Standard Script 楷書 kǎi shū

仁 者 愛 人

【仁】里仁為美【論語第四・里仁篇・第 1 節】*The Analects, Chapter 4, Li-Ren, Verse 1*

It is virtuous manners which constitute the excellence of a neighborhood.

10

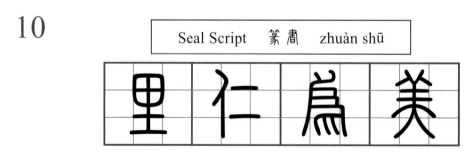

Seal Script 篆書 zhuàn shū

里 仁 為 美

**Clerical Script　隸書　lì shū**

**Cursive Script　草書　cǎo shū**

**Running Script　行書　xíng shū**

**Standard Script　楷書　kǎi shū**

關於【道德】的三個論語名言：
Three top quotes about "Virtues":

朝聞道，夕死可矣。

If a man in the morning hear the right way, he may die in the evening without regret.

【論語第四・里仁篇・第 8 節】 *The Analects, Chapter 4 Li-Ren, Verse 8*


德不孤，必有鄰。

Virtue is not left to stand alone. He who practices it will have neighbors.

【論語第四・里仁篇・第 25 節】 *The Analects, Chapter 4 Li-Ren, Verse 25*


巧言亂德。小不忍，則亂大謀。

Specious words confound virtue. Want of forbearance in small matters confounds great plans.

【論語第十五・衛靈公篇・第 27 節】 *The Analects, Chapter 15 Wei-Ling-Gong, Verse 27*

## (一) 逐字翻譯

**Learn the original text and its meaning**

子曰：「朝聞道，夕死可矣。」

zǐ yuē: zhāo wén dào, xī sǐ kě yǐ.

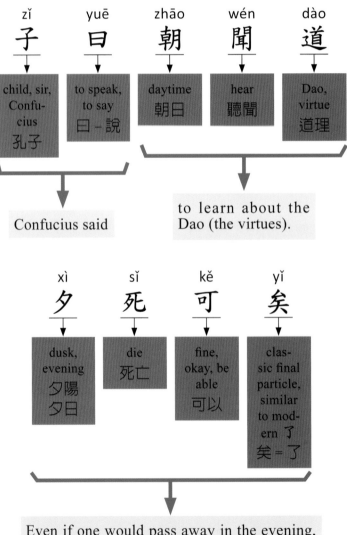

| zǐ 子 | yuē 曰 | zhāo 朝 | wén 聞 | dào 道 |
|---|---|---|---|---|
| child, sir, Confucius 孔子 | to speak, to say 曰－說 | daytime 朝日 | hear 聽聞 | Dao, virtue 道理 |

Confucius said

to learn about the Dao (the virtues).

| xì 夕 | sǐ 死 | kě 可 | yǐ 矣 |
|---|---|---|---|
| dusk, evening 夕陽 夕日 | die 死亡 | fine, okay, be able 可以 | classic final particle, similar to modern 了 矣＝了 |

Even if one would pass away in the evening, it is not too late to learn the Dao (virtues).

The Master said, "If a man in the morning hear the right way, he may die in the evening without regret." *Never too late to learn (or do) the right thing.*

## ㈡白話解釋原文
## Explanation with the modern text

朝聞道，夕死可矣。

The Master said, "If a man in the morning hear the right way, he may die in the evening without regret."

### 1.白話解釋

孔子說：如果一個人在早上學會了「道」，即使就算是在晚上就死了，也不會有後悔了。學習或做對的事情永遠不會太晚。

Confucius said: "A person who learned about "The Ways" (Dao) in the morning could die in the night without any regret. It's never too late to learn or do the right thing.

一個人如果在死之前能夠學懂了什麼是「道德」，那麼他死了也不會有遺憾。

If a person learned about "Dao" right before he passed away, then we could say that he died without any regrets.

### 2.生詞

| | 生詞<br>Vocabulary | 拼音<br>Pin Yin | 英文<br>English | 詞類<br>Part of Speech |
|---|---|---|---|---|
| 1 | 即使 | jí shǐ | even if | conjunction phrase |
| 2 | 就算 | jiù suàn | even if | conjunction phrase |
| 3 | 在…之前 | zài … zhī qián | before | preposition phrase |
| 4 | 學懂 | xué dǒng | to learn and to comprehend | verb |
| 5 | 後悔 | hòu huǐ | to regret | verb |
| 6 | 遺憾 | yí hàn | regret | noun |
| 7 | 道 | dào | the ways, the method, the virtues | noun |
| 8 | 道德 | dào dé | virtues | noun |

## (三) 延伸對話與生詞
## Extended learning with sentence practices

1. 會話

A：為了我們的地球環境，出門購物時，我會記得準備環保購物袋，不再使用一次性的塑膠袋了。

For the sake of the environment of our earth, I will remember to bring with me a reusable shopping bag. I will not use the disposable plastic bags offered by the shops.

B：現在開始不用一次性的塑膠袋，就能夠救世界嗎？

Do you think we can save our world by not using disposable plastic shopping bags now?

A：為了地球的未來，做對的事情，永遠不會太晚。

Yes, for the sake of our earth, it is never too late to do the right thing.

2. 生詞

| | 生詞<br>Vocabulary | 拼音<br>Pin Yin | 英文<br>English | 詞類<br>Part of Speech |
|---|---|---|---|---|
| 1 | 地球 | dì qiú | the earth | noun |
| 2 | 環境 | huán jìng | environment | noun |
| 3 | 購物 | gòu wù | to shop | verb |
| 4 | 環保 | huán bǎo | environmental protection | noun |
| 5 | 購物袋 | gòu wù dài | shopping bag | noun |
| 6 | 使用 | shǐ yòng | to use | verb |
| 7 | 一次性 | yī cì xìng | one time use, disposable | noun |
| 8 | 塑膠袋<br>塑料袋 | sù jiāo dài<br>sù liào dài | plastic bags | noun |

| | 生詞<br>Vocabulary | 拼音<br>Pin Yin | 英文<br>English | 詞類<br>Part of Speech |
|---|---|---|---|---|
| 9 | 救世界 | jiù shì jiè | to help the world | verb |
| 10 | 未來 | wèi lái | future | noun |
| 11 | 永遠 | yǒng yuǎn | forever | adjective |

## ㈣ 孔子故事
### Stories about Confucius' life and his teaching

孔子一直持守的道是什麼？（吾道一以貫之。）

What was the pervading core value in Confucius' teaching?

孔子説：「曾參啊！我的做人的道理是用一個基本『道德』貫通的。」曾子説：「是。」孔子走後，其他的學生問曾子：「老師説的基本的『道德』是什麼？」曾子説：「老師説的『道德』，就是忠恕。」

The Master said, "Shen, my doctrine is that of an all-pervading unity." The disciple Zeng replied, "Yes." The Master went out, and the other disciples asked, saying, "What do his words mean?" Zeng said, "The doctrine of our master is to be true to the principles of our nature and the benevolent exercise of them to others, this and nothing more."

【原文出處 Reference】

子曰：「參乎！吾道一以貫之。」曾子曰：「唯。」子出。門人問曰：「何謂也？」曾子曰：「夫子之道，忠恕而已矣。」
【論語第四・里仁篇・第 15 節】 *The Analects, Chapter 4 Li-Ren, Verse 15*

## ㈤ 論語名言的現代價值評論
## Commentary about this ancient text with modern values

Ancient Text：朝聞道，夕死可矣。

The Master said, "If a man in the morning hear the right way, he may die in the evening without regret." (It is important to do the right thing, no matter how close it is near the end of one's life - better late than never.)

【論語第四 · 里仁篇 · 第 8 節】*The Analects, Chapter 4 Li-Ren, Verse 8*

**Modern Values Commentary by: Dr. Panetha Theodosia Nychis Ott**

The importance of moral development is a prevalent theme throughout the *Analects*. Confucius' concern in the cultivation of virtuous behavior. A person who engages in learning and leads a life of virtue, which may be developed through the study of the Six Arts described elsewhere in this book, will be at peace upon death. It is never too late for a person to discover and to practice virtuous behavior. People who lead a life of virtue will die with no regrets or doubts. Once again, there is a connection drawn between virtue and learning/knowledge/ wisdom. Embracing virtue and practicing it results in inner peace.

Dr. Panetha Theodosia Nychis Ott
Director of Admission, International Recruitment
Office of College Admission
Brown University 美國布朗大學招生部主任

## ㈥ 模擬口語考試討論話題
## Suggested topics for oral proficiency interview (OPI)

朝聞道，夕死可矣。
"If a man in the morning hear the right way, he may die in the evening without

regret."

【模擬口試練習】

1. 請談談你對道德標準的看法。什麼是有道德的行為？什麼是不道德的行為？

Please talk about your opinion on virtues and ethics. What action is considered ethical and what action is considered unethical?

【中級、高級 – 描述／敘述 Intermediate to Advanced Level – can narrate and describe】

【優秀級 – 表達個人意見和申述抽象觀念 Superior Level – can support opinion and discuss abstract concept】

2. 你曾經看過一個犯過錯的人，後來決定改過自新，重新做一個好人的例子嗎？請說一個這方面的故事。

Please describe a story about someone who committed a crime or made a mistake, then later redeemed himself/herself.

【中級、高級 – 描述／敘述 Intermediate to Advanced Level – can narrate and describe】

---

名言二
Quote 2
## 德不孤，必有鄰。
**Virtue is not left to stand alone. He who practices it will have neighbors.**

---

## (一) 逐字翻譯
## Learn the original text and its meaning

子曰：「德不孤，必有鄰。」
zǐ yuē: dé bù gū, bì yǒu lín.

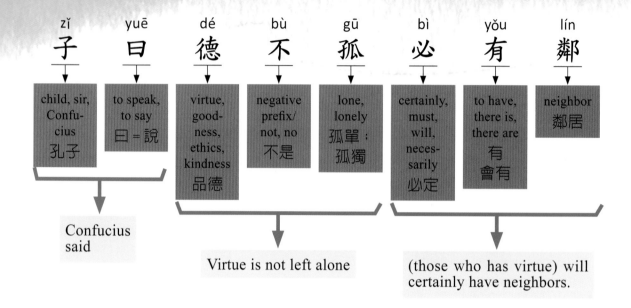

| zǐ 子 | yuē 曰 | dé 德 | bù 不 | gū 孤 | bì 必 | yǒu 有 | lín 鄰 |
|---|---|---|---|---|---|---|---|
| child, sir, Confucius 孔子 | to speak, to say 曰＝說 | virtue, goodness, ethics, kindness 品德 | negative prefix/not, no 不是 | lone, lonely 孤單：孤獨 | certainly, must, will, necessarily 必定 | to have, there is, there are 有 會有 | neighbor 鄰居 |

Confucius said

Virtue is not left alone

(those who has virtue) will certainly have neighbors.

## (二) 白話解釋原文
### Explanation with the modern text

子曰：「德不孤，必有鄰。」

The Master said, "Virtue is not left to stand alone. He who practices it will have neighbors."

### 1. 白話解釋

一個有道德的人，是不會孤獨的，一定會有人喜歡和他在一起。

A virtuous person will not stand alone. Someone would surely like to be associated with him.

### 2. 生詞

| | 生詞 Vocabulary | 拼音 Pin Yin | 英文 English | 詞類 Part of Speech |
|---|---|---|---|---|
| 1 | 道德 | dào dé | virtue, ethics | noun |
| 2 | 孤獨 | gū dú | lonely | adjective |
| 3 | 和… 在一起 | hé … zài yī qǐ | to be with someone | preposition phrase |

## ㈢ 延伸對話與生詞
### Extended learning with sentence practices

1. 會話

A：下學期我會搬到大學的宿舍去住。不知道我和室友會不會成爲好朋友。

Next semester, I will move to the residence hall (dormitory) in my college. I wonder if my roommates and I will become good friends.

B：你放心！你的品行道德良好，你的室友一定會和妳和平相處。

No problem! (Don't worry!) You have a great personality. Your roommates will definitely get along with you peacefully.

2. 生詞

| | 生詞<br>Vocabulary | 拼音<br>Pin Yin | 英文<br>English | 詞類<br>Part of Speech |
|---|---|---|---|---|
| 1 | 搬到 | bān dào | to move to somewhere | verb |
| 2 | 宿舍 | sù shè | dormitory | noun |
| 3 | 室友 | shì yǒu | roommate | noun |
| 4 | 品行 | pǐn xìng | conduct | noun |
| 5 | 良好 | liáng hǎo | good, fine | adjective |
| 6 | 和平 | hé píng | peacefully | adverb |
| 7 | 相處 | xiāng chǔ | to get along | verb |

## ㈣ 孔子故事
### Stories about Confucius' life and his teaching

孔子對生死的看法（未知生，焉知死？）

Confucius' view about the living and the death.

　　季路問孔子怎樣祀奉鬼神，孔子說：「人都不能侍奉好，還談什麼侍奉鬼神？」季路又問：「請問死是怎麼回事？」孔子回答：「『生』的意義都不懂了，還談什麼懂得『死』？」

Ji Lu asked about serving the spirits of the dead. The Master said, "While you are not able to serve the living men, how can you serve their spirits after death?" Ji Lu added, "I venture to ask about death?" Confucius answered, "While you do not know life, how can you know about death?"

【原文出處 Reference】

> 季路問事鬼神，子曰：「未能事人，焉能事鬼？」「敢問死？」曰：「未知生，焉知死？」
> 【論語第十一 · 先進篇 · 第 12 節】 *The Analects, Chapter 11 Xian-Jin, Verse 12*

## ㈤ 論語名言的現代價值評論
### Commentary about this ancient text with modern values

Ancient Text：子曰：「德不孤，必有鄰。」

> Confucius said:"Virtue is not left to stand alone. He who practices it will have neighbors."

【論語第四 · 里仁篇 · 第 25 節】 *The Analects, Chapter 4 Li-Ren, Verse 25*

**Modern Values Commentary by: Dianne D. Miles**

Empathy and respect are virtues that strengthen friendships and other social relationships. When the people around you realize that they will be treated kindly by you, automatically, without their having to prove their worth first, then a true dialog starts between you. I've learned this myself, that there are certain people who I always welcome into my space, knowing I can relax and will be understood, and that I will be treated as someone with inherent worth without having to explain myself. Receiving that type of kindness from others has made me want to offer it myself. It makes every type of connection easier, even if it's just a casual interaction. Treating people with kind respect removes a barrier of remoteness, and when you are easily approachable, real communication can begin right away. If you have the humility to realize that people are in situations you know nothing about, the same way that others don't know what challenges you might be having at the same time, it becomes easy to have empathy. When your friends see that you assume the best of them, they tend to live up to it, and assume the same of you. This is what strengthens friendships.

Dianne D. Miles

Program Assistant

Department of World Languages and Cultures

The College of New Jersey, USA

Ancient Text：子曰：「德不孤，必有鄰。」

Confucius said:"Virtue is not left to stand alone. He who practices it will have neighbors."

【論語第四・里仁篇・第 25 節】 *The Analects, Chapter 4 Li-Ren, Verse 25*

**Modern Values Commentary by: Dr. Shouwen Pan**

Confucius said, "A man of virtue will never be lonely, and will surely have people around him 德不孤，必有鄰 ." What did Confucius mean?

The concept of virtue (dé 德 ) appeared in the early days of the Zhou dynasty and was understood as the attribute of Heaven (tiān 天 ). It is what Heaven gives to a man (rén 人 ) when Heaven creates him. It is thus the medium of "the unity of Heaven and man," the ultimate goal of personal cultivation. As a poem from the *Book of Odes* goes:

Heaven produces the teeming multitude.

As there are things, there are their specific principles.

When the people keep to their normal nature,

They will love excellent virtue.

As a devoted advocate of the Zhou ideals, Confucius declared, "Heaven produced the virtue that is in me." He believed that virtue has miraculous power, saying "He who possesses great virtue will certainly receive the appointment of

Heaven" and "A virtuous ruler is like the north polar star, which remains in its place while all the other stars revolve around it."

However, as Confucius noticed clearly, the superior men are different from the inferior men, because the superior men cultivate virtue, while the inferior men materialize virtue. In the real world, the virtuous people may not be rewarded; they may even be marginalized. It is possible that Confucius made the remark on virtue to encourage his disciples to stay optimistic in loneliness. At the same time, Confucius may also encourage them to get involved in the social life and cultivate virtue in the concrete human affairs, as he said, "When a man pursues the Way and yet remains away from man, his course cannot be considered the Way." He believed that in pursuing the Way "a man of virtue will never be alone and can always attract followers."

Dr. Shouwen Pan

Instructor at China Institute, NYC, USA

## ㈥ 模擬口語考試討論話題
## Suggested topics for oral proficiency interview (OPI)

子曰：「德不孤，必有鄰。」

"The Master said, "Virtue is not left to stand alone. He who practices it will have neighbors."

【模擬口試練習】

1. 品德好的人，他的朋友和鄰居們一定會喜歡他。你贊成這個說法嗎？關於有道德的人會受到朋友的喜歡，請舉一個你自己曾經有過的經驗。

   A virtuous person will always be welcome and well-liked by friends or neighbors. Can you share an example related to your own experience of seeing a virtuous man being welcome by his friends?

   【中級、高級 – 描述／敘述 Intermediate to Advanced Level – can narrate and describe】

2. 孔子說：「一個國家如果重視道德，這個國家一定能有很多友邦。」請你
   舉一個這樣的例子，來說明這個道理。

   Confucius said: "A country which values virtues and ethics would have many
   allies providing their support." Can you share an example to support this
   statement?

   【中級、高級 – 描述 / 敘述 Intermediate to Advanced Level – can narrate and
   describe】

## 名言三　巧言亂德。小不忍，則亂大謀。
### Quote 3　Specious words confound virtue. Want of forbearance in small matters confounds great plans.

## ㈠逐字翻譯
## Learn the original text and its meaning

巧言亂德。小不忍，則亂大謀。
qiǎo yán luàn dé. xiǎo bù rěn, zé luàn dà móu.

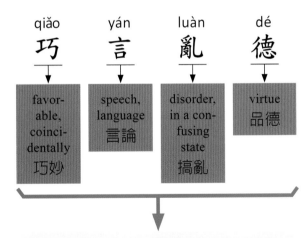

Specious words confound (baffle) virtue.

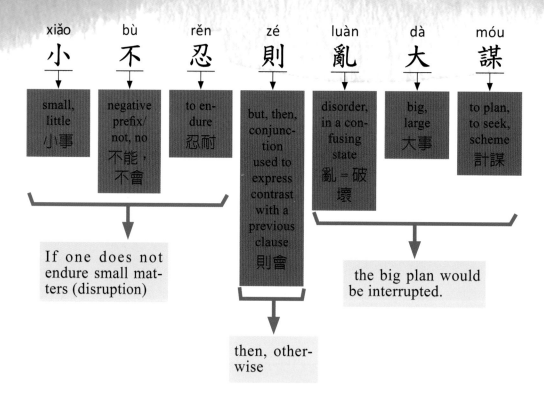

小 xiǎo — small, little 小事

不 bù — negative prefix/ not, no 不能，不會

忍 rěn — to endure 忍耐

則 zé — but, then, conjunction used to express contrast with a previous clause 則會

亂 luàn — disorder, in a confusing state 亂＝破壞

大 dà — big, large 大事

謀 móu — to plan, to seek, scheme 計謀

If one does not endure small matters (disruption)

then, otherwise

the big plan would be interrupted.

## (二) 白話解釋原文
## Explanation with the modern text

巧言亂德。小不忍，則亂大謀。

The Master said, "Specious words confound virtue. Want of forbearance in small matters confounds great plans."

### 1. 白話解釋

孔子說：「一個人說話如果不真實誠懇的話，很容易就會攪亂了他的道德水準。小事情不忍耐就會搞亂了大計劃。」

Confucius: "If a person speaks specious words, his credibility will be untrustworthy. If a person cannot hold his temper on small matters, his big plan will be disrupted."

## 2. 生詞

| | 生詞<br>Vocabulary | 拼音<br>Pin Yin | 英文<br>English | 詞類<br>Part of Speech |
|---|---|---|---|---|
| 1 | 真實 | zhēn shí | real, true | adjective |
| 2 | 誠懇 | chéng kěn | sincere | adjective |
| 3 | 容易 | róng yì | easy | adjective |
| 4 | 攪亂 | jǎo luàn | to mess up | verb |
| 5 | 道德 | dào dé | virtue | noun |
| 6 | 水準 | shuǐ zhǔn | standard | noun |
| 7 | 忍耐 | rěn nài | to endure | verb |
| 8 | 計劃 | jì huà | to plan | verb |

## (三) 延伸對話與生詞
### Extended learning with sentence practices

### 1. 會話

A：妳先不要生氣，忍耐一點別口出惡言。小事情如果不忍耐，也會破壞關係和計劃。

Do not be angry. Hold your temper. Do not spread bad words. If you do not hold your temper toward small matters, the relationship and overall plan can be affected negatively.

B：可是我受不了他常常散佈謠言攻擊我啊！

I cannot stand that he is constantly spreading rumors about me.

### 2. 生詞

| | 生詞<br>Vocabulary | 拼音<br>Pin Yin | 英文<br>English | 詞類<br>Part of Speech |
|---|---|---|---|---|
| 1 | 生氣 | shēng qì | upset, angry | adjective |
| 2 | 忍耐 | rěn nài | to endure | verb |
| 3 | 破壞 | pò huài | to destroy, to disrupt | Verb |

| | 生詞<br>**Vocabulary** | 拼音<br>**Pin Yin** | 英文<br>**English** | 詞類<br>**Part of Speech** |
|---|---|---|---|---|
| 4 | 關係 | guān xì | relationship | noun |
| 5 | 受不了 | shòu bù liǎo | cannot stand it | verb phrase |
| 6 | 散佈 | sàn bù | to spread | verb |
| 7 | 謠言 | yáo yán | rumor | noun |
| 8 | 攻擊 | gong jī | to attack | verb |
| 9 | 口出惡言 | kǒu chû è yán | to verbally attack someone with slander | Verb phrase |

## ㈣ 孔子故事
### Stories about Confucius' life and his teaching

孔子不談論的事是什麼？（子不語：怪、力、亂、神。）

What topics Confucius did not want to discuss about?

　　孔子不談論：怪異、暴力、變亂、鬼神這類的主題。

　　The subjects on which the Master did not talk were extraordinary things, feats of strength, disorder, and spiritual beings.

【原文出處 Reference】

子不語：怪、力、亂、神。
【論語第七・述而篇・第 21 節】*The Analects, Chapter 7 Xu-Er, Verse 21*

孔子對於鬼神的態度（敬鬼神而遠之）

What is Confucius' opinion about the spiritual beings?

　　樊遲問什麼是明智，孔子說：「做事順應民心，尊重鬼神卻遠離鬼神，就算明智了。」

　　Fan Chi asked what constituted wisdom. The Master said, "To give one's self earnestly to the duties due to men, and, while respecting spiritual beings, to keep aloof from them, may be called wisdom."

【原文出處 Reference】

> 樊遲問知，子曰：「務民之義，敬鬼神而遠之，可謂知矣。」
> 【論語第六・雍也篇・第 22 節】*The Analects, Chapter 6 Yong-Ye, Verse 22*

## ㈤ 論語名言的現代價值評論
## Commentary about this ancient text with modern values

Ancient Text：巧言亂德。小不忍，則亂大謀。

Specious words confound virtue. Want of forbearance in small matters confounds great plans.

【論語第十五・衛靈公篇・第 27 節】*The Analects, Chapter 15 Wei-Ling-Gong, Verse 27*

**Modern Values Commentary by: Dr. Benjamin Rifkin**

People young and old sometimes struggle with an impulse to speak or act, when doing so can actually complicate already challenging situations. As I look back on my own life, I cannot count the number of times when I responded impulsively rather than more wisely exercising patience to listen attentively, reflect thoughtfully, and consider multiple perspectives. As an educator, one of my goals is to help students understand the cultural perspectives and practices of people from diverse backgrounds, including perspective taking, empathy, and compassion, to understand that the world is not a simple place of binary truths and falsehoods, but a complex place with many shades of nuanced greys. This is more important than ever, since in the era of the instantaneity of social media, many people often rush to engage anonymously online in situations or problems without knowing the fuller context or the deeper background of that situation or problem. They don't stop to ask participants in that very situation or problem about their perspectives, experiences, and thoughts and don't bother to truly listen to and consider them, but react, rather, on the basis of a video or sound clip that could have been purposefully edited to support a particular ideological perspective. People sometimes repost false information without checking its validity or the reliability of its source, contributing to the dissemination of hate and anger, sometimes directed at a single individual undeserving of this negative attention, sometimes directed at entire religious, ethnic, or racial groups (who are of course undeserving of hate). Confucius's analects, from thousands of years ago, is particularly helpful for us today: We should take time to investigate and reflect before we click "post" lest our specious words confound virtue and ultimately confound the greatest plan for humanity: peace among all nations and respect for all people.

Benjamin Rifkin, PhD

Professor of Russian and

Dean of Hofstra College of Liberal Arts and Sciences,

Hofstra University

## ㈥ 模擬口語考試討論話題
## Suggested topics for oral proficiency interview (OPI)

巧言亂德。小不忍，則亂大謀。

The Master said, "Specious words confound virtue. Want of forbearance in small matters confounds great plans."

【模擬口試練習】

1. 你覺得從一個人說話的方式可以看出那個人的性格嗎？請說說你認識的兩個不同性格的人，他們的說話內容和方式，跟他們的性格有什麼關係？

   Can you observe a person's characteristics by listening to the content and the style of their speech? Please give two examples to explain speech styles which can give you a hint of the speaker's characteristics.

   【中級、高級 – 描述／敘述 Intermediate to Advanced Level – can narrate and describe】

   【高級 – 說明比較 Advanced Level – can compare】

2. 如果你的上司喜歡別人稱讚他／她，不喜歡別人說他／她做錯了。有一天你發現他／她做錯一件事，而且對公司造成了很嚴重的負面影響，你會怎麼跟上司說？

Does your supervisor like to be praised by others or dislike others to criticize them? If one day, you found an error your supervisor made which can affect the company, how would you rectify the situation?

【中級、高級 – 描述／敘述 Intermediate to Advanced Level – can narrate and describe】

【優秀級 – 假設情境申述 Superior Level – can hypothesize】

【德】德不孤必有鄰【論語第四‧里仁篇‧第 25 節】*The Analects, Chapter 4 Li-Ren, Verse 25*

Virtue is not left to stand alone. He who practices it will have neighbors.

## 11

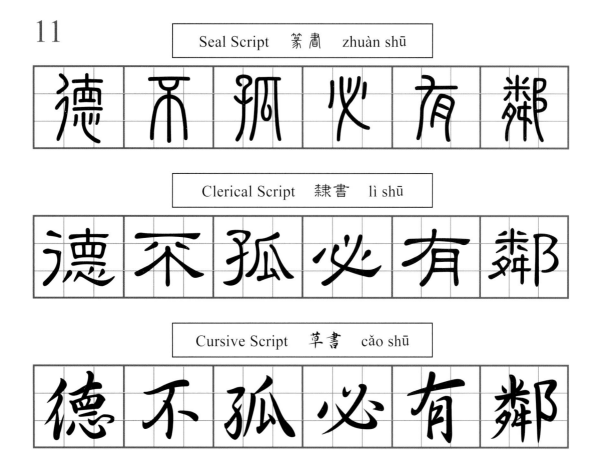

Seal Script　篆書　zhuàn shū

Clerical Script　隸書　lì shū

Cursive Script　草書　cǎo shū

Running Script 　行書　xíng shū

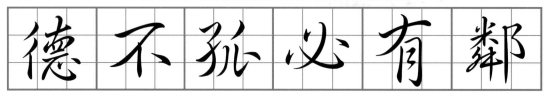

Standard Script 　楷書　kǎi shū

第十章 【政治】 zhèng zhì

Chapter 10   Quotes related to politics

## 關於【政治】的三個論語名言：

### Three top quotes about "Government and Good Leaders":

君君、臣臣、父父、子子。

There is government, when the prince is prince, and the minister is minister; when the father is father, and the son is son.

【論語第十二 · 顏淵篇 · 第 11 節】 *The Analects, Chapter 12 Yan-Yuan, Verse 11*

其身正，不令而行；其身不正，雖令不從。

When a prince's personal conduct is correct, his government is effective without the issuing of orders. If his personal conduct is not correct, he may issue orders, but they will not be followed.

【論語第十三 · 子路篇 · 第 6 節】 *The Analects, Chapter 13  Zi-Lu, Verse 6*

不在其位，不謀其政。

He who is not in any particular office has nothing to do with plans for the administration of its duties.

【論語第十四 · 憲問篇 · 第 26 節】 *The Analects, Chapter 14 Xian-Wen, Verse 26*

名言一　君君、臣臣、父父、子子。

Quote 1

"There is government, when the prince is prince, and the minister is minister; when the father is father, and the son is son."

## ㈠逐字翻譯
### Learn the original text and its meaning

君君、臣臣、父父、子子。
Jūn jūn chén chén fù fù zǐ zǐ.

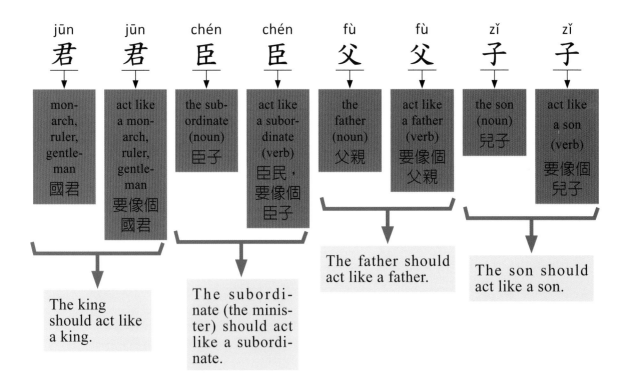

## ㈡白話解釋原文
### Explanation with the modern text

君君、臣臣、父父、子子。
(Below is the entire paragraph of this quote.)

全段原文：

齊景公問政於孔子。孔子對曰：「君君，臣臣，父父，子子。」公曰：「善哉！信如君不君，臣不臣，父不父，子不子，雖有粟，吾得而食諸？」

The duke Jing, of Qi, asked Confucius about government. Confucius replied, "There is government, when the prince is prince, and the minister is minister; when the father is father, and the son is son." "Good!" said the duke; "if, indeed, the prince be not prince, the minister be not minister, the father be not father, and the son be not son, although I have my revenue, can I enjoy it?"

全段白話：

齊景公請教孔子關於政治的事。孔子回答：「當國君做國君該做的事，臣子做臣子該做的事，父親做父親該做的事，兒子做兒子該做的事，這樣就能夠有一個很好的政府。」

齊景公回答說：「您說得真好！要是一個國君不像個國君（沒做到國君該做的事），臣子不像個臣子，父親不像個父親，兒子不像個兒子（如果是這樣）的話，雖然這個國家有食物，但我會吃得到嗎？」

## 1. 白話解釋

一個國君的行為就要像一個國君，一個臣子的行為就要像一個臣子，一個父親的行為就要像一個父親，一個兒子的行為就要像一個兒子。

The King should act like a king and a minister should act like a minister. A father should act like a father and a son should act like a son.

## 2. 生詞

| | 生詞<br>Vocabulary | 拼音<br>Pin Yin | 英文<br>English | 詞類<br>Part of Speech |
|---|---|---|---|---|
| 1 | 國君 | guó jūn | emperor, king | noun |
| 2 | 行為 | xíng wéi | actions, conducts | noun |
| 3 | 就要 | jiù yào | must | adverb |
| 4 | 像 | xiàng | to be like | verb |
| 5 | 臣子 | chén zǐ | state official, subject in dynasty | noun |

## ㈢ 延伸對話與生詞
### Extended learning with sentence practices

1. 會話

　　A：這個兒子對他的爸爸說話的樣子，好像他是他爸爸的爸爸。

　　　The son talks to his father as if he is his father's father.

　　B：是啊！太不像話了！他應該要更尊敬他的爸爸。

　　　Indeed, it is truly inappropriate. He should respect his father more.

2. 生詞

| | 生詞<br>Vocabulary | 拼音<br>Pin Yin | 英文<br>English | 詞類<br>Part of Speech |
|---|---|---|---|---|
| 1 | 對…說話 | duì … shuō huà | to speak to someone | verb |
| 2 | …的樣子 | … de yàng zǐ | the appearance | noun |
| 3 | 不像話 | bú xiàng huà | ridiculous | adjective |
| 4 | 應該 | yīng gāi | should | auxiliary verb |
| 5 | 更 | gèng | more | adverb |
| 6 | 尊敬 | zūn jìng | to respect | verb |

## ㈣ 孔子故事
### Stories about Confucius' life and his teaching

孔子周遊列國

Confucius traveled around the states to advocate his political ideas.

　　孔子的志向一直是想從政，他希望能協助君王以「禮樂治國」。雖然孔子在魯國做了一些行政的工作，可是魯國的國君一直沒有能好好地採用孔子的意見。在五十五歲時，孔子決定帶著學生離開魯國到其他國家周遊，希望能遇到有一位國君能採用孔子的政治主張。

　　孔子去了很多國家，周遊列國的時間總共有 14 年，卻沒有得到一個好的官職。孔子在 68 歲的時候才回到了魯國。73 歲的時候，孔子生病過世了。

Confucius' career plan was always to become a political advisor. He wished to assist kings to rule a country and to cultivate citizens with Rites and Music. Although Confucius served in the State of Lu for some official jobs, the King of Lu never accepted Confucius' suggestions. At age of 55, Confucius decided to take his students to travel around the states, hoping to meet a king who would adopt Confucius' political ideas. Confucius traveled for 14 years around many states, never having a suitable governmental position. He returned to the State of Lu when he was 68. He passed away at the age of 73.

【原文出處 Reference】

已而去魯，斥乎齊，逐乎宋、衛，困於陳蔡之間，於是反魯。
【史記‧孔子世家‧第 5 節】 *Shiji, Kongzi Shijia, Verse 5*
孔子之去魯凡十四歲而反乎魯。
【史記‧孔子世家‧第 56 節】 *Shiji, Kongzi Shijia, Verse 56*
孔子年七十三，以魯哀公十六年四月己丑卒。
【史記‧孔子世家‧第 76 節】 *Shiji, Kongzi Shijia, Verse 76*

## ㈤ 論語名言的現代價值評論
### Commentary about this ancient text with modern values

Ancient Text：君君臣臣，父父子子。

There is government, when the prince acts like a prince, and the minister acts like a minister; when the father acts like a father, and the son acts like a son.

【論語第十二‧顏淵篇‧第 11 節】 *The Analects, Chapter 12 Yan-Yuan, Verse 11*

**Modern Values Commentary by: Jun H. Choi**

Democracy or authoritarianism? This question continues to be debated in the Twenty First Century as global power centers attempt to expand their sphere of influence by selling their form of government as the better one.

As a former American Mayor of a midsize city, I, of course, believe strongly in promoting representative democracy as the most stable and prosperous form of government. However, democracy has its challenges when there is a crisis and when effective, efficient government matters. In America's case, the growing gap between the haves and the have-nots (among the largest gaps in inequality among the world's advanced nations) and political extremism are limiting the ability of its representative leaders and citizens to fix its systemic problems.

Regardless of your view of the optimal form of government, Confucius' words are wise beyond his time. Government only works in the long term when its leaders act like selfless, enlightened public servants who make decisions based on the public interest, and citizens act responsibly, not only in their own individual interest to live a fulfilling life, with a recognition that their actions affect the behavior of others.

When someone doesn't act in this manner, there is a societal cost that everyone pays for in the long run – lost productivity, criminal justice costs, social welfare costs and degradation of our environment. When the rule of law is not followed, both legally and in principle, or the rule itself is viewed as inequitable, there is a loss of trust and social capital. When parents don't responsibly raise their children with positive values, their children and society both pay a cost for their children not acting within acceptable norms. When corporations pollute, although legal at the time, the environment suffers and everyone, including other nations and governments, pay a heavy cost.

In essence, Confucius recognized more than 2,500 years ago that an ideal society depends on the collaboration of its citizenry – everyone has a role and society functions best when everyone plays their role with integrity and a recognition that each and every citizen plays an important role to improve the quality of life of its entire citizenry.

Jun H. Choi，崔俊，市長
Former Mayor of Edison, New Jersey
CEO, Menlo Realty Ventures

## ㈥ 模擬口語考試討論話題
## Suggested topics for oral proficiency interview (OPI)

# 君君、臣臣、父父、子子。

The Duke Jing, of Qi, asked Confucius about the government. Confucius replied, "There is government, when the prince is prince, and the minister is minister; when the father is father, and the son is son."

【模擬口試練習】

1. 假設你是一位大公司的高階主管，面對公司員工之間的相處不融洽，身為公司的高階主管的你，會採用什麼管理策略來加強員工之間的團隊精神，並且讓員工願意配合你的領導方式？

   If you were a manager/supervisor in a large-size company where your staff are not having a good morale or teamwork. What managing strategy would you adapt to improve the teamwork among your staff members and agree to comply to your leadership style?

   【優秀級 - 假設情境申述 Superior Level - can hypothesize】

2. 請舉三個例子來說明，你認為一位公司的員工要怎麼做才能和他的主管維持良好的關係？

   Please describe three examples about what an employee / team-member can do to maintain good relationship with their boss / supervisor at the company.

   【中級、高級 – 描述 / 敘述 Intermediate to Advanced Level – can narrate and describe】

3. 請舉三個例子說明，你認為一位公司的主管應該如何與他的員工維持良好的關係？

   Please describe three examples about what a supervisor can do to maintain good relationship with his employees / team-members.

   【中級、高級 – 描述 / 敘述 Intermediate to Advanced Level – can narrate and describe】

4. 請討論國家領導（總統）、政府官員對人民的責任。

   Please discuss the responsibilities of the nation's leader (the president) or the politician to the people.

【中級、高級 – 描述／敘述 Intermediate to Advanced Level – can narrate and describe】

【優秀級 – 表達個人意見和申述抽象觀念 Superior Level – can support opinion and discuss abstract concept】

---

名言二　其身正，不令而行；其身不正，雖令不從。

Quote 2
When a prince's personal conduct is correct, his government is effective without the issuing of orders. If his personal conduct is not correct, he may issue orders, but they will not be followed.

---

## ㈠逐字翻譯
## Learn the original text and its meaning

其身正，不令而行；
qí shēn zhèng, bú lìng ér xíng.

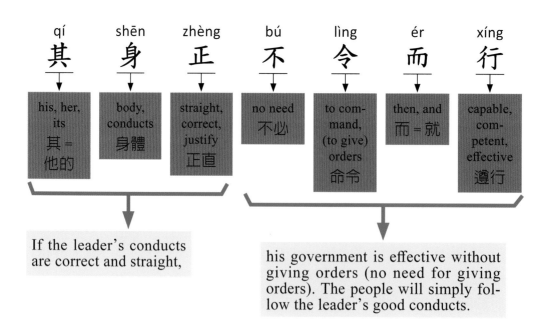

其身不正，雖令不從。

qí shēn bú zhèng, suī lìng bù cóng.

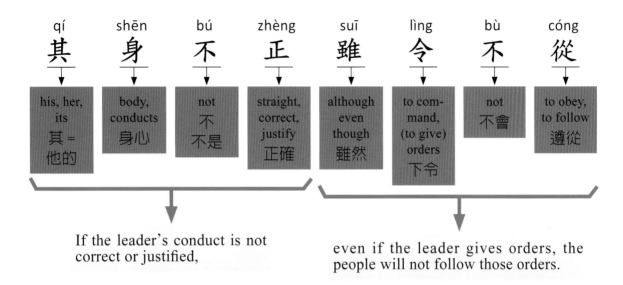

| qí<br>其 | shēn<br>身 | bú<br>不 | zhèng<br>正 | suī<br>雖 | lìng<br>令 | bù<br>不 | cóng<br>從 |
|---|---|---|---|---|---|---|---|
| his, her, its<br>其 =<br>他的 | body, conducts<br>身心 | not<br>不是 | straight, correct, justify<br>正確 | although even though<br>雖然 | to command, (to give) orders<br>下令 | not<br>不會 | to obey, to follow<br>遵從 |

If the leader's conduct is not correct or justified,

even if the leader gives orders, the people will not follow those orders.

When a prince's personal conduct is correct, his government is effective without the issuing of orders. If his personal conduct is not correct, he may issue orders, but they will not be followed.

## ㈡ 白話解釋原文
### Explanation with the modern text

子曰：「其身正，不令而行，其身不正，雖令不從。」

When a prince's personal conduct is correct, his government is effective without the issuing of orders. If his personal conduct is not correct, he may issue orders, but they will not be followed.

### 1.白話解釋

孔子說：「如果領導人自己的行為正當，即使領導人不下達命令，人民也會做好自己的行為；然而，如果領導人自己的行為不正當，即使對人民下了命令，人民也不會服從。」

Confucius said: "As long as the leader's conduct is correct, his people will be obedient even if he does not give order. If the leader's actions are not correct, the people will not follow his orders even when he gives his command.

## 2.生詞

| | 生詞<br>Vocabulary | 拼音<br>Pin Yin | 英文<br>English | 詞類<br>Part of Speech |
|---|---|---|---|---|
| 1 | 領導人 | lǐng dǎo rén | leader | noun |
| 2 | 行為 | xíng wéi | conduct | noun |
| 3 | 正當 | zhèng dāng | decent, rightful | adjective |
| 4 | 正直 | zhèng zhí | upright, honest | adjective |
| 5 | 即使 | jí shǐ | even if | conjunction phrase |
| 6 | 下達 | xià dá | to give order | verb |
| 7 | 命令 | mìng lìng | order | noun |
| 8 | 人民 | rén mín | people, citizen | noun |
| 9 | 服從 | fú cóng | to obey | verb |
| 10 | 然而 | rán ér | however | conjunction phrase |

# ㈢ 延伸對話與生詞
## Extended learning with sentence practices

### 1.會話

A：我們這個單位的主管，每天早上八點就來上班了。

Our supervisor of the unit comes to work every morning before 8:00AM.

B：難怪你們所有的員工都很準時，不敢遲到。

No wonder all your workers are very punctual, and they are never late.

A：是啊，看到領導「以身作則」，大家不必等領導下命令，就會做好行動了。

Indeed, the leader set a good example with his own actions. Everyone would simply follow his example, no need for any orders given.

## 2. 生詞

| 生詞<br>Vocabulary | 拼音<br>Pin Yin | 英文<br>English | 詞類<br>Part of Speech |
|---|---|---|---|
| 1 | 單位 | dān wèi | unit | noun |
| 2 | 主管 | zhǔ guǎn | supervisor | noun |
| 3 | 難怪 | nán guài | no wonder | conjunction phrase |
| 4 | 員工 | yuán gōng | employee, worker | noun |
| 5 | 準時 | zhǔn shí | punctual | adjective |
| 6 | 遲到 | chí dào | late | adjective |
| 7 | 以身作則 | yǐ shēn zuò zé | setting an example | verb |
| 8 | 行動 | xíng dòng | actions | noun |

## ㈣ 孔子故事

### Stories about Confucius' life and his teaching.

### 孔子為什麼離開魯國？

### Why Confucius leave his home country (Lu State)?

孔子幫助季桓子治理魯國，齊國人卻送來一些歌女，季桓子接受了，和歌女歡樂了三天不上朝。於是，孔子覺得很失望，就離開了魯國開始周遊列國尋求實現政治理想的機會。

While Confucius was assisting the administration of Ji-Huan (Duke of Lu), the people of Qi (a neighboring state) sent a group of female musical dancers as gift to the Duke of Lu, which the Duke of Lu, Ji Huan, received and enjoyed the company of these dancers for three days without holding court. Confucius was disappointed seeing the situation; therefore, he departed his homeland (Lu) to start traveling around the states in hoping to find another opportunity to be a political adviser for a better suitable king.

> 齊人歸女樂，季桓子受之，三日不朝。孔子行。
> 【論語第十八・微子篇・第 04 節】*The Analects, Chapter 18 Wei-Zi, Verse 04*

## 孔子 68 歲回到魯國
## Confucius returned to Lu at the age of 68.

　　孔子 68 歲終於回到魯國（西元前 484 年），他不想當官了，他專心修訂了六經中的《詩》、《書》、《禮》、《樂》、《春秋》，和繼續教導學生。

　　At age of 68, Confucius returned to the State of Lu (484 B.C.E.). He did not pursue any official governmental position; instead, he devoted his time on editing the Six Classics Books and continued his teaching.

　　【六經】Six Classics, namely: Book of Songs 詩經、Book of History 尚書、Book of Rites 儀禮、the lost Book of Music 樂經、Book of Changes 易經、Spring and Autumn Annals 春秋。

【原文出處 Reference】

> 【史記・孔子世家・第 5，59，60，62，85 節】*Shiji, Kongzi Shijia, Verse 5, 59, 60, 62, 85*

## ㈤ 論語名言的現代價值評論
## Commentary about this ancient text with modern values

Ancient Text：其身正，不令而行；其身不正，雖令不從。

　　　　　　"When a prince's personal conduct is correct, his government is effective without the issuing of orders. If his personal conduct is not correct, he may issue orders, but they will not be followed."

【論語第十三・子路篇・第 6 節】*The Analects, Chapter 13 Zi-Lu, Verse 6*

**Modern Values Commentary by: Alexander D'Andrea**

Confucius notes the prince's "personal conduct" when teaching about how an effective government should operate. In other words, when a prince is not corrupt and is benevolent, the people will be in good standing with the country. His words can also be interpreted as "lead by example." If a prince is kind to his subjects, they will be kind to each other.

There is no better example in American politics than that of our first President, George Washington. The precedent of stepping down as President after two terms revolutionized leadership. This decision set in motion the idea of a peaceful transition of power in the American political world. His farewell address was not an order, but rather consisted of wise parting words and warnings. Washington was not only successful because his character was strong and he gained the trust of his people, but because he catalyzed them to gain the trust of each other.

Confucius' words are especially useful, in that they can be applied outside of government terms. For instance, when parents set a poor example, then no matter how many times they may ask their child to do a chore, they will refuse. However, if a child's parents are good role models, they will complete their chores without even being asked.

Alexander D'Andrea

Political Science Major, 杜宏敬

The College of New Jersey, USA

## ㈥ 模擬口語考試討論話題
### Suggested topics for oral proficiency interview (OPI)

其身正，不令而行；其身不正，雖令不從。

The Master said, "When a prince's personal conduct is correct, his government is effective without the issuing of orders. If his personal conduct is not correct, he may issue orders, but they will not be followed."

【模擬口試練習】

1. 請用例子來說明「以身作則」在管理上的效應。

   Please discuss cases of "leading by example" to explain its effects for management.

   【中級、高級 – 描述／敘述 Intermediate to Advanced Level – can narrate and describe】

2. 你覺得領導者需不需要用自己的行為來設典範，還是他們應該享有不同的禮遇？請解釋你的意見。

   Do you think the leaders need to act as a model to set examples or should they enjoy various privileges? Please share your opinion on this issue.

   【優秀級 – 表達個人意見和申述抽象觀念 Superior Level – can support opinion and discuss abstract concept】

3. 如果你是你的國家的領導人（總統），你會對你的國家做什麼政策上的改變？請舉三個例子說明。

   If you were the president (the leader) of your country, what policies or changes would you implement for your country? Please make three examples.

   【優秀級 – 假設情境申述 Superior Level – can hypothesize】

名言三　不在其位，不謀其政。
Quote 3　"He who is not in any particular office has nothing to do with plans for the administration of its duties."

(一) 逐字翻譯
**Learn the original text and its meaning**

不在其位，不謀其政。
bú zài qí wèi, bù móu qí zhèng.

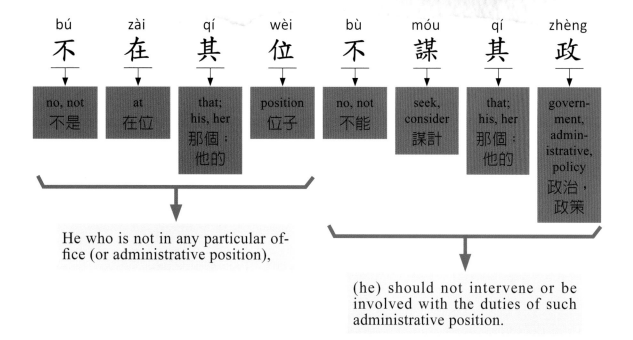

He who is not in any particular office has nothing to do with plans for the administration of its duties.

## ㈡ 白話解釋原文
**Explanation with the modern text**

不在其位，不謀其政。

He who is not in any particular office has nothing to do with plans for the administration of its duties.

全段原文：

子曰：「不在其位，不謀其政。」曾子曰：「君子思不出其位。」

The Master said, "He who is not in any particular office has nothing to do with plans for the administration of its duties." The philosopher Zeng said, "The superior man, in his thoughts, does not go out of his place."

1.白話解釋

孔子說：「不在那個職位，就不要考慮那個職位上的事。」曾子說：「君子考慮問題時，不應該超過自己的職權範圍。」

Confucius said: "If you are not at the position of any particular office, you should not meddle with the business of that office." Zeng-Zi said: "A gentleman should not scrutinize matters outside of his own position."

自己如果不在那個職位，就不應該介入干涉那個職位的事務。

If not in the position, one should not intervene in the matters belonging to that position.

2.生詞

| | 生詞<br>Vocabulary | 拼音<br>Pin Yin | 英文<br>English | 詞類<br>Part of Speech |
|---|---|---|---|---|
| 1 | 職位 | zhí wèi | position | noun |
| 2 | 考慮 | kǎo lǜ | to consider | verb |
| 3 | 超過 | chāo guò | to exceed | verb |
| 4 | 職權 | zhí quán | authority | noun |
| 5 | 範圍 | fàn wéi | range | noun |
| 6 | 介入 | jiè rù | to intervene | verb |
| 7 | 干涉 | gān shè | to meddle, to control | verb |
| 8 | 事務 | shì wù | matters | noun |

## ㈢ 延伸對話與生詞
**Extended learning with sentence practices**

1.會話

A：我覺得我們的老闆對員工太嚴格了。

I think our boss is too strict to the employees.

B：你別批評你的老闆了。你不是在那個職位，不要介入。因為你不知道那個工作有多困難，還是先把自己的工作做好吧！這就是孔子說的「不在其位，不謀其政」。

You should not criticize your boss. You should not intervene since you are not in that position. You do not know the difficulty of being in that position. You should focus on your own job. That is why Confucius said: "He who is not in any particular office has nothing to do with plans for the administration of its duties."

## 2. 生詞

| | 生詞<br>**Vocabulary** | 拼音<br>**Pin Yin** | 英文<br>**English** | 詞類<br>**Part of Speech** |
|---|---|---|---|---|
| 1 | 老闆 | lǎo bǎn | boss, supervisor | noun |
| 2 | 員工 | yuán gōng | employee | noun |
| 3 | 嚴格 | yán gé | strict | adjective |
| 4 | 批評 | pī píng | to criticize | verb |
| 5 | 介入 | jiè rù | to intervene | verb |
| 6 | 工作 | gōng zuò | work | noun |
| 7 | 困難 | kùn nán | difficult | adjective |

## ㈣ 孔子故事
### Stories about Confucius' life and his teaching

孔子認為死後留下好名聲是很重要的

Confucius considered it is important to leave a good fame after one's death.

孔子説：「君子害怕死後，人們不會再記得他的名聲。」

The Master said, "The superior man dislikes the thought of his name not being mentioned after his death."

【原文出處 Reference】

子曰：「君子疾沒世而名不稱焉。」
【論語第十五·衛靈公篇·第二十節】*The Analects, Chapter 15 Wei-Ling-Gong, Verse 20*

## 麒麟被抓後死了，孔子也在 73 歲去世
After Qin-Ling was captured, Confucius passed away at age 73.

有一次魯哀公打獵，捕到了一隻野獸，以為這是很不吉祥的怪物，就叫孔子來看。孔子看了說，這是「麒麟」。麒麟是很稀少特有的吉祥動物。孔子看到麒麟被殺了，覺得很難過，孔子最好的學生顏淵也死了，孔子說這是老天的意思。孔子說：「我的日子也快結束了。但是我不會埋怨天，也不會責備人。」兩年後，孔子就死了。孔子活到 73 歲（公元前 479 年）。

King of Lu hunted in the wilderness, captured an unusual animal, thinking it was an inauspicious creature. They asked Confucius to see it. Confucius said: "This is a Qi-Ling, the auspicious heavenly animal." After this incident, Confucius said to his disciple, Zi-Gong, "My time is ending, heaven wants me to die. The heavenly animal, Qi-Ling, was captured and my time is ending." Confucius continued: "I am not complaining or blaming on anyone. I know heaven knows how hard I have committed to life-long learning." Two years later, Confucius passed away at age 73 (479 B.C.E.).

【原文出處 Reference】

> 魯哀公十四年春，狩大野。叔孫氏車子鉏商獲獸，以為不祥。仲尼視之，曰：「麟也。」取之。曰：「河不出圖，雒不出書，吾已矣夫！」顏淵死，孔子曰：「天喪予！」及西狩見麟，曰：「吾道窮矣！」喟然嘆曰：「莫知我夫！」子貢曰：「何為莫知子？」子曰：「不怨天，不尤人，下學而上達，知我者其天乎！」
> 【史記‧孔子世家‧第 71 節】*Shiji, Kongzi Shijia, Verse 71*
> 孔子年七十三，以魯哀公十六年四月己丑卒。
> 【史記‧孔子世家‧第 56 & 76 節】*Shiji, Kongzi Shijia, Verse 56 & 76*

## 《論語》是孔子的學生記錄孔子教學時的對話和孔子所教的哲學思想
The Analects - compiled by Confucius' disciples to record the master's thoughts and his teaching

孔子去世後，他的弟子把孔子教學生的思想，以及和學生說的話都記下來，整理編成了《論語》。

After Confucius passed away, his disciples recorded the teaching of Confucius, as well as the dialogues they had with Confucius. It was the Analects.

論語總共有 20 篇，492 章，1 萬 2 千多字。

There are 20 chapters, 492 verses, more than 12,000 words.

論語 20 章的名字是以那章的第一句名言的前兩個字（或是三個字）做爲章名。

The 20 Chapters (Books) were named with the first two or three characters of the first verse in that chapter.

【原文出處 Reference】

> 論語者，孔子應答弟子時人及弟子相與言而接聞於夫子之語也。當時弟子各有所記。夫子既卒，門人相與輯而論篡，故謂之論語。
> 東漢班固【漢書・藝文志・第 115 節】 *Han-Shu, Yi-Wen-Zhi, Verse 115.* By Ban-Gu, Eastern Han

## 論語 20 章名
## Chapters' Names of the Analects

| Chapter 1 | Xue-Er | 學而 xué ér |
|---|---|---|
| Chapter 2 | Wei-Zheng | 為政 wéi zhèng |
| Chapter 3 | Ba-Yi | 八佾 bā yì |
| Chapter 4 | Li-Ren | 里仁 lǐ rén |
| Chapter 5 | Gong-Ye-Chang | 公冶長 gōng yě cháng |
| Chapter 6 | Yong-Ye | 雍也 yōng yě |
| Chapter 7 | Shu-Er | 述而 shù ér |
| Chapter 8 | Tai-Bo | 泰伯 tài bó |
| Chapter 9 | Zi-Han | 子罕 zǐ hǎn |
| Chapter 10 | Xiang-Dang | 鄉黨 xiāng dǎng |
| Chapter 11 | Xian-Jin | 先進 xiān jìn |
| Chapter 12 | Yan-Yuan | 顏淵 yán yuan |
| Chapter 13 | Zi-Lu | 子路 zǐ lù |

| Chapter 14 | Xian-Wen | 憲問 xiàn wèn |
|---|---|---|
| Chapter 15 | Wei-Ling-Gong | 衛靈公 wèi líng gong |
| Chapter 16 | Zi-Shi | 季氏 jì shì |
| Chapter 17 | Yang-Huo | 陽貨 yáng huò |
| Chapter 18 | Wei-Zi | 微子 wēi zǐ |
| Chapter 19 | Zi-Zhang | 子張 zǐ zhāng |
| Chapter 20 | Yao-Yue | 堯曰 yáo yuē |

## ㈤ 論語名言的現代價值評論
### Commentary about this ancient text with modern values

Ancient Text：子曰：為政以德，譬如北辰，居其所而眾星共之。

Confucius said: "He who exercises government by means of his virtue may be compared to the north polar star, which keeps its place, and all the stars turn towards it."

【論語第二 · 為政篇 · 第 1 節】 *The Analects, Chapter 2 Wen-Zheng, Verse 01*

**Modern Values Commentary by: Dr. Lenard Goodman**

I found this Confucius proverb on the leadership to be extremely applicable to our modern world. It is insightful in many ways, that, as I read it, I--as someone who adores Chinese culture but is neither a native Chinese speaker, nor someone who understand all the beauty of Chinese philosophy, can nevertheless understand the relevant philosophy, and apply it to my broader understanding of the world in which I live more than two thousand years after Confucius' time. For example, when I read in Chapter 2, that Confucius said: *He who exercises government by means of his virtue may be compared to the north polar star, which keeps its place and all the stars turn towards it"* I realized that it is still extremely comparable to the society that I have seen in my life, whether in my family growing up, the schools I attended, the University in which I have taught now for over 45 years, or now in my family life in which I first became a husband, then a father, and now most recently a grandfather, what makes one successful is by taking one's best qualities and working always to make them even better. By serving as the best role model, we can be, we in turn inspire those who look up to us. Whether they be for our children, grandchildren, current or former students, or faculty colleague, or simply someone we met during our lives, we should always work hard in obtaining the best virtues that bring true peace and happiness to our society.

Leonard Goodman, Ph.D. CPA, 郝廉禮 教授

Professor, Vice Chair and Director of the Undergraduate Accounting

Program-New Brunswick at the Rutgers University Business School

## ㈥ 模擬口語考試討論話題
## Suggested topics for oral proficiency interview (OPI)

## 不在其位，不謀其政。

He who is not in any particular office has nothing to do with plans for the administration of its duties.

【模擬口試練習】

1. 請用例子說明什麼是「管閒事」？什麼是「干涉」別人的事情？

   Please share an example of "busy-body" or an example of someone "meddling" in others' matters.

   【中級、高級 – 描述／敘述 Intermediate to Advanced Level – can narrate and describe】

2. 請列出三個政府單位的職位，並且說明看他們負責的工作。

   Please list three governmental positions and describe their respective jobs and duties.

   【中級、高級 – 描述／敘述 Intermediate to Advanced Level – can narrate and describe】

3. 在民主的國家制度中，執政者或地方政府首長（如州長、市長）的職位都是由人民用選票選出來的。你認為這種選舉制度有什麼優點，有什麼缺點？請舉出三個關於「選舉制度」的優點和三個缺點。

In democratic countries, citizens can exercise their voting rights to decide the ruling party and their leaders of the local government (such as the governors or the mayors.) Please share your opinion on the election policy. List three advantages of the citizens' voting rights and three disadvantages which come with the election.

【優秀級 – 表達個人意見和申述抽象觀念 Superior Level – can support opinion and discuss abstract concept】

【政治】君臣父子【論語第十二 · 顏淵篇 · 第 11 節】 *The Analects, Chapter 12 Yan-Yuan, Verse 11*

The prince should act like a prince, and the minister should act like a minister, the father should act like a father, and the son should act like a son.

12

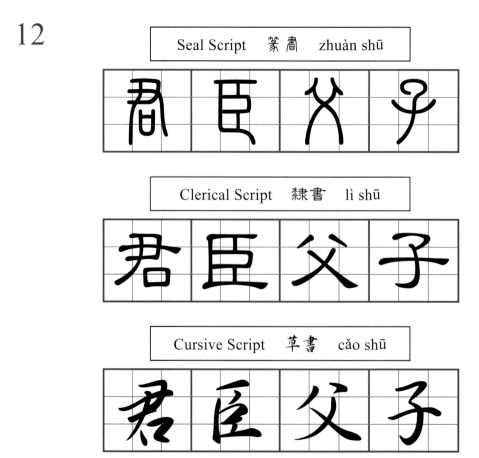

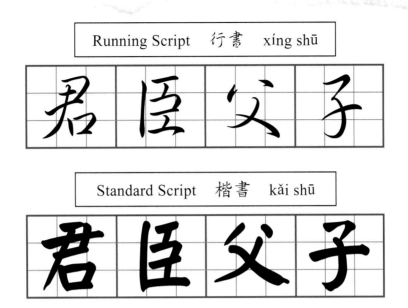

【政治】為政以德【論語第二 · 為政篇 · 第 1 節】 *The Analects, Chapter 2, Wei-Zheng, Verse 1*

Exercise government by means of his virtue

13

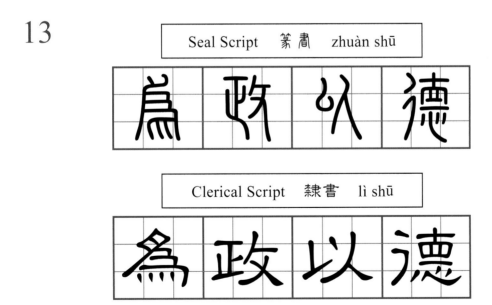

【政治】世界大同【禮記·禮運篇·第 1 節】*Li-Ji, Chapter Li-Yun Verse 1*
The world as the Grand Union.

14

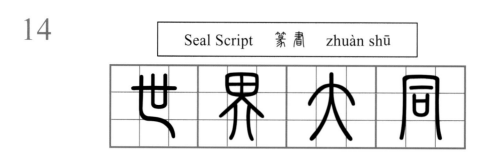

Clerical Script　隸書　lì shū

世界大同

Cursive Script　草書　cǎo shū

世界大同

Running Script　行書　xíng shū

世界大同

Standard Script　楷書　kǎi shū

世界大同

# 附錄

Supplements

# 附錄一
## 生詞延伸學習
### 漢語水平考試（HSK）和華語文能力測驗（TOCFL）
### Extended Vocabulary Learning on HSK & TOCFL

#### 第一章　【孝順】名言一

父母在，不遠遊，遊必有方。

While his parents are alive, the son may not go abroad to a distance. If he does go abroad, he must have a fixed place to which he goes.

| 父 | 母 | 在 | 不 | 遠（远） | 遊（游） | 必 | 有 | 方 |
|---|---|---|---|---|---|---|---|---|

| | 父<br>fù | 漢語水平考試<br>HSK | 拼音<br>Pin Yin | 英文翻譯<br>English | 詞類<br>Part of Speech | 華語文<br>能力測驗<br>TOCFL |
|---|---|---|---|---|---|---|
| 1 | 父親 | 父亲（四級） | fù qīn | father | Noun | 基礎級<br>Level 2 |
| 2 | 父母 | 父母 | fù mǔ | parents | Noun | 基礎級<br>Level 2 |
| 3 | 祖父 | 祖父（六級） | zǔ fù | grandfather | Noun | 進階級<br>Level 3 |
| 4 | 伯父 | 伯父 | bó fù | uncle | Noun | 基礎級<br>Level 2 |
| 5 | 師父 | 师父 | shī fu | Master | Noun | 高階級<br>Level 4 |

| | 母<br>mǔ | 漢語水平考試<br>HSK | 拼音<br>Pin Yin | 英文翻譯<br>English | 詞類<br>Part of Speech | 華語文<br>能力測驗<br>TOCFL |
|---|---|---|---|---|---|---|
| 1 | 母親 | 母亲（四級） | mǔ qīn | mother | Noun | 基礎級<br>Level 2 |

| | 母<br>mǔ | 漢語水平考試<br>HSK | 拼音<br>Pin Yin | 英文翻譯<br>English | 詞類<br>Part of Speech | 華語文<br>能力測驗<br>TOCFL |
|---|---|---|---|---|---|---|
| 2 | 父母 | 父母 | fù mǔ | parents | Noun | 基礎級<br>Level 2 |
| 3 | 祖母 | 祖母 | zǔ mǔ | grand-mother | Noun | 進階級<br>Level 3 |
| 4 | 伯母 | 伯母（六級） | bó mǔ | aunt | Noun | 基礎級<br>Level 2 |
| 5 | 師母 | 师母 | shī mǔ | master | Noun | 高階級<br>Level 4 |
| 6 | 字母 | 字母（五級） | zì mǔ | letter | Noun | 高階級<br>Level 4 |
| 7 | 母語 | 母语（六級） | mǔ yǔ | mother tongue | Noun | 基礎級<br>Level 2 |

| | 在<br>zài | 漢語水平考試<br>HSK | 拼音<br>Pin Yin | 英文翻譯<br>English | 詞類<br>Part of Speech | 華語文<br>能力測驗<br>TOCFL |
|---|---|---|---|---|---|---|
| 1 | 現在 | 现在（一級） | xiàn zài | now | Noun | 準備級一級<br>Novice 1 |
| 2 | 實在 | 实在（四級） | shí zài | really | Vs | 進階級<br>Level 3 |
| 3 | 在乎 | 在乎（五級） | zài hū | to care | Vst | 高階級<br>Level 4 |
| 4 | 內在 | 内在（六級） | nà zài | inner | Noun | 流利級<br>Level 5 |
| 5 | 外在 | 外在 | wài zài | external | Noun | 流利級<br>Level 5 |
| 6 | 正在 | 正在（二級） | zhèng zài | doing something | Adv | NA |

| 不<br>bù, bú | 漢語水平考試<br>HSK | 拼音<br>Pin Yin | 英文翻譯<br>English | 詞類<br>Part of Speech | 華語文<br>能力測驗<br>TOCFL |
|---|---|---|---|---|---|
| 1 | 對不起 | 对不起（一級） | duì bù qǐ | sorry | phrase | 準備級一級<br>Novice 1 |
| 2 | 不錯 | 不错 | bú cuò | not bad | Vs | 準備級二級<br>Novice 2 |
| 3 | 不客氣 | 不客气（一級） | bú kè qì | you're welcome | phrase | 入門級<br>Level 1 |
| 4 | 不同 | 不同 | bù tóng | different | Vs | 基礎級<br>Level 2 |
| 5 | 不久 | 不久 | bù jiǔ | soon | Noun | 基礎級<br>Level 2 |
| 6 | 不好意思 | 不好意思 | bù hǎo yì sī | apologetic | phrase | 入門級<br>Level 1 |
| 7 | 差不多 | 差不多（四級） | chà bù duō | almost | Adv | 基礎級<br>Level 2 |

| 遠（远）<br>yuǎn | 漢語水平考試<br>HSK | 拼音<br>Pin Yin | 英文翻譯<br>English | 詞類<br>Part of Speech | 華語文<br>能力測驗<br>TOCFL |
|---|---|---|---|---|---|
| 1 | 永遠 | 永远（四級） | yǒng yuǎn | forever and always | Adv | 進階級<br>Level 3 |
| 2 | 跳遠 | 跳远 | tiào yuǎn | long jump | Vi | 高階級<br>Level 4 |
| 3 | 遠大 | 远大 | yuǎn dà | manificant | Vs | 高階級<br>Level 4 |
| 4 | 長遠 | 长远 | zhǎng yuǎn | long | Vs | 流利級<br>Level 5 |
| 5 | 遙遠 | 遥远（六級） | yáo yuǎn | distant, far | Vs | 流利級<br>Level 5 |

| 遠（远）yuǎn | 漢語水平考試 HSK | 拼音 Pin Yin | 英文翻譯 English | 詞類 Part of Speech | 華語文能力測驗 TOCFL |
|---|---|---|---|---|---|
| 6 遠方 | 远方 | yuǎn fāng | distance | Noun | NA |
| 7 遠景 | 远景 | yuǎn jǐng | vision | Noun | 流利級 Level 5 |

| 遊（游）yóu | 漢語水平考試 HSK | 拼音 Pin Yin | 英文翻譯 English | 詞類 Part of Speech | 華語文能力測驗 TOCFL |
|---|---|---|---|---|---|
| 1 導遊 | 导游（四級） | dǎo yóu | tourist guide | Noun | 高階級 Level 4 |
| 2 遊戲 | 游戏（三級） | yóu xì | game | Noun | 基礎級 Level 2 |
| 3 遊行 | 游行 | yóu xíng | parade | Vi | 高階級 Level 4 |
| 4 旅遊 | 旅游（二級） | lǚ yóu | tourism | Noun | 進階級 Level 3 |
| 5 遊客 | 游客 | yóu kè | tourist | Noun | 進階級 Level 3 |
| 6 遊玩 | 游玩 | yóu wán | to play | V | NA |
| 7 遊覽 | 游览（五級） | yóu lǎn | to tour | V | 流利級 Level 5 |
| 8 周遊 | 周游 | zhōu yóu | to travel around | V | 流利級 Level 5 |
| 9 游泳 | 游泳（二級） | yóu yǒng | to swim | V-sep | 入門級 Level 1 |

| 必<br>bì | 漢語水平考試<br>HSK | 拼音<br>Pin Yin | 英文翻譯<br>English | 詞類<br>Part of Speech | 華語文<br>能力測驗<br>TOCFL |
|---|---|---|---|---|---|
| 1 | 不必 | 不必 | bú bì | not necessary | Vaux | 基礎級<br>Level 2 |
| 2 | 必要 | 必要（五級） | bì yào | necessary | Noun | 進階級<br>Level 3 |
| 3 | 必須 | 必须（三級） | bì xū | have to | Vs-attr | 基礎級<br>Level 2 |
| 4 | 何必 | 何必（五級） | hé bì | why bother | Adv | 高階級<br>Level 4 |
| 5 | 必然 | 必然（五級） | bì rán | inevitable | Adv | 流利級<br>Level 5 |
| 6 | 必要 | 必要（五級） | bì yào | necessary | Vs | 進階級<br>Level 3 |
| 7 | 何必 | 何必（五級） | hé bì | why bother | Adv | 高階級<br>Level 4 |
| 8 | 未必 | 未必（五級） | wèi bì | not necessarily | Adv | 流利級<br>Level 5 |
| 9 | 勢必 | 势必（六級） | shì bì | bound to | Adv | 流利級<br>Level 5 |
| 10 | 必定 | 必定 | bì dìng | must | Adv | 流利級<br>Level 5 |

| 有<br>yǒu | 漢語水平考試<br>HSK | 拼音<br>Pin Yin | 英文翻譯<br>English | 詞類<br>Part of Speech | 華語文<br>能力測驗<br>TOCFL |
|---|---|---|---|---|---|
| 1 | 有時候 | 有时候 | yǒu shí hòu | sometimes | Adv | 入門級<br>Level 1 |
| 2 | 有用 | 有用 | yǒu yòng | it works | Vs | 入門級<br>Level 1 |

| 有<br>yǒu | 漢語水平考試<br>HSK | 拼音<br>Pin Yin | 英文翻譯<br>English | 詞類<br>Part of<br>Speech | 華語文<br>能力測驗<br>TOCFL |
|---|---|---|---|---|---|
| 3 | 有空 | 有空 | yǒu kòng | available | Vs | 入門級<br>Level 1 |
| 4 | 所有 | 所有（四級） | suǒ yǒu | all | Det | 入門級<br>Level 1 |
| 5 | 沒有 | 没有（一級） | méi yǒu | do not have | Ptc | 準備級一<br>級 Novice<br>1 |
| 6 | 具有 | 具有 | jù yǒu | to have | Vst | 進階級<br>Level 3 |
| 7 | 擁有 | 拥有 | yǒng yǒu | to have | Vst | 進階級<br>Level 3 |
| 8 | 有趣 | 有趣（四級） | yǒu qù | interesting | Vs | 基礎級<br>Level 2 |

| 方<br>fāng | 漢語水平考試<br>HSK | 拼音<br>Pin Yin | 英文翻譯<br>English | 詞類<br>Part of<br>Speech | 華語文<br>能力測驗<br>TOCFL |
|---|---|---|---|---|---|
| 1 | 方便 | 方便（三級） | fāng biàn | convenience | Vs | 準備級二級<br>Novice 2 |
| 2 | 地方 | 地方（三級） | dì fāng | local | Noun | 準備級二級<br>Novice 2 |
| 3 | 方法 | 方法（四級） | fāng fǎ | method | Noun | 入門級<br>Level 1 |
| 4 | 方向 | 方向（四級） | fāng xiàng | direction | Noun | 基礎級<br>Level 2 |
| 5 | 大方 | 大方（五級） | dà fāng | generous | Vs | 進階級<br>Level 3 |

| | 方<br>fāng | 漢語水平考試<br>HSK | 拼音<br>Pin Yin | 英文翻譯<br>English | 詞類<br>Part of<br>Speech | 華語文<br>能力測驗<br>TOCFL |
|---|---|---|---|---|---|---|
| 6 | 對方 | 对方（五級） | duì fāng | the other side | Noun | 進階級<br>Level 3 |
| 7 | 方面 | 方面（四級） | fāng shì | aspect | Noun | 基礎級<br>Level 2 |

## 第一章　【孝順】名言二

父母唯其疾之憂。

Parents are anxious lest their children should be sick.

| 父 | 母 | 唯 | 其 | 疾 | 之 | 憂 |
|---|---|---|---|---|---|---|
| CH1-1 | CH1-1 | | | | | |

| | 唯<br>wéi | 漢語水平考試<br>HSK | 拼音<br>Pin Yin | 英文翻譯<br>English | 詞類<br>Part of<br>Speech | 華語文<br>能力測驗<br>TOCFL |
|---|---|---|---|---|---|---|
| 1 | 唯一 | 唯一（五級） | wéi yī | only | Vs-attr | 高階級<br>Level 4 |
| 2 | 唯獨 | 唯独（六級） | wéi dú | the only | Adj/adv | NA |

| | 其<br>qí | 漢語水平考試<br>HSK | 拼音<br>Pin Yin | 英文翻譯<br>English | 詞類<br>Part of<br>Speech | 華語文<br>能力測驗<br>TOCFL |
|---|---|---|---|---|---|---|
| 1 | 其他 | 其他（三級） | qí tā | other | Det | 入門級<br>Level 1 |
| 2 | 其次 | 其次（四級） | qí cì | secondly | Conj | 進階級<br>Level 3 |
| 3 | 其實 | 其实（三級） | qí shí | in fact | Adv | 基礎級<br>Level 2 |

| | 其 qí | 漢語水平考試 HSK | 拼音 Pin Yin | 英文翻譯 English | 詞類 Part of Speech | 華語文能力測驗 TOCFL |
|---|---|---|---|---|---|---|
| 4 | 其中 | 其中（四級） | qí zhōng | among them | Det | 基礎級 Level 2 |
| 5 | 尤其 | 尤其（四級） | yóu qí | especially | Adv | 基礎級 Level 2 |
| 6 | 極其 | 极其（五級） | jí qí | extremely | Adv | 高階級 Level 4 |
| 7 | 與其 | 与其（五級） | yǔ qí | instead of | Conj | 高階級 Level 4 |
| 8 | 其餘 | 其余（五級） | qí yú | the remaining | Det | 高階級 Level 4 |

| | 疾 jí | 漢語水平考試 HSK | 拼音 Pin Yin | 英文翻譯 English | 詞類 Part of Speech | 華語文能力測驗 TOCFL |
|---|---|---|---|---|---|---|
| 1 | 疾病 | 疾病（六級） | jí bìng | disease | Noun | 高階級 Level 4 |

| | 之 zhī | 漢語水平考試 HSK | 拼音 Pin Yin | 英文翻譯 English | 詞類 Part of Speech | 華語文能力測驗 TOCFL |
|---|---|---|---|---|---|---|
| 1 | 之＝的 | 之（四級） | zhī | possessive term | Noun | NA |
| 2 | 之後 | 之后 | zhī hòu | afterwards | Noun | 進階級 Level 3 |
| 3 | 之前 | 之前 | zhī qián | prior to | Noun | 進階級 Level 3 |
| 4 | 總而言之 | 总而言之（六級） | zǒng ér yán zhī | all in all | Conj | 進階級 Level 3 |

| | 之<br>zhī | 漢語水平考試<br>HSK | 拼音<br>Pin Yin | 英文翻譯<br>English | 詞類<br>Part of<br>Speech | 華語文<br>能力測驗<br>TOCFL |
|---|---|---|---|---|---|---|
| 5 | 總之 | 总之（五級） | zǒng zhī | in short | Conj | 進階級<br>Level 3 |
| 6 | 之間 | 之间 | zhī jiān | between,<br>among | Noun | 進階級<br>Level 3 |

| | 憂<br>yōu | 漢語水平考試<br>HSK | 拼音<br>Pin Yin | 英文翻譯<br>English | 詞類<br>Part of<br>Speech | 華語文<br>能力測驗<br>TOCFL |
|---|---|---|---|---|---|---|
| 1 | 憂鬱 | 忧郁（六級） | yōu yù | depressed | Vs | 高階級<br>Level 4 |
| 2 | 後顧之憂 | 后顾之忧<br>（六級） | hòu gù<br>zhī yōu | Concern,<br>worried-<br>ness | Noun | NA |
| 3 | 無憂無慮 | 无忧无虑<br>（六級） | wú yōu<br>wú lǜ | worry-free | adj | NA |
| 4 | 憂心 | 忧心 | yōu xīn | worry | verb | NA |
| 5 | 憂慮 | 忧虑 | yōu lǜ | concern,<br>worry | Noun | NA |
| 6 | 憂傷 | 忧伤 | yōu<br>shāng | sadness | Noun | NA |

## 第一章 【孝順】名言三

父母之年，不可不知，一則以喜，一則以懼。

The years of parents may by no means not be kept in the memory, as an occasion at once for joy and for fear.

| 父 | 母 | 之 | 年 | 不 | 可 | 不 | 知 |
|---|---|---|---|---|---|---|---|
| CH1-1 | CH1-1 | CH1-2 | | CH1-1 | | CH1-1 | |

| 一 | 則 | 以 | 喜 | 一 | 則 | 以 | 懼（惧） |
|---|---|---|---|---|---|---|---|
|  |  |  |  | 重複 | 重複 | 重複 |  |

| 年<br>nián | 漢語水平考試<br>HSK | 拼音<br>Pin Yin | 英文翻譯<br>English | 詞類<br>Part of Speech | 華語文能力測驗<br>TOCFL |
|---|---|---|---|---|---|
| 1 今年 | 今年 | jīn nián | jīn nián | Noun | 準備級一級 Novice 1 |
| 2 明年 | 明年 | míng nián | míng nián | Noun | 準備級二級 Novice 2 |
| 3 去年 | 年（一級） | qùn ián | qù nián | Noun | 準備級二級 Novice 2 |
| 4 年級 | 年級（三級） | nián jí | nián jí | Noun | 入門級 Level 1 |
| 5 當年 | 当年 | dāng nián | dāng nián | Noun | 進階級 Level 3 |
| 6 年代 | 年代（五級） | nián dài | nián dài | Noun | 進階級 Level 3 |

| 可<br>kě | 漢語水平考試<br>HSK | 拼音<br>Pin Yin | 英文翻譯<br>English | 詞類<br>Part of Speech | 華語文能力測驗<br>TOCFL |
|---|---|---|---|---|---|
| 1 可以 | 可以（二級） | kě yǐ | can | Vaux | 準備級一級 Novice 1 |
| 2 可是 | 可是（四級） | kě shì | but | Conj | 準備級一級 Novice 1 |
| 3 可能 | 可能（二級） | kě néng | may | Vaux | 準備級二級 Novice 2 |
| 4 可愛 | 可爱（三級） | kě ài | lovely | Vs | 入門級 Level 1 |

| | 可<br>kě | 漢語水平考試<br>HSK | 拼音<br>Pin Yin | 英文翻譯<br>English | 詞類<br>Part of Speech | 華語文<br>能力測驗<br>TOCFL |
|---|---|---|---|---|---|---|
| 5 | 可憐 | 可怜（四級） | kě lián | pathetic | Vs | 進階級<br>Level 3 |
| 6 | 可怕 | 可怕（五級） | kě pà | scary, terrible | Vs | 基礎級<br>Level 2 |

| | 知<br>zhī | 漢語水平考試<br>HSK | 拼音<br>Pin Yin | 英文翻譯<br>English | 詞類<br>Part of Speech | 華語文<br>能力測驗<br>TOCFL |
|---|---|---|---|---|---|---|
| 1 | 知道 | 知道（二級） | zhī dào | know | Vst | 準備級一級<br>Novice 1 |
| 2 | 通知 | 通知（四級） | tōng zhī | to notify | V | 進階級<br>Level 3 |
| 3 | 知識 | 知识（四級） | zhī shì | knowledge | Noun | 基礎級<br>Level 2 |
| 4 | 須知 | 须知（六級） | xū zhī | notice | Noun | 高階級<br>Level 4 |
| 5 | 不知不覺 | 知觉（六級） | bù zhī<br>bùj ué | unconsciously | Adv | 流利級<br>Level 5 |
| 6 | 知足常樂 | 知足常乐<br>（六級） | zhī zú<br>cháng lè | contented | Vs | 知足（流利級 Level 5） |

| | 一<br>yī | 漢語水平考試<br>HSK | 拼音<br>Pin Yin | 英文翻譯<br>English | 詞類<br>Part of Speech | 華語文<br>能力測驗<br>TOCFL |
|---|---|---|---|---|---|---|
| 1 | 一 | 一（一級） | yī | One | Number | 準備級一級<br>Novice 1 |
| 2 | 一點 | 一点儿（一級） | yī diǎn(r) | a little | Det | 準備級二級<br>Novice 2 |

| | 一<br>yī | 漢語水平考試<br>HSK | 拼音<br>Pin Yin | 英文翻譯<br>English | 詞類<br>Part of Speech | 華語文<br>能力測驗<br>TOCFL |
|---|---|---|---|---|---|---|
| 3 | 一些 | 一些（一級） | yī xiē | some | Det | 準備級二級<br>Novice 2 |
| 4 | 一樣 | 一样（三級） | yī yàng | same | Vs | 準備級二級<br>Novice 2 |
| 5 | 一起 | 一起（二級） | yī qǐ | together | Adv | 準備級二級<br>Novice 2 |
| 6 | 一半 | 半（三級） | yī bàn | half | Det | 入門級<br>Level 1 |
| 7 | 一定 | 一定（三級） | yī dìng | for sure | Adv | 準備級二級<br>Novice 2 |
| 8 | 一會兒 | 一会儿（三級） | yī huǐ ér | a while | Noun | 入門級<br>Level 1 |
| 9 | 一直 | 一直（三級） | yī zhí | always | Adv | 入門級<br>Level 1 |
| 10 | 一般 | 一般（三級） | yī bān | general | Vs | 基礎級<br>Level 2 |

| | 則<br>zé | 漢語水平考試<br>HSK | 拼音<br>Pin Yin | 英文翻譯<br>English | 詞類<br>Part of Speech | 華語文<br>能力測驗<br>TOCFL |
|---|---|---|---|---|---|---|
| 1 | 否則 | 否則（四級） | fǒu zé | otherwise | Conj | 進階級<br>Level 3 |
| 2 | 規則 | 规则（五級） | guī zé | rule，<br>regulations | Noun | 高階級<br>Level 4 |
| 3 | 原則 | 原则（五級） | yuán zé | principle | Noun | 高階級<br>Level 4 |

| 則 zé | 漢語水平考試 HSK | 拼音 Pin Yin | 英文翻譯 English | 詞類 Part of Speech | 華語文 能力測驗 TOCFL |
|---|---|---|---|---|---|
| 4 | 原則上 | 原則上 | yuán zé shàng | in principle | Adv | 高階級 Level 4 |
| 5 | 法則 | 法則 | fǎ zé | law, regulations | Noun | 流利級 Level 5 |
| 6 | 準則 | 准則（六級） | zhǔn zé | guidelines | Noun | 流利級 Level 5 |

| 以 yǐ | 漢語水平考試 HSK | 拼音 Pin Yin | 英文翻譯 English | 詞類 Part of Speech | 華語文 能力測驗 TOCFL |
|---|---|---|---|---|---|
| 1 | 可以 | 可以（二級） | kě yǐ | can | Vaux | 準備級一級 Novice 1 |
| 2 | 以前 | 以前（三級） | yǐ qián | before | Noun | 準備級一級 Novice 1 |
| 3 | 以後 | 以后 | yǐ hòu | after | Noun | 準備級一級 Novice 1 |
| 4 | 以來 | 以来（五級） | yǐ lái | since | Noun | 進階級 Level 3 |

| 喜 xǐ | 漢語水平考試 HSK | 拼音 Pin Yin | 英文翻譯 English | 詞類 Part of Speech | 華語文 能力測驗 TOCFL |
|---|---|---|---|---|---|
| 1 | 喜歡 | 喜欢（一級） | xǐ huān | like | Vst | 準備級一級 Novice 1 |
| 2 | 恭喜 | 恭喜（五級） | gōng xǐ | congratu-lations | V | 進階級 Level 3 |
| 3 | 喜愛 | 喜爱 | xǐ ài | favorite | Vst | 進階級 Level 3 |

| 喜<br>xǐ | 漢語水平考試<br>HSK | 拼音<br>Pin Yin | 英文翻譯<br>English | 詞類<br>Part of<br>Speech | 華語文<br>能力測驗<br>TOCFL |
|---|---|---|---|---|---|
| 4 | 歡喜 | 欢喜 | huān xǐ | joy | Vs | 高階級<br>Level 4 |
| 5 | 可喜 | 可喜 | kě xǐ | gratifying | Vs | 高階級<br>Level 4 |
| 6 | 喜劇 | 喜剧 | xǐ jù | comedy | Noun | 高階級<br>Level 4 |

| 懼（惧）<br>jù | 漢語水平考試<br>HSK | 拼音<br>Pin Yin | 英文翻譯<br>English | 詞類<br>Part of<br>Speech | 華語文<br>能力測驗<br>TOCFL |
|---|---|---|---|---|---|
| 1 | 恐懼 | 恐惧（六級） | kǒng jù | fear | Vs | 流利級<br>Level 5 |
| 2 | 畏懼 | 畏惧（六級） | wèi jù | fear, to be scared | Noun | NA |

## 第二章　【朋友】名言一

四海之內，皆兄弟也。

To the superior and benevolent man (educated person), all within the four seas will be his brothers.

| 四 | 海 | 之 | 內 | 皆 | 兄 | 弟 | 也 |
|---|---|---|---|---|---|---|---|
| | | CH1-2 | | | | | |

| 四<br>sì | 漢語水平考試<br>HSK | 拼音<br>Pin Yin | 英文翻譯<br>English | 詞類<br>Part of<br>Speech | 華語文<br>能力測驗<br>TOCFL |
|---|---|---|---|---|---|
| 1 | 四 | 四（一級） | sì | four | Noun | 準備級一級<br>Novice 1 |

| | 四<br>sì | 漢語水平考試<br>HSK | 拼音<br>Pin Yin | 英文翻譯<br>English | 詞類<br>Part of Speech | 華語文能力測驗<br>TOCFL |
|---|---|---|---|---|---|---|
| 2 | 四處 | 四处 | sì chǔ | around | Adv | 高階級<br>Level 4 |
| 3 | 四方 | 四方 | sì fāng | four directions, everywhere | Noun | 高階級<br>Level 4 |
| 4 | 四季 | 四季 | sì jì | four seasons | Noun | 高階級<br>Level 4 |
| 5 | 四週 | 四周 | sì zhōu | all around | Noun | 高階級<br>Level 4 |

| | 海<br>hǎi | 漢語水平考試<br>HSK | 拼音<br>Pin Yin | 英文翻譯<br>English | 詞類<br>Part of Speech | 華語文能力測驗<br>TOCFL |
|---|---|---|---|---|---|---|
| 1 | 海 | 海 | hǎi | sea | Noun | 入門級<br>Level 1 |
| 2 | 海邊 | 海边 | hǎi biān | seaside | Noun | NA |
| 3 | 海報 | 海报 | hǎi bào | poster | Noun | 進階級<br>Level 3 |
| 4 | 海灘 | 海滩 | hǎi tān | beach | Noun | 進階級<br>Level 3 |
| 5 | 海洋 | 海洋（四級） | hǎi yáng | ocean | Noun | 進階級<br>Level 3 |
| 6 | 海關 | 海关（五級） | hǎi guān | customs | Noun | 高階級<br>Level 4 |

| 内<br>nèi | 漢語水平考試<br>HSK | 拼音<br>Pin Yin | 英文翻譯<br>English | 詞類<br>Part of Speech | 華語文<br>能力測驗<br>TOCFL |
|---|---|---|---|---|---|
| 1 | 内衣 | 内衣 | nèi yī | underwear | Noun | 基礎級<br>Level 2 |
| 2 | 國内 | 国内 | guó nèi | domestic | Noun | 進階級<br>Level 3 |
| 3 | 内容 | 内容（四級） | nèi róng | content | Noun | 進階級<br>Level 3 |
| 4 | 以内 | 以内 | yǐ nèi | within | Noun | NA |
| 5 | 内部 | 内部（五級） | nèi bù | interNAl | Noun | 高階級<br>Level 4 |
| 6 | 内地 | 内地 | nèi dì | mainland | Noun | 高階級<br>Level 4 |

| 皆<br>jiē | 漢語水平考試<br>HSK | 拼音<br>Pin Yin | 英文翻譯<br>English | 詞類<br>Part of Speech | 華語文<br>能力測驗<br>TOCFL |
|---|---|---|---|---|---|
| 1 | 皆 | 皆（六級） | jiē | all | Adv | 流利級<br>Level 5 |
| 2 | 皆可 | 皆可 | jiē kě | both | Adv | NA |
| 3 | 皆有 | 皆有 | jiē yǒu | all have | Adv | NA |
| 4 | 皆知 | 皆知 | jiē zhī | well-known | Adv | NA |

| 兄<br>xiōng | 漢語水平考試<br>HSK | 拼音<br>Pin Yin | 英文翻譯<br>English | 詞類<br>Part of Speech | 華語文<br>能力測驗<br>TOCFL |
|---|---|---|---|---|---|
| 1 | 兄弟 | 兄弟（五級） | xiōng dì | brothers | Noun | 基礎級<br>Level 2 |
| 2 | 弟兄 | 弟兄 | dì xiong | brother,<br>buddy | Noun | 流利級<br>Level 5 |

| 兄<br>xiōng | 漢語水平考試<br>HSK | 拼音<br>Pin Yin | 英文翻譯<br>English | 詞類<br>Part of<br>Speech | 華語文<br>能力測驗<br>TOCFL |
|---|---|---|---|---|---|
| 3 | 兄妹 | 兄妹 | xiōng mèi | older brother and younger sister | Noun | NA |

| 弟<br>dì | 漢語水平考試<br>HSK | 拼音<br>Pin Yin | 英文翻譯<br>English | 詞類<br>Part of<br>Speech | 華語文<br>能力測驗<br>TOCFL |
|---|---|---|---|---|---|
| 1 | 弟弟 | 弟弟（二級） | dì dì | little brother | Noun | 準備級一級<br>Novice 1 |
| 2 | 兄弟 | 兄弟（五級） | xiōng dì | brothers | Noun | 基礎級<br>Level 2 |
| 3 | 徒弟 | 徒弟（六級） | tú dì | apprentice | Noun | 流利級<br>Level 5 |
| 4 | 子弟 | 子弟 | zǐ dì | disciples | Noun | 流利級<br>Level 5 |

| 也<br>yě | 漢語水平考試<br>HSK | 拼音<br>Pin Yin | 英文翻譯<br>English | 詞類<br>Part of<br>Speech | 華語文<br>能力測驗<br>TOCFL |
|---|---|---|---|---|---|
| 1 | 也 | 也（二級） | yě | and, also | Adv | 準備級一級<br>Novice 1 |
| 2 | 也許 | 也许（四級） | yě xǔ | maybe | Adv | 基礎級<br>Level 2 |
| 3 | 也好 | 也好 | yě hǎo | fine, as well | Conj | 進階級<br>Level 3 |

# 第二章 【朋友】名言二

與朋友交，言而有信。

In our interaction with friends, one's words should be sincere.

| 與（与） | 朋 | 友 | 交 | 言 | 而 | 有 | 信 |
|---|---|---|---|---|---|---|---|
|  |  |  |  |  |  | CH1-1 |  |

| | 與<br>yǔ | 漢語水平考試<br>HSK | 拼音<br>Pin Yin | 英文翻譯<br>English | 詞類<br>Part of Speech | 華語文能力測驗<br>TOCFL |
|---|---|---|---|---|---|---|
| 1 | 與 | 与（四級） | yǔ | with | Conj | 進階級<br>Level 3 |
| 2 | 參與 | 参与（五級） | cān yǔ | to participate | Verb | 高階級<br>Level 4 |
| 3 | 與其 | 与其（五級） | yǔ qí | instead of | Conj | 高階級<br>Level 4 |
| 4 | 與會 | 与会 | yǔ huì | to attend | Vi | 流利級<br>Level 5 |

| | 朋<br>péng | 漢語水平考試<br>HSK | 拼音<br>Pin Yin | 英文翻譯<br>English | 詞類<br>Part of Speech | 華語文能力測驗<br>TOCFL |
|---|---|---|---|---|---|---|
| 1 | 朋友 | 朋友（一級） | péng yǒu | friend | Noun | 準備級一級<br>Novice 1 |
| 2 | 小朋友 | 小朋友 | xiǎo péng yǒu | kids, children | Noun | 入門級<br>Level 1 |
| 3 | 好朋友 | 好朋友 | hǎo péng yǒu | good friend | Noun | NA |
| 4 | 老朋友 | 老朋友 | lǎo péng yǒu | old friend | Noun | NA |

| 友<br>yǒu | 漢語水平考試<br>HSK | 拼音<br>Pin Yin | 英文翻譯<br>English | 詞類<br>Part of Speech | 華語文<br>能力測驗<br>TOCFL |
|---|---|---|---|---|---|
| 1 | 朋友 | 朋友（一級） | péng yǒu | friend | Noun | 準備級一級<br>Novice 1 |
| 2 | 交友 | 交友 | jiāo yǒu | to make friends | Vi | 進階級<br>Level 3 |
| 3 | 友誼 | 友谊（四級） | yǒu yí | friendship | Noun | 進階級<br>Level 3 |
| 4 | 校友 | 校友 | xiào yǒu | alumni | Noun | 高階級<br>Level 4 |
| 5 | 友好 | 友好（四級） | yǒu hǎo | friendly | Vs | 高階級<br>Level 4 |
| 6 | 筆友 | 笔友 | bǐ yǒu | pen pal | Noun | 流利級<br>Level 5 |

| 交<br>jiāo | 漢語水平考試<br>HSK | 拼音<br>Pin Yin | 英文翻譯<br>English | 詞類<br>Part of Speech | 華語文<br>能力測驗<br>TOCFL |
|---|---|---|---|---|---|
| 1 | 交 | 交（四級） | jiāo | to cross | Verb | 入門級<br>Level 1 |
| 2 | 交通 | 交通（四級） | jiāo tōng | traffic | Noun | 基礎級<br>Level 2 |
| 3 | 交流 | 交流（四級） | jiāo liú | to communicate with | Vi | 進階級<br>Level 3 |
| 4 | 交友 | 交友 | jiāo yǒu | to make friends | Vi | 進階級<br>Level 3 |
| 5 | 交換 | 交换（五級） | jiāo huàn | to exchange | Verb | 高階級<br>Level 4 |
| 6 | 交際 | 交际（五級） | jiāo jì | to associate with | Vi | 高階級<br>Level 4 |

| 言 yán | 漢語水平考試 HSK | 拼音 Pin Yin | 英文翻譯 English | 詞類 Part of Speech | 華語文能力測驗 TOCFL |
|---|---|---|---|---|---|
| 1 語言 | 语言（四級） | yǔ yán | language | Noun | 入門級 Level 1 |
| 2 留言 | 留言 | liú yán | to leave a message | Vi | 進階級 Level 3 |
| 3 總而言之 | 总而言之 | zǒng ér yán zhī | all in all | Conj | 進階級 Level 3 |
| 4 發言 | 发言（五級） | fā yán | to speak | V-sep | 高階級 Level 4 |
| 5 言論 | 言论（六級） | yán lùn | speech | Noun | 流利級 Level 5 |
| 6 謠言 | 谣言（六級） | yáo yán | rumor | Noun | 流利級 Level 5 |
| 7 寓言 | 寓言（六級） | yù yán | fable | Noun | 流利級 Level 5 |

| 而 ér | 漢語水平考試 HSK | 拼音 Pin Yin | 英文翻譯 English | 詞類 Part of Speech | 華語文能力測驗 TOCFL |
|---|---|---|---|---|---|
| 1 而且 | 不但……而且……（三級） | bú dàn ér qiě | not only but also | Conj | 基礎級 Level 2 |
| 2 反而 | 反而 | fǎn ér | instead | Conj | 進階級 Level 3 |
| 3 而已 | 而已 | ér yǐ | that's it | Ptc | 高階級 Level 4 |
| 4 然而 | 然而（四級） | rán ér | however | Conj | 高階級 Level 4 |

| | 信<br>xìn | 漢語水平考試<br>HSK | 拼音<br>Pin Yin | 英文翻譯<br>English | 詞類<br>Part of<br>Speech | 華語文<br>能力測驗<br>TOCFL |
|---|---|---|---|---|---|---|
| 1 | 信 | | xìn | letter | Noun | 入門級<br>Level 1 |
| 2 | 信封 | 信封（四級） | xìn fēng | envelope | Noun | 入門級<br>Level 1 |
| 3 | 相信 | 相信（三級） | xiāng xìn | to believe | Vst | 入門級<br>Level 1 |
| 4 | 信用卡 | 信用卡（三級） | xìn yòng qiǎ | credit card | Noun | 入門級<br>Level 1 |
| 5 | 信心 | 信心（四級） | xìn xīn | confidence | Noun | 進階級<br>Level 3 |
| 6 | 自信 | 自信（四級） | zì xìn | self-confidence | Noun | 進階級<br>Level 3 |

## 第二章 【朋友】名言三

老者安之，朋友信之，少者懷之。

My wishes are, to provide the aged comfort; to show the friends sincerity; to treat the young tenderly.

| 老 | 者 | 安 | 之 | 朋 | 友 | 信 | 之 |
|---|---|---|---|---|---|---|---|
| | | | CH1-2 | CH2-2 | CH2-1 | | CH1-2 |

| 少 | 者 | 懷（怀） | 之 |
|---|---|---|---|
| | | | CH1-2 |

| | 老<br>lǎo | 漢語水平考試<br>HSK | 拼音<br>Pin Yin | 英文翻譯<br>English | 詞類<br>Part of<br>Speech | 華語文<br>能力測驗<br>TOCFL |
|---|---|---|---|---|---|---|
| 1 | 老師 | 老师（一級） | lǎo shī | teacher | Noun | 準備級一級<br>Novice 1 |

| | 老<br>lǎo | 漢語水平考試<br>HSK | 拼音<br>Pin Yin | 英文翻譯<br>English | 詞類<br>Part of Speech | 華語文<br>能力測驗<br>TOCFL |
|---|---|---|---|---|---|---|
| 2 | 老闆 | 老板（五級） | lǎo bǎn | boss | Noun | 入門級<br>Level 1 |
| 3 | 老人 | 老人 | lǎo rén | old man | Noun | 入門級<br>Level 1 |
| 4 | 老公 | 老公 | lǎo gōng | husband | Noun | 進階級<br>Level 3 |
| 5 | 老虎 | 老虎（四級） | lǎo hǔ | tiger | Noun | 進階級<br>Level 3 |
| 6 | 老婆 | 老婆（五級） | lǎo pó | wife | Noun | 進階級<br>Level 3 |

| | 者<br>zhě | 漢語水平考試<br>HSK | 拼音<br>Pin Yin | 英文翻譯<br>English | 詞類<br>Part of Speech | 華語文<br>能力測驗<br>TOCFL |
|---|---|---|---|---|---|---|
| 1 | 記者 | 记者（四級） | jì zhě | reporter | Noun | 進階級<br>Level 3 |
| 2 | 讀者 | 读者 | dú zhě | reader | Noun | 進階級<br>Level 3 |
| 3 | 作者 | 作者（四級） | zuò zhě | author | Noun | 進階級<br>Level 3 |
| 4 | 或者 | 或者（三級） | huò zhě | or | Conj | 基礎級<br>Level 2 |
| 5 | 患者 | 患者（六級） | huàn zhě | patient | Noun | 流利級<br>Level 5 |

| | 安<br>ān | 漢語水平考試<br>HSK | 拼音<br>Pin Yin | 英文翻譯<br>English | 詞類<br>Part of<br>Speech | 華語文<br>能力測驗<br>TOCFL |
|---|---|---|---|---|---|---|
| 1 | 安靜 | 安靜（三級） | ān jìng | quiet，<br>silent | Vs | 進階級<br>Level 3 |
| 2 | 安全 | 安全（四級） | ān quán | to be safe | Vs | 基礎級<br>Level 2 |
| 3 | 安定 | 安定 | ān dìng | to secure | Vs | 進階級<br>Level 3 |
| 4 | 安排 | 安排（四級） | ān pái | to arrange | Noun | 進階級<br>Level 3 |
| 5 | 安心 | 安心 | ān xīn | peace of<br>mind | Vs | 進階級<br>Level 3 |
| 6 | 平安 | 平安（五級） | píng ān | safe | Vs | 進階級<br>Level 3 |

| | 少<br>shào, shǎo | 漢語水平考試<br>HSK | 拼音<br>Pin Yin | 英文翻譯<br>English | 詞類<br>Part of<br>Speech | 華語文<br>能力測驗<br>TOCFL |
|---|---|---|---|---|---|---|
| 1 | 少年<br>shào | 少年 | shào nián | young man | Noun | 高階級<br>Level 4 |
| 2 | 少女<br>shào | 少女 | shào nǚ | young lady | Noun | 高階級<br>Level 4 |
| 3 | 青少年<br>shào | 青少年（五級） | qīng shào nián | juvenile | Noun | 進階級<br>Level 3 |
| 4 | 多少<br>shǎo | 多少（一級） | duō shǎo | how many | Noun | 高階級<br>Level 4 |
| 5 | 少 shǎo | 少（一級） | shǎo | less | Vs-pred | 準備級二級<br>Novice 2 |

| | 少<br>shào, shǎo | 漢語水平考試<br>HSK | 拼音<br>Pin Yin | 英文翻譯<br>English | 詞類<br>Part of<br>Speech | 華語文<br>能力測驗<br>TOCFL |
|---|---|---|---|---|---|---|
| 6 | 減少<br>shǎo | 减少（四級） | jiǎn shǎo | to reduce | Vpt | 進階級<br>Level 3 |
| 7 | 至少<br>shǎo | 至少（四級） | zhì shǎo | at least | Adv | 進階級<br>Level 3 |
| 8 | 缺少<br>shǎo | 缺少（四級） | quē shǎo | lack of | Verb,<br>Adj. | 高階級<br>Level 4 |

| | 懷（怀）<br>huái | 漢語水平考試<br>HSK | 拼音<br>Pin Yin | 英文翻譯<br>English | 詞類<br>Part of<br>Speech | 華語文<br>能力測驗<br>TOCFL |
|---|---|---|---|---|---|---|
| 1 | 懷念 | 怀念（五級） | huái niàn | to miss | Vst | 高階級<br>Level 4 |
| 2 | 懷孕 | 怀孕（五級） | huái yùn | pregNAncy | Vi | 高階級<br>Level 4 |
| 3 | 關懷 | 关怀（六級） | guān huái | care | Vst | 流利級<br>Level 5 |
| 4 | 懷疑 | 怀疑（四級） | huái yí | doubt | Vst | 高階級<br>Level 4 |
| 5 | 滿懷 | 满怀 | mǎn huái | to be full of | Vst | 流利級<br>Level 5 |

## 第三章 【君子或小人】名言一

君子不器。

The Master said, "The accomplished scholar is not a utensil."

| 君 | 子 | 不 | 器 |
|---|---|---|---|
| | | CH1-1 | |

| 君<br>jūn | 漢語水平考試<br>HSK | 拼音<br>Pin Yin | 英文翻譯<br>English | 詞類<br>Part of Speech | 華語文<br>能力測驗<br>TOCFL |
|---|---|---|---|---|---|
| 1 | 國君 | 国君 | guó jūn | moNArch | Noun | 流利級<br>Level 5 |
| 2 | 君主 | 君主 | jūn zhǔ | emperor | Noun | NA |
| 3 | 君子 | 君子（六級） | jūn zǐ | Gentleman | Noun | NA |

| 子<br>zǐ | 漢語水平考試<br>HSK | 拼音<br>Pin Yin | 英文翻譯<br>English | 詞類<br>Part of Speech | 華語文<br>能力測驗<br>TOCFL |
|---|---|---|---|---|---|
| 1 | 孩子 | 孩子 | hái zǐ | child | Noun | 準備級二級<br>Novice 2 |
| 2 | 車（子） | 车子 | chē<br>(zǐ) | car | Noun | 準備級一級<br>Novice 1 |
| 3 | 兒子 | 儿子（一級） | ér zǐ | son | Noun | 準備級二級<br>Novice 2 |
| 4 | 房子 | 房子 | fáng zǐ | house | Noun | 準備級二級<br>Novice 2 |
| 5 | 褲子 | 裤子 | kù zǐ | pants | Noun | NA |
| 6 | 電子郵件 | 电子邮件<br>（三級） | diàn zǐ<br>yóu jiàn | e-mail | N | 入門級<br>Level 1 |

| 不<br>bú, bù | 漢語水平考試<br>HSK | 拼音<br>Pin Yin | 英文翻譯<br>English | 詞類<br>Part of Speech | 華語文<br>能力測驗<br>TOCFL |
|---|---|---|---|---|---|
| 1 | 不斷 | 不断（五級） | bú duàn | non-stop,<br>continue | Adv | 進階級<br>Level 3 |
| 2 | 不過 | 不过（四級） | bú guò | but | Adv | 入門級<br>Level 1 |

| 不<br>bú, bù | 漢語水平考試<br>HSK | 拼音<br>Pin Yin | 英文翻譯<br>English | 詞類<br>Part of<br>Speech | 華語文<br>能力測驗<br>TOCFL |
|---|---|---|---|---|---|
| 3 不見了 | 不见得（五級） | bú jiàn le | gone,<br>disappear | Vp | NA |
| 4 不好意思 | 不好意思<br>（五級） | bú hǎo<br>yì sī | sorry | phrase | 入門級<br>Level 1 |
| 5 不得了 | 不得了（五級） | bú dé le | terrible,<br>terrific | Vs | 基礎級<br>Level 2 |

| 器<br>qì | 漢語水平考試<br>HSK | 拼音<br>Pin Yin | 英文翻譯<br>English | 詞類<br>Part of<br>Speech | 華語文<br>能力測驗<br>TOCFL |
|---|---|---|---|---|---|
| 1 容器 | 容器（六級） | róng qì | container | Noun | 流利級<br>Level 5 |
| 2 陶器 | 陶器 | táo qì | pottery | Noun | 流利級<br>Level 5 |
| 3 玉器 | 玉器 | yù qì | jade | Noun | 流利級<br>Level 5 |
| 4 樂器 | 乐器（五級） | yuè qì | musical<br>instrument | Noun | 基礎級<br>Level 2 |
| 5 機器 | 机器（五級） | jī qì | machine | Noun | 進階級<br>Level 3 |

## 第三章　【君子或小人】名言二

君子求諸己，小人求諸人。

What the superior man seeks, is in himself. What the mean man seeks, is in others.

| 君 | 子 | 求 | 諸<br>（诸） | 己 | 小 | 人 | 求 | 諸<br>（诸） | 人 |
|---|---|---|---|---|---|---|---|---|---|
| CH3-1 | CH3-1 | | | | | | 重複 | 重複 | 重複 |

| 求<br>qiú | 漢語水平考試<br>HSK | 拼音<br>Pin Yin | 英文翻譯<br>English | 詞類<br>Part of Speech | 華語文<br>能力測驗<br>TOCFL |
|---|---|---|---|---|---|
| 1 要求 | 要求（三級） | yào qiú | a claim<br>a request | Noun | 基礎級<br>Level 2 |
| 2 請求 | 请求（五級） | qǐng qiú | to request | Verb | 進階級<br>Level 3 |
| 3 需求 | 需求（六級） | xū qiú | a demand | Noun | 進階級<br>Level 3 |
| 4 追求 | 追求（五級） | zhuī qiú | to pursue | Verb | 進階級<br>Level 3 |
| 5 求學 | 求学 | qiú xué | to study | Vi | 流利級<br>Level 5 |
| 6 求婚 | 求婚 | qiú hūn | to propose | V-sep | 高階級<br>Level 4 |
| 7 謀求 | 谋求（六級） | móu qiú | to seek | Verb | NA |

| 諸（诸）<br>zhū | 漢語水平考試<br>HSK | 拼音<br>Pin Yin | 英文翻譯<br>English | 詞類<br>Part of Speech | 華語文<br>能力測驗<br>TOCFL |
|---|---|---|---|---|---|
| 1 諸多 | 诸多 | zhū duō | many | Det | 流利級<br>Level 5 |
| 2 諸位 | 诸位（六級） | zhū wèi | everyone,<br>each person | Noun | NA |

| 己<br>jǐ | 漢語水平考試<br>HSK | 拼音<br>Pin Yin | 英文翻譯<br>English | 詞類<br>Part of Speech | 華語文<br>能力測驗<br>TOCFL |
|---|---|---|---|---|---|
| 1 自己 | 自己（三級） | zì jǐ | oneself | Noun | 準備級二級<br>Novice 2 |

| 己 jǐ | | 漢語水平考試 HSK | 拼音 Pin Yin | 英文翻譯 English | 詞類 Part of Speech | 華語文能力測驗 TOCFL |
|---|---|---|---|---|---|---|
| 2 | 各抒己見 | 各抒己见（六級） | gè shū jǐ jiàn | express one's opinions | Noun | NA |

| 小 xiǎo | | 漢語水平考試 HSK | 拼音 Pin Yin | 英文翻譯 English | 詞類 Part of Speech | 華語文能力測驗 TOCFL |
|---|---|---|---|---|---|---|
| 1 | 小姐 | 小姐（一級） | xiǎo jiě | miss | Noun | 準備級二級 Novice 2 |
| 2 | 小時 | 小时（二級） | xiǎo shí | hour | Noun | 準備級一級 Novice 1 |
| 3 | 小孩 | 小孩 | xiǎo hái | child | Noun | 準備級一級 Novice 1 |
| 4 | 小心 | 小心（三級） | xiǎo xīn | be careful | Vs, Adj | 入門級 Level 1 |
| 5 | 小吃 | 小吃（四級） | xiǎo chī | sNAck | Noun | 準備級二級 Novice 2 |
| 6 | 小麥 | 小麦（五級） | xiǎo mài | wheat | Noun | 高階級 Level 4 |
| 7 | 小氣 | 小气（五級） | xiǎo qì | stingy | Vs, Adj | 高階級 Level 4 |
| 8 | 小說 | 小说（四級） | xiǎo shuō | fiction, novel | Noun | 進階級 Level 3 |

| | 人<br>rén | 漢語水平考試<br>HSK | 拼音<br>Pin Yin | 英文翻譯<br>English | 詞類<br>Part of Speech | 華語文<br>能力測驗<br>TOCFL |
|---|---|---|---|---|---|---|
| 1 | 人 | 人（一級） | rén | people | Noun | 準備級一級<br>Novice 1 |
| 2 | 別人 | 別人（三級） | bié rén | other people | Noun | 入門級<br>Level 1 |
| 3 | 個人 | 个人（五級） | gè rén | persoNAl | Noun | 進階級<br>Level 3 |
| 4 | 成人 | 成人（五級） | chéng rén | adult | Noun | 高階級<br>Level 4 |
| 5 | 主人 | 主人（五級） | zhǔ rén | host | Noun | 基礎級<br>Level 2 |
| 6 | 客人 | 客人（三級） | kè rén | guest | Noun | 入門級<br>Level 1 |
| 7 | 敵人 | 敌人（五級） | dí rén | enemy | Noun | 進階級<br>Level 3 |
| 8 | 情人 | 情人 | qíng rén | lover | Noun | 進階級<br>Level 3 |
| 9 | 工人 | 工人（五級） | gōng rén | worker | Noun | 入門級<br>Level 1 |

## 第三章　【君子或小人】名言三

君子謀道不謀食。

The object of the superior man is truth. Food is not his object.

| 君 | 子 | 謀（谋） | 道 | 不 | 謀（谋） | 食 |
|---|---|---|---|---|---|---|
| CH3-1 | CH3-1 | | | CH1-1 | CH3-3 | |

| 謀（谋）<br>móu | 漢語水平考試<br>HSK | 拼音<br>Pin Yin | 英文翻譯<br>English | 詞類<br>Part of<br>Speech | 華語文<br>能力測驗<br>TOCFL |
|---|---|---|---|---|---|
| 1 | 參謀 | 参谋（六級） | cān móu | staff | Noun | 流利級<br>Level 5 |
| 2 | 謀求 | 谋求（六級） | móu qiú | to seek | Vi | NA |
| 3 | 陰謀 | 阴谋（六級） | yīn móu | conspiracy | Noun | 流利級<br>Level 5 |
| 4 | 謀生 | 谋生 | móu shēng | make a living | Vi | 流利級<br>Level 5 |

| 道<br>dào | 漢語水平考試<br>HSK | 拼音<br>Pin Yin | 英文翻譯<br>English | 詞類<br>Part of<br>Speech | 華語文<br>能力測驗<br>TOCFL |
|---|---|---|---|---|---|
| 1 | 知道 | 知道（二級） | zhī dào | to know | Vst | 準備級一級<br>Novice 1 |
| 2 | 街道 | 街道（三級） | jiē dào | street | Noun | 高階級<br>Level 4 |
| 3 | 道歉 | 道歉（四級） | dào qiàn | to apologize | V-sep | 進階級<br>Level 3 |
| 4 | 味道 | 味道（四級） | wèi dào | to taste | Noun | 入門級<br>Level 1 |
| 5 | 難道 | 难道（四級） | nán dào | could it be that？ | Adv | 高階級<br>Level 4 |
| 6 | 道德 | 道德（五級） | dào dé | moral | Noun | 進階級<br>Level 3 |

| | 食<br>shí | 漢語水平考試<br>HSK | 拼音<br>Pin Yin | 英文翻譯<br>English | 詞類<br>Part of<br>Speech | 華語文<br>能力測驗<br>TOCFL |
|---|---|---|---|---|---|---|
| 1 | 食物 | 食物（五級） | shí wù | food | Noun | 準備級二級<br>Novice 2 |
| 2 | 糧食 | 粮食（五級） | liáng shí | food | Noun | 高階級<br>Level 4 |
| 3 | 飲食 | 饮食（六級） | yǐn shí | diet | Noun | 高階級<br>Level 4 |
| 4 | 美食 | 美食 | měi shí | gourmet | Noun | 高階級<br>Level 4 |
| 5 | 零食 | 零食（五級） | líng shí | sNAcks | Noun | NA |
| 6 | 素食 | 素食（六級） | sù shí | vegetarian<br>food | Noun | 高階級<br>Level 4 |

## 第四章　【學習】名言一

知之為知之，不知為不知，是知也。

When you know a thing, to hold that you know it; and when you do not know a thing, to allow that you do not know it - this is how to obtain knowledge.

| 知 | 之 | 為 | 知 | 之 |
|---|---|---|---|---|
| CH1-3 | CH1-2 | | CH1-3 | CH1-2 |

| 不 | 知 | 為（为） | 不 | 知 | 是 | 知 | 也 |
|---|---|---|---|---|---|---|---|
| CH1-1 | CH1-3 | CH4-1 | CH1-1 | CH1-3 | | CH1-3 | CH2-1 |

| | 知<br>zhī | 漢語水平考試<br>HSK | 拼音<br>Pin Yin | 英文翻譯<br>English | 詞類<br>Part of<br>Speech | 華語文<br>能力測驗<br>TOCFL |
|---|---|---|---|---|---|---|
| 1 | 知道 | 知道（二級） | zhī dào | know | Vst | 準備級一級<br>Novice 1 |

| | 知<br>zhī | 漢語水平考試<br>HSK | 拼音<br>Pin Yin | 英文翻譯<br>English | 詞類<br>Part of<br>Speech | 華語文<br>能力測驗<br>TOCFL |
|---|---|---|---|---|---|---|
| 2 | 通知 | 通知（四級） | tōng zhī | to notify | V | 進階級<br>Level 3 |
| 3 | 知識 | 知识（四級） | zhī shì | knowledge | Noun | 基礎級<br>Level 2 |
| 4 | 須知 | 须知（六級） | xū zhī | notice | Noun | 高階級<br>Level 4 |
| 5 | 不知不覺 | 不知不觉 | bù zhī bù jué | unconsciously | Adv | 流利級<br>Level 5 |
| 6 | 知足 | 知足常乐<br>（六級） | zhī zú | feeling contented | Vs | 流利級<br>Level 5 |

| | 為（为）<br>wéi, wèi | 漢語水平考試<br>HSK | 拼音<br>Pin Yin | 英文翻譯<br>English | 詞類<br>Part of<br>Speech | 華語文<br>能力測驗<br>TOCFL |
|---|---|---|---|---|---|---|
| 1 | 為什麼 | 为什么（二級） | wèi shén me | why | Vs | 準備級二級<br>Novice 2 |
| 2 | 因為 | 因为（二級） | yīn wéi | because | Conj | 準備級二級<br>Novice 2 |
| 3 | 認為 | 认为（三級） | rèn wéi | to think | V | 入門級<br>Level 1 |
| 4 | 為了 | 为了（三級） | wèi liǎo | in order to | Prep | NA |
| 5 | 行為 | 行为（五級） | xíng wéi | behavior | Noun | 進階級<br>Level 3 |
| 6 | 以為 | 以为（四級） | yǐ wéi | to think | V | 入門級<br>Level 1 |
| 7 | 成為 | 成为（四級） | chéng wéi | to become | Vpt | 高階級<br>Level 4 |

| 為（为）<br>wéi, wèi | | 漢語水平考試<br>HSK | 拼音<br>Pin Yin | 英文翻譯<br>English | 詞類<br>Part of Speech | 華語文<br>能力測驗<br>TOCFL |
|---|---|---|---|---|---|---|
| 8 | 為難 | 为难（六級） | wéi nán | embar-rassed | Vs | 高階級<br>Level 4 |
| 9 | 作為 | 作为（五級） | zuò wéi | to be as | Vst | 高階級<br>Level 4 |

| 是<br>shì | | 漢語水平考試<br>HSK | 拼音<br>Pin Yin | 英文翻譯<br>English | 詞類<br>Part of Speech | 華語文<br>能力測驗<br>TOCFL |
|---|---|---|---|---|---|---|
| 1 | 是 | 是（一級） | shì | to be | Vst | 準備級一級<br>Novice 1 |
| 2 | 可是 | 可是 | kě shì | but | Conj | 準備級一級<br>Novice 1 |
| 3 | 還是 | 是（三級） | hái shì | or | Conj | 準備級一級<br>Novice 1 |
| 4 | 總是 | 总是（三級） | zǒng shì | always | Adv | 入門級<br>Level 1 |
| 5 | 或是 | 或是 | huò shì | or | Conj | 入門級<br>Level 1 |
| 6 | 但是 | 虽然⋯但是<br>（二級） | dàn shì | but | Conj | 入門級<br>Level 1 |
| 7 | 要是 | 要是（四級） | yào shì | if | Conj | 入門級<br>Level 1 |
| 8 | 倒是 | 倒是 | dǎo shì | but | Adv | 進階級<br>Level 3 |
| 9 | 就是 | 就是 | jiù shì | just | Conj | 進階級<br>Level 3 |
| 10 | 老是 | 老是 | lǎo shì | always | Adv | 進階級<br>Level 3 |

| | 是<br>shì | 漢語水平考試<br>HSK | 拼音<br>Pin Yin | 英文翻譯<br>English | 詞類<br>Part of<br>Speech | 華語文<br>能力測驗<br>TOCFL |
|---|---|---|---|---|---|---|
| 11 | 是非 | 是非（六級） | shì fēi | right or<br>wrong | Noun/<br>Adjective | 高階級<br>Level 4 |

## 第四章　【學習】名言二

溫故而知新，可以為師矣。

If a man keeps cherishing his old knowledge, so as continually to be acquiring new, he may be a teacher of others.

| 溫 | 故 | 而 | 知 | 新 | 可 | 以 | 為(为) | 師(师) | 矣 |
|---|---|---|---|---|---|---|---|---|---|
| | | | CH1-3 | | CH1-3 | CH1-3 | CH4-1 | | |

| | 溫<br>wēn | 漢語水平考試<br>HSK | 拼音<br>Pin Yin | 英文翻譯<br>English | 詞類<br>Part of<br>Speech | 華語文<br>能力測驗<br>TOCFL |
|---|---|---|---|---|---|---|
| 1 | 溫暖 | 温暖（五級） | wēn nuǎn | warm | Vs | 進階級<br>Level 3 |
| 2 | 溫度 | 温度 | wēn dù | temperature | Noun | 進階級<br>Level 3 |
| 3 | 氣溫 | 气温 | qì wēn | temperature | Noun | 進階級<br>Level 3 |
| 4 | 溫柔 | 温柔（五級） | wēn róu | tender | Vs | 進階級<br>Level 3 |
| 5 | 體溫 | 体温 | tǐ wēn | body temperature | Noun | 高階級<br>Level 4 |
| 6 | 溫和 | 温和 | wēn hé | mild | Vs | 高階級<br>Level 4 |
| 7 | 溫帶 | 温带（六級） | wēn dài | temperate zone | Noun | 流利級<br>Level 5 |

| 溫<br>wēn | 漢語水平考試<br>HSK | 拼音<br>Pin Yin | 英文翻譯<br>English | 詞類<br>Part of<br>Speech | 華語文<br>能力測驗<br>TOCFL |
|---|---|---|---|---|---|
| 8 | 溫泉 | 温泉 | wēn quán | spa | Noun | 基礎級<br>Level 2 |
| 9 | 溫習 | 温习 | wēn xí | review | V | 流利級<br>Level 5 |
| 10 | 溫馴 | 温驯 | wēn xùn | tame | Vs | 流利級<br>Level 5 |

| 故<br>gù | 漢語水平考試<br>HSK | 拼音<br>Pin Yin | 英文翻譯<br>English | 詞類<br>Part of<br>Speech | 華語文<br>能力測驗<br>TOCFL |
|---|---|---|---|---|---|
| 1 | 故事 | 故事（三級） | gù shì | story | Noun | 入門級<br>Level 1 |
| 2 | 故意 | 故意（四級） | gù yì | deliberately | Vs | 進階級<br>Level 3 |
| 3 | 故鄉 | 故乡（六級） | gù xiāng | hometown | Noun | 高階級<br>Level 4 |
| 4 | 緣故 | 缘故（六級） | yuán gù | reason | Noun | 高階級<br>Level 4 |
| 5 | 事故 | 事故 | shì gù | accident | Noun | 流利級<br>Level 5 |

| 而<br>ér | 漢語水平考試<br>HSK | 拼音<br>Pin Yin | 英文翻譯<br>English | 詞類<br>Part of<br>Speech | 華語文<br>能力測驗<br>TOCFL |
|---|---|---|---|---|---|
| 1 | 一般而言 | 一般而言 | yī bān ér yán | generally speaking | Conj | 高階級<br>Level 4 |
| 2 | 因而 | 因而（五級） | yīn ér | thus | Conj | 高階級<br>Level 4 |

| | 而 ér | 漢語水平考試 HSK | 拼音 Pin Yin | 英文翻譯 English | 詞類 Part of Speech | 華語文能力測驗 TOCFL |
|---|---|---|---|---|---|---|
| 3 | 從而 | 反而（五級） | cóng ér | thereby | Conj | 流利級 Level 5 |
| 4 | 而是 | 而是 | ér shì | （not）…but… | Conj | 流利級 Level 5 |
| 5 | 而 | 而（四級） | ér | and | Conj | 進階級 Level 3 |
| 6 | 進而 | 进而（六級） | jìn ér | and then | Conj | 流利級 Level 5 |

| | 新 xīn | 漢語水平考試 HSK | 拼音 Pin Yin | 英文翻譯 English | 詞類 Part of Speech | 華語文能力測驗 TOCFL |
|---|---|---|---|---|---|---|
| 1 | 新 | 新（二級） | xīn | new | Vs | 準備級二級 Novice 2 |
| 2 | 新年 | 新年 | xīn nián | new year | Noun | 入門級 Level 1 |
| 3 | 新聞 | 新闻（三級） | xīn wén | news | Noun | 基礎級 Level 2 |
| 4 | 新鮮 | 新鲜（三級） | xīn xiān | fresh | Vs | 基礎級 Level 2 |
| 5 | 重新 | 重新（四級） | zhòng xīn | re-do | Adv | 進階級 Level 3 |
| 6 | 新生 | 新生 | xīn shēng | re-born | Noun | 進階級 Level 3 |
| 7 | 新郎 | 新郎（六級） | xīn láng | bride-groom | Noun | 高階級 Level 4 |
| 8 | 新娘 | 新娘（六級） | xīn niáng | bride | Noun | 高階級 Level 4 |

# 第四章 【學習】名言三

三人行，必有我師焉。

When I walk along with two others, they may serve me as my teachers.

| 三 | 人 | 行 | 必 | 有 | 我 | 師（师） | 焉 |
|---|---|---|---|---|---|---|---|
|  |  | CH3-2 | CH1-1 | CH1-1 |  |  | N/A |

| | 三<br>sān | 漢語水平考試<br>HSK | 拼音<br>Pin Yin | 英文翻譯<br>English | 詞類<br>Part of Speech | 華語文能力測驗<br>TOCFL |
|---|---|---|---|---|---|---|
| 1 | 三 | 三（一級） | sān | three | Noun | 準備級一級<br>Novice 1 |
| 2 | 三明治 | 三明治 | sān míng zhì | sandwich | Noun | 入門級<br>Level 1 |
| 3 | 三角形 | 三角形 | sān jiǎo xíng | triangle | Noun | 高階級<br>Level 4 |
| 4 | 再三 | 再三（五級） | zài sān | repeatedly | Adv | 高階級<br>Level 4 |

| | 行<br>háng, xíng | 漢語水平考試<br>HSK | 拼音<br>Pin Yin | 英文翻譯<br>English | 詞類<br>Part of Speech | 華語文能力測驗<br>TOCFL |
|---|---|---|---|---|---|---|
| 1 | 自行車 | 自行车（三級） | zì xíng chē | bicycle | Noun | 入門級<br>Level 1 |
| 2 | 銀行<br>（hang） | 银行（三級） | yín háng | bank | Noun | 入門級<br>Level 1 |
| 3 | 旅行 | 旅行（四級） | lǚ xíng | to travel | Vi | 入門級<br>Level 1 |
| 4 | 行李 | 行李 | xíng lǐ | baggage | Noun | 基礎級<br>Level 2 |

| 行<br>háng, xíng | | 漢語水平考試<br>HSK | 拼音<br>Pin Yin | 英文翻譯<br>English | 詞類<br>Part of Speech | 華語文<br>能力測驗<br>TOCFL |
|---|---|---|---|---|---|---|
| 5 | 流行 | 流行（四級） | liú xíng | popular | Vs | 基礎級<br>Level 2 |
| 6 | 進行 | 进行（四級） | jìn xíng | to conduct | V | 進階級<br>Level 3 |
| 7 | 舉行 | 举行（四級） | jǔ xíng | to hold | V | 進階級<br>Level 3 |

| 我<br>wǒ | | 漢語水平考試<br>HSK | 拼音<br>Pin Yin | 英文翻譯<br>English | 詞類<br>Part of Speech | 華語文<br>能力測驗<br>TOCFL |
|---|---|---|---|---|---|---|
| 1 | 我 | 我（一級） | wǒ | I | Noun | 準備級一級<br>Novice 1 |
| 2 | 我們 | 我 （一級） | wǒ men | we | Noun | 準備級一級<br>Novice 1 |
| 3 | 自我 | 自我 | zì wǒ | self | Noun | 高階級<br>Level 4 |

| 師（师）<br>shī | | 漢語水平考試<br>HSK | 拼音<br>Pin Yin | 英文翻譯<br>English | 詞類<br>Part of Speech | 華語文<br>能力測驗<br>TOCFL |
|---|---|---|---|---|---|---|
| 1 | 老師 | 老师（一級） | lǎo shī | teacher | Noun | 準備級一級<br>Novice 1 |
| 2 | 教師 | 教师 | jiāo shī | teacher | Noun | 進階級<br>Level 3 |
| 3 | 廚師 | 厨师 | chú shī | chef | Noun | 進階級<br>Level 3 |
| 4 | 律師 | 律师（四級） | lǜ shī | lawyer | Noun | 進階級<br>Level 3 |

| 師（师）<br>shī | | 漢語水平考試<br>HSK | 拼音<br>Pin Yin | 英文翻譯<br>English | 詞類<br>Part of<br>Speech | 華語文<br>能力測驗<br>TOCFL |
|---|---|---|---|---|---|---|
| 5 | 師父 | 师父 | shī fù | master | Noun | 高階級<br>Level 4 |
| 6 | 師傅 | 师傅（四級） | shī fù | master | Noun | 高階級<br>Level 4 |

## 第五章　【禮】名言一

不知禮，無以為立。

Without an acquaintance with the rules of Propriety, it is impossible for the character to be established.

| 不 | 知 | 禮（礼） | 無（无） | 以 | 為（为） | 立 |
|---|---|---|---|---|---|---|
| CH1-1 | CH1-3 | | | CH1-3 | CH4-1 | |

| 禮（礼）<br>lǐ | | 漢語水平考試<br>HSK | 拼音<br>Pin Yin | 英文翻譯<br>English | 詞類<br>Part of<br>Speech | 華語文<br>能力測驗<br>TOCFL |
|---|---|---|---|---|---|---|
| 1 | 禮物 | 礼物（三級） | lǐ wù | gift | Noun | 入門級<br>Level 1 |
| 2 | 禮拜 | 礼拜 | lǐ bài | worship,<br>（a）week | Noun | 入門級<br>Level 1 |
| 3 | 禮拜天 | 礼拜天（四級） | lǐ bài tiān | Sunday | Noun | 準備級二級<br>Novice 2 |
| 4 | 禮貌 | 礼貌（四級） | lǐ mào | courtesy | Noun | 基礎級<br>Level 2 |
| 5 | 婚禮 | 婚礼（五級） | hūn lǐ | wedding | Noun | 進階級<br>Level 3 |
| 6 | 禮堂 | 礼堂 | lǐ táng | hall | Noun | 進階級<br>Level 3 |

| 禮（礼）<br>lǐ | 漢語水平考試<br>HSK | 拼音<br>Pin Yin | 英文翻譯<br>English | 詞類<br>Part of<br>Speech | 華語文<br>能力測驗<br>TOCFL |
|---|---|---|---|---|---|
| 7 | 禮節 | 礼节（六級） | lǐ jié | etiquette | Noun | 流利級<br>Level 5 |

| 無（无）<br>wú | 漢語水平考試<br>HSK | 拼音<br>Pin Yin | 英文翻譯<br>English | 詞類<br>Part of<br>Speech | 華語文<br>能力測驗<br>TOCFL |
|---|---|---|---|---|---|
| 1 | 無聊 | 无聊（四級） | wú liáo | bored | Vs | 基礎級<br>Level 2 |
| 2 | 無法 | 无法 | wú fǎ | uNAble to | Adv | 進階級<br>Level 3 |
| 3 | 無論如何 | 无论（四級） | wú lùn rú hé | anyway | Conj | 進階級<br>Level 3 |
| 4 | 無窮 | 无无（六級） | wú qióng | endless | Vs | 進階級<br>Level 3 |
| 5 | 無所謂 | 无所谓（五級） | wú suǒ wèi | (it) does not matter | Vs | 進階級<br>Level 3 |
| 6 | 毫無 | 毫无（六級） | háo wú | nothing | Conj | 高階級<br>Level 4 |

| 為（为）<br>wéi, wèi | 漢語水平考試<br>HSK | 拼音<br>Pin Yin | 英文翻譯<br>English | 詞類<br>Part of<br>Speech | 華語文<br>能力測驗<br>TOCFL |
|---|---|---|---|---|---|
| 1 | 為什麼 | 为什么（二級） | wèi shí me | why | Vs | 準備級二級<br>Novice 2 |
| 2 | 因為 | 因为……所以……（二級） | yīn wèi | because | Conj | 準備級二級<br>Novice 2 |

| 為（为）<br>wéi, wèi | | 漢語水平考試<br>HSK | 拼音<br>Pin Yin | 英文翻譯<br>English | 詞類<br>Part of Speech | 華語文<br>能力測驗<br>TOCFL |
|---|---|---|---|---|---|---|
| 3 | 認為 | 认为（三級） | rèn wéi | to think | V | 入門級<br>Level 1 |
| 4 | 為了 | 为了（三級） | wèi le | in order to | Prep | NA |
| 5 | 以 … 為主 | 以 … 为主 | yǐ …. wéi zhǔ | mainly | Vs | NA |
| 6 | 行為 | 行为（五級） | xíng wéi | behavior | Noun | 進階級<br>Level 3 |
| 7 | 成為 | 成为（四級） | chéng wéi | to become | Vpt | 高階級<br>Level 4 |

| 立<br>lì | | 漢語水平考試<br>HSK | 拼音<br>Pin Yin | 英文翻譯<br>English | 詞類<br>Part of Speech | 華語文<br>能力測驗<br>TOCFL |
|---|---|---|---|---|---|---|
| 1 | 建立 | 建立（五級） | jiàn lì | to set up | V | 進階級<br>Level 3 |
| 2 | 立刻 | 立刻（五級） | lì kè | immediately | Adv | 基礎級<br>Level 2 |
| 3 | 成立 | 成立（五級） | chéng lì | to established | Adv | 高階級<br>Level 4 |
| 4 | 獨立 | 独立（五級） | dú lì | independent | Vs | 高階級<br>Level 4 |
| 5 | 對立 | 对立（六級） | duì lì | opposition | Vs | 高階級<br>Level 4 |
| 6 | 公立 | 公立 | gōng lì | public | Vs-attr | 高階級<br>Level 4 |
| 7 | 中立 | 中立（六級） | zhōng lì | neutral | Vs | 流利級<br>Level 5 |

## 第五章　【禮】名言二

君使臣以禮，臣事君以忠。

A prince should employ his minister according to according to the rules of propriety; ministers should serve their prince with faithfulness.

| 君 | 使 | 臣 | 以 | 禮（礼） | 臣 | 事 | 君 | 以 | 忠 |
|---|---|---|---|---|---|---|---|---|---|
| CH3-1 | | | CH1-3 | CH5-1 | | | CH3-1 | CH1-3 | |

| | 使<br>shǐ | 漢語水平考試<br>HSK | 拼音<br>Pin Yin | 英文翻譯<br>English | 詞類<br>Part of Speech | 華語文<br>能力測驗<br>TOCFL |
|---|---|---|---|---|---|---|
| 1 | 使得 | 使得 | shǐ dé | to give effect to | Vst | 進階級<br>Level 3 |
| 2 | 使用 | 使用（四級） | shǐ yòng | to use | V | 進階級<br>Level 3 |
| 3 | 即使 | 即使（四級） | jí shǐ | even if | Conj | 高階級<br>Level 4 |
| 4 | 促使 | 促使（五級） | cù shǐ | to prompt | Vst | 流利級<br>Level 5 |
| 5 | 大使 | 大使（四級） | dà shǐ | ambassa-dor | N | 流利級<br>Level 5 |
| 6 | 假使 | 假使 | jiǎ shǐ | if | Conj | 流利級<br>Level 5 |
| 7 | 使命 | 使命（六級） | shǐ mìng | mission | N | 流利級<br>Level 5 |

| | 臣<br>chén | 漢語水平考試<br>HSK | 拼音<br>Pin Yin | 英文翻譯<br>English | 詞類<br>Part of Speech | 華語文<br>能力測驗<br>TOCFL |
|---|---|---|---|---|---|---|
| 1 | 大臣 | 大臣（六級） | dà chén | state official or subject in a dyNAsty | noun | NA |

| | 事 shì | 漢語水平考試 HSK | 拼音 Pin Yin | 英文翻譯 English | 詞類 Part of Speech | 華語文能力測驗 TOCFL |
|---|---|---|---|---|---|---|
| 1 | 同事 | 同事（三級） | tóng shì | colleague | Noun | 進階級 Level 3 |
| 2 | 故事 | 故事（三級） | gù shì | story | Noun | 入門級 Level 1 |
| 3 | 事情 | 事情（二級） | shì qíng | thing | Noun | 入門級 Level 1 |
| 4 | 懂事 | 懂（二級） | dǒng shì | sensible | Vs | 進階級 Level 3 |
| 5 | 事實 | 事实（五級） | shì shí | fact | Noun | 進階級 Level 3 |
| 6 | 事業 | 事业（六級） | shì yè | a business, a career | Noun | 進階級 Level 3 |

| | 忠 zhōng | 漢語水平考試 HSK | 拼音 Pin Yin | 英文翻譯 English | 詞類 Part of Speech | 華語文能力測驗 TOCFL |
|---|---|---|---|---|---|---|
| 1 | 效忠 | 效忠 | xiào zhōng | allegiance | V | 流利級 Level 5 |
| 2 | 忠實 | 忠实（六級） | zhōng shí | loyal | Vs | 流利級 Level 5 |
| 3 | 忠心 | 忠心 | zhōng xīn | loyalty | Noun | NA |
| 4 | 忠誠 | 忠（六級） | zhōng chéng | loyalty | Noun | NA |

# 第五章　【禮】名言三

上好禮，則民莫敢不敬。

If a superior man love propriety, the people will not dare not to be reverent.

| 上 | 好 | 禮（礼） | 則 | 民 | 莫 | 敢 | 不 | 敬 |
|---|---|---|---|---|---|---|---|---|
|   |   | CH5-1 | CH1-3 |   |   |   | CH1-1 |   |

| | 上<br>shàng | 漢語水平考試<br>HSK | 拼音<br>Pin Yin | 英文翻譯<br>English | 詞類<br>Part of Speech | 華語文<br>能力測驗<br>TOCFL |
|---|---|---|---|---|---|---|
| 1 | 早上 | 早上（二級） | zǎo shàng | morning | Noun | 準備級一級<br>Novice 1 |
| 2 | 上午 | 上午（一級） | shàng wǔ | morning | Noun | 準備級一級<br>Novice 1 |
| 3 | 晚上 | 晚上（二級） | wǎn shàng | at night | Noun | 準備級一級<br>Novice 1 |
| 4 | 上課 | 上课 | shàng kè | class | V-sep | 準備級一級<br>Novice 1 |
| 5 | 上面 | 上面 | shàng miàn | above | Noun | NA |
| 6 | 上班 | 上班（二級） | shàng bān | to work | V-sep | 入門級<br>Level 1 |

| | 好<br>hào, (hǎo) | 漢語水平考試<br>HSK | 拼音<br>Pin Yin | 英文翻譯<br>English | 詞類<br>Part of Speech | 華語文<br>能力測驗<br>TOCFL |
|---|---|---|---|---|---|---|
| 1 | 愛好 | 爱好（三級） | ài hào | hobby | Vst | 高階級<br>Level 4 |
| 2 | 喜好 | 喜好 | xǐ hào | preferences | Noun | NA |

| 好<br>hào, (hǎo) | | 漢語水平考試<br>HSK | 拼音<br>Pin Yin | 英文翻譯<br>English | 詞類<br>Part of Speech | 華語文<br>能力測驗<br>TOCFL |
|---|---|---|---|---|---|---|
| 3 | 好客 | 好客（五級） | hào kè | hospitable | Vs | 高階級<br>Level 4 |
| 4 | 好奇 | 好奇（五級） | hào qí | curious | Vs | 高階級<br>Level 4 |
| 5 | 嗜好 | 嗜好 | shì hào | hobby | Noun | 流利級<br>Level 5 |

| 民<br>mín | | 漢語水平考試<br>HSK | 拼音<br>Pin Yin | 英文翻譯<br>English | 詞類<br>Part of Speech | 華語文<br>能力測驗<br>TOCFL |
|---|---|---|---|---|---|---|
| 1 | 民國 | 民国 | mín guó | Republic of ChiNA | Noun | 進階級<br>Level 3 |
| 2 | 民族 | 民族（四級） | mín zú | NAtion | Noun | 進階級<br>Level 3 |
| 3 | 人民 | 人民 | rén mín | people | Noun | 進階級<br>Level 3 |
| 4 | 殖民地 | 殖民地（六級） | zhí mín dì | colony | Noun | 進階級<br>Level 3 |
| 5 | 居民 | 居民（六級） | jū mín | residents | Noun | 高階級<br>Level 4 |
| 6 | 民間 | 民间（六級） | mín jiān | folk area | Noun | 高階級<br>Level 4 |
| 7 | 農民 | 农民（五級） | nóng mín | farmer | Noun | 高階級<br>Level 4 |

| 勇<br>yǒng | 漢語水平考試<br>HSK | 拼音<br>Pin Yin | 英文翻譯<br>English | 詞類<br>Part of<br>Speech | 華語文<br>能力測驗<br>TOCFL |
|---|---|---|---|---|---|
| 1 勇敢 | 勇敢（四級） | yǒng gǎn | brave | Vs | 進階級<br>Level 3 |
| 2 不敢當 | 不敢当（六級） | bú gǎn dāng | being<br>humble | Vs | 高階級<br>Level 4 |

| 敬<br>jìng | 漢語水平考試<br>HSK | 拼音<br>Pin Yin | 英文翻譯<br>English | 詞類<br>Part of<br>Speech | 華語文<br>能力測驗<br>TOCFL |
|---|---|---|---|---|---|
| 1 尊敬 | 尊敬（五級） | zūn jìng | to respect | Vst | 進階級<br>Level 3 |
| 2 敬愛 | 敬爱 | jìng ài | to admire<br>with respect | Vst | 高階級<br>Level 4 |
| 3 敬酒 | 敬酒 | jìng jiǔ | to toast | V-sep | 高階級<br>Level 4 |
| 4 敬禮 | 敬礼（六級） | jìng lǐ | to salute | V-sep | 高階級<br>Level 4 |
| 5 恭敬 | 恭敬（六級） | gōng jìng | respectful | Vs | 流利級<br>Level 5 |
| 6 敬佩 | 敬佩 | jìng pèi | to admire | Vst | 流利級<br>Level 5 |
| 7 敬業 | 敬业（六級） | jìng yè | dedicated | Vi | NA |

## 第六章　【快樂】名言一之 A

學而時習之，不亦說（悅 yuè）乎？

Is it not pleasant to learn with a constant perseverance and application?

| 學(学) | 而 | 時 | 習(习) | 之 | 不 | 亦 | 說(悅) | 乎 |
|---|---|---|---|---|---|---|---|---|
|  | CH2-2 |  |  | CH1-2 | CH1-1 |  |  |  |

| 學（学）<br>xué | 漢語水平考試<br>HSK | 拼音<br>Pin Yin | 英文翻譯<br>English | 詞類<br>Part of<br>Speech | 華語文<br>能力測驗<br>TOCFL |
|---|---|---|---|---|---|
| 1 學校 | 学校（一級） | xué xiào | school | Noun | 準備級一級<br>Novice 1 |
| 2 學習 | 学习（一級） | xué xí | to study | V | 入門級<br>Level 1 |
| 3 科學 | 科学（四級） | kē xué | science | Noun | 進階級<br>Level 3 |
| 4 同學 | 同学（一級） | tóng xué | classmate | Noun | 準備級一級<br>Novice 1 |
| 5 學生 | 学生（一級） | xué shēng | student | Noun | 準備級一級<br>Novice 1 |
| 6 學費 | 学费 | xué fèi | tuition | Noun | 進階級<br>Level 3 |
| 7 留學 | 留学（五級） | liú xué | to study abroad | Vi | 進階級<br>Level 3 |
| 8 哲學 | 哲学（五級） | zhé xué | philosophy | Noun | 進階級<br>Level 3 |
| 9 學問 | 学问（五級） | xué wèn | knowledge | Noun | 進階級<br>Level 3 |
| 10 文學 | 文学（五級） | wén xué | literature | Noun | 進階級<br>Level 3 |
| 11 化學 | 化学（五級） | huà xué | chemistry | Noun | 高階級<br>Level 4 |
| 12 學術 | 学术（五級） | xué shù | academic | Noun | 高階級<br>Level 4 |
| 13 教學 | 教学（三級） | jiāo xué | to teach | Vi | 高階級<br>Level 4 |
| 14 學位 | 学位（六級） | xué wèi | degree | Noun | 高階級<br>Level 4 |

| | 學（学）xué | 漢語水平考試 HSK | 拼音 Pin Yin | 英文翻譯 English | 詞類 Part of Speech | 華語文能力測驗 TOCFL |
|---|---|---|---|---|---|---|
| 15 | 學分 | 学分 | xué fēn | credit | Noun | 流利級 Level 5 |
| 16 | 學科 | 学科 | xué kē | subject | Noun | 流利級 Level 5 |
| 17 | 學年 | 学年 | xué nián | school year | Noun | 流利級 Level 5 |

| | 時（时）shí | 漢語水平考試 HSK | 拼音 Pin Yin | 英文翻譯 English | 詞類 Part of Speech | 華語文能力測驗 TOCFL |
|---|---|---|---|---|---|---|
| 1 | 小時 | 小时（三級） | xiǎo shí | hour | Noun | 準備級一級 Novice 1 |
| 2 | 時間 | 时间（三級） | shí jiān | time | Noun | 準備級一級 Novice 1 |
| 3 | 平時 | 平时（四級） | píng shí | regular time | Adv | 進階級 Level 3 |
| 4 | 暫時 | 暂时（四級） | zàn shí | temporary | Adj | 進階級 Level 3 |
| 5 | 準時 | 准时（四級） | zhǔn shí | on time | Adj | 進階級 Level 3 |
| 6 | 按時 | 按时（四級） | àn shí | timely | Adv | 高階級 Level 4 |
| 7 | 當時 | 当时（四級） | dāng shí | at that time | Adv | 基礎級 Level 2 |
| 8 | 時光 | 时光（六級） | shí guāng | time | Noun | 流利級 Level 5 |

| 時（时）<br>shí | 漢語水平考試<br>HSK | 拼音<br>Pin Yin | 英文翻譯<br>English | 詞類<br>Part of<br>Speech | 華語文<br>能力測驗<br>TOCFL |
|---|---|---|---|---|---|
| 9 | 時髦 | 时髦（五級） | shí máo | fashioN-Able | Adj | 流利級<br>Level 5 |
| 10 | 即時 | 即时 | jí shí | Immediate-ly, promptly | Adv | 流利級<br>Level 5 |
| 11 | 時效 | 时效 | shí xiào | time limit/<br>effective<br>time frame | Noun | 流利級<br>Level 5 |
| 12 | 時差 | 时差（六級） | shí chā | jet lag | Noun | 基礎級<br>Level 2 |
| 13 | 頓時 | 顿时（六級） | dùn shí | Suddenly | Adv | 流利級<br>Level 5 |

| 習（习）<br>xí | 漢語水平考試<br>HSK | 拼音<br>Pin Yin | 英文翻譯<br>English | 詞類<br>Part of<br>Speech | 華語文<br>能力測驗<br>TOCFL |
|---|---|---|---|---|---|
| 1 | 學習 | 学习（一級） | xué xí | to learn, to study | Verb | 入門級<br>Level 1 |
| 2 | 練習 | 练习（四級） | liàn xí | to practice | Noun or Verb | 入門級<br>Level 1 |
| 3 | 習慣 | 习惯（三級） | xí guàn | habit, ac-customed | Noun or Verb | 入門級<br>Level 1 |
| 4 | 複習 | 复习（四級） | fù xí | to review | Verb | 進階級<br>Level 3 |
| 5 | 預習 | 预习（四級） | yù xí | to preview | V | 進階級<br>Level 3 |

| 習（习）<br>xí | | 漢語水平考試<br>HSK | 拼音<br>Pin Yin | 英文翻譯<br>English | 詞類<br>Part of Speech | 華語文<br>能力測驗<br>TOCFL |
|---|---|---|---|---|---|---|
| 6 | 補習 | 补习 | bǔ xí | to review or to have lessons after regular school | V-sep | 高階級<br>Level 4 |
| 7 | 實習 | 实习（五級） | shí xí | to intern | Vi | 流利級<br>Level 5 |
| 8 | 溫習 | 温习 | wēn xí | to review | V | 流利級<br>Level 5 |
| 9 | 演習 | 演习（六級） | yǎn xí | to rehearse | Vi | 流利級<br>Level 5 |
| 10 | 習俗 | 习俗（六級） | xí sú | custom | Noun | NA |

| 亦<br>yì | | 漢語水平考試<br>HSK | 拼音<br>Pin Yin | 英文翻譯<br>English | 詞類<br>Part of Speech | 華語文<br>能力測驗<br>TOCFL |
|---|---|---|---|---|---|---|
| 1 | 亦 | 亦（六級） | yì | also | Adv | 流利級<br>Level 5 |
| 2 | 亦是 ＝<br>也是 | | | | | |

| 悅<br>yuè | | 漢語水平考試<br>HSK | 拼音<br>Pin Yin | 英文翻譯<br>English | 詞類<br>Part of Speech | 華語文<br>能力測驗<br>TOCFL |
|---|---|---|---|---|---|---|
| 1 | 喜悅 | 喜悦（六級） | xǐ yuè | joy | Vs | 流利級<br>Level 5 |
| 2 | 取悅 | 取悦 | qǔ yuè | to please | V | 流利級<br>Level 5 |

| | 乎<br>hū | 漢語水平考試<br>HSK | 拼音<br>Pin Yin | 英文翻譯<br>English | 詞類<br>Part of Speech | 華語文<br>能力測驗<br>TOCFL |
|---|---|---|---|---|---|---|
| 1 | 似乎 | 似乎（五級） | sì hū | to seem to | Adv | 進階級<br>Level 3 |
| 2 | 合乎 | 合乎 | hé hū | fit | Vst | 高階級<br>Level 4 |
| 3 | 幾乎 | 几乎（三級） | jǐ hū | almost | Adv | 高階級<br>Level 4 |
| 4 | 在乎 | 在乎 | zài hū | to care | Vst | 高階級<br>Level 4 |

## 第六章　【快樂】名言一之 B

有朋自遠方來，不亦樂（lè - happiness）乎？

Is it not delightful to have friends coming from distant quarters?

| 有 | 朋 | 自 | 遠<br>（远） | 方 | 來 | 不 | 亦 | 樂<br>（乐） | 乎 |
|---|---|---|---|---|---|---|---|---|---|
| CH1-1 | CH2-2 | | CH1-1 | CH1-1 | | CH1-1 | CH<br>6-6-1 | | CH<br>6-1-1 |

| | 自<br>zì | 漢語水平考試<br>HSK | 拼音<br>Pin Yin | 英文翻譯<br>English | 詞類<br>Part of Speech | 華語文<br>能力測驗<br>TOCFL |
|---|---|---|---|---|---|---|
| 1 | 自行車 | 自行车（三級） | zì xíng chē | bicycle | Noun | 入門級<br>Level 1 |
| 2 | 自己 | 自己（三級） | zì jǐ | oneself | Noun | 準備級二級<br>Novice 2 |
| 3 | 親自 | 亲自（五級） | qīn zì | persoNAlly | Adv | 進階級<br>Level 3 |

| | 自 zì | 漢語水平考試 HSK | 拼音 Pin Yin | 英文翻譯 English | 詞類 Part of Speech | 華語文能力測驗 TOCFL |
|---|---|---|---|---|---|---|
| 4 | 自從 | 自从（五級） | zì cóng | since | Prep | 進階級 Level 3 |
| 5 | 自動 | 自动（五級） | zì dòng | automatic | Vs | 進階級 Level 3 |
| 6 | 自然 | 自然（四級） | zì rán | NAtural | Vs | 基礎級 Level 2 |
| 7 | 自殺 | 自杀 | zì shā | to suicide | Vi | 進階級 Level 3 |

| | 來 lái | 漢語水平考試 HSK | 拼音 Pin Yin | 英文翻譯 English | 詞類 Part of Speech | 華語文能力測驗 TOCFL |
|---|---|---|---|---|---|---|
| 1 | 進來 | 进来 | jìn lái | to come in | Vi | NA |
| 2 | 起來 | 起来（三級） | qǐ lái | to stand up | Vp | 進階級 Level 3 |
| 3 | 後來 | 后来（三級） | hòu lái | later | N | 入門級 Level 1 |
| 4 | 出來 | 出来 | chū lái | to come out | Vi | NA |
| 5 | 原來 | 原来（四級） | yuán lái | origiNAlly | Adv | 基礎級 Level 2 |
| 6 | 本來 | 本来（四級） | běn lái | origiNAlly | Adv | 入門級 Level 1 |
| 7 | 從來 | 从来（四級） | cóng lái | ever | Adv | 基礎級 Level 2 |

| 樂（乐）<br>lè (yuè) | | 漢語水平考試<br>HSK | 拼音<br>Pin Yin | 英文翻譯<br>English | 詞類<br>Part of<br>Speech | 華語文<br>能力測驗<br>TOCFL |
|---|---|---|---|---|---|---|
| 1 | 音樂<br>（yuè） | 音乐（三級） | yīn yuè | music | Noun | 入門級<br>Level 1 |
| 2 | 樂團<br>（yuè） | 乐团 | yuè tuán | orchestra | Noun | 進階級<br>Level 3 |
| 3 | 樂隊<br>（yuè） | 乐队 | yuè duì | band | Noun | 流利級<br>Level 5 |
| 4 | 快樂<br>（lè） | 快乐（二級） | kuài lè | happy | Vs | 準備級二級<br>Novice 2 |
| 5 | 樂器<br>（yuè） | 乐器（五級） | yuè qì | musical<br>instrument | Noun | 基礎級<br>Level 2 |
| 6 | 吃喝玩樂<br>（lè） | 吃喝玩乐 | chī hē<br>wán lè | fun | Vi | 進階級<br>Level 3 |
| 7 | 可樂<br>（lè） | 可乐 | kě lè | coke | Noun | 基礎級<br>Level 2 |

## 第六章　【快樂】名言二

知（智）者樂水，仁者樂山。

The wise find pleasure in water; the virtuous find pleasure in hills.

| 知（智） | 者 | 樂（乐） | 水 | 仁 | 者 | 樂（乐） | 山 |
|---|---|---|---|---|---|---|---|
| | CH2-3 | CH6-1-2 | | | CH2-3 | CH6-1-2 | |

| 知（智） | 者 | 動（动） | 仁 | 者 | 靜 |
|---|---|---|---|---|---|
| CH1-3 | CH2-3 | | repeat | CH2-3 | |

| | 智 zhì | 漢語水平考試 HSK | 拼音 Pin Yin | 英文翻譯 English | 詞類 Part of Speech | 華語文能力測驗 TOCFL |
|---|---|---|---|---|---|---|
| 1 | 智慧 | 智慧（五級） | shuǐ guǒ | intelligence | Noun | 進階級 Level 3 |
| 2 | 明智 | 明智 | | wise | Vs | 流利級 Level 5 |
| 3 | 理智 | 理智（六級） | qì shuǐ | Intellect | Vs | 流利級 Level 5 |
| 4 | 智力 | 智力（六級） | rè shuǐ | Intelligence | Noun | 流利級 Level 5 |
| 5 | 智能 | 智能（六級） | shuǐ jiǎo | dumplings | Noun | NA |
| 6 | 智商 | 智商（六級） | shuǐ píng | Intelligence quotient (Q) | Noun | NA |
| 7 | 才智 | 才智 | | wit, intellect | Noun | 流利級 Level 5 |
| 8 | 機智 | 机智（六級） | kāi shuǐ | wit | Noun | NA |

| | 水 shuǐ | 漢語水平考試 HSK | 拼音 Pin Yin | 英文翻譯 English | 詞類 Part of Speech | 華語文能力測驗 TOCFL |
|---|---|---|---|---|---|---|
| 1 | 水果 | 水果（一級） | shuǐ guǒ | fruit | Noun | 準備級二級 Novice 2 |
| 2 | 開水 | 开水（五級） | kāi shuǐ | boiling water | Noun | 基礎級 Level 2 |
| 3 | 汽水 | 汽水 | qì shuǐ | soda | Noun | 基礎級 Level 2 |
| 4 | 熱水 | 热水 | rè shuǐ | hot water | Noun | 進階級 Level 3 |
| 5 | 水餃 | 水饺 | shuǐ jiǎo | dumplings | Noun | 進階級 Level 3 |

| 水<br>shuǐ | 漢語水平考試<br>HSK | 拼音<br>Pin Yin | 英文翻譯<br>English | 詞類<br>Part of<br>Speech | 華語文<br>能力測驗<br>TOCFL |
|---|---|---|---|---|---|
| 6 | 水平 | 水平（三級） | shuǐ<br>píng | level | Noun | 進階級<br>Level 3 |

| 仁<br>rén | 漢語水平考試<br>HSK | 拼音<br>Pin Yin | 英文翻譯<br>English | 詞類<br>Part of<br>Speech | 華語文<br>能力測驗<br>TOCFL |
|---|---|---|---|---|---|
| 1 | 仁愛 | 仁爱 | rén ài | kindness,<br>benevo-<br>lence | Noun | 流利級<br>Level 5 |

| 山<br>shān | 漢語水平考試<br>HSK | 拼音<br>Pin Yin | 英文翻譯<br>English | 詞類<br>Part of<br>Speech | 華語文<br>能力測驗<br>TOCFL |
|---|---|---|---|---|---|
| 1 | 山區 | 山区 | shān qū | mountain<br>area | Noun | 進階級<br>Level 3 |
| 2 | 登山 | 登山 | dēng<br>shān | mountain-<br>eering | V-sep | 高階級<br>Level 4 |
| 3 | 山地 | 山地 | shān dì | mountain | Noun | 高階級<br>Level 4 |
| 4 | 山峰 | 山峰 | shān<br>fēng | mountain<br>peak | Noun | 流利級<br>Level 5 |
| 5 | 山谷 | 山谷 | shān gǔ | valley | Noun | 流利級<br>Level 5 |
| 6 | 山脈 | 山脉（六級） | shān mài | mountain<br>range | Noun | 流利級<br>Level 5 |
| 7 | 爬山 | 爬山（三級） | pá shān | climbing | V | NA |

| 動（动）dòng | | 漢語水平考試 HSK | 拼音 Pin Yin | 英文翻譯 English | 詞類 Part of Speech | 華語文能力測驗 TOCFL |
|---|---|---|---|---|---|---|
| 1 | 運動 | 运动（二級） | yùn dòng | exercise | V，N | 準備級 二級 |
| 2 | 動物 | 动物（三級） | dòng wù | animal | Noun | NA |
| 3 | 活動 | 活动（四級） | huó dòng | activity | Vi | 進階級 Level 3 |
| 4 | 感動 | 感动（四級） | gǎn dòng | to be moved | Vs | 進階級 Level 3 |
| 5 | 行動 | 行动（五級） | xíng dòng | action | Noun | 進階級 Level 3 |
| 6 | 自動 | 自动（五級） | zì dòng | automatic | Vs | 進階級 Level 3 |
| 7 | 主動 | 主动（六級） | zhǔ dòng | initiative | Vs | 進階級 Level 3 |
| 8 | 動手 | 动手（六級） | dòng shǒu | hands-on | Vs | 高階級 Level 4 |
| 9 | 動作 | 动作（六級） | dòng zuò | action, movement | Noun | 高階級 Level 4 |
| 10 | 勞動 | 劳动（五級） | láo dòng | labor | V | 高階級 Level 4 |
| 11 | 震動 | 振动（五級） | zhèn dòng | vibration | Vi | 高階級 Level 4 |
| 12 | 動機 | 动机（六級） | dòng jī | motive | Noun | 流利級 Level 5 |
| 13 | 衝動 | 冲动（六級） | chōng dòng | impulse | Noun | 流利級 Level 5 |
| 14 | 動力 | 动力（六級） | dòng lì | power | Noun | 流利級 Level 5 |

| | 動（动）dòng | 漢語水平考試 HSK | 拼音 Pin Yin | 英文翻譯 English | 詞類 Part of Speech | 華語文能力測驗 TOCFL |
|---|---|---|---|---|---|---|
| 15 | 動態 | 动态（六級） | dòng tài | movement, development | Noun | 流利級 Level 5 |

| | 靜 jìng | 漢語水平考試 HSK | 拼音 Pin Yin | 英文翻譯 English | 詞類 Part of Speech | 華語文能力測驗 TOCFL |
|---|---|---|---|---|---|---|
| 1 | 安靜 | 安静（三級） | ān jìng | to be quiet | Vs | 進階級 Level 3 |
| 2 | 冷靜 | 冷静（四級） | lěng jìng | calm | Vs | 高階級 Level 4 |
| 3 | 平靜 | 平静（五級） | píng jìng | calm | Vs | 高階級 Level 4 |
| 4 | 動靜 | 动静（六級） | dòng jìng | movement | Noun | 流利級 Level 5 |
| 5 | 靜脈 | 静脉 | jìng mài | vein | Noun | 流利級 Level 5 |
| 6 | 清靜 | 清净 | qīng jìng | quiet | Vs | 流利級 Level 5 |

## 第六章 【快樂】名言三

知之者不如好之者，好之者不如樂（lè）之者。

They who know the truth are not equal to those who love it, and they who love it are not equal to those who delight in it.

| 知 | 之 | 者 | 不 | 如 | 好 hào | 之 | 者 |
|---|---|---|---|---|---|---|---|
| CH1-3 | CH1-2 | CH2-3 | CH1-1 | | CH5-3 | CH1-2 | CH2-3 |

| 好 hào | 之 | 者 | 不 | 如 | 樂（乐） | 之 | 者 |
|---|---|---|---|---|---|---|---|

| 好<br>hào, (hǎo) | 漢語水平考試<br>HSK | 拼音<br>Pin Yin | 英文翻譯<br>English | 詞類<br>Part of Speech | 華語文<br>能力測驗<br>TOCFL |
|---|---|---|---|---|---|
| 1 愛好 | 愛好（三級） | ài hào | hobby | Vst | 高階級 |
| 2 喜好 | 喜好 | xǐ hào | preferences | Noun | NA |
| 3 好客 | 好客（五級） | hào kè | hospitable | Vs | 高階級 |
| 4 好奇 | 好奇（五級） | hào qí | curious | Vs | 高階級 |
| 5 嗜好 | 嗜好 | shì hào | hobby | Noun | 流利級 |

| 如<br>rú | 漢語水平考試<br>HSK | 拼音<br>Pin Yin | 英文翻譯<br>English | 詞類<br>Part of Speech | 華語文<br>能力測驗<br>TOCFL |
|---|---|---|---|---|---|
| 1 如果 | 如果（三級） | rú guǒ | in case | Conj | 入門級<br>Level 1 |
| 2 比如 | 比如（四級） | bǐ rú | such as | Prep | 進階級<br>Level 3 |
| 3 不如 | 不如（五級） | bù rú | not as good as | Conj | 進階級<br>Level 3 |
| 4 假如 | 假如（五級） | jiǎ rú | if | Conj | 進階級<br>Level 3 |
| 5 例如 | 例如（四級） | lì rú | for example | Prep | 基礎級<br>Level 2 |
| 6 如下 | 如下 | rú xià | as follows | Vs | 進階級<br>Level 3 |
| 7 如意 | 心如意（六級） | rú yì | as wish | Vs | 進階級<br>Level 3 |

| | 如<br>rú | 漢語水平考試<br>HSK | 拼音<br>Pin Yin | 英文翻譯<br>English | 詞類<br>Part of<br>Speech | 華語文<br>能力測驗<br>TOCFL |
|---|---|---|---|---|---|---|
| 8 | 無論如何 | 无论如何 | wú lùn rú<br>hé | anyway | Conj | 進階級<br>Level 3 |
| 9 | 如何 | 如何（五級） | rú hé | how | Adv | 高階級<br>Level 4 |
| 10 | 如今 | 如今（五級） | rú jīn | today，<br>presently | Noun | 高階級<br>Level 4 |
| 11 | 如同 | 如同（五級） | rú tóng | as, same | Vst | 高階級<br>Level 4 |
| 12 | 如此 | 如此 | rú cǐ | in this way | Adv | 進階級<br>Level 3 |
| 13 | 譬如 | 譬如（六級） | pì rú | for example | Prep | 流利級<br>Level 5 |

## 第七章　【音樂】名言一

興於詩，立於禮，成於樂（yuè - music）。

It is by the Odes that the mind is aroused. It is by the Rules of Propriety that the character is established. It is from Music that the finish is received.

| 興(兴) | 於(于) | 詩(诗) | 立 | 於(于) | 禮(礼) | 成 | 於 | 樂(乐) |
|---|---|---|---|---|---|---|---|---|
| | | | CH5-1 | | CH5-1 | | | CH6-1 |

| | 興（兴）<br>xīng, xìng | 漢語水平考試<br>HSK | 拼音<br>Pin Yin | 英文翻譯<br>English | 詞類<br>Part of<br>Speech | 華語文<br>能力測驗<br>TOCFL |
|---|---|---|---|---|---|---|
| 1 | 興奮 | 兴奋（四級） | xìng fèn | to be<br>excited | Vs | 進階級<br>Level 3 |
| 2 | 新興 | 新兴 | xīn xīng | newly<br>established | Vs-attr | 高階級<br>Level 4 |

| 興（兴）<br>xīng, xìng | | 漢語水平考試<br>HSK | 拼音<br>Pin Yin | 英文翻譯<br>English | 詞類<br>Part of Speech | 華語文<br>能力測驗<br>TOCFL |
|---|---|---|---|---|---|---|
| 3 | 興建 | 兴建 | xīng jiàn | to build | V | 流利級<br>Level 5 |
| 4 | 興隆 | 兴奋（四級） | xīng lóng | prosperous | Vs | 流利級<br>Level 5 |
| 5 | 興起 | 兴起 | xīng qǐ | to rise | Vpt | 流利級<br>Level 5 |
| 6 | 高興 | 高兴（一級） | gāo xìng | happy | Vs | 入門級<br>Level 1 |
| 7 | 興趣 | 兴趣（三級） | xìng qù | interest | Noun | 基礎級<br>Level 2 |

| 於（于）<br>yú | | 漢語水平考試<br>HSK | 拼音<br>Pin Yin | 英文翻譯<br>English | 詞類<br>Part of Speech | 華語文<br>能力測驗<br>TOCFL |
|---|---|---|---|---|---|---|
| 1 | 由於 | 由于（四級） | yóu yú | due to | Conj | 進階級<br>Level 3 |
| 2 | 於是 | 于是（四級） | yú shì | therefore | Conj | 進階級<br>Level 3 |
| 3 | 在於 | 在于（五級） | zài yú | as far as | Vst | 進階級<br>Level 3 |
| 4 | 至於 | 至于（五級） | zhì yú | as for | Prep | 進階級<br>Level 3 |
| 5 | 終於 | 终于（三級） | zhōng yú | at last, fiNAlly | Adv | 進階級<br>Level 3 |
| 6 | 等於 | 等于（五級） | děng yú | equal to | Vst | 高階級<br>Level 4 |

| 於（于）<br>yú | 漢語水平考試<br>HSK | 拼音<br>Pin Yin | 英文翻譯<br>English | 詞類<br>Part of<br>Speech | 華語文<br>能力測驗<br>TOCFL |
|---|---|---|---|---|---|
| 7 | 對於 | 对于（四級） | duì yú | with regards to, regarding | Prep | 高階級<br>Level 4 |
| 8 | 關於 | 关于（三級） | guān yú | concerning, about | Prep | 高階級<br>Level 4 |

| 詩（诗）<br>shī | 漢語水平考試<br>HSK | 拼音<br>Pin Yin | 英文翻譯<br>English | 詞類<br>Part of<br>Speech | 華語文<br>能力測驗<br>TOCFL |
|---|---|---|---|---|---|
| 1 | 詩人 | 诗人 | shī rén | poet | Noun | 高階級<br>Level 4 |
| 2 | 詩歌 | 诗（五級） | shī gē | poetry | Noun | NA |

| 成<br>chéng | 漢語水平考試<br>HSK | 拼音<br>Pin Yin | 英文翻譯<br>English | 詞類<br>Part of<br>Speech | 華語文<br>能力測驗<br>TOCFL |
|---|---|---|---|---|---|
| 1 | 成功 | 成功（四級） | chéng gōng | success | Vs | 基礎級<br>Level 2 |
| 2 | 成績 | 成（三級） | chéng jī | grades | Noun | 入門級<br>Level 1 |
| 3 | 變成 | 变成 | biàn chéng | to become | Vpt | 進階級<br>Level 3 |
| 4 | 成果 | 成果（五級） | chéng guǒ | results | Noun | 進階級<br>Level 3 |
| 5 | 成就 | 成就（五級） | chéng jiù | achieve-ment | Noun | 進階級<br>Level 3 |
| 6 | 成熟 | 成熟（五級） | chéng shú | mature | Vs | 進階級<br>Level 3 |

| | 成<br>chéng | 漢語水平考試<br>HSK | 拼音<br>Pin Yin | 英文翻譯<br>English | 詞類<br>Part of Speech | 華語文<br>能力測驗<br>TOCFL |
|---|---|---|---|---|---|---|
| 7 | 成長 | 成长（五級） | chéng zhǎng | growing up | Vs | 進階級<br>Level 3 |
| 8 | 成本 | 成本（六級） | chéng běn | cost | Noun | 高階級<br>Level 4 |

## 第七章　【音樂】名言二

歌樂者，仁之和也。

Singing and music are the harmony of humanity.

| 歌 | 樂（乐） | 者 | 仁 | 之 | 和 | 也 |
|---|---|---|---|---|---|---|
| CH6-1 | CH2-3 | CH6-2 | CH1-2 | CH5-4 | CH2-1 |

| | 歌<br>gē | 漢語水平考試<br>HSK | 拼音<br>Pin Yin | 英文翻譯<br>English | 詞類<br>Part of Speech | 華語文<br>能力測驗<br>TOCFL |
|---|---|---|---|---|---|---|
| 1 | 唱歌 | 唱歌（二級） | chàng gē | to sing | V-sep | 準備級二級<br>Novice 2 |
| 2 | 歌曲 | 歌曲 | gē qǔ | song | Noun | 進階級<br>Level 3 |
| 3 | 歌星 | 歌星 | gē xīng | singer | Noun | 進階級<br>Level 3 |
| 4 | 歌劇 | 歌剧 | gē jù | opera | Noun | 高階級<br>Level 4 |
| 5 | 歌手 | 歌手 | gē shǒu | singer | Noun | 高階級<br>Level 4 |
| 6 | 歌頌 | 歌颂（六級） | gē sòng | to praise | Verb | 流利級<br>Level 5 |

# 第七章　【音樂】名言三

子與人歌而善，必使反之，而後和之。

When the Master was in company with a person who was singing, if he sang well, he would make him repeat the song, while he accompanied it with his own voice.

| 子 | 與<br>（与） | 人 | 歌 | 而 | 善 | 必 | 使 | 反 | 之 |
|---|---|---|---|---|---|---|---|---|---|
| CH3-1 | CH2-2 | CH3-2 | CH7-2 | | | CH-1 | | | CH1-2 |

| 而 | 後<br>（后） | 和 | 之 |
|---|---|---|---|
| | | CH5-4 | CH1-2 |

| | 而<br>ér | 漢語水平考試<br>HSK | 拼音<br>Pin Yin | 英文翻譯<br>English | 詞類<br>Part of Speech | 華語文能力測驗<br>TOCFL |
|---|---|---|---|---|---|---|
| 1 | 而且 | 不但……而且……（三級） | ér qiě | also | Conj | 基礎級<br>Level 2 |
| 2 | 反而 | 反而（五級） | fǎn ér | instead of | Conj | 進階級<br>Level 3 |
| 3 | 總而言之 | 总而言之 | zǒng ér yán zhī | all in all | Conj | 進階級<br>Level 3 |
| 4 | 而已 | 而已（六級） | ér yǐ | That's it | Ptc | 高階級<br>Level 4 |
| 5 | 然而 | 然而（四級） | rán ér | however | Conj | 高階級<br>Level 4 |
| 6 | 一般而言 | 一般而言 | yī bān ér yán | generally speaking | Conj | 高階級<br>Level 4 |
| 7 | 因而 | 因而（五級） | yīn ér | thus | Conj | 高階級<br>Level 4 |

| 善<br>shàn | 漢語水平考試<br>HSK | 拼音<br>Pin Yin | 英文翻譯<br>English | 詞類<br>Part of<br>Speech | 華語文<br>能力測驗<br>TOCFL |
|---|---|---|---|---|---|
| 1 | 改善 | 改善（五級） | gǎi shàn | to improve | V | 進階級<br>Level 3 |
| 2 | 善於 | 善于（五級） | shàn yú | to be good at | Vst | 高階級<br>Level 4 |
| 3 | 妥善 | 妥善（六級） | tuǒ shàn | proper | Vs | 高階級<br>Level 4 |
| 4 | 完善 | 完善（五級） | wán shàn | perfect | Vs | 高階級<br>Level 4 |
| 5 | 慈善 | 慈善（六級） | cí shàn | charitable | Vs | 流利級<br>Level 5 |
| 6 | 行善 | 行善 | xíng shàn | practice charitable activities | Vi | 流利級<br>Level 5 |
| 7 | 善良 | 善良（五級） | shàn liáng | kindness, kind | N or Vs | NA |

| 反<br>shàn | 漢語水平考試<br>HSK | 拼音<br>Pin Yin | 英文翻譯<br>English | 詞類<br>Part of<br>Speech | 華語文<br>能力測驗<br>TOCFL |
|---|---|---|---|---|---|
| 1 | 反而 | 反而（五級） | fǎn ér | on the contrary | Conj | 進階級<br>Level 3 |
| 2 | 相反 | 相反（四級） | xiāng fǎn | opposite | Vs | 進階級<br>Level 3 |
| 3 | 反對 | 反对（四級） | fǎn duì | disagree. oppose | Vst | 高階級<br>Level 4 |
| 4 | 反覆 | 反复（五級） | fǎn fù | repeat | Adv | 高階級<br>Level 4 |

| | 反 shàn | 漢語水平考試 HSK | 拼音 Pin Yin | 英文翻譯 English | 詞類 Part of Speech | 華語文 能力測驗 TOCFL |
|---|---|---|---|---|---|---|
| 5 | 反映 | 反映（五級） | fǎn yìng | to reflect | V | 高階級 Level 4 |
| 6 | 反應 | 反应（五級） | fǎn yìng | re respond to | Vi | 高階級 Level 4 |
| 7 | 反正 | 反正（五級） | fǎn zhèng | anyway | Adv | 高階級 Level 4 |
| 8 | 反抗 | 反抗（六級） | fǎn kàng | to resist | V | 高階級 Level 4 |
| 9 | 反面 | 反面（六級） | fǎn miàn | the opposite side | N | 高階級 Level 4 |
| 10 | 反問 | 反问（六級） | fǎn wèn | rebutt, ask a question in return | V | 高階級 Level 4 |

| | 後（后） shàn | 漢語水平考試 HSK | 拼音 Pin Yin | 英文翻譯 English | 詞類 Part of Speech | 華語文 能力測驗 TOCFL |
|---|---|---|---|---|---|---|
| 1 | 後（面） | 后面（一級） | hòu (mìan) | the back side | N | 準備級二級 Novice 2 |
| 2 | 後來 | 后来（三級） | hòu lái | afterwards | N | 基礎級 Level 2 |
| 3 | 最後 | 最后（三級） | zuì hòu | in the last | N | 入門級 Level 1 |
| 4 | 然後 | 然后（三級） | rán hòu | then, afterwards | Adv | 準備級二級 Novice 2 |
| 5 | 背後 | 后背（五級） | bèi hòu | in the back, backside | N | 進階級 Level 3 |

| | 後（后）shàn | 漢語水平考試 HSK | 拼音 Pin Yin | 英文翻譯 English | 詞類 Part of Speech | 華語文能力測驗 TOCFL |
|---|---|---|---|---|---|---|
| 6 | 以後 | 以后 | yǐ hòu | in the future, afterwards | N | 準備級一級 Novice 1 |
| 7 | 之後 | 之后 | zhī hòu | afterwards, then | N | 進階級 Level 3 |
| 8 | 後代 | 后代（六級） | hòu dài | future (younger) generationg | N | 高階級 Level 4 |
| 9 | 後果 | 后果（五級） | hòu guǒ | result | N | 高階級 Level 4 |
| 10 | 後悔 | 后悔（四級） | hòu huǐ | to regret | Vs | 高階級 Level 4 |
| 11 | 落後 | 落后（五級） | luò hòu | to fall behind | Vpt | 高階級 Level 4 |
| 12 | 後天 | 后天 | hòu tiān | the day after tomorrow | N | 準備級二級 Novice 2 |

## 第八章 【仁】名言一

己所不欲，勿施於人。

Not to do to others as you would not wish done to yourself.

| 己 | 所 | 不 | 欲 | 勿 | 施 | 於（于） | 人 |
|---|---|---|---|---|---|---|---|
| CH3-2 | | CH1-1 | | | | | CH3-2 |

| | 己 jǐ | 漢語水平考試 HSK | 拼音 Pin Yin | 英文翻譯 English | 詞類 Part of Speech | 華語文能力測驗 TOCFL |
|---|---|---|---|---|---|---|
| 1 | 自己 | 自己（三級） | zì jǐ | oneself | Noun | 準備級二級 Novice 2 |

| 己 jǐ | | 漢語水平考試 HSK | 拼音 Pin Yin | 英文翻譯 English | 詞類 Part of Speech | 華語文 能力測驗 TOCFL |
|---|---|---|---|---|---|---|
| 2 | 各抒己見 | 各抒己见（六級） | gè shū jǐ jiàn | Each person expresses their own opinion. | phrase | NA |

| 所 suǒ | | 漢語水平考試 HSK | 拼音 Pin Yin | 英文翻譯 English | 詞類 Part of Speech | 華語文 能力測驗 TOCFL |
|---|---|---|---|---|---|---|
| 1 | 所以 | 因为……所以……（二級） | yīn wèi … suǒ yǐ | therefore | Conj | 準備級二級 Novice 2 |
| 2 | 廁所 | 厕所（四級） | cè suǒ | toilet | Noun | 入門級 Level 1 |
| 3 | 所有 | 所有 | suǒ yǒu | all | Det | 入門級 Level 1 |
| 4 | 所謂 | 所谓 | suǒ wèi | so-called | Vs-attr | 進階級 Level 3 |
| 5 | 無所謂 | 无所谓（五級） | wú suǒ wèi | it doesn't matter | Vs | 進階級 Level 3 |
| 6 | 場所 | 所（六級） | chǎng suǒ | location | Noun | 高階級 Level 4 |

| 欲 yù | | 漢語水平考試 HSK | 拼音 Pin Yin | 英文翻譯 English | 詞類 Part of Speech | 華語文 能力測驗 TOCFL |
|---|---|---|---|---|---|---|
| 1 | 欲望 | 欲望（六級） | yù wàng | desire | Noun | NA |

| | 勿<br>wù | 漢語水平考試<br>HSK | 拼音<br>Pin Yin | 英文翻譯<br>English | 詞類<br>Part of Speech | 華語文<br>能力測驗<br>TOCFL |
|---|---|---|---|---|---|---|
| 1 | 勿 | 勿（五級） | wù | do not | Adv | 高階級<br>Level 4 |

| | 施<br>shī | 漢語水平考試<br>HSK | 拼音<br>Pin Yin | 英文翻譯<br>English | 詞類<br>Part of Speech | 華語文<br>能力測驗<br>TOCFL |
|---|---|---|---|---|---|---|
| 1 | 施工 | 施工 | shī gōng | construc-tion | Vi | 高階級<br>Level 4 |
| 2 | 措施 | 措施（五級） | cuò shī | measures | Noun | 高階級<br>Level 4 |
| 3 | 實施 | 实施（六級） | shí shī | to implement | Verb | 高階級<br>Level 4 |
| 4 | 設施 | 设施（五級） | shè shī | facility | Noun | 流利級<br>Level 5 |
| 5 | 施肥 | 施肥 | shī féi | to fertilize | V-sep | 流利級<br>Level 5 |
| 6 | 施行 | 施行 | shī háng | Implement | Verb | 流利級<br>Level 5 |

## 第八章　【仁】名言二

巧言令色，鮮以仁。

Fine words and an insinuating appearance are seldom associated with true virtue.

| 巧 | 言 | 令 | 色 | 鮮（鲜） | 以 | 仁 |
|---|---|---|---|---|---|---|
| | CH2-2 | | | | CH1-3 | CH6-2 |

| 巧<br>qiǎo | | 漢語水平考試<br>HSK | 拼音<br>Pin Yin | 英文翻譯<br>English | 詞類<br>Part of<br>Speech | 華語文<br>能力測驗<br>TOCFL |
|---|---|---|---|---|---|---|
| 1 | 巧克力 | 巧克力 | qiǎo kè lì | chocolate | Noun | 準備級二級<br>Novice 2 |
| 2 | 技巧 | 技巧（六級） | jì qiǎo | skill | Noun | 進階級<br>Level 3 |
| 3 | 巧妙 | 巧妙（五級） | qiǎo miào | clever | Vs | 高階級<br>Level 4 |
| 4 | 湊巧 | 湊巧 | còu qiǎo | by coinci-dence | Vs | 流利級<br>Level 5 |
| 5 | 巧合 | 巧合 | qiǎo hé | coinci-dence | Noun | 流利級<br>Level 5 |
| 6 | 恰巧 | 恰巧（六級） | qià qiǎo | coinciden-tally | adv | NA |

| 令<br>lìng | | 漢語水平考試<br>HSK | 拼音<br>Pin Yin | 英文翻譯<br>English | 詞類<br>Part of<br>Speech | 華語文<br>能力測驗<br>TOCFL |
|---|---|---|---|---|---|---|
| 1 | 命令 | 命令（五級） | mìng lìng | command | Noun | 高階級<br>Level 4 |
| 2 | 法令 | 法令 | fǎ lìng | decree | Noun | 流利級<br>Level 5 |
| 3 | 禁令 | 禁令 | jìn lìng | ban | Noun | 流利級<br>Level 5 |
| 4 | 司令 | 司令（六級） | sī lìng | commander | Noun | 流利級<br>Level 5 |
| 5 | 指令 | 指令（六級） | zhǐ lìng | instruction | Noun | NA |

| | 色<br>sè | 漢語水平考試<br>HSK | 拼音<br>Pin Yin | 英文翻譯<br>English | 詞類<br>Part of<br>Speech | 華語文<br>能力測驗<br>TOCFL |
|---|---|---|---|---|---|---|
| 1 | 顏色 | 顏色（二級） | yán sè | color | Noun | 入門級<br>Level 1 |
| 2 | 黃色 | 黃色 | huáng sè | yellow | Noun | 入門級<br>Level 1 |
| 3 | 白色 | 白色 | bái sè | white | Noun | 入門級<br>Level 1 |
| 4 | 藍色 | 蓝色 | lán sè | blue | Noun | 基礎級<br>Level 2 |
| 5 | 綠色 | 绿色 | lǜ sè | green | Noun | 基礎級<br>Level 2 |
| 6 | 特色 | 特色（五級） | tè sè | features | Noun | 進階級<br>Level 3 |
| 7 | 景色 | 景色（四級） | jǐng sè | view | Noun | 高階級<br>Level 4 |
| 8 | 出色 | 出色（五級） | chū sè | outstanding | Vs | 高階級<br>Level 4 |
| 9 | 角色 | 角色（五級） | jiǎo/jué sè | character | Noun | 進階級<br>Level 3 |

| 鮮（鲜）<br>xiān (1st tone)<br>fresh<br>xiǎn (3rd tone) rare,<br>very few | 漢語水平考試<br>HSK | 拼音<br>Pin Yin | 英文翻譯<br>English | 詞類<br>Part of<br>Speech | 華語文<br>能力測驗<br>TOCFL |
|---|---|---|---|---|---|
| 1 新鮮 | 新鮮（三級） | xīn xiān | fresh | Vs | 基礎級<br>Level 2 |

| 鮮（鲜）xiān (1st tone) fresh xiǎn (3rd tone) rare, very few | | 漢語水平考試 HSK | 拼音 Pin Yin | 英文翻譯 English | 詞類 Part of Speech | 華語文能力測驗 TOCFL |
|---|---|---|---|---|---|---|
| 2 | 海鮮 | 海鮮（五級） | hǎi xiān | seafood | N | 基礎級 Level 2 |
| 3 | 鮮花 | 鮮花 | xiān huā | fresh flowers | N | 高階級 Level 4 |
| 4 | 鮮奶 | 鮮奶 | xiān nǎi | fresh milk | N | 高階級 Level 4 |
| 5 | 鮮血 | 鮮血 | xiān xuè | blood | N | 高階級 Level 4 |
| 6 | 鮮明 | 鮮明（六級） | xiān míng | bright | Vs | 流利級 Level 5 |
| 7 | 鮮艷 | 鮮艳（五級） | xiān yàn | bright and colorful | Vs | NA |

## 第八章　【仁】名言三

克己復禮仁。

To subdue one's self and return to propriety, is perfect virtue.

| 克 | 己 | 復（复） | 禮（礼） | 為（为） | 仁 |
|---|---|---|---|---|---|
| | CH3-2 | | CH5-1 | CH4-1 | CH6-2 |

| 克 kè | 漢語水平考試 HSK | 拼音 Pin Yin | 英文翻譯 English | 詞類 Part of Speech | 華語文能力測驗 TOCFL |
|---|---|---|---|---|---|
| 1　巧克力 | 巧克力（四級） | qiǎo kè lì | chocolate | Noun | 準備級二級 Novice 2 |

| | 克 kè | 漢語水平考試 HSK | 拼音 Pin Yin | 英文翻譯 English | 詞類 Part of Speech | 華語文能力測驗 TOCFL |
|---|---|---|---|---|---|---|
| 2 | 公克 | 公克 | gōng kè | gram | Measure word | 進階級 Level 3 |
| 3 | 克服 | 克服（五級） | kè fú | conquer | Vpt | 進階級 Level 3 |
| 4 | 克制 | 克制（六級） | kè zhì | to restraint | Verb | 流利級 Level 5 |
| 5 | 坦克 | 坦克 | tǎn kè | tank | Noun | 流利級 Level 5 |

| | 復（复） fù | 漢語水平考試 HSK | 拼音 Pin Yin | 英文翻譯 English | 詞類 Part of Speech | 華語文能力測驗 TOCFL |
|---|---|---|---|---|---|---|
| 1 | 恢復 | 恢复（五級） | huī fù | to restore | Vpt | 進階級 Level 3 |
| 2 | 報復 | 报复（六級） | bào fù | to revenge | Verb | 流利級 Level 5 |
| 3 | 復甦 | 复苏 | fù sū | to recover (economic) | Vp | 流利級 Level 5 |
| 4 | 復原 | 复原 | fù yuán | to recover | Vp | 流利級 Level 5 |
| 5 | 康復 | 康复 | kāng fù | recovery | Vp, noun | 流利級 Level 5 |

# 第九章　【道德】名言一

朝聞道，夕死可矣。

If a man in the morning hear the right way, he may die in the evening without regret.

| 朝 | 聞（闻） | 道 | 夕 | 死 | 可 | 矣 |
|---|---|---|---|---|---|---|
| | | | | | CH1-3 | N/A |

| | 朝<br>cháo, zhāo | 漢語水平考試<br>HSK | 拼音<br>Pin Yin | 英文翻譯<br>English | 詞類<br>Part of<br>Speech | 華語文<br>能力測驗<br>TOCFL |
|---|---|---|---|---|---|---|
| 1 | 朝 | 朝（五級） | cháo | towards | Prep | 高階級<br>Level 4 |
| 2 | 朝向 | 朝向 | cháo xiàng | towards | Prep | NA |
| 3 | 朝氣 | 朝气 | zhāo qì | vitality | Noun | 流利級<br>Level 5 |
| 4 | 朝代 | 朝代（六級） | cháo dài | dyNAsty | Noun | NA |

| | 聞（闻）<br>wén | 漢語水平考試<br>HSK | 拼音<br>Pin Yin | 英文翻譯<br>English | 詞類<br>Part of<br>Speech | 華語文<br>能力測驗<br>TOCFL |
|---|---|---|---|---|---|---|
| 1 | 聞 | 闻（五級） | wén | to smell | Verb | 基礎級<br>Level 2 |
| 2 | 新聞 | 新闻（三級） | xīn wén | news | Noun | 基礎級<br>Level 2 |
| 3 | 聞名 | 闻名 | wén míng | famous | Vst | 流利級<br>Level 5 |
| 4 | 見聞 | 见闻（六級） | jiàn wén | knowledge | Noun | NA |

| 道<br>dào | | 漢語水平考試<br>HSK | 拼音<br>Pin Yin | 英文翻譯<br>English | 詞類<br>Part of<br>Speech | 華語文<br>能力測驗<br>TOCFL |
|---|---|---|---|---|---|---|
| 1 | 知道 | 知道 | zhī dào | to know | Vst | 準備級一級<br>Novice 1 |
| 2 | 味道 | 味道（四級） | wèi dào | to taste | Vst | 入門級<br>Level 1 |
| 3 | 道德 | 道德（五級） | dào dé | moral | Noun | 進階級<br>Level 3 |
| 4 | 道教 | 道教 | dào jiāo | Taoism | Noun | 進階級<br>Level 3 |
| 5 | 道理 | 道理（五級） | dào lǐ | reason | Noun | 進階級<br>Level 3 |
| 6 | 道歉 | 道歉（四級） | dào qiàn | to apologize | V-sep | 進階級<br>Level 3 |
| 7 | 道路 | 道路 | dào lù | the way | Noun | 高階級<br>Level 4 |
| 8 | 人道 | 人道（六級） | rén dào | humanitari-<br>anism | Noun | 流利級<br>Level 5 |

| 夕<br>xī | | 漢語水平考試<br>HSK | 拼音<br>Pin Yin | 英文翻譯<br>English | 詞類<br>Part of<br>Speech | 華語文<br>能力測驗<br>TOCFL |
|---|---|---|---|---|---|---|
| 1 | 除夕 | 除夕（五級） | chú xī | New Year's<br>Eve | Noun | 基礎級<br>Level 2 |
| 2 | 夕陽 | 夕阳（六級） | xī yáng | sunset | Noun | NA |

| 死<br>sǐ | 漢語水平考試<br>HSK | 拼音<br>Pin Yin | 英文翻譯<br>English | 詞類<br>Part of Speech | 華語文能力測驗<br>TOCFL |
|---|---|---|---|---|---|
| 1 | 死 | 死（四級） | sǐ | to die | Vp | 基礎級<br>Level 2 |
| 2 | 死亡 | 死亡（六級） | sǐ wáng | death | noun | 高階級<br>Level 4 |
| 3 | 該死 | 该死 | gāi sǐ | damned | Vs | 流利級<br>Level 5 |
| 4 | 生死 | 生死 | shēng sǐ | life and death | Noun | 流利級<br>Level 5 |

## 第九章　【道德】名言二

德不孤，必有鄰。

Virtue is not left to stand alone. He who practices it will have neighbors.

| 德 | 不 | 孤 | 必 | 有 | 鄰（邻） |
|---|---|---|---|---|---|
| | CH1-1 | | CH1-1 | CH1-1 | |

| 德<br>dé | 漢語水平考試<br>HSK | 拼音<br>Pin Yin | 英文翻譯<br>English | 詞類<br>Part of Speech | 華語文能力測驗<br>TOCFL |
|---|---|---|---|---|---|
| 1 | 道德 | 道德（五級） | dào dé | virtue, ethics | Noun | 進階級<br>Level 3 |
| 2 | 品德 | 品德（六級） | pǐn dé | moral character | Noun | 高階級<br>Level 4 |

| 孤<br>gū | 漢語水平考試<br>HSK | 拼音<br>Pin Yin | 英文翻譯<br>English | 詞類<br>Part of Speech | 華語文能力測驗<br>TOCFL |
|---|---|---|---|---|---|
| 1 | 孤單 | 孤单 | gū dān | alone | Vs | 高階級<br>Level 4 |

| | 孤<br>gū | 漢語水平考試<br>HSK | 拼音<br>Pin Yin | 英文翻譯<br>English | 詞類<br>Part of Speech | 華語文能力測驗<br>TOCFL |
|---|---|---|---|---|---|---|
| 2 | 孤獨 | 孤独（六級） | gū dú | lonely | Vs | 流利級<br>Level 5 |
| 3 | 孤兒 | 孤儿 | gū ér | orphan | Noun | 流利級<br>Level 5 |
| 4 | 孤立 | 孤立（六級） | gū lì | isolated | Vs | 流利級<br>Level 5 |

| | 鄰（邻）<br>lín | 漢語水平考試<br>HSK | 拼音<br>Pin Yin | 英文翻譯<br>English | 詞類<br>Part of Speech | 華語文能力測驗<br>TOCFL |
|---|---|---|---|---|---|---|
| 1 | 鄰居 | 邻居（三級） | lín jū | neighbor | Noun | 基礎級<br>Level 2 |
| 2 | 鄰里 | 邻里 | lín lǐ | neighbor-hood | Noun | 流利級<br>Level 5 |

## 第九章　【道德】名言三

巧言亂德。小不忍，則亂大謀。

Specious words confound virtue. Want of forbearance in small matters confounds great plans.

| 巧 | 言 | 亂（乱） | 德 |
|---|---|---|---|
| Ch8-2 | Ch8-2 | | |

| 小 | 不 | 忍 | 則 | 亂（乱） | 大 | 謀（谋） |
|---|---|---|---|---|---|---|
| CH3-2 | CH1-1 | | CH1-3 | | | CH3-3 |

| 巧<br>qiǎo | 漢語水平考試<br>HSK | 拼音<br>Pin Yin | 英文翻譯<br>English | 詞類<br>Part of<br>Speech | 華語文<br>能力測驗<br>TOCFL |
|---|---|---|---|---|---|
| 1 | 巧克力 | 巧克力（四級） | qiǎo kè lì | chocolate | Noun | 準備級二級<br>Novice 2 |
| 2 | 技巧 | 技巧（六級） | jì qiǎo | skill | Noun | 進階級<br>Level 3 |
| 3 | 巧妙 | 巧妙（五級） | qiǎo miào | clever | adj | 高階級<br>Level 4 |
| 4 | 湊巧 | 湊巧 | còu qiǎo | by coincidence | Vs | 流利級<br>Level 5 |
| 5 | 巧合 | 巧合 | qiǎo hé | coincidence | noun | 流利級<br>Level 5 |

| 亂<br>luàn | 漢語水平考試<br>HSK | 拼音<br>Pin Yin | 英文翻譯<br>English | 詞類<br>Part of<br>Speech | 華語文<br>能力測驗<br>TOCFL |
|---|---|---|---|---|---|
| 1 | 混亂 | 混乱 | hún luàn | confusion | noun | 進階級<br>Level 3 |
| 2 | 亂 | 乱（四級） | luàn | chaos | noun | 基礎級<br>Level 2 |
| 3 | 動亂 | 动乱 | dòng luàn | turmoil | noun | 流利級<br>Level 5 |
| 4 | 胡亂 | 胡乱（六級） | hú luàn | casually | Adv | 流利級<br>Level 5 |
| 5 | 紊亂 | 紊乱 | wěn luàn | to disorder | Vs | 流利級<br>Level 5 |
| 6 | 戰亂 | 战乱 | zhàn luàn | war | Noun | 流利級<br>Level 5 |
| 7 | 搗亂 | 乱（六級） | dǎo luàn | to make trouble | Vp | NA |

| | 忍<br>rěn | 漢語水平考試<br>HSK | 拼音<br>Pin Yin | 英文翻譯<br>English | 詞類<br>Part of<br>Speech | 華語文<br>能力測驗<br>TOCFL |
|---|---|---|---|---|---|---|
| 1 | 忍 | 忍 | rěn | to endure | Vs | 進階級<br>Level 3 |
| 2 | 忍耐 | 忍耐（六級） | rěn nài | patience | noun | 進階級<br>Level 3 |
| 3 | 忍不住 | 忍不住（五級） | rěn bú zhù | can't help | Vs | 高階級<br>Level 4 |
| 4 | 忍受 | 忍受（六級） | rěn shòu | to endure | Vst | 高階級<br>Level 4 |
| 5 | 堅忍 | 坚忍 | jiān rěn | persevering | Vs | 流利級<br>Level 5 |
| 6 | 忍痛 | 忍痛 | rěn tòng | reluctantly,<br>to suffer | Vs | 流利級<br>Level 5 |

| | 大<br>dà | 漢語水平考試<br>HSK | 拼音<br>Pin Yin | 英文翻譯<br>English | 詞類<br>Part of<br>Speech | 華語文<br>能力測驗<br>TOCFL |
|---|---|---|---|---|---|---|
| 1 | 大學 | 大学 | dà xué | the<br>university | Noun | 準備級一級<br>Novice 1 |
| 2 | 大家 | 大家（二級） | dà jiā | everyone | Noun | 準備級二級<br>Novice 2 |
| 3 | 大人 | 大人 | dà rén | grown-up's | Noun | 入門級<br>Level 1 |
| 4 | 大學生 | 大学生 | dà xué shēng | college<br>students | Noun | 基礎級<br>Level 2 |
| 5 | 大樓 | 大厦（五級） | dà lóu | building | Noun | 入門級<br>Level 1 |
| 6 | 大衣 | 大衣 | dà yī | overcoat | Noun | 入門級<br>Level 1 |

| 大 dà | 漢語水平考試 HSK | 拼音 Pin Yin | 英文翻譯 English | 詞類 Part of Speech | 華語文 能力測驗 TOCFL |
|---|---|---|---|---|---|
| 7 | 大聲 | 大声 | dà shēng | loudly | adv | NA |

| 謀 móu | 漢語水平考試 HSK | 拼音 Pin Yin | 英文翻譯 English | 詞類 Part of Speech | 華語文 能力測驗 TOCFL |
|---|---|---|---|---|---|
| 1 | 參謀 | 参谋（六級） | cān móu | advisor, staff officer | Noun | 流利級 Level 5 |
| 2 | 謀生 | 谋生 | móu shēng | to make a living | Vi | 流利級 Level 5 |
| 3 | 陰謀 | 阴谋（六級） | yīn móu | conspiracy | Noun | 流利級 Level 5 |
| 4 | 謀殺 | 谋杀（六級） | móu shā | to murder | Vi | NA |
| 5 | 謀求 | 谋求（六級） | móu qiú | to seek | Vi | NA |

## 第十章　【政治】名言一

君君、臣臣、父父、子子。

There is government, when the prince is prince, and the minister is minister; when the father is father, and the son is son.

| 君 | 臣 | 父 | 子 |
|---|---|---|---|
| CH3-1 | CH5-2 | CH1-1 | CH3-1 |

| 臣 chén | 漢語水平考試 HSK | 拼音 Pin Yin | 英文翻譯 English | 詞類 Part of Speech | 華語文 能力測驗 TOCFL |
|---|---|---|---|---|---|
| 1 | 大臣 | 大臣（六級） | dà chén | state official or subject in a dyNAsty | noun | NA |

# 第十章 【政治】名言二

其身正，不令而行；其身不正，雖令不從。

When a prince's personal conduct is correct, his government is effective without the issuing of orders. If his personal conduct is not correct, he may issue orders, but they will not be followed.

| 其 | 身 | 正 | 不 | 令 | 而 | 行 |
|---|---|---|---|---|---|---|
| CH1-2 | | | CH1-1 | CH8-2 | | CH4-3 |

| 其 | 身 | 不 | 正 | 雖（虽） | 令 | 不 | 從（从） |
|---|---|---|---|---|---|---|---|
| CH1-2 | | CH1-1 | | | CH8-2 | CH1-1 | |

| | 身<br>shēn | 漢語水平考試<br>HSK | 拼音<br>Pin Yin | 英文翻譯<br>English | 詞類<br>Part of Speech | 華語文<br>能力測驗<br>TOCFL |
|---|---|---|---|---|---|---|
| 1 | 身體 | 身体（二級） | shēn tǐ | body | Noun | 準備級二級<br>Novice 2 |
| 2 | 單身 | 单身 | dān shēn | single | Vs | 進階級<br>Level 3 |
| 3 | 本身 | 本身（六級） | běn shēn | itself | Noun | 高階級<br>Level 4 |
| 4 | 全身 | 全身 | quán shēn | whole body | Noun | 進階級<br>Level 3 |
| 5 | 身邊 | 身边 | shēn biān | at one's side | Noun | 基礎級<br>Level 2 |
| 6 | 身高 | 身高 | shēn gāo | height | Noun | 基礎級<br>Level 2 |
| 7 | 健身 | 健身（五級） | shēn shàng | fitness | Vi | 流利級<br>Level 5 |
| 8 | 出身 | 出身（六級） | chū shēn | family back-ground | Vpt | 高階級<br>Level 4 |

| 正 zhèng | 漢語水平考試 HSK | 拼音 Pin Yin | 英文翻譯 English | 詞類 Part of Speech | 華語文能力測驗 TOCFL |
|---|---|---|---|---|---|
| 1 正在 | 正在（四級） | zhèng zài | doing | Adv | NA |
| 2 真正 | 真正（四級） | zhēn zhèng | real | Adv | 進階級 Level 3 |
| 3 正常 | 正常（四級） | zhèng cháng | normal | Vs | 基礎級 Level 2 |
| 4 正確 | 正确（四級） | zhèng què | correct | Vs | 進階級 Level 3 |
| 5 正式 | 正式（四級） | zhèng shì | formal | Vs | 基礎級 Level 2 |
| 6 反正 | 反正（四級） | fǎn zhèng | anyway | Adv | 高階級 Level 4 |
| 7 改正 | 改正（四級） | gǎi zhèng | to correct a mistake | V | 高階級 Level 4 |

| 而 ér | 漢語水平考試 HSK | 拼音 Pin Yin | 英文翻譯 English | 詞類 Part of Speech | 華語文能力測驗 TOCFL |
|---|---|---|---|---|---|
| 1 而且 | 不但……而且……（三級） | ér qiě | not only, but also | Conj | 基礎級 Level 2 |
| 2 而 | 而（四級） | ér | but | Conj | 進階級 Level 3 |
| 3 反而 | 反而（五級） | fǎn ér | instead of | Conj | 進階級 Level 3 |
| 4 總而言之 | 总而言之 | zǒng ér yán zhī | in short, briefly speaking | Conj | 進階級 Level 3 |

| 而 ér | | 漢語水平考試 HSK | 拼音 Pin Yin | 英文翻譯 English | 詞類 Part of Speech | 華語文 能力測驗 TOCFL |
|---|---|---|---|---|---|---|
| 5 | 而已 | 而已（六級） | ér yǐ | only, just | Ptc | 高階級 Level 4 |
| 6 | 然而 | 然而（四級） | rán ér | however | Conj | 高階級 Level 4 |
| 7 | 一般 而言 | 一般而言 | yī bān ér yán | general speaking | Conj | 高階級 Level 4 |
| 8 | 因而 | 因而（五級） | yīn ér | therefore | Conj | 高階級 Level 4 |

| 雖（虽）suī | | 漢語水平考試 HSK | 拼音 Pin Yin | 英文翻譯 English | 詞類 Part of Speech | 華語文 能力測驗 TOCFL |
|---|---|---|---|---|---|---|
| 1 | 雖然 | 虽然……但 是……（二級） | suī rán | although | Conj | 入門級 Level 1 |
| 2 | 雖說 | 虽说 | suī shuō | although | Conj | 流利級 Level 5 |

| 從（从）cóng | | 漢語水平考試 HSK | 拼音 Pin Yin | 英文翻譯 English | 詞類 Part of Speech | 華語文 能力測驗 TOCFL |
|---|---|---|---|---|---|---|
| 1 | 從 | 从（二級） | cóng | from | Prep | 準備級二級 Novice 2 |
| 2 | 從前 | 从前（五級） | cóng qián | before | Noun | 入門級 Level 1 |
| 3 | 從不 | 从不 | cóng bú | never | Adv | 進階級 Level 3 |
| 4 | 從來 | 从来（四級） | cóng lái | ever | Adv | 基礎級 Level 2 |

| 從（从）<br>cóng | | 漢語水平考試<br>HSK | 拼音<br>Pin Yin | 英文翻譯<br>English | 詞類<br>Part of Speech | 華語文<br>能力測驗<br>TOCFL |
|---|---|---|---|---|---|---|
| 5 | 從小 | 从小 | cóng xiǎo | since childhood | Adv | 進階級<br>Level 3 |
| 6 | 自從 | 自从（五級） | zì cóng | since | Prep | 進階級<br>Level 3 |
| 7 | 從此 | 从此（五級） | cóng cǐ | since then | Adv | 高階級<br>Level 4 |

## 第十章 【政治】名言三

不在其位，不謀其政。

He who is not in any particular office has nothing to do with plans for the administration of its duties.

| 不 | 在 | 其 | 位 | 不 | 謀（谋） | 其 | 政 |
|---|---|---|---|---|---|---|---|
| CH1-1 | CH1-1 | CH1-2 | | CH1-1 | CH9-3 | CH1-2 | |

| 位<br>wèi | | 漢語水平考試<br>HSK | 拼音<br>Pin Yin | 英文翻譯<br>English | 詞類<br>Part of Speech | 華語文<br>能力測驗<br>TOCFL |
|---|---|---|---|---|---|---|
| 1 | 座位 | 座位（四級） | zuò wèi | seat | Noun | 基礎級<br>Level 2 |
| 2 | （一）<br>位 | 位（三級） | (yī )wèi | （Measure word for person） | Measure word | 準備級一級<br>Novice 1 |
| 3 | 地位 | 地位（五級） | dì wèi | status | Noun | 進階級<br>Level 3 |
| 4 | 各位 | 各位 | gè wèi | everybody | Noun | 進階級<br>Level 3 |

| 位 wèi | 漢語水平考試 HSK | 拼音 Pin Yin | 英文翻譯 English | 詞類 Part of Speech | 華語文能力測驗 TOCFL |
|---|---|---|---|---|---|
| 5 | 位置 | 位置（五級） | wèi zhì | position | Noun | 進階級 Level 3 |
| 6 | 位子 | 位子 | wèi zǐ | seat | Noun | 基礎級 Level 2 |
| 7 | 學位 | 学位（六級） | xué wèi | degree | Noun | 高階級 Level 4 |

| 政 zhèng | 漢語水平考試 HSK | 拼音 Pin Yin | 英文翻譯 English | 詞類 Part of Speech | 華語文能力測驗 TOCFL |
|---|---|---|---|---|---|
| 1 | 政治 | 政治（五級） | zhèng zhì | politics | Noun | 進階級 Level 3 |
| 2 | 政策 | 政策（六級） | zhèng cè | policy | Noun | 高階級 Level 4 |
| 3 | 政黨 | 政党 | zhèng dǎng | political party | Noun | 高階級 Level 4 |
| 4 | 政府 | 政府（五級） | zhèng fǔ | government | Noun | 高階級 Level 4 |
| 5 | 財政 | 政（六級） | cái zhèng | fiNAnces | Noun | 流利級 Level 5 |
| 6 | 行政 | 行政（六級） | xíng zhèng | administrative | Noun | 流利級 Level 5 |

# 附錄二
# 美國總統在演說中引用中文古名言之實例
## World Leaders Quoting the Analects or Chinese Proverb

## 實例 1

shè wǒ qí shuí?

捨我其誰？

Lord, reform Thy world, beginning with me.

### Franklin D. Roosevelt 富蘭克林・羅斯福 總統

美國第三十二任總統 32nd President of the United States: 1933-1945

演說 Speech：Remarks to the Management-Labor Conference.

日期 Date：December 17, 1941

引用名言 Proverb quoted：捨我其誰？ Lord, reform Thy world, beginning with me.

原文出處 Ancient text cited from：【孟子・公孫丑下】 *Mencius*

美國總統檔案來源 The American Presidency Project link:

【演說內容 Speech】

　　And so I was just thinking of an old idea of self-discipline an old Chinese proverb—of a Chinese Christian. He prayed every day—he had been told to pray to our kind of God—and his prayer was: "Lord, reform Thy world, beginning with me." It is rather a nice line for us all to keep in the back of our heads.

【名言翻譯 Translation】

捨我其誰？ Lord, reform Thy world, beginning with me.

如欲平治天下，當今之世，捨我其誰也？

If it wished this, in today's world, who is there besides me to bring it about?

| | 生詞<br>Vocabulary | 拼音<br>Pin Yin | 英文翻譯<br>English | 詞類<br>Part of<br>Speech | 華語文<br>能力測驗<br>TOCFL |
|---|---|---|---|---|---|
| 1 | 捨 | （捨得）<br>shě de | to give up / to abandon | Vst | 高階級<br>Level 4 |
| 2 | 我 | wǒ | I / me / my | N | 準備級一級<br>Novice1 |
| 3 | 其 | qí | his / her / its / their (refers to sth preceding it) | N | 高階級<br>Level 4 |
| 4 | 誰 | shéi | who | N | 準備級一級<br>Novice1 |

# 實例 2

qiān lǐ zhī xíng shǐ yú zú xià.

千里之行始於足下。

A journey of a thousand miles must begin with a single step.

**John F. Kennedy** 約翰‧甘迺迪 總統

美國第三十五任總統 35th President of the United States: 1961-1963

1. 演說 Speech：Remarks on the White House Lawn at a Reception for Foreign Students

日期 Date：May 10, 1961

引用名言 Proverb quoted：千里之行始於足下。A journey of a thousand miles must begin with a single step.

原文出處 Ancient text cited from：【道德經・64 章】，*Dao-De Jing, Chapter 64*

美國總統檔案來源 The American Presidency Project link:

President John F. Kennedy mentioned this Chinese proverb in his Remarks on the White House Lawn at a Reception for Foreign Students, May 10, 1961. The President spoke from a bandstand erected on the South Lawn at the White House. The guests included about 1,000 foreign students, representing 73 nations, who were attending colleges in the Washington, D.C., area.

## 【演說內容 Speech】

"The Chinese have an old proverb that to begin a voyage of a thousand miles requires the first step. I believe that we've taken more than the first step in this country, that we are moving ahead. But I realize we have a long way to go to build a free and open country here, and free and open societies around the world."

## 2. **John F. Kennedy** 約翰・甘迺迪 總統

演說 Speech：Radio and Television Address to the American People on the Nuclear Test Ban Treaty

日期 Date：July 26, 1963

引用名言 Proverb quoted：千里之行始於足下。A journey of a thousand miles must begin with a single step.

原文出處 Ancient text cited from：【道德經・第 64 章】，*Dao-De Jing, Chapter 64*

美國總統檔案來源 The American Presidency Project link:

【演說內容 Speech】

But now, for the first time in many years, the path of peace may be open. No one can be certain what the future will bring. No one can say whether the time has come for an easing of the struggle. But history and our own conscience will judge us harsher if we do not now make every effort to test our hopes by action, and this is the place to begin. According to the ancient Chinese proverb, "A journey of a thousand miles must begin with a single step."

My fellow Americans, let us take that first step. Let us, if we can, step back from the shadows of war and seek out the way of peace. And if that journey is a thousand miles, or even more, let history record that we, in this land, at this time, took the first step.

【名言翻譯 Translation】

千里之行始於足下。A journey of a thousand miles must begin with a single step.

| | 生詞<br>Vocabulary | 拼音<br>Pin Yin | 英文翻譯<br>English | 詞類<br>Part of<br>Speech | 華語文<br>能力測驗<br>TOCFL |
|---|---|---|---|---|---|
| 1 | 千 | qiān | thousand | N | 準備級<br>一級<br>Novice1 |
| 2 | 里 | lǐ | mile | M | 進階級<br>Level 3 |
| 3 | 之 | zhī | Possessive particle, literary equivalent of 的 | Ptc | 高階級<br>Level 4 |
| 4 | 行 | xíng | to walk / to travel (V)<br>a visit / journey (N) | Vs | 入門級<br>Level 1 |
| 5 | （開）始 | （開始）<br>kāi shǐ | to begin (verb),<br>beginning (N) | Vp | 入門級<br>Level 1 |

| | 生詞<br>Vocabulary | 拼音<br>Pin Yin | 英文翻譯<br>English | 詞類<br>Part of<br>Speech | 華語文<br>能力測驗<br>TOCFL |
|---|---|---|---|---|---|
| 6 | （在）於 | （在於）<br>zài yú | in / at / from /<br>because | Vst | 流利級<br>Level 5 |
| 7 | 足 | zú | foot | N / Vs | 高階級<br>Level 4 |
| 8 | 下 | xià | down / downwards /<br>below / lower | Det | 基礎級<br>Level 2 |

# 實例 3

rù qí sú, cóng qí lìng.

入其俗，從其令。

When you enter a country, inquire as to what is forbidden; when you cross a boundary, ask about the customs.

## Lyndon B. Johnson 林登・約翰遜 總統

美國第三十六任總統 *36th President of the United States: 1963-1969*

演說 Speech：The President's Response to Remarks of Welcome by Prime Minister Pearson at Vancouver International Airport, British Columbia

日期 Date：September 16, 1964

引用名言 Proverb quoted：入其俗，從其令。When you enter a country, inquire as to what is forbidden; when you cross a boundary, ask about the customs.

原文出處 Ancient text cited from：【莊子・山木】 *Zhuang-Zi, Chapter Shan-Mu*

美國總統檔案來源 The American Presidency Project link：

【演說內容 Speech】

I think I will be guided by an old Chinese proverb: "When you enter a country, inquire as to what is forbidden; when you cross a boundary, ask about the customs." Well, I have made careful inquiries and I will eat the salmon and praise the B.C. Lions.

【名言翻譯 Translation】

入其俗，從其令。When you enter a country, inquire as to what is forbidden; when you cross a boundary, ask about the customs.

| | 生詞<br>Vocabulary | 拼音<br>Pin Yin | 英文翻譯<br>English | 詞類<br>Part of<br>Speech | 華語文能力<br>測驗<br>TOCFL |
|---|---|---|---|---|---|
| 1 | 入 | rù | to enter | V | 高階級<br>Level 4 |
| 2 | 其 | qí | his / her / its / their (refers to sth preceding it) | N | 高階級<br>Level 4 |
| 3 | 俗 | sú | custom / convention / popular / common | Vs | 高階級<br>Level 4 |
| 4 | 從 | (從)<br>cóng ；<br>（服從）<br>fú cóng | to follow / to obey / to engage in (an activity) | V | 準備級二級<br>Novice 2<br>流利級<br>Level 5 |
| 5 | 其 | qí | his / her / its / their (refers to sth preceding it) | N | 高階級<br>Level 4 |
| 6 | （命）令 | mìng lìng<br>（命令） | to order / to command (V. or N) | N | 進階級<br>Level 3 |

# 實例 4

tiān xià tóng guī ér shū tú, yí zhì ér bǎi lù.

天下同歸而殊途，一致而百慮。

There are many paths up the mountain, but the view from the top is always the same.

## Lyndon B. Johnson 林登‧約翰遜 總統

美國第三十六任總統 *36th President of the United States: 1963-1969*

演說 Speech：Remarks at the 175th Anniversary Convocation of Georgetown University

日期 Date：December 03, 1964

引用名言 Proverb quoted：天下同歸而殊途，一致而百慮。There are many paths up the mountain, but the view from the top is always the same.

原文出處 Ancient text cited from：【周易】*Book of Zhou-Yi (Book of Changes, I-Ching)*

美國總統檔案來源 The American Presidency Project link：

【演說內容 Speech】

　　A Chinese proverb says there are many paths up the mountain, but the view from the top is always the same. We are always ready to look for a better or easier path, but we intend to climb to the summit.

【名言翻譯 Translation】

天下同歸而殊途，一致而百慮。There are many paths up the mountain, but the view from the top is always the same.

| | 生詞<br>Vocabulary | 拼音<br>Pin Yin | 英文翻譯<br>English | 詞類<br>Part of<br>Speech | 華語文<br>能力測驗<br>TOCFL |
|---|---|---|---|---|---|
| 1 | 天下 | tiān xià | land under heaven /<br>the whole world | N | 進階級<br>Level 3 |
| 2 | 同 | tóng | like / same / similar /<br>together / alike | adv | 進階級<br>Level 3 |
| 3 | 歸 | guī | to return / to go<br>back to / (of a<br>responsibility) to be<br>taken care of by / to<br>belong to | V | 流利級<br>Level 5 |
| 4 | 殊 | tè shū<br>（特殊） | different / unique /<br>special / | Vs | 進階級<br>Level 3 |
| 5 | 途 | tú jīng<br>（途徑） | way / route / road | N | 高階級<br>Level 4 |
| 6 | 一致 | yí zhì | unanimous / identical<br>(views or opinions) | Vs | 高階級<br>Level 4 |
| 7 | 百 | bǎi | hundred | N | 準備級一級<br>Novice1 |
| 8 | 慮 | lǜ | to think over / to<br>consider / anxiety | V | 高階級<br>Level 4 |

# 實例 5

hǎi nèi cún zhī jǐ, tiān yá ruò bǐ lín.

海內存知己，天涯若比鄰。

To feel a closeness to a friend or loved one, despite being separated by a great distance.

## Ronald Reagan 雷諾‧雷根 總統

美國第四十任總統 *40th President of the United States: 1981-1989*

演說 Speech：Toast at a Dinner Hosted by President Li Xiannian of China in Beijing

日期 Date：April 26, 1984

引用名言 Proverb quoted：海內存知己，天涯若比鄰。Although we reside in far corners of the world, having a good friend is akin to having a good neighbor.

原文出處 Ancient text cited from：唐朝王勃【送杜少府之任蜀州】Tang Poet, Wang Bo

美國總統檔案來源 The American Presidency Project link:

President Ronald Reagan mentioned this quote during his Toast at a Dinner Hosted by President Li Xiannian of China in Beijing on April 26, 1984.

【演說內容 Speech】

"Many centuries ago, Wang Po, a famous Chinese poet-philosopher, wrote, 'Although we reside in far corners of the world, having a good friend is akin to having a good neighbor.'"

【名言翻譯 Translation】

海內存知己，天涯若比鄰。Although we reside in far corners of the world, having a good friend is akin to having a good neighbor.

| | 生詞<br>Vocabulary | 拼音<br>Pin Yin | 英文翻譯<br>English | 詞類<br>Part of<br>Speech | 華語文<br>能力測驗<br>TOCFL |
|---|---|---|---|---|---|
| 1 | 海 | hǎi | ocean | N | 入門級<br>Level 1 |

| | 生詞<br>Vocabulary | 拼音<br>Pin Yin | 英文翻譯<br>English | 詞類<br>Part of Speech | 華語文<br>能力測驗<br>TOCFL |
|---|---|---|---|---|---|
| 2 | 內 | nèi | inside | N | 基礎級<br>Level 2 |
| 3 | 存 | cún | keep, save, exist | V | 基礎級<br>Level 2 |
| 4 | 知己 | zhī jǐ | soul mate | N | NA |
| 5 | 天涯 | tiān yá | faraway places | N | NA |
| 6 | 若 | ruò | as if | Conj | 流利級<br>Level 5 |
| 7 | 比 | bǐ | alike, compare to | Prep | 準備級二級<br>Novice 2 |
| 8 | 鄰 | lín jū<br>（鄰居） | neighbor | N | 基礎級<br>Level 2 |

## 實例 6

qián rén zāi shù, hòu rén chéng liáng.

前人栽樹，後人乘涼。

One generation plants a tree, the next sits in its shade.

### George H. W. Bush 喬治・布希 總統

美國第四十一任總統 *41st President of the United States: 1989-1993*

演說 Speech：Toast at the Welcoming Banquet in Beijing

日期 Date：February 25, 1989

引用名言 Proverb quoted：前人栽樹，後人乘涼。One generation plants a tree; the next sits in its shade.

原文出處 Ancient text cited from：晚清【黃繡球】Late Qing novel, *Yellow Silk Ball*

美國總統檔案來源 The American Presidency Project link:

President George Bush mentioned this quote to praise the thousands of years of Chinese culture in his Toast at a Dinner Hosted by President Li Xiannian of China in Beijing in 1989

【演說內容 Speech】

George Bush: There's a Chinese proverb that says: "One generation plants a tree; the next sits in its shade."

【名言翻譯 Translation】

前人栽樹，後人乘涼。One generation plants a tree; the next sits in its shade.

| | 生詞<br>Vocabulary | 拼音<br>Pin Yin | 英文翻譯<br>English | 詞類<br>Part of Speech | 華語文能力測驗<br>TOCFL |
|---|---|---|---|---|---|
| 1 | 前人 | qián rén | ancestors | N | NA |
| 2 | 栽 | zāi | plant | V | 流利級<br>Level 5 |
| 3 | 樹 | shù | tree | N | 入門級<br>Level 1 |
| 4 | 後人 | hòu rén | descendants | N | NA |
| 5 | 乘 | chéng | to ride on (a transportation); to enjoy | V | 基礎級<br>Level 2 |
| 6 | 涼 | liáng | coolness | Vs | 基礎級<br>Level 2 |

# 實例 7

dà dào zhī xíng yě, tiān xià wéi gōng.

大道之行也，天下為公。

When the great way is followed, all under heaven will be equal.

## William J. Clinton 威廉‧克林頓 總統

美國第四十二任總統 *42nd President of the United States: 1993-2001*

演說 Speech：Remark by the President in welcoming ceremony, South Gate of the Old City, Xian, China

日期 Date：June 25, 1998

引用名言 Proverb quoted：大道之行也，天下為公 When the great way is followed, all under heaven will be equal.

原文出處 Ancient text cited from：【禮記‧禮運篇‧第 1 節】 *Li-Ji, Chapter Li-Yun, Verse 1*

美國總統檔案來源 The American Presidency Project link:

President William J. Clinton mentioned this quote from 【禮記‧禮運篇】 *Li-Ji, Chapter Li-Yun*, in his remarks at the Arrival Ceremony in Xi'an, China, June 25, 1998.

【演說內容 Speech】

Let us give new meaning to the words written in the ancient Book of Rites, what you call the Li Shi: When the great way is followed, all under heaven will be equal.

【名言翻譯 Translation】

大道之行也，天下爲公。When the great way is followed, all under heaven will be equal.

| 生詞<br>Vocabulary | 拼音<br>Pin Yin | 英文翻譯<br>English | 詞類<br>Part of Speech | 華語文能力測驗<br>TOCFL |
|---|---|---|---|---|
| 1 | 大道 | dà dào | The great way, the ultimate way | N | 流利級<br>Level 5 |
| 2 | 之 | zhī | Possessive particle, literary equivalent of 的 | Ptc | 高階級<br>Level 4 |
| 3 | 行 | xíng | to do, to function | Vs | 入門級<br>Level 1 |
| 4 | 也 | yě | Final particle, affirmative | ptc | 準備級一級<br>Novice 1 |
| 5 | 天下 | tiān xià | The universe, the world | N | 進階級<br>Level 3 |
| 6 | 為 | wéi | Is, be | Prep | 進階級<br>Level 3 |
| 7 | 公 | gōng yòng<br>（公用） | Belonged to everyone, fair | Vs-attr | 高階級<br>Level 4 |

## 實例 8

mín wéi bāng běn, běn gù bāng níng.

民為邦本，本固邦寧。

The people should be cherished, the people are the root of a country; the root firm, the country is tranquil.

**George Walker Bush** 喬治・沃克・布希 總統

美國第四十三任總統 *43rd President of the United States: 2001-2009*

演說 Speech：President discusses Freedom and Democracy in Kyoto, Japan

日期 Date：November 16, 2005

引用名言 Proverb quoted：民為邦本，本固邦寧。The people are the root of a country；the root firm, the country is tranquil.

原文出處 Ancient text cited from：【尚書】 *Shang-Shu*

美國總統檔案來源 The American Presidency Project link：

President George W. Bush quoted【尚書】 *Shang-Shu* to illustrate the importance of people's contribution during his remarks in Kyoto, November 16, 2005.

【演說內容 Speech】

George W. Bush: "Thousands of years before Thomas Jefferson or Abraham Lincoln, a Chinese poet wrote that, "the people should be cherished, the people are the root of a country; the root firm, the country is tranquil.""

【名言翻譯 Translation】

民為邦本，本固邦寧。The people are the root of a country; the root firm, the country is tranquil.

| | 生詞 Vocabulary | 拼音 Pin Yin | 英文翻譯 English | 詞類 Part of Speech | 華語文能力測驗 TOCFL |
|---|---|---|---|---|---|
| 1 | 民 | rén mín （人民） | people | N | 進階級 Level 3 |
| 2 | 為 | wéi | is | Prep | 進階級 Level 3 |
| 3 | 邦 | bāng | country, state | N | N/A |
| 4 | 本 | běn | foundation, root | N | 準備級二級 Novice2 |
| 5 | 固 | jiān gù （堅固） | surely, firm, solid | Vs | 流利級 Level 5 |

| | 生詞<br>**Vocabulary** | 拼音<br>**Pin Yin** | 英文翻譯<br>**English** | 詞類<br>**Part of**<br>**Speech** | 華語文<br>能力測驗<br>**TOCFL** |
|---|---|---|---|---|---|
| 6 | 寧 | ān níng<br>（安寧） | peace, tranquil | Vs | 流利級<br>Level 5 |

## 實例 9

yù sù zé bù dá.

欲速則不達。

More haste, less speed.

### George W. Bush 喬治 · 沃克 · 布希 總統

美國第四十三任總統 *43rd President of the United States: 2001-2009*

演說 Speech：The President's News Conference With President Jiang Zemin of China in Beijing

日期 Date：February 21, 2002

引用名言 Proverb quoted：欲速則不達。More haste, less speed.

原文出處 Ancient text cited from：【論語 · 子路篇 · 第十七節】，*The Analects, Chapter Zi-Lu, verse 17*

美國總統檔案來源 The American Presidency Project link:

【演說內容 Speech】

Let me conclude by quoting a Chinese proverb: "**More haste, less speed.**" Despite the fact that sometimes you will have problems that cry out for immediate solution, yet patience is sometime also necessary. Or perhaps I could quote another Chinese old saying to describe the situation: "One cannot expect to dig a well with one spade." So we need to make continuous our unlimiting efforts to fight terrorism.

【名言翻譯 Translation】

欲速則不達。More haste, less speed.

| | 生詞<br>**Vocabulary** | 拼音<br>**Pin Yin** | 英文翻譯<br>**English** | 詞類<br>**Part of Speech** | 華語文<br>能力測驗<br>**TOCFL** |
|---|---|---|---|---|---|
| 1 | 欲 | yù | to intend to, to want to | V | N/A |
| 2 | 速 | gāo sù<br>（高速） | to speed up, fast speed | Vs-attr | 進階級<br>Level 3 |
| 3 | 則 | zé | (conjunction used to express contrast with a previous clause) but / then | Adv | 高階級<br>Level 4 |
| 4 | 不 | bù | not / no | Adv | 準備級一級<br>Novice1 |
| 5 | 達 | dǐ dá<br>（抵達） | to attain / to reach/ to arrive | V | 流利級<br>Level 5 |

## 實例 10

wēn gù ér zhī xīn.

溫故而知新。

Consider the past you shall know the future.

**Barack Obama** 貝拉克‧歐巴馬 總統

美國第四十四任總統 *44th President of the United States: 2009-2017*

演說 Speech：Remarks by President Barack Obama at Town Hall Meeting with Future Chinese Leaders

日期 Date：November 16, 2009

引用名言 Proverb quoted：溫故而知新。Consider the past, and you shall know the future.

原文出處 Ancient text cited from：【論語・為政・第 11 節】，*The Analects, Chapter Wei-Zheng, verse 11*

美國總統檔案來源 The American Presidency Project link:

When President Obama visited China in 2009, he quoted a Chinese proverb from The Analects in his speech to a group of Chinese students in Shanghai.

【演說內容 Speech】

There is a Chinese proverb: "Consider the past, and you shall know the future." Surely, we have known setbacks and challenges over the last 30 years. Our relationship has not been without disagreement and difficulty. But the notion that we must be adversaries is not predestined, not when we consider the past.

【名言翻譯 Translation】

溫故而知新。Consider the past, and you shall know the future.

| | 生詞<br>**Vocabulary** | 拼音<br>**Pin Yin** | 英文翻譯<br>**English** | 詞類<br>**Part of Speech** | 華語文<br>能力測驗<br>**TOCFL** |
|---|---|---|---|---|---|
| 1 | 溫 | wēn xí<br>（溫習） | to review/ to keep warm | Vs | 高階級<br>Level 4 |

| | 生詞<br>Vocabulary | 拼音<br>Pin Yin | 英文翻譯<br>English | 詞類<br>Part of<br>Speech | 華語文<br>能力測驗<br>TOCFL |
|---|---|---|---|---|---|
| 2 | 故 | gù shi<br>（故事） | former / old | N | 入門級<br>Level 1 |
| 3 | 而 | ér | and / as well as / and so / (indicates causal relation) | Conj | 進階級<br>Level 3 |
| 4 | 知 | zhī | to know / to be aware | Vst | 進階級<br>Level 3 |
| 5 | 新 | xīn | new / newly | Vs | 準備級二級<br>Novice2 |

# 實例 11

yī nián shù gǔ, shí nián shù mù, bǎi nián shù rén.

一年樹穀，十年樹木，百年樹人。

If you want 1 year of prosperity, then grow grain. If you want 10 years of prosperity, then grow trees. But if you want 100 years of prosperity, then you grow people.

**Barack Obama** 貝拉克‧歐巴馬 總統

美國第四十四任總統 *44th President of the United States: 2009-2017*

演說 Speech：Remarks at a State Dinner Honoring President Hu Jintao of China

日期 Date：January 19, 2011

引用名言 Proverb quoted：一年之計，莫如樹穀；十年之計，莫如樹木；終身之計，莫如樹人。

If you want 1 year of prosperity, then grow grain. If you want 10 years of prosperity, then grow trees. But if you want 100 years of prosperity, then you grow people.

原文出處 Ancient text cited from：【管子‧權修‧第 11 節】*Guan-Zi, Chapter Quan-Xiu, verse 11*

美國總統檔案來源 The American Presidency Project link:

【演說內容 Speech】

I'm told that there is a Chinese proverb that says: "If you want 1 year of prosperity, then grow grain. If you want 10 years of prosperity, then grow trees. But if you want 100 years of prosperity, then you grow people."

To our people, the citizens of the People's Republic of China and the United States of America: May they grow together in friendship, may they prosper together in peace, and may they realize their dream of the future for themselves, for their children, and for their grandchildren.

【名言翻譯 Translation】

一年樹穀，十年樹木，百年樹人。

一年之計，莫如樹穀；十年之計，莫如樹木；終身之計，莫如樹人。

If you want 1 year of prosperity, then grow grain. If you want 10 years of prosperity, then grow trees. But if you want 100 years of prosperity, then you grow people.

| | 生詞<br>Vocabulary | 拼音<br>Pin Yin | 英文翻譯<br>English | 詞類<br>Part of Speech | 華語文<br>能力測驗<br>TOCFL |
|---|---|---|---|---|---|
| 1 | 年 | nián | year | M | 準備級<br>一級 |
| 2 | 之 = 的 | zhī | possessive particle, literary equivalent of 的 | Ptc | 高階級<br>Level 4 |
| 3 | 計畫 / 劃 | jìhuà | to plan | V / N | 入門級<br>Level 1 |

| | 生詞<br>Vocabulary | 拼音<br>Pin Yin | 英文翻譯<br>English | 詞類<br>Part of<br>Speech | 華語文<br>能力測驗<br>TOCFL |
|---|---|---|---|---|---|
| 4 | 莫 | mò | do not / there is none who | adv | N/A |
| 5 | 如 | rú | as / as if / such as | Conj | 進階級<br>Level 3 |
| 6 | 樹 | shù | tree (n), to plant (v) | V | 入門級<br>Level 1 |
| 7 | 穀 | gǔ | grain / corn | N | N/A |
| 8 | 木 | mù | wood | N | 進階級<br>Level 3 |
| 9 | 人 | rén | person, human | N | 準備級一級 Novice1 |

# 實例 12

hǎi nà bǎi chuān.

海納百川。

An ocean admits all rivers, one is to be inclusive to all things.

**Joseph R. Biden** 喬瑟夫 · 拜登 總統

美國第四十六任總統 *46th President of the United States: 2021-present*

演說 Speech：Remarks by the Vice President and Chinese Vice President Xi at a U.S.-China Business Roundtable in Beijing, China

日期 Date：August 19, 2011

引用名言 Proverb quoted：海納百川。As an ocean admits all rivers, one is to be inclusive to all things.

原文出處 Ancient text cited from：

1.海納百川。【說文解字】 *Shuowen Jiezi*

2.海不辭水，故能成其大。【管子‧形勢解‧第 36 節】 *Guan-Zi, Chapter Xing-Shi-Jie, Verse 36*

美國總統檔案來源 The American Presidency Project link:

【演說內容 Speech】

　　We need to be mutually inclusive. A Chinese proverb reads, as an ocean admits all rivers, one is to be inclusive to all things.

　　Given the big size and rapid expansion of our business cooperation, it's only natural that we have some differences and frictions in our cooperation. But we need to approach them with an inclusive mind, and we need to properly handle these differences through equal consultations in compliance with the law of the market and WTO rules. We should not politicize or sensationalize the trade issues.

【名言翻譯 Translation】

海納百川。As an ocean admits all rivers, one is to be inclusive to all things.

| | 生詞 Vocabulary | 拼音 Pin Yin | 英文翻譯 English | 詞類 Part of Speech | 華語文能力測驗 TOCFL |
|---|---|---|---|---|---|
| 1 | 海 | hǎi | ocean, sea | N | 入門級 Level 1 |
| 2 | 納 | nà rù（納入） | to receive / to accept / to enjoy / to bring into | V | 流利級 Level 5 |
| 3 | 百 | bǎi | hundred / numerous / all kinds of | N | 準備級一級 Novice1 |
| 4 | 川 | chuān | river / creek | N | N/A |

# 附錄三
## 東西方古代哲學家對照年誌圖
### Timeline of Western and Chinese philosophers

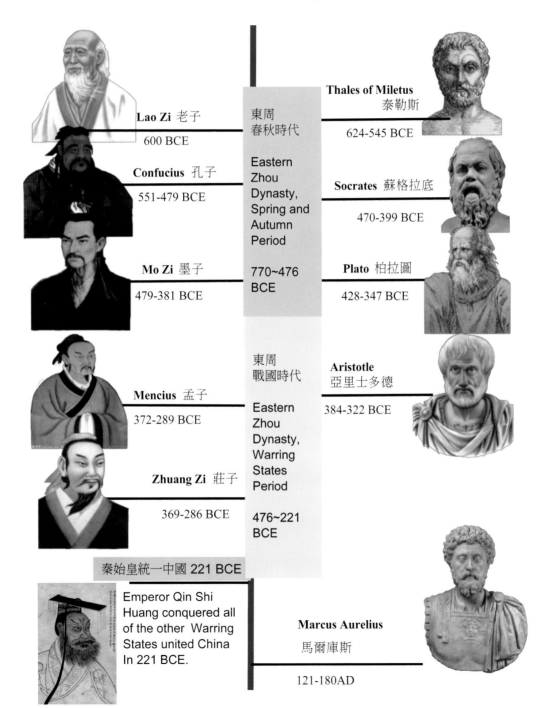

**Lao Zi** 老子
600 BCE

**Confucius** 孔子
551-479 BCE

**Mo Zi** 墨子
479-381 BCE

東周
春秋時代

Eastern
Zhou
Dynasty,
Spring and
Autumn
Period

770~476
BCE

**Thales of Miletus**
泰勒斯
624-545 BCE

**Socrates** 蘇格拉底
470-399 BCE

**Plato** 柏拉圖
428-347 BCE

**Mencius** 孟子
372-289 BCE

**Zhuang Zi** 莊子
369-286 BCE

東周
戰國時代

Eastern
Zhou
Dynasty,
Warring
States
Period

476~221
BCE

**Aristotle**
亞里士多德
384-322 BCE

秦始皇統一中國 221 BCE

Emperor Qin Shi
Huang conquered all
of the other Warring
States united China
In 221 BCE.

**Marcus Aurelius**
馬爾庫斯
121-180AD

Note

Note

國家圖書館出版品預行編目資料

古文今用一洋弟子學《論語》／劉亮吟著. --
初版. -- 臺北市：五南圖書出版股份有限
公司, 2023.03
　　面；　公分
　　ISBN 978-626-317-355-2（平裝）

1.漢語　2.讀本

802.86　　　　　　　　　　110018594

1XKY 華語系列

# 古文今用──洋弟子學《論語》

作　　　者 ― 劉亮吟

發 行 人 ― 楊榮川

總 經 理 ― 楊士清

總 編 輯 ― 楊秀麗

副總編輯 ― 黃惠娟

責任編輯 ― 陳巧慈

封面設計 ― 姚孝慈

出 版 者 ― 五南圖書出版股份有限公司

地　　　址：106台北市大安區和平東路二段339號4樓

電　　　話：(02)2705-5066　　傳　　真：(02)2706-6100

網　　　址：https://www.wunan.com.tw

電子郵件：wunan@wunan.com.tw

劃撥帳號：01068953

戶　　　名：五南圖書出版股份有限公司

法律顧問　林勝安律師

出版日期　2023年3月初版一刷

定　　　價　新臺幣520元

# 經典永恆・名著常在

## 五十週年的獻禮 —— 經典名著文庫

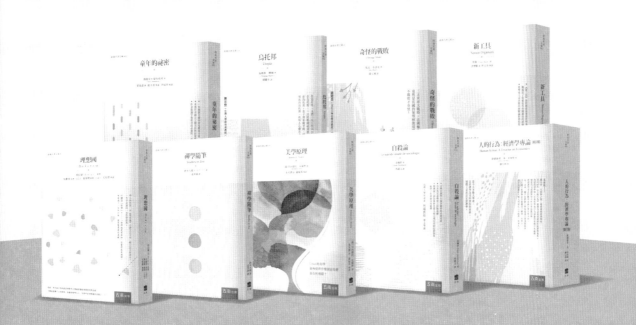

五南，五十年了，半個世紀，人生旅程的一大半，走過來了。

思索著，邁向百年的未來歷程，能為知識界、文化學術界作些什麼？

在速食文化的生態下，有什麼值得讓人雋永品味的？

歷代經典・當今名著，經過時間的洗禮，千錘百鍊，流傳至今，光芒耀人；

不僅使我們能領悟前人的智慧，同時也增深加廣我們思考的深度與視野。

我們決心投入巨資，有計畫的系統梳選，成立「經典名著文庫」，

希望收入古今中外思想性的、充滿睿智與獨見的經典、名著。

這是一項理想性的、永續性的巨大出版工程。

不在意讀者的眾寡，只考慮它的學術價值，力求完整展現先哲思想的軌跡；

為知識界開啟一片智慧之窗，營造一座百花綻放的世界文明公園，

任君遨遊、取菁吸蜜、嘉惠學子！